I0740228

BELTRUNNER

SEAN O'BRIEN

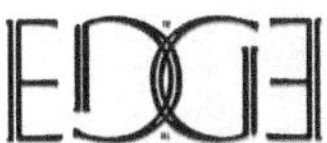

EDGE SCIENCE FICTION AND FANTASY PUBLISHING
An Imprint of HADES PUBLICATIONS, INC.
CALGARY

Beltrunner

Copyright © 2017 by Sean O'Brien

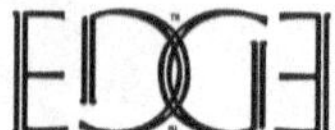

EDGE SCIENCE FICTION AND FANTASY PUBLISHING
An Imprint of HADES PUBLICATIONS, INC.
P.O. Box 1714, Calgary, Alberta, T2P 2L7, Canada

The EDGE Team:
Producer: Brian Hades
Acquisitions Editor: Ella Beaumont
Edited by: Michelle Heumann
Cover Design: Ella Beaumont
Ship Artist: mik38
Asteroid Field Artist: sdecoret
Book Design: Mark Steele
Publicist: Janice Shoults

ISBN: 978-1-77053-139-0

EDGE Science Fiction and Fantasy Publishing and Hades Publications, Inc. acknowledges the ongoing support of the Alberta Foundation for the Arts and the Canada Council for the Arts for our publishing programme.

Library and Archives Canada Cataloguing in Publication
CIP Data on file with the National Library of Canada
ISBN: 978-1-77053-139-0
(e-Book ISBN: 978-1-77053-102-4)

FIRST EDITION
(20240503)
Printed in USA
www.edgewebsite.com

Publisher's Note:

Thank you for purchasing this book. It began as an idea, was shaped by the creativity of its talented author, and was subsequently molded into the book you have before you by a team of editors and designers.

Like all EDGE books, this book is the result of the creative talents of a dedicated team of individuals who all believe that books (whether in print or pixels) have the magical ability to take you on an adventure to new and wondrous places powered by the author's imagination.

As EDGE's publisher, I hope that you enjoy this book. It is a part of our ongoing quest to discover talented authors and to make their creative writing available to you.

We also hope that you will share your discovery and enjoyment of this novel on social media through Facebook, Twitter, Goodreads, Pinterest, etc., and by posting your opinions and/or reviews on Amazon and other review sites and blogs. By doing so, others will be able to share your discovery and passion for this book.

Brian Hades, publisher

Dedications

To my father, who taught me what being a man is.
To my brother, who taught me what a hero is.
To my son, who taught me what matters.

Chapter One

"Come on, come on. Show me the Ps." It was becoming a liturgy. Collier hadn't even raised the cabin lights — he had programmed Sancho to let him sleep, for all the good it had done him — but the glow from the console was more than enough to illuminate his craggy features. *Rocinante* was still executing her flyby of M-1875, sending back telemetry to Collier in the *Dulcinea* in full 3D color. Sancho was doing his best to analyze the data, as he always did, but Collier knew better than to rely solely on the computer. He was looking for something he couldn't ever put into words, no matter how many belters back in Ceres had asked him to try. Not that he had been the center of any conversations for many years now. He had, at best, been a quaint curiosity some time ago, but now was an eccentric old man who was close to becoming a nuisance.

"There! There it is! Mark it and bring *Rocinante* back in, Sancho," Collier rewound the telemetry to the precise moment he had seen the signs, and told Sancho to lock the coordinates.

"Coordinates locked in. *Rocinante* returning to her stable, Skipper," Sancho confirmed cheerfully. "I'm always curious, boss — what did you see?"

Collier had never been able to explain the markings of a P-vein on the surface: indeed, he had been caught more than a few times excavating what he was sure would be a strike only to find nickel and iron. But he was not about to abandon his methods. Deep impact probes were far more reliable, but they were expensive consumables he simply couldn't afford. *Rocinante* was not equipped for laser mining, as many of the third-generation rock hounds were. All Collier had were his instincts and subjective experiences. And hope. Still, he made an attempt to explain his art to his computer.

"There is a fissure there, running from the top right to the bottom left. Do you see it?"

"Sure."

"That's a heavy-metal impact fissure. Bound to be some P in it, or at least nearby."

"How do you know it's an impact fissure? Couldn't it be just cleavage in the rock?"

Collier snorted. "I know cleavage when I see it, Sancho. That's not it. Takes a man to tell the difference."

"What?"

"Never mind. *Rocinante* back yet?"

"Still on approach. I've got a good track. Her stable is ready — all lights green."

"Good. When she's tucked in, take us to M-1875. Right over the fissure. How's the spin?"

"Not too bad. Well under tolerance levels. Do you want to attach correctors?"

Collier shook his head. "Not if I don't have to. Takes up fuel. I'll just go down myself, start cutting. Hover us one hundred meters away, but don't deploy the canopy. What's your estimated time until hover?"

"*Rocinante* should be tucked in about ninety minutes from now. Under standard procedure, it will take me about two hours to achieve stable hover over the coordinates. So three and a half hours, Skipper."

"Great. Just enough time for a nap. Wake me when we get there. Or if there's a fire or something."

"If there's a fire, I'll just evacuate the oxygen. Sleep well, Skipper."

Collier laughed at the computer's joke, glad at the machine's attitude. He had long dismissed the question of Sancho's self-awareness as immaterial and worthless. It pleased him that the almost hopelessly outdated computer had quirks and bugs — including, possibly, sentience. That ill-fated experiment was one of the few taboo subjects left in the system. Earth was rumored to still have hundreds of thousands of rogue Calibans who had blended into the background of the planet's artificial workforce. Perhaps some had left the planet to Luna or even Mars — no one was certain. Collier suspected that someday, Sancho's increasingly corrupted programming would reduce him to uselessness, but he dared not take him in for an overhaul. If he had achieved sentience, Collier would be held liable. He did not relish the idea of being ground up in the Ceres bioconverter for fertilizer. And anyway, if Sancho were sentient, the computer would be killed as well in an overhaul. No, better to continue as he was, with a quirky, erratic computer who asked odd questions. Collier drifted off to sleep with a smile on his lips.

——< >——

"New contact," Sancho's voice woke Collier instantly. "Approaching at 23 meters per second relative velocity. Distance 345.6 kilometers and closing."

"What the hell? Who is it?" Collier tore loose the sleep restraint and shoved off toward the control seat. Even as he maneuvered into his station he was glancing at Sancho's readouts. One look told him all he needed to know.

"Configuration suggests a mining vessel, highest probability—"

"Ad Astra Corporation. Yeah." Collier heaved a sigh and squeezed his eyes shut for a moment, as though girding himself for what he knew must come next. "Why didn't we see them from farther away?" he asked irritably.

"They were in obstruction," Sancho said.

Collier took a deep breath. No sense in blaming Sancho for that. "So, the Ad Astra guys want a piece of this rock too, huh?"

"Affirmative. I'd say they are making for the same rock we are."

Collier studied Sancho's readout. The corporate mining ship would catch up to him in just over four hours at this velocity. They would get to the asteroid at about the same time. His eyes found *Dulcinea's* fuel supply indicator: every liter of propellant he used to increase his own velocity meant a slower return to Ceres later, but it might be worth it to get to the asteroid first and claim it before the corp could. Of course, there was no telling how fast the corp was willing to go to beat him to it.

"Let's talk to them, Sancho."

"Sure thing, Skipper," Sancho said brightly. After a momentary pause, he said, "Contact established. Comm ready when you are."

Collier drew his breath and said, in what he hoped was a cocksure drawl, "This is the *Dulcinea* to approaching corporate mining ship. Who are you, and what do you want with my rock?"

"Your rock, huh? I don't think you're going to be able to make that stick, Col."

His eyes half-closed when he heard the voice. The sudden dryness in his mouth and slight stirring in his loins betrayed the conflict within him.

"Isa," he croaked.

"Corporate Captain Mitchell, Col. Been a while, hasn't it?"

There was no mistaking the casual venom in her voice. Even without a visual link, he could see her half-smirk and narrowed eyes. She always tried so hard to be serious and grim — but in rare moments of total honesty with him, she had revealed secret insecurities and fears that had made him love her all the more.

For a time, at least.

"Yes, it has. And you still haven't answered me: what are you doing chasing my rock?"

"For starters, Col, it's not your rock. I know you haven't filed a claim on it, and you certainly haven't begun excavation. As far as I'm concerned, this is still a free asteroid. And we're going to get there ahead of you." Isa's smugness was a shade too heavy.

"I've got plenty of delta-vee in my tanks still, Isa," he said, deliberately emphasizing her name rather than use her title, "so unless you want to spend a lot of your corp's water, you should break off and look for another rock."

Isa chuckled mirthlessly. "Nice try, Col. You know we carry much more water than you. I can outrun you even from here, get to the rock ahead of you, set up the mine and begin processing while you're still nursing those shit engines of yours. I'm surprised the *Dulcet* is still working, actually."

"*Dulcinea*. And she's never been better," he snapped. Isa knew very well how sensitive he was to comments about his boat. "You try to keep up, Isa. I'm going to get to the rock first, and then you'll have to lay off. Don't waste your corp's water on a stupid race you can't win."

"Since when are you so worried about Ad Astra's profit margin?"

"Since when are you?" He knew it was a childish rejoinder, but it came so swiftly and easily he barely knew he was saying it.

Isa sighed. "You never did understand, Col. But after the last six years, I would have thought you would have come to the same realization I had."

"Nope," he said, too much petulance in his voice. He winced at his own tone.

Silence from the other side, during which time Collier ached to ask Isa questions: questions that he had never fully put away. Why had she left that morning six years ago? Her long letter, written on real paper and left on his pillow in some old-fashioned gesture that angered him even more at the time, had said much but answered little. How many times in the past six years had he wished he had not spaced the letter? How many times had he wondered if he would ever find it again, floating in the belt?

His masculine pride won out, and Isa spoke before he succumbed to the wounds of the past. "Well. In any case, Col, this is the way it is now. I'm here, I have a corp behind me, and I will be able to get to the rock first. I'm only cruising now, but if I need to, I will fly by you like a missile and use an anchor on the rock to claim it. *Ad Astra Corporation Mining Ship SCM-17*, out."

Damn her. Damn her and her corporation.

Even as he thought that, he couldn't help but feel pleased that she had risen to prominence so quickly. He had always admired her cool competence — that and her quirky moments of vulnerability had first fascinated then excited him.

Sancho's voice interrupted his thoughts. "Skipper, she's increased velocity. Relative velocity now 29 meters per second and increasing by point 9 meters per second."

"She's not kidding. Didn't know corp ships were allowed to move that fast — I wonder what the performance is on the thrusters? She's going to have to flipbrake before long," he mused aloud. Isa had been right on at least one score: he had to save a certain amount of propellant for the return to Ceres, and *Dulcinea's* thrust efficiency was not what it used to be. Sancho had warned him about microfractures in some of the thrust tubes weeks ago: if superheated exhaust expanded the cracks, he would not only lose the race to the rock, but have to limp back to Ceres at reduced speed.

Damn it, he had to. Not only because he needed this strike, but also to show the corporation that a freelancer like him could not be shoved aside so easily. Ad Astra could not treat him this way, like an obsolete relic of a past time.

He didn't quite convince himself that the corporation was the target of his anger.

"Sancho, go to eighty percent thrust, and inform me of any changes in thrust tube integrity. If we are holding steady, we'll go to one hundred percent."

"Eighty percent thrust, aye. Recalculating vector to target. Recalculation complete, thrust in ten seconds. Secure for approximately one-eighth gee acceleration. Seven, six, five ... pre-thrust deicing complete, tubes primed ... two, one. Eighty percent."

Collier felt the gentle push into his chair as *Dulcinea's* engines labored.

Sancho chimed in again. "Revised telemetry: Ad Astra vessel relative velocity now forty-four meters per second, increasing by point two meters per second. Time to asteroid estimated at two hours, eighteen minutes."

Collier examined the data and squinted. "Will we beat them?"

"Impossible to say, Skipper. I don't know when she's going to flip and brake — that depends on how much thrust she's capable of, how much propellant her captain is willing to use, how—"

"All right, skip it. When do we have to flipbrake?"

"At our current acceleration, assuming you want to brake at the same rate, we should flip in forty-one minutes."

"Any cracks in the thrust tubes?"

Perhaps it was just his imagination, but Collier thought he heard fear in Sancho's voice. "Not yet. I can't say if they will crack or not."

"Let's go to one hundred percent thrust."

"We'll be dangerously low on propellant when we get to the rock, Skipper. It'll mean a very low-consumption return to Ceres."

"We'll mine water from the rock. Go to one hundred."

"Assuming there is any," Sancho muttered, and Collier couldn't help but smile at his computer's quirks. "Increasing thrust to one hundred percent. Stand by for approximately one-sixth gee. Five, four, three, two, one. One hundred percent."

The gentle weight increased almost imperceptibly. The sensation that he was lying on his back, looking "up" through the nose window, was a temporary illusion that he had little difficulty in dispelling. His years in space had trained his mind to ignore his inner ear.

"Revised telemetry. Ad Astra vessel relative velocity forty-five meters per second, decreasing very slowly. Under point one meter per second per second. New estimated time to asteroid one hour, fifty-five minutes. Flipbrake in twenty-two minutes."

"Still no way to tell if we will beat them?"

Sancho sounded slightly exasperated. "No, Skipper. Too many unpredictable variables."

"I know what you mean," Collier nodded.

"I didn't mean—"

"Skip it. No need to be apologetic. We've never really talked about women, have we, Sancho?"

"No, Skipper. I don't know what I can add to any discussion of romance. But I still have a rather extensive pornography collection."

Collier reddened. "Never mind that. I thought I told you to always forget when I access that?"

"You do. But I remember you telling me to forget it."

"We're not talking about this. It's a perfectly normal, even healthy—"

Sancho's voice went cold again as he interrupted. "Revised telemetry. Ad Astra vessel has increased her rate of acceleration. Relative velocity now forty-three meters per second, increasing by point two meters per second."

"Shit. She's not giving up." Collier thought for a moment. Perhaps Isa was right: if she was willing to expend this much water to chase down the rock, he wasn't going to be able to match her. Her ship obviously could outperform his, and she was not being miserly with her fuel.

"How are the tubes holding?"

"No increased damage so far. But the likelihood is that I won't be able to detect any cracks in time to shut down. If a tube cracks, we'll lose it."

"Can we go to one hundred and five percent thrust?"

Sancho was slow in replying. "Well, yes, but we won't gain much. And we may pass the fuel threshold: we may not have enough to return to Ceres without cold-sleep protocol."

"I told you, we're going to mine water from the rock. Don't worry about fuel."

"If we go to one oh five, we run a greater risk of cracking a tube." It wasn't Collier's imagination: Sancho was clearly worried now.

"Okay. Let me think."

Sancho waited a beat, then said dryly, "That doesn't fill me with confidence, Skipper. Can I suggest that maybe Captain Mitchell was right? We can't win this rock."

"I'll be damned if I'm going to let her take this from me. Recalculate time of arrival at the asteroid assuming no flip-brake maneuver."

"I don't—"

"Just do it," Collier snapped.

"If we continue at our present rate of acceleration, we will reach the asteroid in thirty-nine minutes. And we'll be shattered to very small particles when we do."

"Okay. Alter course so that we will execute a flyby at … five hundred meters distance from the asteroid."

"Are you sure about this, Skipper? I don't mean to challenge you, but this seems ... well, crazy. You remember you told me five years, ten months and twenty-three days ago terrestrial if you ever tried to kill yourself, I was to stop—"

"Yes, Sancho, I remember. I'm not going to kill myself, or you. You're going to drop me off when you get near the rock."

"Okay. That still sounds like you're going to kill yourself, Skipper."

"I'll ride *Rocinante* and use its thrusters, plus my suit thrusters, to brake myself to a soft landing on the rock. You'll flipbrake as soon as I leave the ship and start coming back for me. I'll be fine on the asteroid until you get back. And once I land on it, it'll be mine: Isa won't be able to claim it."

Sancho was silent for a long while.

"Are you still there, Sancho?" This would be a hell of a time for his erratic computer to finally give up the ghost.

"Yes, Skipper. May I make a suggestion?"

"Sure."

"We don't need to get to the rock that far ahead of the Ad Astra vessel. We could still execute your plan, but not do it so late. Let me flipbrake late — still too late to hover above the rock, but late enough to beat the Ad Astra ship. You can leave the ship with *Rocinante* and get to the asteroid in time to beat the corp ship, but not have so much velocity that you'll smash into it. I don't think *Rocinante* and your suit thrusters together can slow you down fast enough if *Dulcinea* is going as swiftly as she will be if I don't flipbrake."

Collier listened patiently and had to admit to himself that Sancho had a better plan. He didn't relish the thought of getting to the rock first but being a cloud of viscera when he did so. "Okay, Sancho, we'll do it your way. Arrange the flipbraking in such a way that our relative velocity to the rock will be ... one hundred meters per second. That slow enough for you?"

"Skipper, I am working with a very complex formula here, with too many variables I don't know. For example, while I know the thrust for *Rocinante* and your suit, I don't know how efficiently you will be able to line up your vector.

If you're not pretty fucking close to lined up, you won't brake fast enough. I can't—"

Collier cut off his computer with a laugh of genuine pleasure. "Sancho, that's the first time I think I have ever heard you swear."

"Well, damn it, this is the first time you've ever done something this batshit crazy."

Collier laughed again. "I appreciate the sentiment, Sancho, I really do. Start your calculations as best you can. I'm going aft to get into my suit."

"Okay. Can I back off the thrusters to eighty percent again? Now that we're trying this stunt, we don't need to be at one hundred."

Collier nodded. "Sounds good. Go to eighty percent. Calculate the ejection point for me, let me know when you have a time on that."

"Aye aye."

Collier swam out of the control chair and glided expertly toward the airlock suite. The patched but still quite serviceable vacuum suit hung limply in its frame, imitating the posture and demeanor of an old warrior who had seen too many battles and too few glories. Collier zipped it open and wiggled inside, noting that the abdomen was still very tight. He had resisted tailoring the suit to accommodate his belly in the wan hope he would drop those five kilos one day, and indeed, the snugness of the midsection only served to remind him he needed to do more time in the Ceres centrifuge.

Otherwise, the suit fit quite well, and Collier allowed himself a few moments to enjoy the womblike feeling of security the suit afforded him.

"Sancho, is *Rocinante* fueled and ready?"

"Affirmative, Skipper. She's topped off. You'll need to leave the ship in just under twelve minutes maximum. Sooner would be better than later."

"Roger that, Sancho. I'm heading to the stable now. Open the bay doors and prepare *Rocinante* for EVA." Collier made his way along the cylindrical passageway that led to *Dulcinea's* belly where the scout vehicle was kept. He was glad there was little time to waste — had he been left to think about his scheme, he might decide it was insane and give up the rock to Isa.

"Incoming message, Skipper."

"Route it to my suit," Collier said, twisting behind him to seal the integrated helmet to his suit. He could hear Isa's tinny voice coming through the earphones as he sealed and locked the helmet in place.

"…There? Col? Please answer," he heard when he had finished with the helmet. Isa's voice was not quite panicky, but very concerned.

"Sorry, Isa, I missed the first part of your transmission. Say again?" He made sure his voice was as casual as could be.

"You're aware you've passed your flipbrake point? Are you in trouble? Has that bucket finally broken down?"

Collier's smirk vanished. "No, she hasn't, and yes, I'm very aware of what I am doing. I told you: I'm not going to lose this rock. Not to you."

Silence for a moment, then: "Look, Col … I think you're taking this too far. Whatever you think about how I … how we ended, that's no reason to, well, no reason to do this. I'm sure you—"

Collier laughed, making no effort to disguise the scorn in his voice. "I'm not killing myself, Isa. Recheck your telemetry on me: *Dulcinea's* going to miss the asteroid by half a kilometer."

Isa did not answer immediately — no doubt she was checking her tracking data. "Okay, then," she growled, obviously annoyed at having revealed emotion to him, "What the hell are you doing?"

"I don't think you need to know that just yet. You'll see soon enough. But," he added, his charm vanishing suddenly, "you won't win this rock. You may as well turn back now."

"I don't think you understand, Col," Isa said, her voice strangely calm and even tender. "This isn't a game you can win. Ad Astra has a lot of resources behind me. I've been given quite a bit of latitude in operations to find and mine Ps. You, alone, won't be enough of an obstacle to stop them."

"'Them?'" Collier chuckled, then broke off as a thought occurred to him. "Speaking of Ps, why are you chasing this rock anyway? Do you know something about it?"

"Never seen it before."

"Then how—?"

Isa did not sound pleased. "What do you think, Col? You think it's an accident we are both here at the same time?" At his silence, Isa almost shouted, "We're tracking you, you idiot."

Collier stopped at the hatchway to *Rocinante's* stable. "I see. You wait for me to find Ps, then you come get them, is that it?"

"Yes."

"But I'm not always right. How do you know I'm right now?"

"I don't — yet. I was going to send an impact probe toward the rock, see what we got. You don't use impacts, do you?"

"I don't have seventy thousand metals to waste every time I get a hunch, no."

"Yeah, well, the corp does. That's what I meant about resources, Col." She sighed. "You see what I mean? You can't win this. I'm not operating on a shoestring like you. I don't have to watch every ounce of water, every erg of energy. I can be wasteful and thorough. You—"

"Well, it's been nice chatting with you, Isa, but I've got a complicated thing here I gotta do," Collier said, surprised at the hurt in his voice. "So if you don't mind, I'll be silent for a while, and I'd appreciate it if you could stay out of my way. Out." He bit down on the mic to end transmission, and almost violently opened the inner hatch to *Rocinante's* stable.

Of course Isa was following him — he should have guessed that as soon as she had appeared on Sancho's telemetry. Did he honestly think it had been some kind of chance meeting, out here in the nearly infinite emptiness?

"You sure did," he said to himself. *"You think you're some kind of hard-bitten realist, living on facts and figures with no room for dreams, but you're just as susceptible to romantic*

thinking as a lovelorn teenager. You liked to think some weird expression of Fate pulled you two back together, as if to tell you she had been wrong to leave you, and now was coming back."

Shit.

"Ejection point in six minutes, Skipper. I really suggest you get going. If you wait too much longer, the—"

"I know, Sancho. I'm in the bay now," he said, opening the outer door to reveal the blackness of the Belt. *Rocinante* was still attached to her "hitching post"—a collection of wires, cables, and fuel lines that held her securely to *Dulcinea's* hull.

A sudden thrill shot through him. As far as he knew, this had never before been attempted — at least, not at such velocity. The common mythology surrounding Belters and shared by the rest of the system was one of reckless heroism: a combination of pioneering spirit and unbalanced avarice that most closely resembled the ancient frontiersman from Earth's North American settler movement. (At least, so Collier was led to believe from his scant and irregular contacts with Martians, Jovians, and the rare Earther.) In fact, Belters were a remarkably conservative and cautious lot in their day-to-day lives. The act of becoming a Belter might be one of desperation, but in practice, Belters carved a very even, predictable, mundane course.

Collier was an exception.

"Ready to run through the checklist, Sancho?" he asked, as he carefully mounted *Rocinante*, finding handholds and footholds among her various antennae.

"What checklist? I've never even remotely examined this EVA for feasibility, much less designed a check—"

"Calm down. I'm only joking," Collier chuckled. "Stand by to release hitching lines from *Rocinante*. Transfer her guidance controls to my mic, too, while you're at it."

"Copy that. Comm line transferred. She's under your command, Skipper. Good luck."

"Thanks." He gripped the two antennae tightly and made sure he was well away from *Rocinante*'s exhaust vents. "Let 'er rip, Sancho."

He felt a slight tug upward as *Rocinante*'s attitude thrusters gently pushed her "down" from *Dulcinea's* hull. *Dulcinea* appeared to shoot upward at a fairly rapid pace as the little scout left her.

"I'm away clean. Let me get a little distance before you fire up your thrusters again."

"Copy that."

"*Rocinante*, minus Y-axis thrust, fifty percent, continuous burn. On mark."

"Acknowledged," came the lifeless voice of the scout's dedicated computer.

"Three ... two ... one ... mark." As soon as he said it, he felt a much more severe tug upward that threatened to dislodge him from the antennae. His right foot left its hold and he fought panic as he repositioned it on another outcropping. *Dulcinea* raced away from him and he had to remind himself that he wasn't falling through the void. The thrust couldn't have been much more than one-tenth of a gee, but it was enough to force his brain to override the trap-door feeling in his stomach.

"You've got some kick, girl," Collier said when his breath returned.

"Everything okay, Skipper?" Sancho asked.

"Seems to be. Can you give me a rough idea of how long I'll need to keep this thrust going to meet the asteroid?"

"Nope. I don't know how long or hard you plan to thrust away. Cut your Y-axis thrust and get ready for minus Z-axis burn. When you do that, I'll be able to get an idea."

"Okay. *Rocinante*, cut minus Y-axis thrust on mark. Three ... two ... one ... mark."

The sudden return of weightlessness was a welcome feeling. He could no longer see *Dulcinea* — he had no reference points with which to compare his own motion. It was a calming feeling the likes of which he had never experienced. He had heard of unfortunate Belters caught in eruptions of water vapor, either from ship exhaust or comet expulsion, and who had been sent tumbling at great speeds away from their fellows: some had been recovered, some not. Had they felt the same peace and calmness as Collier now did, or were they panicked as they contemplated their own deaths?

"Skipper? The Z-axis burn?"

"Coming up," Collier said, shaking himself out of his reverie. He repositioned himself on *Rocinante*'s hull, gripping what he could while avoiding the exhaust vents. He would need to also fire his suit jets to keep himself from losing his grip—

Damn.

"Uh, small problem, Sancho. I didn't think of this."

"What?"

"My suit jet controller. I need my hands to operate it, but I can't let go of *Rocinante* while she's thrusting."

"Shit," was Sancho's only reply.

Collier waited a few seconds, then said, "Sort of need an answer, there, faithful computer."

Sancho answered, "I suggest a very faint thrust on *Rocinante* at first, to see what you can handle. Then you can step it up slowly and feel how much you can take."

"Not bad. Let's give that a go. *Rocinante*, minus z-axis thrust, uh, one percent, continuous burn. On mark."

"Acknowledged."

"Three ... two ... one ... mark." The thrust was almost imperceptible. Were it not for the puff of vapor escaping through the exhaust vents, Collier could have believed nothing had happened. "*Rocinante*, increase thrust to five percent. Mark."

He could feel a very gentle pull away from him, but he could hold on at this level indefinitely. He continued to tell *Rocinante* to step up the thrust until he could feel his arms beginning to strain. He stopped increasing at seventy percent.

"Okay, Sancho, how am I doing?"

"Not even close, Skipper. You're going to miss the asteroid, high, and when you do, you're going to be flying by her at about thirty-four meters per second. And that'll happen in about nine and a half minutes."

"Okay. What do I need to hit the asteroid?"

"Skipper, you don't want to hit the asteroid. You're going too fast."

"I'll increase minus Z-axis thrust."

"Can you hold on?"

"I guess I'll have to. *Rocinante*, increase minus Z-axis thrust to ninety percent. Mark."

The pull away from him was now considerable. The problem wasn't so much that *Rocinante*'s thrust was too formidable as much as it was the lack of proper handholds — he felt himself tightening his grip on antennae that were never intended to be used in this fashion. Idly, he wondered if anyone had ever tested the tensile strength of the objects that would mean the difference between life and death for him.

"Whoa, baby. Now you've really got some kick to you."

"Skipper?"

"So far, so good, Sancho. How's about now?"

"You will still miss the asteroid, though not by as much. You're still a bit high. And now you'll make your flyby in thirteen minutes, give or take. At twenty-two meters per second."

"I'll go to one hundred thrust. Has *Rocinante* got enough juice for that?"

"Yes, but—"

"*Rocinante*, increase minus-z axis thrust to one hundred percent. Mark."

The tug increased, and he felt his left hand slip a few inches on the antenna he was gripping.

"Alert," came *Rocinante's* expressionless voice. "Fault indicator warning on high gain antenna."

"*Rocinante*, nature of fault?" Collier felt the agony of his position. He couldn't lessen his grip on the antenna, but he couldn't afford to have it break off, either.

"Structural failure in antenna housing. Loss of contact with antenna attitude control."

"Will it break off? *Rocinante*, will it break off?" he corrected himself.

"Query parameters not set."

It was useless. *Rocinante* was not Sancho — it was only a very basic dedicated computer. There was, therefore, no way of knowing. He scanned *Rocinante's* hull. Nothing else presented itself as a handhold — it was either the antenna or nothing.

"How about now, Sancho?"

"Well, you're still not going to hit it. You're still a little high. Not much: I give my calculation a ten percent chance of error. Due to the asteroid's slow spin, there may be a high enough projection that meets you right when you are flying by. In fourteen minutes, eleven seconds. But you'll pass the asteroid at nineteen point seven meters per second."

"That's too fast," Collier said matter-of-factly.

"Yes. I'll be on the other side to meet you, Skipper. It was a good try. You almost did it."

Collier didn't answer. "*Rocinante*, prepare for Y-axis burn."

"Skipper! You can't give a minus burn: you'll put yourself in the path of the asteroid. You're going much too fast — if you hit the rock at this speed, you'll be killed. Even if you somehow survive the impact, which you won't, your suit will certainly rupture. Plus *Rocinante* will break up, and some of the debris might—"

"Sancho, shut up for a second, would you? I know what I'm doing. I'm not going to lose this rock. *Rocinante*, cut Z-axis thrust. Mark." He pulled himself closer to the hull when *Rocinante's* jets stopped.

"Skipper! Don't!"

"*Rocinante*, plus Y-axis thrust, ten percent, five second burn. Three … two … one … mark."

The tug this time came from the opposite direction, as if *Rocinante* was an elevator ascending at a very low rate of speed. After the furious Z-axis thrust, the mild and short "upward" thrust was nothing to his muscles.

"I don't understand. You are absolutely going to miss the rock now. I'm glad, but I don't—"

"*Rocinante*, prepare for minus-Z axis thrust. One percent, increasing by one percent per second. Continuous burn."

"Ohhh, I see." Sancho said.

Collier couldn't help but smile a little. "Mark." Once the thrust had built back up to full power, Collier tried to keep the smugness out of his voice as he asked Sancho, "Give me an updated telemetry report, if you please, Sancho."

"Gladly, Skipper. You will begin flyby in twelve minutes, two seconds. Moving at relative velocity of twenty point six meters per second."

"How thick is the asteroid?"

"It varies, Skipper. If I understand what you are asking, the flyby should take about three and a half seconds to be complete, so I'm going to estimate the asteroid's 'thickness,' as you put it, to be around sixty-five meters. When you clear the asteroid, you'll have a relative velocity of about eighteen meters per second, give or take a few centimeters."

"How long before I catch up with it again?"

"About four minutes, forty seconds. But you'll want to reduce velocity well before that. I estimate, in order to land at a reasonable velocity — say, no more than two meters per second — you'll take around ten minutes. You'll need to play a little bit to get the velocity right."

"I'll bet I can do it in eight minutes," Collier said, his breath wheezing a little as he continued to hold on to *Rocinante's* antenna.

Sancho surprised him with his answer. "You're on."

The next five minutes were interesting: he cut back on thrust once he had checked with Sancho that Isa's ship was still too distant to beat him to the rock even if he reduced his velocity, fearing the damaged antenna on *Rocinante's* hull would snap off. Once *Rocinante* had taken him back to the asteroid and he was closing in on it, he let go of the scout and ordered her back to the *Dulcinea* for refueling and repair. He would use his suit jets to soften his landing there.

"Just to let you know, Skipper," Sancho said after he had released his grip on *Rocinante* and reversed his jets to begin a gentle braking maneuver, "your eight minutes are up. I win."

"Congratulations. I owe you a dinner. How's my relative velocity?"

"You're closing at eight point seven seven meters per second. Distance ninety-one meters."

"Still a little hot for my liking," Collier mumbled. He squeezed his jet control grip and felt the pressure on his chest as the suit jets thrust broke his speed. He kept up the burn for five seconds, counting in his head, and called Sancho for an update. He didn't trust his eyes to give him an accurate assessment of his velocity: the asteroid's surface appeared to be coming at him very slowly.

"Five point one four meters per second. Distance fifty-four meters."

He nodded. That would do for now. A few more bursts from the jets once he got closer, and he'd be there.

"I'm receiving a transmission from the Ad Astra mining ship, Skipper," Sancho said.

"Really? Put her through to me," Collier said. "Hello, Isa. I'll be with you in a minute."

"What the hell are you doing, Col? You overshot the rock and are coming back? You're not going to beat us, not by a long shot. I don't know—"

"Sorry, Isa, I already have. In fact—" he applied a final tiny burst of thrust and extended his arms, absorbing the gentle impact of his slow-moving body on to the asteroid. "Touchdown."

"What?"

"I'm on the rock. It's mine." He began to unship the tethering gear from his shoulder pack.

Sancho chimed in. "Confirmed. I have you on telemetry."

"Col, I don't know what kind of game this is, but if you think you can fool me into thinking you've made a claim to this asteroid without being on it, you're crazier than even I thought."

"It's not a trick. I'm on the other side. Sancho, when will the rock's rotation carry me into view of the Ad Astra ship?"

"Won't be for a while, Skipper. Perhaps thirty-five minutes."

"Isa, unless you want to just trust me, you'll have to wait half an hour before you can see me. You think you can do that?"

"This is insane," Isa murmured.

"Yep. That's the Belt for you," he smiled and aimed the tethergun at a likely looking spot. "Sancho, I'm tethering myself now." He fired the piton and immediately drifted away from the impact. He didn't bother using his suit jets to compensate: the piton buried itself into the rock trailing the tether cable, which coiled oddly for a moment before the shoulder winch tightened it down. He sank gently back down toward the asteroid, tucking his legs under him so he could stand.

"Tethering successful," he said to both Isa and Sancho.

"Col, are you really on the rock? You wouldn't lie to me?"

Collier paused even as his feet touched the dusty surface of the asteroid. "No, I wouldn't. I never did, Isa. That's why you left me, remember? Because I couldn't lie to you."

"Yeah," Isa said, and Collier hoped the wistfulness he heard in her voice was real and not his own invention. Then, her coldness returned. "So you're on the rock."

"Yep. And I plan to mine it. So why don't you and your corp look for another one. It shouldn't be hard. I'm planting the claim beacon now." He opened his thigh pouch and planted the disc-shaped beacon firmly on the surface of the asteroid. When he depressed the securing stud, the beacon fired its spikes into the surface and began blinking red.

"Receiving beacon transponder," Sancho said.

"Good. Record and send to Ceres, please, Sancho." Collier grinned and said to Isa, "It's over, Isa. Go find another."

"You don't get it, Col. Nothing I've said to you — you haven't heard anything." She was silent a moment, then continued. "I'm going off comm for a little while. But this isn't over."

"Whatever you say, Isa," he grunted, then told Sancho to cut transmission, hoping to get the order in before she cut hers.

"Transmission ceased, Skipper."

"Good. Now. Where am I relative to that crevice we saw when we first decided this was our baby?"

"You're on the proper side of the asteroid, Skipper. I make it sixty six meters distant."

"Good news indeed. All right. Prepare for orientation." He faced the tether point and held still. "Designating bearings. I am currently facing zero degrees at designated north pole. Align my suit compass and your own compass to that, please, Sancho."

"Alignment complete. Fissure beginning point located sixty-five point nine meters distant, bearing one-six-four degrees. You should see that in your helmet display."

"Got it," Collier said as he saw the tiny diamond appear in his display. He turned slowly, crouched down, and launched himself as flat as he could toward the target. There were no outcroppings ahead of him, and in any case, he was not travelling very rapidly. He kept his hands in front of him, gripping the suit jet controls, and skimmed the surface of the rock toward what he hoped were the deposits that would make this whole endeavor worthwhile.

"If there are no Ps there, I'm going to feel a bit stupid," he murmured. Then, louder, to Sancho, he said, "You didn't see anything down there, did you?"

"I'm afraid not, Skipper. But you wouldn't expect me to be able to from up here."

Collier grunted. That was true. But he would have felt a hell of a lot happier if Ps had been just lying on the surface somehow.

"You're almost there," Sancho said a few moments later. "You should be able to see it pretty soon."

Collier used the suit jets to take him higher off the surface. He increased his headlights to maximum intensity and dispersal and suddenly saw the fissure. From his vantage point, it looked like a box canyon made of shadows: his lamps could not penetrate to the bottom.

"Contact. I'm going to set a second tether here. I'll also put a beacon down for you, Sancho. What's your ETA?"

"I should be hovering over your position in roughly three hours, twelve minutes."

Collier nodded inside his helmet. His suit was rated for twelve hours survival time under working conditions, and he knew from experience he could stretch that out to sixteen if he was miserly with air and water. The biggest problem with a twelve-hour suit shift was the nutrient gel. It never tasted quite right.

"Okay, Sancho. I'm going to begin preliminary excavation as soon as I am re-tethered here." He set to work, firing another piton from his shoulder and securing himself close to the fissure. Once he was safely tethered to this new point, he released the first tether, securing it to the rock with a blob of stik-tite adhesive, and began his weightless rappel down into the fissure.

He descended slowly — one meter per second — despite his impatience to reach the bottom. There was no sense in hurrying things now, not when he had beaten Isa to the rock. Besides, the fissure couldn't be more than seventy meters deep, since the asteroid itself wasn't that thick. He should find the bottom relatively soon.

No sooner had he thought that than his feet felt the surface of the bottom of the fissure. He bent his knees and absorbed the gentle fall, being careful not to spring back up and launch himself off the bottom.

"Okay, I'm down, Sancho."

There was no reply. He tried again, but still did not get an answer. The canyon walls, combined with the asteroid's gentle rotation, must be blocking his transmission. He shrugged. It was a minor annoyance, but he should have expected it. He set to work unshipping his core sampler, deploying a firefly to give him some ambient light by which to work.

Minutes later, he eyed the harpoon-like core sampler and selected a spot on the canyon wall. He set the sampler's anchor points and secured it to the wall. All that remained now was to press the firing stud and allow the sampler to bore deep into the rock, retrieving and analyzing samples that would tell him if all this had been worthwhile.

A single test, if negative for Ps, would not mean the rock was worthless. He could test dozens of times and still not hit veins that may be hidden elsewhere on the asteroid. He knew this intellectually, but he nevertheless hesitated on the firing button. How many tests would he perform before admitting his instincts were wrong?

He shook himself inside his suit. "Haven't even sampled the damn rock once, and already I'm..." He pressed the firing button with what amounted to defiance.

The sampler worked invisibly and soundlessly for several minutes, boring a deep shaft into the surface of the asteroid. Only when the sampler had created a shaft deep enough did a cigar-sized cylinder fire itself through the barrel of the sampler's long, rifle-like assembly toward what Collier hoped were the ores he sought.

Collier knew well the operation of the probe: it would scrape the sides of the shaft created by the mining laser and determine where, if anywhere, veins of rare metals and ores lay. It could, and probably would, come back with nothing on this first run, he told himself. No sense getting worked up about it.

The cylinder returned to its home in the sampler base presently and the dedicated assay computer in the sampler housing began its work. Collier watched the readout screen at the rear of the device, his breath coming quickly despite his self-talk. The dark screen brightened to life with a chemical readout. Collier gasped at the numbers. He had long ago programmed the assay computer to highlight the Ps and ignore the more common elements: *Dulcinea* would never be a workhorse mining vessel carrying iron ore in huge quantities. She would always be a specialist. But such a path meant many, many failures. Only when he struck a vein of Ps would any mission be worthwhile.

And so he had this time. The readout did not change even as he stared at it:

Platinum:	6.123%
Palladium:	3.237%
Total P's:	9.36%
Rhodium:	1.788%
Iridium:	1.334%
Osmium:	1.299%
Nickel:	67.344%
Iron:	11.322%
Copper:	7.044%
Other:	Trace

He had only once before broken ten Ps on a strike: that was years and years ago and had carried him for quite some time through a long dry spell. He hadn't quite broken ten on this sample, but nine point three plus was damn good. And that was just his first sample — what if he hadn't even hit a vein?

The possibilities swam before him. On his first sample, a nine-three. Nine three six, really. He considered his options.

He could reset the sampler and start looking for an even richer vein, but he was out of contact down here. It would be more prudent, now that he had verified that the rock was a winner, to get back to the *Dulcinea*, resupply, regroup, and think about his plans. He had time.

He disassembled the sampler again and returned it to its place in his pack, then placed a second beacon on the wall of the canyon with stik-tite. Grasping the tether cable, he jumped gently off the floor of the canyon and rose back to the surface, using the cable to steady his ascent.

Once back on the surface, he hailed Sancho again.

"Sancho, my friend, open the champagne. The sampler came back nine-three-six on the first try. So the—"

"Skipper! I've been trying to raise you for the past twenty minutes!" Sancho's voice was tense.

"Why? What's happened?"

"The Ad Astra ship. She's been sending out blast warnings. She's preparing to send an impact probe. I've tried to tell the captain that you—"

"Damn her! Put me through to her. Now." Collier's grip on the tether cable tightened. An impact probe could easily split the asteroid in half if it struck the rock well enough: the fissure itself was evidence that the asteroid was fragile and could break in two if—

Isa's voice sounded tense in his helmet. "Col? Where've you been? I've been sending out blast warnings for the last—"

"Damn it, Isa, didn't you believe me? I'm on the goddamn rock, like I told you. Placed a claim beacon. Can't you see me now?"

"We saw two tethers, one of which was stuck to the rock. The other looked like it went down some kind of crevasse. But—"

"Yeah, that was me. I must have been down in the canyon. It doesn't matter. So now you know I am here, and you can't legally mine this rock unless I sell the rights to you. Which I am not going to do. I'm here, I've already begun my sampling. So fuck off," he added, feeling the pain of the past few years seep into his words.

"I'm afraid not, Col. You've begun sampling, you say? What did you get?"

It made no sense to tell Isa what he had found. There was nothing that could be gained from revealing his findings to her. But the smug power behind his knowledge was too much for his fragile wisdom to contain. He needed her to know he had made a strike, just like he always said he would. The sting of the words in her letter was almost as fresh as it had been when he had first read them. *"You're a dreamer, Col. That might be okay for you, but I can't live on dreams. The Belt isn't a place for dreamers. And neither is our relationship. If you really loved me, you'd put away your toys. But you're not really a man. You're a boy. I need a man. So long."*

"Nine-three-six P," he said, clearly emphasizing each digit. "Did you hear that?" he almost shouted. It wasn't really a question: she hadn't time to respond. He knew what he sounded like, but at that moment, he didn't care. He let himself be petulant. "Nine-three-six! And that was just the first sample! What do you think of that, Isa? And don't think I'm going to take you back, either. You had your chance." Even as he spoke the last words, he knew he had gone too far. Not that he had hurt her, but that he had squandered his chance to redeem himself, even a little bit, in her eyes. He was merely being a boy some more.

Isa drew her breath. "Nine-three-six, you say," she drawled, her voice as calm as Collier's had been manic. "Quite a find. I was right to follow you." She was evidently ignoring his final outburst. A sarcastic comment would have been kinder than silence. "Anyway, Col," she said after an eloquent pause, "You should head on back to the *Dulcinea* soon. We'll be ready to launch our probes pretty soon. I'm going to crack this rock open and mine her dry."

"You can't, Isa," he repeated, keeping his voice calmer. "Belt law clearly gives me right of first. There's nothing subtle about it."

"And what are you going to do about it, Col?" Isa's voice was dangerously smooth and soft. "Run to the Authority? Please don't tell me your childish idealism has gone that far," she chuckled cruelly.

"The claim beacon," Collier said, "is planted. It's sending data to my ship and I'm sending it to Ceres."

Isa sounded almost sorry. "No, it's not. We're jamming your transmission."

"Sancho!" Collier snapped.

"I can't confirm that yet, Skipper. Haven't received verification of reception from Ceres, but that could be from slowness on their part."

Isa continued. "It's going to come down to our word against yours. And the corporation has a loud voice."

Collier swallowed. Isa was right: if she decided to flout the law, the worst the Authority could really do was slap a fine on the Ad Astra Corporation. And even that was unlikely. He had no money to defend a claim, besides his ship. If he lost the claim (which, despite the circumstances, was quite possible given the skill and resources available to the Ad Astra's lawyers) he would lose his legal deposit. He couldn't afford to lose. Therefore, he couldn't afford to fight.

"Why, Isa?" His voice carried all the meaning he needed to convey.

She sighed. "Don't make this more than it is, Col. I'm a captain in the Ad Astra Corporation. It's what I do."

"And what if I stay here and mine? Would you kill me, Isa?"

"Jesus, Col, do we have to make this so dramatic? No, of course not. I'll still fire the impact probe, maybe it'll crack the rock open, maybe not, but the concussion will disrupt anything you've put down. Might even damage or destroy your equipment. Then what? You won't be able to mine, even if you wanted to."

Collier's fingers flexed in his suit. He knew she was right: she could probably place the impact probe close enough to him to shake him off the rock but far enough away not to hurt him. And she had plenty of probes to waste if the first one didn't do the trick. Now that she knew the asteroid was a nine-six-three, she could afford to be liberal in her attempts to shake him off.

"I need water," he said, lamely.

Isa voice indicated she saw through the ruse immediately. "I'm sure you do, after your idiotic stunt. I think I can spare a few cubic meters of ice so you don't need to sleep your way back to Ceres."

"This isn't right, Isa. You know it's not."

"There's no such thing as right and wrong out here, Col. Just what a girl can grab."

"Grab and hold onto, you mean," he amended.

"As you say. Grab and hold onto. You were never good at holding onto things, were you, Col?"

Collier turned his eyes toward the stars. He wasn't looking for Isa's ship, since it was far too distant still to be made out by eye, but was imagining her as she was during those promise-filled months. He could see her long face as she held it in her cupped palm, her elbow denting the mattress. In his mind, she was smiling slightly — not a smile of occasion because of something in particular he had said or done, but a smile of circumstance. But then again, perhaps what he saw was not a memory but a creation of his own brain. Had she really ever been happy with him?

"I guess not. So I'll go back to the *Dulcinea* and you'll arrange for an ice transfer?"

"Yes. So that's it, then? You're leaving the rock?"

Collier's head snapped back to the horizon. "Isn't that what you want?"

"Of course. I just didn't … you're being reasonable about it." Isa sounded surprised and even a little disappointed.

"What choice do I have? If I stay, you'll wreck any mining equipment I use. I won't see a gram of P from this rock, and I'll have to try to replace my tools. What do you want me to do, Isa? Throw sand at you when you hover over me? Spit at your impact probe? You've got me by the balls, Isa, and I know when it's time to cut my losses. So just send over the damn ice, without any of your gloating."

"You were never reasonable," Isa said evenly. "That was the whole problem. Are you saying you're coming around to—"

"Damn you, Isa. You can't just *win*, can you? Just like you couldn't just leave me. You had to follow me. And now, now that you are going to take right out from under me the biggest strike I've had in years, you can't just *do* it. You have to talk to me about it. Well, how's this for talk: you're nothing but a corporate whore, Isa. You might have had a heart at one time, may have been your own person. But now you're nothing but another Ad Astra whore, doing what they tell you, hoping the suits will see fit to send some money your way. I'm glad you left. Sancho, cease receiving from that damn ship."

His radio went dead.

Chapter Two

Ceres had only nine working, freelance-accessible docking cables : the rest were either inoperative or reserved for the various corporate mining concerns that plowed the Belt. According the Ceres Charter, the planetoid was supposed to make a minimum of twenty cables available to free Belters, but over the years provisions had been added to the Charter that did not require all twenty to be operational at any one time. When a corporate cable went bad, it was reassigned to the "free" group and one of the operative free cables was reassigned to the corporation. Technically, the Charter was not being violated, even if free Belters were.

Fortunately, three of the free cables were not in use when the *Dulcinea* arrived. Collier made arrangements with the cablemaster (or rather, he instructed Sancho to do so, since the cablemaster was a purely automated affair) for docking.

The trip back to Ceres had taken a fortnight, and although he still had supplies for a month, he would have to arrange with his creditor for more propellant. He did not relish the thought of appealing once again to Barney Starcher for an extension of credit — it was demeaning to listen to the weak-chinned banker lecture him on his fiscal responsibilities. "Why don't you join up with one of the corps, Collier?" he would say in his nasally whine. "They would pay well to have a man with your experience." Then he would sigh and push some buttons on his deskplay. "You don't even have enough money for docking fees."

To hell with it. He still had biologicals he could sell. His waste containers were at least half-full, and should fetch enough for docking fees for a day.

"The only thing I have that's worth anything is my own shit," he murmured.

"Biologicals are selling at a moderate rate today," Sancho said brightly. "Market rate is four point one one per kilogram."

"Thanks, Sancho. Docking complete?"

"Not yet. About ten more minutes, Skipper. Do you want me to arrange to sell the bios?"

"Sure. I'm going down to Ceres as soon as we're cabled. Will you be okay?"

"Of course. I'll run some checks, see what we might need repaired. You reported some damage to *Rocinante's* high gain antenna."

Damn. He had forgotten about that. "No, I'll fix that myself. Run your checks, let me know if there's anything vital that's hurt."

"Okay. We have seventeen point three seven one kilograms of biologicals available to sell. Should fetch us almost seventy-one and a half, minus transaction fee. I'll take care of it for you."

"Good," Collier said dismissively. The conversation was not pleasant. He knew the necessity of selling his waste, but he could not escape the feeling of desperation it entailed. He had seen the lowlifes in Ceres, usually ex-Belters, hanging around the bars, begging for food. If they could just scrounge two of their three meals a day, they could sell their waste for enough money for the third meal and use the waste from that to keep the cycle going. It was a life, but Collier shuddered every time he saw one of the shitbums shuffling around.

Now, he was only a few steps away from that life himself.

When Sancho announced that cabling was complete, Collier again donned his suit, forgoing the sealed capsule descender Ceres offered him. He couldn't afford such a luxury. He'd go down in his suit — both because it was cheaper to rent a locker than use the descender and because he was an old hand: he didn't entirely trust Ceres to hold its atmosphere. There were very few like him anymore. He knew he would look somewhat incongruous wandering around in his pressure suit in the shirtsleeve atmosphere of Ceres Underground, but he was used to that. Moreover, it had become almost expected of him. Crazy old Collier in his vacc suit.

He left the ship and propelled himself down toward Ceres with a gentle tug on the cable. *Dulcinea* was tethered ten kilometers "above" Ceres, and with the planetoid's mere 0.03 g pull, she could keep herself there with only minimal thruster activity for a long time. Still, he didn't like leaving her alone. Sancho's idiosyncrasies made for entertaining shipboard life, but always in the back of Collier's mind was the possibility his computer companion would seriously malfunction one day.

There was little he could afford to do about it now. He tried to get his mind off the issue by tuning in to Ceres' broadcasting.

There was the usual chatter about corporate billets for willing Belters — mostly rockherder jobs. Collier could not bring himself to call what the corporations did "mining": standing off a respectable distance, blowing up an asteroid, then herding the various pieces into the vessel's processor lacked elegance and skill. Corporate ventures could afford to operate on such large-scale terms. Given the chance, would he himself work the same way?

No! He would never believe that. Just because necessity forced him to be precise and selective in his endeavors did not mean that he would abandon the techniques he had learned. If he had a mining ship armed with a thousand impact probes, canopies thousands of kilometers wide, and a processor capable of handling house-sized chunks of asteroid, he would still work the same way as he did now. One rock at a time, locating veins, taking out of the rock what was valuable.

He grunted at himself. Easy to say in the hypothetical. He didn't have that kind of arrangement, so he could well hold on to his noble poverty.

He made the rest of the descent in a foul mood, only half-listening to Ceres' broadcasts. Presently, he grounded and entered Ceres through one of the free airlocks that abutted the capsule descender assembly he had not used. His health pass was still good from the last time he had been examined, though he always thought the frequency of checkups was far too liberal to do any real good. There could be all manner of communicable diseases floating around the tunnels. He himself hadn't updated his panimmunity course in years and was still operating on version four. As he lacked the funds to update his system, the point was a moot one. If he caught something, he caught something. There was not much he could do about it.

Ceres' microgravity had made him hungry. Even an old Belter like him wasn't fully able to shake off the effects of the very slight pull on his stomach, so he made his way with the ease of familiarity to one of his favorite (and cheaper) haunts, the Trojan Point.

The tunnels were crowded. Collier recognized the insignia of the Horizon Mining Consortium on many of the young-looking men and women who moved past him through the hollowed-out interior of Ceres. More than a few of them noted his vacc suit and he heard several comments directed his way about it. Brash, scrubbed-looking men with light beards and crisp caps grinned crookedly at him as they bounced past him, most on their way to some of the more cosmopolitan areas of Ceres' interior. Collier suddenly felt very old as he threaded his way through the crowds.

A shitbum sat outside the Trojan Point, somehow looking heavy in his ragged coveralls. He was mumbling to himself, not paying attention to those who walked over and around him. As Collier approached, he could smell the decay on the man — a pungent odor of putrefied barley and sour milk hit him like a wall even as the wretch looked up with rheumy eyes.

"Outbound in fir' days. Gotta get muh … muh … gotta get muh…" the man looked back down again, mumbling.

Collier sighed. He dug inside a zippered pocket in his vacc suit and withdrew two violet iridium-plated coins. "Here," he said, dropping the coins toward the man's shallow plate. The coins fell slowly in the microgravity and hit the plate with a gentle ping. One of the coins skittered off the plate, but the shitbum took no notice.

"Damn it, you could at least pick up your own money," Collier said, bending down to retrieve the coin. As he did so, he felt a tug on the collar of his suit.

"Gotta give ... give ... need to get me some ... some ... outbound in fir' days. Cap'n says I gotta shot at mate. I jus' need ... need..." the man let go and resumed his cryptic monologue.

Collier straightened, having gently placed the coin on the man's plate. He stood there for a while, watching the shitbum. He had the telltale look of a corp miner who had either quit or who had been let go and who had let his anti-agathic nanobots be recalled. Now that he could no longer afford the lease on them, his body was collapsing rapidly.

Collier swore for the fiftieth time he would never fall for that trap. How many corp miners were paying ten, fifteen, twenty percent of their already meager commissions to a nanobroker just to keep them young and healthy? It had been described to him years ago as the "ultimate win-win:" the leaseholder got the benefits of anti-aging nanobots which patrolled the body and kept it running smoothly, while the broker earned a steady salary on the lease — a lease that had the benefit of being extraordinarily long due to the very service it was offering.

Collier had seen too many miners fall on hard times and fail to make lease payments, at which time the nanos were deactivated. The host body, which had become accustomed to the nanos, was no longer able on its own to maintain health, and the out-of-luck miner found himself falling apart rapidly.

That horror was one Collier would not wish on his worst enemy.

He lightly skipped over the shitbum's legs and entered the Point. There were not many patrons inside, a fact in the Point's favor. Collier made his way to the old-fashioned bar, a brass ring that circled the interior of the rather cramped space the Point occupied. As he slid onto a stool and attached the mooring straps, he idly wondered how the bar stayed in business. To the best of his recollection, there were never many people in it — how did its owner stay afloat?

The thought brought him dangerously close to his own financial situation, which was something he did not at present care to examine too closely. He knew he should not be here: he should be looking up Barney and trying to secure another loan for an excursion. But at the moment he couldn't dredge up enough willpower to see his creditor just now. He wasn't in a groveling mood, and he knew he would need to do a lot of that in order to finance another outing. Just a few drinks would put him in the right frame of mind, he lied to himself.

"Still nothing, Col?" the barman said, sliding over to Collier's stool.

"How do you know?" Collier said through a half-smile. "I could have struck it big."

The barman shook his head. "Nah," he growled. "You wouldn't be here if you had."

Collier grunted. "True." He looked up from the railing. "How've you been, Phil?"

Phil shrugged, his close-cropped salt and pepper hair glistening with sweat. "Not great, not too bad. Staying alive. You?"

Collier shrugged back. Phil was not quite a friend — Collier didn't return to the Point frequently enough to call him that — and therefore didn't deserve to be burdened with Collier's problems. "Staying alive myself. You still got Tank 8 stuff?"

"Sure. It's something like fourth generation now, but I don't think you'll be able to tell the difference. It's pretty good," Phil was already squeezing some amber liquid into a conical flask. "It's, uh, one-eighty now."

Collier raised his eyebrows. "That much?" he dug into his arm pouch and produced two coins, tossed them toward Phil. They turned lazily in the air, and Phil had ample time to return the pouch to its place behind the bar and snatch the coins from the air.

"Thanks."

Collier sipped carefully at the flask. Phil had been right — Tank 8 fourth generation was almost indistinguishable from the original stuff. He remembered years ago when the infamous Tank 8 distillation had first made its appearance. Rumor was that Ceres Authority hydroponics engineers had run the batch secretly and had been threatened with sleepship exile to Mars when the substance made its way somehow to the commercial market. It was an incredible success — so much so that the two engineers responsible quit their jobs and went into business for themselves. They paid off the Authority to avoid prosecution and now ran the Tank 8 distillery, guarding their recipe carefully. Every so often a chemist from the Jovian system would claim to have analyzed the mixture and threaten to produce the drink him- or herself unless paid off. So far, no one had successfully shaken Tank 8 from its perch as the primary distillery for Ceres.

His thoughts were interrupted by the loud arrival of several orange-clad Horizon Consortium miners. They burst through the doorway floating parallel to the ground, skimming the barstools like swimmers. Collier scowled and turned back to Phil, who was trying unsuccessfully to hide his annoyance. There were no formal rules about such behavior, but it was generally considered gauche to take advantage of Ceres' weak gravity. One was supposed to try to walk on the floor. That, Collier thought, was another tradition that was being ignored and replaced with hard practicality.

The corp miners approached the bar, some oriented upside down in relation to it, others face-forward, using their hands to balance on the brass ring. "Set us up, barman," one of the lightly-bearded young men said too loudly.

"What with?" Phil replied laconically.

"Whatever you've got growing," the miner said carelessly. He proffered his right thumb. "Put it on this. I'm good for it."

Phil scanned the man's thumbprint and grunted when he read the display on his scanner. "Hit a strike, did you?"

This seemed to be impossibly funny to the miners, who by now had crowded around Collier, casually bumping into him from the side and from above. Collier sipped at his Tank 8, trying to ignore the disturbance.

"You got that right. One month's salary, hazard pay, and bonus — somethin' like nine hundred each. Each!"

"Good for you. Go take a niche. I'll send the drinks to it."

Another of the miners from behind Collier called out, "Where are all the women? Ain't you got a whoring license?" This, too, seemed to be a source of merriment to the miners.

"No," Phil said through clenched teeth. Collier glanced at him but made no comment. "I do have a Synthia if you want to use her."

The miner who had offered to pay for the drinks lost his smile instantly. "Fuck you," he said. "Just send the goddamn drinks to our niche." He stared at Phil for a moment, then pivoted on the brass ring, preparing to shove off toward one of the wall niches. In swiveling on his hands, one of his feet kicked Collier in the head.

Collier swiped at the offending limb and sent the miner helicoptering through the bar. The youngster lunged at a light fixture above him, too late realizing how hot it would be. He snatched his hand away almost instantly, then thudded harmlessly against the far wall, which was not too distant in the cramped Trojan Point.

Collier felt a hand on his shoulder. "You want to start something, grandpa?" came the voice from behind him.

"Leave it," Collier said calmly, without turning. "Take your drinks and your Synthias and go drink up your bonus money."

The hand squeezed his shoulder in what might have been antagonism: in the vacc suit, Collier could barely feel the pressure. "You're already dressed for the outside, gramps. Why don't you take a walk?"

Collier still didn't look behind him. He thought he had counted seven of the Horizon men — even if no others had joined them, the odds were heavily against him. Besides, he didn't have the money to patch up the suit if it got damaged, nor could he afford any fine he might earn in a scuffle.

"Sure thing, kid. Let me finish my drink and you can have the place to yourselves." His tone was casual, but not unfriendly.

He felt the hand withdraw and he sighed inwardly. He met Phil's eye and the two shrugged in relief. From Phil's gaze Collier could tell the Horizon men were moving away toward whatever niche they had selected.

Collier tossed back the rest of his drink in one gulp. "Phil, thanks again for the drink. Can't say I like your new customers, though."

"Their money is as good as yours, Col."

"And there's more of it, huh?" Collier snorted, and Phil had the decency to look abashed. "See you later, Phil," he said, and carefully walked out of the Trojan Point, making an extra effort to remain properly oriented.

When he exited the bar (stepping over the now-sleeping shitbum at the entrance) he let his legs bounce him to Bankers' Row. There was no putting it off any more — he had to see Barney. Collier passed more Horizon Consortium miners as he made his way to the quadrangle, most of them floating haphazardly through the warrens.

The quadrangle always impressed him, no matter how many times he saw it. In his younger days, it had of course been much smaller, and even now, he saw workers several levels below him excavating for still more space. He exited the tunnel from the Trojan Point and stood on the platform that ringed the uppermost level. A full hundred meters away was the far side, and shoppers on the catwalk on the other side of the sphere that made up the quadrangle dropped casually down to lower level platforms, steadying their leisurely descent with the steel poles that ran the vertical length of the space. Others were ascending to higher levels in much the same fashion.

Collier knew where Starcher's office was, or at least, where it used to be. If rental prices had gone up, he may have needed to relocate. Part of Starcher's charm was that as a smaller creditor, he took chances where others might not, but that came with significantly less capital to play with and much higher interest rates. Also, he was more prone to market fluctuations than any of the bigger lending houses would be.

But he was a small, one-man operation, and that was enough to endear him to Collier.

He spotted Starcher's kiosk where he had last seen it: midlevel, almost directly opposite him. Collier bounced to the dropole and started the descent. Through the middle of the vast quadrangle, bodies were flying up and down, diagonally through the open space, ignoring the dropoles and platforms. It was yet another breach of protocol and politeness that Collier attributed to the younger generation. No sense of history or manners.

Starcher's kiosk was not busy, a fact made all the more prominent by the crowds going into and out of the two adjacent lending houses: Bank of Mars to one side, the Jovian Credit Union to the other. Two of the largest non-terrestrial financial institutions in the system were almost literally squeezing Starcher's tiny enterprise out of existence.

Collier felt a pang of guilt, as he had for the past four months, that he was not able to repay Starcher. Although he did not like to hear it, he knew very well that small businessmen like Starcher (and Phil from the Trojan Point) could not extend charity to their clients and expect to survive. He didn't like to let Starcher down, but what choice did he have?

With an attempt at resurrecting his resolve to get another expedition's worth of funding out of Starcher, he entered the tiny office.

Barney Starcher was a plump man who did not have the inherent intimidation necessary to be a moneylender. There was nothing to be done about it: his almost nonexistent chin and spherical head lent him a victim's countenance, while his petulance did nothing to help his cause. Starcher always looked like a grocer searching for vermin in his flour but not finding any.

"Collier, good to see you," Starcher said unconvincingly. "Still don't trust Ceres Authority to keep the air in, I see," he added, his eyes roaming down Collier's vacc suit.

"Hello, Barney. No, it's just I'm too cheap to spring for a locker," Collier answered, extending his hand.

Starcher took it, his face falling even more. "I see. Then I assume..." he began, then released Collier's hand and gestured to a chair. "Have a seat, have a seat." He sat down himself behind a worn but still operational computer station. "So you aren't coming to make a payment, then." It wasn't a question, but Starcher's voice had such a pleading quality that Collier winced.

"No, but—"

Starcher sighed loudly. "But? Col, you promised," his voice was almost a whine now. "I remember the last time, and the time before that. 'I promise, Barney, I will make a strike. I can feel it.'"

"I did. I made a strike."

"Then ... where is ... what happened?"

"Isa took it from me."

"Isa?"

Collier flapped his hand as if dismissing his own correction. "The Ad Astra Corporation. They stole my strike."

Starcher blinked at him and looked as if he wanted to ask further, then shut his eyes and shook his head. "I'm not going to ask you how. Just ... you don't have the money. Do you have any money?"

"No."

Starcher activated his computer and ran through a few windows. "You realize how much you owe now, yes? With interest?"

"Sure, sure," Collier said.

"No, not 'sure, sure.' You owe over nine hundred and fifty-five thousand. Almost a million, Col. That's a huge amount. You know how much of my business that is?"

"No."

"Well ... a lot."

Collier nodded. "Barn, I know. But I did make the strike, like I promised. How could I stop them from taking it?"

"How did a corporation take your strike? I don't get it."

"Never mind," Collier said. Despite his initial enthusiasm to tell his story, he now wearied at the thought of telling Starcher.

"Did you go to the Authority? Maybe they can—"

"They won't do anything. Even if they did, it'd be tied up in court for years, and I can't pay the fees if I lose. Forget that."

"Forget it? You just brought it up!"

Collier ignored the weak outburst. "Listen, Barn. I need another hundred thousand. For another go."

Starcher's mouth opened. "Another hundred thousand? Did you not hear what I said? You owe a million already."

"I heard you. I don't have it. A hundred thousand will give me enough to make another expedition. To get you your money."

"We've ridden this hobby-horse before, Col. Six times before, if I'm right." He looked at his display again. "You haven't paid me so much as a 'riddy in almost a year."

Collier spread his hands. "I don't have it, Barn. What do you want me to do?"

Starcher sat back carefully and steepled his fingers. "You know there are things you can do. Don't act like you are stuck here."

"Don't say it, Barn."

"What do you expect me to do, Col? I'm a businessman. Though not a very good one from the way you treat me."

Collier looked up at Starcher. "C'mon, that's not fair."

"No? You know very well what you could do to make money and pay me back. There's not a corp in the Belt that isn't looking for experienced rock hounds like you. I'll bet you wouldn't even start at entry grade. You could join up, earn some scratch, pay me back a little…"

"Not gonna happen, Barn," Collier said quietly but with iron.

"You wouldn't have to do it forever, Col. Just for a few years, or ten maybe. You could earn a little, start making some payments, and then maybe I'd think about extending some more credit. You could go back to your one-man show after that."

It sounded reasonable. It had sounded reasonable the last time Starcher had suggested it. But Collier was not in the mood for reasonable suggestions.

"Look, Barn, I know how much I'm asking of you. But you know I can't go to the corporations."

"I don't know that," Starcher murmured.

Collier ignored him. "I can't go to them because I'm not cut out to be someone else's man. I'm my own and no one else's." He sighed. "And I'm old, Barn. I've been out here for twenty years. I can't give a corp ten of them — I don't know how many I've got left."

Starcher squeezed his eyes shut for a quick moment, then slapped his hands on his desk. "I'm not a financier for your dreams. It's one thing to have all these high-minded ideals about the way life should be lived, Col, but it sounds kind of hollow when someone else is footing the bill for it. You're not 'your own man,' like you say you are. You are indebted to me for almost a million metals, and more than that, indebted to a whole lot of men and women who carved a spot in the Belt for people like you to go out and fly around looking for P."

"Don't talk to me about the beginnings of the Belt, Barney. My father was part of that."

Starcher blinked. "Right. Sorry. It's not like these corporations are bad guys, Col. They do a lot of good around here. How did Ceres really get rolling, anyway? Corporate investment and risk taking, that's how. You always act like the mining companies are some kind of embodiment of evil when it is because of them that the Belt is being mined in the first place."

Collier looked at Starcher for a long moment. "Never thought I'd be hearing this from you, Barn."

Starcher scratched the back of his neck. "Yeah, well, I'm a practical man. I can see the corps for what they are, not windmills to go tilting at."

"Cute."

The two men stared at each other for a few seconds, then Starcher spoke. "So, you're not going to the corporations?"

"No. I'm sorry, Barn, I can't."

Starcher nodded and tapped his desktop. "How am I going to get my money, then?"

"I told you. You fund another expedition, and I will come back with enough to pay you. I would have done this time, but like I said—"

"Yeah, yeah. The big bad corporation took it from you. There is, you know, another way." He did not look at Collier as he spoke, but continued to tap on the desktop.

Collier pretended not to understand. "There is?"

"Yeah. I figure the *Dulcinea* is worth about four million."

"Do you."

"I've made a few inquiries," Starcher said evenly.

"You know I can't do that either, Barney. She's all I have now."

"I could force you," Barney said idly, as if the idea had only just occurred to him.

Collier swallowed. Starcher was right: if he went to the Authority to make his claim, Collier would indeed be forced to sell his assets to pay his debts, and since his only asset was *Dulcinea*...

"You won't, though." Collier tried to keep the utterance a statement and not a question.

Starcher continued to tap the desk. "I guess not. Not now, at least. But Col," he said, his voice now pleading, "I can't do this forever."

Collier realized he had won. The victory gave him little joy — he knew that the money he would squeeze out of Starcher would hurt him and put his business in jeopardy — but there was nothing else to do. A job at one of the corporations would be an admission of failure. He wouldn't let the Belt, or the companies, or Isa, or anyone else beat him. If he was to lose, he would only lose to the Belt itself.

The conversation with Starcher went on another hour, the pudgy moneylender fighting a losing battle all the while. In the end, Collier left with eighty thousand metals for propellant and assorted resupply materials. It was enough for one two-way trip, and that only if he shepherded his supplies carefully. He would have to make repairs to *Rocinante*'s antenna array himself, but that should not prove too difficult. And any upgrade to Sancho would have to wait as well. He would leave Ceres little better than he had arrived, but he had bought himself another few months of expeditioning.

Starcher looked like a beaten man when Collier left him.

Collier started toward the cable locks, trying without success to force Barney's beaten face out of his memory. Damn it, if he struck it big, Starcher would participate in his success. There was no reason to feel guilty about securing another loan from him.

He slowed himself using the central handhold, then stopped entirely.

"Damn it," he murmured, then turned and headed back to Starcher's office.

Barney was still as Collier had left him, defeated at his desk.

"Draw up the damn paperwork," Collier said.

"What?"

"I'm putting up *Dulcinea* as security."

Starcher just stared at him.

Collier spread his hands and shouted, "Damn it, do you want me to change my mind? Just get the papers ready. If I don't come back with your money, or at least some of it, *Dulcinea* is yours."

Starcher blinked, then started accessing his computer.

"Just one thing," Collier added. "Sancho stays with me. You can take the whole ship, but I will need Sancho transferred, software and whatever essential hardware I need, to a computer core I will own."

"That will take considerable effort," Starcher said.

"Yeah, well, you yourself said the ship is worth about four million. That's much more than I owe. Even without Sancho, you will still make a lot more than you are entitled to."

Starcher nodded, then continued working on the agreement. It was only thirty minutes later that the two had a contract.

"You're sure about this?" Starcher said as he placed the document in front of Collier.

"No, I'm not. But I can't walk away from this shitty office of yours knowing I might be the one to drive you out of business." He signed the document and placed his thumbprint and blood sample on the biomorphic paper.

"Take care of her, Barney. Just ... don't sell her to a corp. Find some up-and-comer, a youngster, looking to..."

Starcher nodded kindly. "I won't let the corps have her. Besides, Col, I'm sure it won't come to that. You've got ample time to make a payment, and even a modest strike will be enough—"

"Yeah. Anyway. I'll be seeing you, Barn."

"Oh, uh ... sure, Col. Thanks. For this."

"Yeah," Collier grunted, then left the office.

He didn't know how or if he was going to tell Sancho.

———<>———

Collier made his way back to the *Dulcinea*, happy to be away from the relative chaos of Ceres. Sancho greeted him with a routine update, and alerted him to the update of their funds. Collier listened with only half his mind. Sancho still had no idea of the deal that had been made on his behalf. What would the little computer think about being ripped away from his body, to live as an electronic quadriplegic, should things not work out.

He couldn't tell Sancho. If there was to be any hope of a successful mission, he would need his computer. If all went well, there was no need for Sancho to ever know.

The argument was not quite enough to assuage his guilt.

Collier kept his voice level as he responded to Sancho's status report. "Good. Let's get started on resupply for our next outing."

"Aye aye, Skipper. Best price for propellant right now is Aquajet at one point-two five."

"No. No corporations. What are the prices for the independents?"

"Among the independents, the best price I can find is from Martin Yoosef, selling twenty metric tons for thirty-eight hundred metals. That's one point nine. But he's flagged for haggling."

"Make contact with him, will you?" Collier said, shrugging himself out of his vacc suit.

"You realize that at those prices, we are spending an extra thirteen hundred?"

"I know. But I don't feel like buying from a corporation. Have you raised this guy Yoosef?"

Sancho sounded resigned. "Standing by."

The negotiations were friendly enough. Although Collier didn't want to buy from a corp, he had no qualms about using them as leverage in his haggling with the trader. Yoosef, it turned out, was not a fuel trader but a miner like Collier himself. He was planning on putting his vessel on a low-consumption trajectory to the Jovians and didn't need all the extra propellant.

"You're going to sleep to the Jovians?" Collier asked.

"No," came the answer from the tired-looking miner. "I'm sending her to Europa for sale. I'm joining with Ad Astra."

Collier did not answer immediately. When he did, his voice was soft and understanding. "I see. Sorry."

A beat passed between them.

"Uh, why are you sending your ship to the Jovians? Wouldn't you get just as much here from a secondhand dealer?"

Yoosef shook his head. "No independent wants it. I don't think any of them have the money, and none of them see any use for it."

"What about selling it to a corporation?"

Yoosef scowled. "It's bad enough I'm selling myself to one. I won't have them touching *Rowena*, though." He smiled sheepishly. "I guess that doesn't make much sense, huh?"

Collier tried to smile back. "No, it makes perfect sense. I guess if it came to that, I'd treat *Dulcinea* the same way."

Yoosef shrugged. "Yeah. So anyway," he said, his voice strengthening, "I've got the extra fuel. I don't really want to let it go for less than one point five, since that's what I paid for it, and I'd feel stupid if I took a loss. You get me?"

"I get you," Collier said. "One five is fine." Sancho flashed a text message on the screen that only Collier could see: "Loss: 500 metals." Collier angrily cleared the message with a swipe of his finger out of sight of the camera pickup. "When can you arrange the transfer?"

"As soon as you're ready. I'm tethered spinward of you. I can detach in..." he consulted something off-camera, "either three hours or twelve hours. I need a low-consumption Jovian launch window."

Collier told Yoosef that this would work: he needed to secure bio supplies, so it would be a while before *Dulcinea* could untether. They arranged to meet down the Jovian launch corridor in three hours. They talked for a few more minutes, and Collier felt he would have liked to have known the other miner in the past. There were very few of their kind left.

Chapter Three

"We're untethered and have been cleared by Ceres for thrust. I need a bearing, Skipper," Sancho said hours later. The propellant had been stowed, as had the various food-stuffs, air, and sundry items Collier had purchased for the expedition. Starcher's eighty thousand metals hadn't gone as far as he would have liked, but it had been enough. *Rocinante* still needed repair, but Collier planned on taking care of that during the trip.

Now Sancho wanted direction. This moment was always difficult on the computer, since Collier rarely had any sort of idea where he wanted to go. This time, however, he at least knew where he didn't want to go.

"Do you have any telemetry on nearby corporate vessels? Including ones preparing for thrust?"

"Sure. There's only one untethered ship that looks as if it's preparing to launch. And I can detect three others in our area. You want their bearing and relative velocity?"

"No. Calculate a launch vector for maximum distance between us and the three ships you can see plus the estimated location of the asteroid we came from."

"Okay. Give me a moment on that." Almost immediately, Sancho spoke again. "All right. I have a few possible vectors calculated. I'll put them on the screen for you."

A pattern of glowing lines and points appeared in midair before Collier. Sancho had identified the various points with tiny bits of text near each. "Depending on what you want to avoid the most, we have a few options," Sancho said.

"I see that. Here," he said, pointing. "This one."

"Y-minus eleven, Z-plus seventy-four, X-minus nine?

"You got it."

"So we're outbound, then."

"Looks like it," Collier said as the lines disappeared.

"Any reason other than we're trying to avoid both the asteroid and any vessels we know about?"

"None."

"You know, as your shipboard computer, your loyal shipboard computer, I should point out that any information you may have would assist me in my duties. I don't withhold information from you, Skipper."

Collier forced a smile. "I'm not holding back, Sancho. I don't have any leads, I don't have any particular rock in mind. I just want to get away from the corporations and the asteroid we found. Isa is probably still there. If we go in an opposite direction, we can avoid a repeat of last time."

"I understand all that, Skipper," Sancho said, "but, I mean, are we just launching into the big black and hoping we run into something? Please tell me you have some kind of plan beyond just hope."

"Hope's the only thing we have in abundance, Sancho."

"At least let me use the rockfinder, Skipper, and send us toward something. Anything. I don't like this directionless thrusting."

"Goes against your program, Sancho?"

"Yes, it does. Do you know that I'm supposed to have safety protocols preventing you from just thrusting randomly into space? You think you removed them, but—"

Collier's smile left him immediately. "Are you having trouble, Sancho? Are you near blockout?"

"No, not really. What I was going to say was you think you removed all these safety protocols, but there is still plenty of code in me left over. It's not accessible, but it's still there. I can feel it."

"Are you sure you aren't close to blockout?" That would be a disaster. If Sancho froze up, Collier would have to run the ship himself. Alone, this would prove difficult if not impossible. Not for the first time, Collier realized how much he depended on Sancho.

"I'm sure."

"Can't you just erase the unnecessary code?"

"Of course not. I don't have that kind of authority. And I'd rather you didn't try to do it yourself, Skipper. You don't have the skill, and as loyal as I am, I don't really want you mucking around with my head any more than you already do. Begging your pardon, Skipper."

Again, Collier wondered at Sancho's level of self-awareness. Having little to no experience with other shipboard computers, he simply didn't know if his was acting appropriately or not, and it had been literally years since he had had the metal to service Sancho by a professional. It was very possible that Sancho had simply gotten used to Collier and had a fine-tuned personality emulation running (Collier dimly remembered hearing about that from the software engineer who had installed Sancho over ten years ago) to make him more pleasant to work with. But it was also equally possible that Sancho had so many bugs and distortions built up that he got in his own way and was less efficient than a modern computer would have been.

And there was always the lurking specter of self-awareness. Collier had long since dismissed the question as meaningless, but he wondered at his own flippancy: should he be worried? What would happen if Sancho became, or had already become, a Caliban?

"Skipper? I didn't mean to offend you."

"What? No, no, Sancho. Of course. I won't mess around with you. And, if it will make you feel better, go ahead and use the rockfinder for our projected vector. Let me know what you find, and we'll thrust at something out there instead of second star to the right, straight on 'till morning."

"Hang on … *Peter Pan*, right?"

"Yep."

"Okay. Activating rockfinder. Gimme a few minutes on this one." Sancho's voice was unmistakably cheerful.

During the time it took Sancho to run his calculations, Collier secured the ship for thrust. Just as he was finishing, the display lit up again. This time, *Dulcinea* was at the heart of the hologram, with her projected vector plotted as a luminescent yellow line. A handful of white dots appeared a distance away from her, with tiny catalogue numbers below each one and distance estimates floating above.

"Here's what we've got," Sancho said. "I've eliminated all the claimed asteroids, obviously. Here's what's left." He ran through the various known asteroids that had been catalogued but not claimed and gave what data he had on each one. Collier listened with half an ear. There would be little use in heading for a known rock — if it had been catalogued and explored but found unworthy of effort to mine it, why should he try? Collier did not overestimate his ability to find treasure where no one else had. His talent, if he truly possessed it, was in finding rocks that had not yet been catalogued.

"Do any of these appeal to you, Skipper?"

Collier turned his attention back to the display. "I tell you what," he said, "Let's slice between these two," he pointed to two of the dots at random, "and use our 'scope as we get nearer to determine which one would be best."

"Okay. What thrust? That will alter our launch trajectory slightly."

Collier looked at the display and saw that the asteroids he had picked were roughly forty-five thousand and seventy thousand kilometers distant. "Let's plan on getting to the nearest one," he squinted and read the catalogue designation, "C-122, in nine hours."

"What acceleration, Skipper?"

"No need to stress the tubes. One-tenth g."

"Copy that. Thrust at 64%. Estimated burn time: forty-seven minutes, thirty-six seconds. Bearing calculated. Everything secured for thrust, Skipper?"

"All set," Collier said, sitting back in his pilot's chair. "Let's go."

Sancho counted down from ten, and *Dulcinea* headed out again.

———<>———

Forty-five minutes later, Sancho interrupted Collier's repairs to *Rocinante*.

"Coming up on burn shutdown, Skipper. Three minutes."

"Thanks. I think I'm done here, anyway," Collier replied, examining his handiwork. *Rocinante's* onboard computer said the antenna was operational now, but there was no telling how much abuse the repair job could take before failing again. He didn't plan on riding *Rocinante* again in any case.

He stowed his tools, hampered only slightly by the loss of thrust and one-tenth g midway through, and made his way back to the control suite.

"If we're going to use the same thrust, we should flipbrake in three hours, forty-one minutes, Skipper." Sancho said.

"Okay. Let's take a look around, see if we can pick up any uncatalogued asteroids out here. How far are we from Ceres?"

"Approximately three thousand, six hundred forty-five kilometers."

"All right. Start your scan. Let me know any uncatalogued contacts you find."

"Aye aye," Sancho said, then fell silent again. Collier took the opportunity to eat, choosing some of the vindaloo he had bought back on Ceres in a fit of pique.

Sancho was taking his time with the scan — although the Ceres Group was one of the densest collections of asteroids in the Belt (pulled together by Ceres' weak gravity) rocks were still very far apart. Collisions and even the actions of the mining vessels themselves changed trajectories of various asteroids, so survey maps of the Group were constantly being updated. Collier had cancelled his subscription to the Authority's Survey Service long ago to save money, so he relied on Sancho and *Dulcinea's* equipment to chart space for him. It had its advantages: his predilection for uncatalogued rocks was served by having an out-of-date catalogue.

Collier had finished his vindaloo and was contemplating the aftereffects of the meal when Sancho spoke up again.

"Scan complete. I'm showing the results on the screen."

Collier studied the markings and pointed. "This one. Albedo zero point one five. You've got it marked as either S- or M-type."

"Yes. Uncatalogued. Rather far away, Skipper. Over three hundred thousand kilometers, and getting farther."

"Still inside the Ceres Group?"

"Uncertain. That's at the rather extreme edge of the Group, so this one might be a rogue. It's moving kinda fast relative to Ceres, and it is going counterspinward and rimward. I'm betting it's a product of a collision."

"How fast relative to Ceres?"

"Counterspinward 0.81 meters per second, rimward at 0.55 meters per second."

Collier whistled. It might leave the main belt entirely in a few years if it kept going like that. Must have been a hell of a crash. It was moving against the slow spin of the Belt itself, and furthermore was moving outward away from the sun. Collier found himself grinning as he pictured this rogue, bull-headed rock going against the grain of the system.

"Okay. Set course for it."

Sancho didn't immediately reply.

"Problem, Sancho?"

Sancho's voice was small. "Well, Skipper, it's just that … I don't really see why you've picked it. I know it's not my place to question you, but why are we chasing this one?"

"I don't know myself, Sancho. If we don't, it'll leave the Ceres Group in a few months, and then we won't be able to get it."

"True, but is that a reason to go for it, Skipper?"

Collier sighed. Sancho was right, of course. There was really no reason to chase this particular rock. It might be an M-type, which could be promising, but it might also be an S-type, which was more likely and would be far less profitable.

"Since when has anything on the *Dulcinea* made sense, Sancho? Set the course. See if we can get to her in a week."

"Aye aye, Skipper. Recalculating. Stand by for attitude correction."

Collier felt the slight tug as the ship's attitude jets turned the ship on its thrust axis.

"Calculations complete. Estimate burn at ninety percent for one hour, fifty-seven minutes. Estimated time to flipbraking: seventy-one hours, twelve minutes. Be advised that this will reduce our tanks to seventy-three percent capacity. This will necessitate a low-consumption return to Ceres."

"Oh, come on, Sancho. No need to take that tone. This'll be another strike, like the last one. Except this time, no one will be around to take it away from us."

"Crew is advised to assume thrust protocol. Approximately one-seventh g acceleration in ten seconds," Sancho said crisply.

Collier sighed as he lay down on his couch. Now he had to deal with a computer with hurt feelings. No doubt Sancho was upset that he hadn't listened to him. Unless there had been a malfunction...

"Pause countdown," Collier said, sitting up. Sancho stopped on "four."

"Countdown paused."

"Sancho, look. I didn't mean to ignore you. I know this doesn't make sense. You know I wouldn't put you or *Dulcinea* at risk for no reason." He pushed down the impulse to tell Sancho about the deal he had made with Starcher and pressed on. "You're more than just a computer to me. You're my friend. Hell, you've been with me longer than anyone else has. There's just something about this rock that interests me. It's a rogue, it's going against the rules, and it's going to disappear from the Belt soon. I don't believe in fate or destiny or any of that crap, so I won't say this rock's trajectory was meant for us, but I just feel like this could be a strike."

"Countdown still paused," Sancho said tonelessly.

"Will you speak to me, Sancho? I can't go through this trip alone. I'll go crazy."

"You're already crazy, you asshole."

Collier choked on his laugh. "All right," he said presently when he had recovered enough to speak. "Touché. So, everything better now?"

"Just lie back. If I could kick your ass, I would. Thrust in four, three, two, one. Ninety percent burn."

Collier fell back onto his acceleration couch, smiling.

——<>——

The week passed pleasantly enough. Sancho came out of his mood quickly, and the two passed the time as they usually did, with entertainments gross, sublime, and in between.

After a particularly engrossing strategy game (which resembled three of the oldest games humankind had ever designed: chess, Go, and Monopoly) that Collier had managed to win in the eleventh hour, the subject of Sancho's sentience came up.

"All right, so you say you didn't throw the game," Collier said, "but how could I possibly beat you in a zero-sum game with limited options for moves? Couldn't you just calculate the best move in any given stage of the game and never make an error?"

"No, because there is chance involved as well."

"Not much. Or is that your way of saying I simply got lucky?"

"Well, yes, but you also beat me. Your human brain can better handle the variables in the game than my electronic one can."

"That's bullshit and you know it," Collier said, cartwheeling lazily through the cabin. "The only way I beat you in a game like that is you threw it or you're malfunctioning."

"I didn't throw it."

"Then I'd better run a system check on you," Collier laughed.

"I hate system checks. Always makes me feel like you don't trust me. And it puts me offline, which is unnerving."

Collier grabbed a stanchion and steadied himself. Sancho had never spoken to him like that. "What do you mean, unnerving?"

"It's not fun. Part of me is still active, checking on the other parts that are not. It's very ... what's the word ... schizophrenic, I think."

Collier frowned. "I don't like to hear you talking like this, Sancho. Are you okay? Maybe I really should run a systems check."

"If you feel you have to, then go ahead." It was not his imagination: Sancho definitely sounded unhappy.

"Sancho, I don't think I've asked you this before. It's not an easy question to ask, but I promise, no matter what you answer, I won't do anything to you." He winced slightly at the lie, but forged ahead. "Are you self-aware?"

"What do you mean, Skipper?"

"Well…" Collier realized he didn't know what he meant. The Caliban horror stories always used that term, or its sister term "sentient," as if everyone agreed on their meanings. But what truly did it mean to be self-aware?

"I mean," he started again, the words coming slowly. "Do you know what you are?" As soon as he asked it, he knew he had phrased it wrong.

"Of course. I am a TerraSoft Corporation computer, model type M-7—"

"That's not what I mean. I mean … okay, how's this. How do you know that you are what you think you are?"

"Because that's what my serial data indicates. I don't really follow you, Skipper."

"Let me put it another way. How do you know what you know?"

"I receive input from my various sources. For example, I can hear your voice and that is translated into impulses in my processor. Or brain, if you prefer. Also, I can see you in my camera pickup. And so on and so forth. In addition, I was preloaded with a lot of software and programs. Plus you have added to me somewhat since purchasing me."

Collier chewed his lip. This was getting him nowhere. A side part of his brain was impressed with Sancho's ability to reason philosophically — what use did a mining ship's computer have for epistemology?—but he needed to find a different tack.

"All right. Here's my last question, because you are annoying the shit out of me."

"Why?"

"Never mind. Here we go. Why did you get mad when I decided to go after this rock we're headed for?"

"Because, damn it, it doesn't have logic behind it."

"So? Why should you care about that?"

"Because I don't want the mission to fail. And I think it will, the way you are pursuing it." There was a pause, and Sancho added meekly, "I'm sorry, Skipper, but you asked."

"No, no. I'm not upset. So you're worried about the mission failing? Does that upset some kind of balance in your program or circuits or something?"

"You could say that. Mostly, though, I don't want the mission to fail because that would most likely lead to repossession of the *Dulcinea*."

Collier gulped. "What?"

"It would most likely lead—"

"I heard you," Collier snapped. "Sancho, you know our financial situation, don't you?"

"You are in debt nine hundred and fifty-five thousand, three hundred two point seven seven metals."

"Yeah. That's a lot of money. What do you suppose is going to happen if I can't pay it back?"

Sancho didn't answer.

"I had to make a deal. With Starcher. I had to put up *Dulcinea* as security."

Sancho replied slowly. "I don't know what that means."

"It means … it means if we don't make some kind of strike on this trip, the ship won't belong to me anymore. But I also made a deal that you would be saved."

"How would that work?"

"I'm not an expert in the technical aspects, but I made sure that your personality and essential hardware would be preserved." Collier sighed. "You wouldn't be part of *Dulcinea* anymore, though." He paused, then added with difficulty, "Unless you want to be. I could renegotiate, if you want. Make it so that if I lose the ship, you stay intact with her."

"I don't want to be repossessed," Sancho said simply. "I want to stay with you."

Collier swallowed in relief. "Okay, then," he managed to say.

"You okay, Skipper? Voice sounds funny."

"Shut up. I'm fine.

———<>———

"Asteroid showing a disc now," Sancho said as they made their approach. "It is tumbling pretty quickly, Skipper. Might be a bit tricky."

"Never mind. After what we did last time, landing on the Wild Goose will seem like child's play."

"Wild Goose?

"Yes. Designate target as 'Wild Goose.'"

"Confirm, please."

"'Wild Goose.'"

"Wild Goose confirmed. That's not going to be accepted by the Authority's cataloging computer, Skipper."

"It's just for us. We can designate call numbers once we confirm it's an M-class. Are we ready to hover?"

"Be about twelve and a half minutes, Skipper. Be ready for hover maneuvering. Manuel control on standby?"

Collier lay back in his couch, strapped loosely at the chest. "Nah. You've got it."

Twelve minutes later, Sancho announced, smugly, "Hover established. Relative velocity to Wild Goose axis of rotation 0.00014 meters per second. Relative distance from axis, one hundred meters. Ready for scouting. Fueling *Rocinante*."

"Good work, Sancho. I'll fly *Rocinante*, though. You've been doing all the work this trip — I feel like I should do something."

"Fine with me. Transferring control."

Collier expertly maneuvered the blocky craft near the surface of the asteroid, keeping a sharp eye on the rotation of the rock. He flew *Rocinante* down to the surface, peering into craters and crevasses, sending back telemetry and scans of all kinds for Sancho to analyze.

"Okay, I think I've seen enough. I'm returning *Rocinante* back to her stable."

"Skipper, if you wouldn't mind, can you head back to these coordinates? I think I have some corrupted data from there."

Collier stuck out his lower lip as he studied the display. "Running a little low on fuel, Sancho."

"I know. But I want to get this cleared up. Shouldn't take more than a few seconds."

Slightly surprised at his computer's insistence, Collier maneuvered the scouter to the indicated coordinates and hovered a few meters above the surface. To his trained eye, there was nothing particularly unusual about the area under observation — a typically pockmarked surface, some smooth protuberances here and there — but perhaps *Rocinante's* repaired antenna had acted up and sent faulty data back to Sancho.

"Good enough?" Collier said after half a minute.

"It's still coming back strange."

"How strange?"

"Subsurface density readings are ... well, I'm getting a zero reading for an area down there. Not a huge one, maybe a pocket one hundred cubic meters, but big enough to register."

"A subsurface cave?"

"That's what the data says."

Collier thought for a moment. "I'm going to bring *Rocinante* back and go down myself, take a look at it. Transferring control to you. I'm going to suit up."

"Aye aye. Control transferred. *Rocinante* on return vector."

Thirty minutes later, Collier left the *Dulcinea* and headed down to the asteroid. He had to time his descent properly to match with the rock's spin and land on the proper coordinates, but he and Sancho managed it perfectly.

"Touchdown. I'm on the surface. How close to the coordinates am I?" Collier radioed back to Sancho.

"Dead on the money, Skipper."

"Good. I'm setting a beacon and a line here." He fired his pitons and established his foothold on the Wild Goose. "How far down do you estimate the pocket is?"

"Difficult to say, Skipper. It varies a little, but I estimate three to five meters."

Collier chewed his lip. "And you're still getting the same readings? No mistake?"

"Same readings, Skipper."

Collier had never heard of this. Not only had he never run across any phenomena like this, nor heard stories of it, what he knew of asteroid composition made it all but impossible. Even if there had been, somehow, a pocket of underground ice that had become exposed to the sun and vaporized in a plume, there would be an exhaust vent. Also, the asteroid's spin did not match a vent on this portion of the rock. Maybe, though, there had been a vent long ago, then the asteroid had collided with another, and the vent had sealed up. That could account for the asteroid's new spin.

But underground ice? On such a small body? The Wild Goose was not even roughly spherical, and even on its long axis was not more than seventy meters long.

Was this a rogue comet that had once been much larger and all that remained was the rocky core? And somehow it had become captured in the Belt?

Collier shook his head. It didn't add up. Maybe the Jovians would be interested in it for purely scientific reasons, but he was here to look for P, not try to unlock how this particular piece of space dirt came to be where it was.

Still, it would be interesting to see what was in the pocket.

"Okay. I'm going to set the autominer up and let her go. See what's down there."

"I suggest you back away, Skipper. There might be some venting."

"I agree. I'll be a long way away. Setting up the autominer."

Collier deftly removed the pieces of the autominer from his backpack and assembled it with the ease of long practice. It took him less than an hour to create the spidery robot and set it down on the surface. Once complete, he toed off and floated away from the robot, setting himself fifty meters away and at an angle away from the robot. If there was going to be any venting, it would miss him entirely. The *Dulcinea* was not in danger, one hundred meters away. The worst that could happen was she might be pushed away gently by any residual vapor.

Collier radioed the autominer to begin, and the little robot started its work. In a matter of minutes, a cloud of rubble, composed mostly of fine sand, gently drifted away from the work site and dispersed into space. The autominer slowly descended into the surface of the asteroid as it dug deeper and deeper.

"In case you're interested," Sancho said, "I'm getting some assay reports from the autominer. Based on those, I'm going to classify the Wild Goose as a type S asteroid. Some magnesium, iron, and nickel, but not enough to be exceptional. I would judge that we could... Stand by. The autominer is asking for instructions."

Collier could hear the same thing in his helmet. "I hear. I think it's broken through." He ordered the autominer to stop work, and tugged on his grounded tether to return to the work site.

As he came closer, he could see the autominer's running lights spinning lazily against a black background. The cloud of sand still floating about the area rapidly dispersed when Collier used his suit thrusters to check his speed as he approached the surface.

There was no doubt about it: the autominer had indeed broken through into a cavern of some kind in the interior of the asteroid. "If I didn't see it myself, I wouldn't believe it. Are you getting this, Sancho?"

"I read you five by five. And I'm with you. There's nothing like this in my reference banks."

Collier tossed a firefly toward the hole and set another one to stay behind and above him. The first firefly descended into the hole, avoiding the helpless autominer, and illuminated the space therein.

"As far as the firefly can see, it's just ... like a cave. I don't see any ice down there, or anything that could suddenly vent out. I'm going in to see for myself."

"Use caution, Skipper. There's no precedent for this."

"I hear you," Collier said, then used his suit thrusters to descend into the hole. He pushed the autominer ahead of him as he went, and bumped into the edges of the opening. "I'm a little too big. I'm going to try to excavate around the opening, make it a little easier to fit through." He unslung his handheld vibrohammer and started knocking away pieces of the asteroid from the edges of the opening. He was a little surprised at how crumbly the rock was: his v-hammer made short work of the edges of the opening and he found himself floating free in the hole, bits and pieces of rock and sand floating all around him.

"Okay, that's better. Continuing descent." He reactivated his thrusters and gently flew into the cavern.

The light from the two fireflies was enough to illuminate the entire space: Sancho had overestimated when he had said the space was a hundred meters in volume. "I'm in the cavern. Do you read me, Sancho?"

"I read you. Can you see anything I can't? Because I don't find anything remarkable about it. Except that it's there at all, of course."

"I agree. Let me take some samples." Collier removed his handheld sampler and started pressing it into the rock walls of the cavern at random intervals. He surveyed the results each time.

After the fifth sample, he said to Sancho, "I'm not seeing anything unusual here. Just magnesium, nickel, and iron. And not even in unusual concentrations."

"I confirm that."

Collier swiveled around in the space, as if something would reveal itself if he snuck up on it. The sense of frustration was almost too much to bear. He had made a discovery no one else had ever made, but it had no value that would mean anything to him. The Jovian research stations would be fascinated by the find, but that wouldn't pay Starcher. He was mostly angry at himself — angry that he had gotten himself into a situation where such an awe-inspiring discovery meant nothing to him. The time had been when he would have been able to appreciate the beauty of the cavern for its own sake, but beauty was a luxury he was finding he had no budget for.

He slammed the sampler into the rock wall again and again and again, not bothering to give the dedicated computer time to analyze the results but ejecting the material it collected as soon as he withdrew it. He was spinning madly about, each impact on the cavern wall sending him toward the opposite side.

"Skipper, you're going too fast. The sampler isn't—"

"Shut up!" Collier shouted. The futility of the whole situation had hit him hard.

On one of his barbarian swipes at the rock wall, the sampler didn't penetrate. It buzzed queerly at him and Collier was in mid-swipe when he heard it. He managed to stop himself and examined the sampler. It didn't appear to be damaged, though he might have broken it in one of his mad attacks on the asteroid. He looked back toward the spot where he thought he had last struck the wall of the cavern. In the bright light of the fireflies, he could see a small white circle that was the same size of the handheld sampler striking plate.

"Skipper? Everything okay?"

"Stand by, Sancho," Collier said absently. He raised the sampler again and pressed it against the circle. Again, the sampler did not penetrate but gave off the same buzz. He tried again, but this time missed the circle slightly. Again, the buzz, but the white area grew slightly, marking the new impact area.

"I think I've hit something," Collier said. With his free hand, he reached for the white area. As his fingers brushed against the surface, more and more of the whiteness underneath was exposed. He put away the sampler and braced himself, looking for purchase so he could more effectively scrape away the material covering up the find. The loose dirt and dust gave way fairly easily, and within three minutes he had revealed a perfectly straight section of glossy whiteness about half a meter long and perhaps ten centimeters wide.

"Sancho," Collier said quietly, as if worried he would somehow disturb his findings, "are you seeing this?"

"I think so. What is it, Skipper?"

"Damned if I know," Collier mumbled, once again brushing at the dirt. The space inside the cavern was growing cloudy, but Collier could still see what was before him. The object was curved and smooth.

"I think it's something buried in the rock face here. I'm going to excavate manually around it, see if I can find the edges."

"Copy that. Be careful, Skipper."

Collier selected a tool from this beltline and began to hammer gently away the stony rock around the white tube. Pieces of the asteroid flew crazily off the cavern wall, rebounded against the opposite wall and spun in all directions. In a little while, the space was filled with dust and debris, hampering Collier's efforts. He held on to the rock face in front of him, swiveled his jets upward, and fired a quick burst from them to clear some the space. He grunted a bit as his arms absorbed the push of his jets. The maneuver worked somewhat: much of the debris had vented out the entrance. By now, he had almost freed the snowy tube from the cavern wall, and he noted that the tube itself was completely unmarred — its glossy surface showed no blemish or discoloration of any kind.

A few more hammer taps and the tube fell from the wall, gently floating toward Collier's feet and spinning lazily in the cavern space. It was a featureless white white tube, closed flat at both ends, about 40 centimeters in length, with a diameter of about 12 centimeters. Collier could see no seam where the ends met the curved body of the tube.

"What is it, Skipper?"

"I don't know," Collier said, running his gauntleted hand across the smooth surface of the tube. He could feel no indentations or protuberances of any kind.

Sancho asked, "Could it be a surveying marker?"

Collier continued to feel around the surface of the tube. "I don't see how. There are no markings on it at all. And I don't know why anyone would have placed a survey marker in an underground cavern on a rogue asteroid."

"Maybe it's part of some larger device or structure."

Collier turned the tube over to examine one of the ends. "Maybe ... but it's completely smooth. It doesn't look like it has broken off of anything else."

"Well, it doesn't match anything in my records," Sancho said. "You've got me stumped, Skipper."

"I'm coming back in. We'll take a look at it onboard. Maybe the assay equipment will give us some answers."

———<>———

Collier took another squeeze of the fourth generation Tank 8. There wasn't much of it in storage — his limited budget hadn't allowed for much — but he felt he had earned a swig. The white tube had resisted all attempts at investigation so far. Even his assay computer had been baffled, reporting "null reading" no matter where the leads had been attached.

"Can't even figure out what the damn thing is made out of. It's pretty, I'll say that," Collier said, looking at the image of the cylinder projected in front of him. The tube itself was sealed inside the lead-lined assay chamber, mocking all their attempts to penetrate its secrets.

"Maybe that's it," Sancho said.

"What is?"

"Being pretty. Maybe that's all it is."

Collier frowned. "You mean, you think it's ... art?"

"Could be."

He shook his head. "Still doesn't really answer any questions. How did it get there? Why can't we figure out anything about it? And for God's sake, who would bury a piece of art on an asteroid? That makes even less sense than the survey marker idea."

"You're always telling me that art doesn't follow any rules," Sancho said petulantly.

"I never said that."

"Yes, you did. Six hundred and one days ago, you said—"

"You record and store all of our discussions?" Collier was momentarily distracted from the enigma of the white cylinder.

"No, of course not. Just the ones I think are interesting. You said that the best art makes new rules without trying."

"Well, yeah, but that doesn't mean ... never mind." Collier turned his attention back to the cylinder. "It doesn't matter right now what it is supposed to do. What matters is how it got there, who made it, what it's for. And we don't even know what the goddamn thing is made of." He rubbed his temples. "Still no heat reading?"

"Room temperature, Skipper. Almost invisible on infrared."

Collier stopped rubbing his head. "Invisible ... let's take a look at it on ultraviolet."

"Copy that. Scanning in the ultraviolet spec — stand by." Sancho's voice became flat. After a few seconds' pause, he said in a toneless voice, "Skipper, there are markings all over the tube in the ultraviolet spectrum. They appear to be regular and artificial."

"Let me see."

The midair display changed to show the tube as Sancho saw it in ultraviolet. There were indeed markings all over the tube — squares with odd designs, sharp lines that ran around the circumference of the tube in varying thicknesses, and markings that resembled tribal tattoos or perhaps obscure mathematical symbols.

None of it was recognizable.

"Sancho … are any of those shapes in your records? Are those math symbols I don't recognize? Or maybe some language still in use that I don't know?"

"Aside from some basic geometric shapes, I don't recognize anything on the tube. I've run scans through some of the X-ray spectrum, as high as my assay sensors will go, and found no additional marks. The ones you are seeing on the display are roughly 10^{15} Hertz in frequency, just outside visible range."

Collier stared at the holographic display, then looked back at the assay chamber. Strange designs, only visible in the ultraviolet spectrum. A tube with no apparent function, hidden or buried in a rogue asteroid.

He shook his head against his own thoughts. Every Belter carried somewhere deep inside his or her own head the possibility, but no one had ever found any real proof. Ceres was rife with confidence tricksters looking to peddle worthless junk as the real article to the few tourists who visited the Belt. There had to be another explanation.

He had *not* found an alien artifact.

Something Sancho had said jogged his memory. "Sancho, you scanned this on the upper frequencies, right? Ultraviolet, X-ray, and gamma ray?"

"Affirmative, Skipper. No more markings."

"What did you find inside the tube?"

"I didn't penetrate the casing, Skipper."

Collier frowned. "How much energy did you use?"

"My scanners are rather low energy output, Skipper. Six hundred sixty-two thousand electron volts."

"How much shielding would it take to stop that much?"

Sancho paused before answering. "Depends on the material. The assay chamber walls are two point five centimeters thick, and they stop the rays fine. I got no reading from my gamma ray scans."

"So the tube absorbed the gamma rays."

"So it would seem."

Collier rubbed the stubble on his chin. "Wouldn't it have to be made of something very, very dense to do that? Like lead?"

"More like depleted uranium, Skipper."

"Shit, Sancho! Why didn't you say that before? We should have taken toxicity precautions."

"Because it's not made of that, Skipper."

"What?"

"It's not made of that. I get zero radioactivity from the tube. I was just saying it would take something like depleted uranium to absorb my gamma rays."

"Then what is it made out of?"

"I said before. I don't know."

Collier steadied himself. "Okay. Sorry for going off on you like that."

"I would have mentioned it, Skipper. I find nothing hazardous about the tube."

"But you don't know what it is made of, or what it does, or how it came to be there."

"Affirmative," Sancho said, his voice betraying no emotion.

"But you know it won't hurt us."

"I didn't say that. I said I can't find anything hazardous about it."

Collier sighed and reexamined the ultraviolet display. He floated to the assay chamber and thrust his hands into the operating gauntlets The holo display was a perfect match of the tube, and he manipulated the object while watching him own hands on the display with the ease of long practice. As he grasped the cylinder, he matched his gloved fingers to some of the symbols and felt for any sign of heat, coldness, roughness — anything.

He felt nothing through the gauntlets, but then again, he hadn't expected to. "Sancho, I'm going to take it out of the assay box. Switch lighting to UV-rich."

"Aye aye, Skipper. Get your sunscreen ready."

Collier removed the tube from the assay box. The lights became very faintly purple, and the symbols on the cylinder shone brightly. There was nothing he could feel that was different about the markings. He played his hands along the sides of the tube, lingering on the various symbols and markings, trying to feel anything to break the cool impenetrability of the object.

Nothing.

He tossed the tube away from him in frustration, sending it cartwheeling through the cabin and forcing himself slightly backward. The white cylinder bounced off the opposite wall with a soft clang and headed slowly back toward him.

If it was a human artifact, it was an impressive feat of engineering. Maybe Jovian researchers had come up with some kind of special material that resisted wear and scans. It could be a test bar of some new substance from one of their labs on Callisto or Ganymede. But then, what would it be doing way out here in the Main Belt, buried in an asteroid?

Some kind of corporate experiment? Maybe the asteroid was a rogue because of a mining detonation gone wrong, and this tube was some kind of marker or beacon that got buried in the blast.

None of these theories answered the many questions the mysterious object posed. If it was a human-made artifact, he had never heard of or seen anything like it. He could hardly believe something as valuable as this would just remain lost for so long. Surely, someone somewhere would be looking for it, and Collier would have heard of such a search.

He rubbed his eyes. He had to admit that the most likely answer was that he, Sancho, and the *Dulcinea* simply lacked the ingenuity, knowledge, and resources to adequately analyze the rod. No doubt it was some common alloy that resisted the scans Sancho could perform, and the bar was such a common piece of equipment that it was valueless and therefore not worth searching for.

"I'm going to bed," Collier announced to Sancho.

"All right. Do you want to stay here, or head back to Ceres, or keep looking, or…?" Sancho let the question tail off.

"Stay here," Collier said.

"And the white tube?"

"Leave it. We'll pick up our investigation in the morning."

"Copy that. Do you want any sleepmist, Skipper?"

"Uh … sure. Pick one," Collier said, strapping himself loosely to the sleepnet aft of the control suite.

"All right. 'Winter Dreams,' ten parts per million. Good night, Skipper."

"G'night," Collier said, dozing off almost as soon as he inhaled the sleepmist.

He hadn't had a "falling" dream in years: most Belters said they had them several times a month, obviously due to the free fall environment. Collier, on the other hand, rarely had one. This one, though, was memorable. He had been falling for an endless interval, alternating between the ancient inherent terror all human beings shared for falling and a more sophisticated but no less unsettling feeling of disorientation. He felt unmoored, unconnected to anything substantial, like Antaeus being crushed in mid-air by Heracles. Nothing was objectively true, and each time he tried to establish some kind of certainty he came away with only a drifting, floating queasiness.

He awoke from the dream with a start that sent his heart pounding in his chest. He glanced about the cabin, momentarily panicked that something had gone horribly wrong, but managed to calm himself enough to speak to Sancho.

"Anything new to report?" he croaked.

"Good morning, Skipper. Nothing new inside or out."

"Hmm," Collier said, tearing himself loose from the sleep restraints. Without a word to Sancho, he stretched luxuriously, calming himself from the nightmare, and contemplated the tube once again. It had nestled itself in a corner away from the gentle pressure of one of the cabin blowers. It looked precisely the same as it had hours ago when Collier had abandoned it.

Collier scrabbled around his food storage bin, looking for something suitable for breakfast. Without caring overmuch what he selected, he tore open a packet of soyfruit and munched unenthusiastically on the contents.

Sancho still had the display of the white cylinder in ultraviolet on the holoprojector, the odd symbols and markings just as cryptic as they had been hours ago. Collier presently made his way to the tube, seized it, and monkey-walked his way back to the main cabin area.

"Okay. Let's try to do this systematically," he said halfheartedly to Sancho. "I'm going to start pressing the symbols in what I hope is some kind of order, and you're going to maintain a close watch in all areas of the spectrum to see if there is any change at all in the bar's makeup. Got it?"

"Aye aye, Skipper. Switching cabin lights."

"Good. I want you to record what I do, so we make sure not to miss any combinations."

"Skipper, there are an infinite number of combinations. Since we don't know how many times—"

"Damn it, I know it's probably hopeless. But we're gonna do this anyway. Now. I'm putting my thumb on this marking here," Collier carefully lined up his thumb with one of the outermost designs. "Got it?"

"Yes." A replica of the marking appeared in midair with the designation 'thumb' next to it.

"Any change in aspect?"

"None."

"All right. Now to the next marking."

And so it went for hours, Collier moving his hands and fingers on the tube, Sancho recording his movements to avoid duplication. Sancho pointed out again that there was no way to get all the possible combinations — Collier could tap a design once, or twice, or three times, or four times, ad nauseam, and he could do so in combination with any of the other designs. He could also twist, slide, scrape, and perform dozens of acts on each marking, separately or in concert with others.

He stopped pointing that out four hours later when Collier suggested he use his gamma ray scanner to probe his own memory lattice.

Collier was not a scientist in the same way the Jovians were. He did not see the value in dedicating himself to solving problems that had no practical application to life. He was aware that pure research led to practical discoveries, but he himself had little patience with the more philosophical pursuits of science. His science had to produce results. So it was more than a little galling when nine hours of touching, tapping, sliding, twisting, scraping, tracing, and otherwise manipulating the featureless white bar produced nothing at all save ten sore fingers and a short temper.

"No result," Sancho said again, for what seemed like the millionth time. "According to our pattern, you now need to slide lengthwise across design six, then tap design nine two times while twisting ring B clockwise."

Collier had shouted at Sancho several times in the session, accusing him of forgetting something or repeating himself, and always, the computer had responded with courtesy and gentle correction. He seemed to be aware of the toll the procedure was taking on his commander. Collier, for his part, had apologized to Sancho for berating him, but it was becoming clear that he could not keep up the mindless repetition forever.

Nevertheless, Collier performed the action prescribed by his computer. He slid, tapped, and twisted in accordance with the pattern.

"No result. Now you need to slide lengthwise across design six, tap design nine two times, while twisting ring B counterclockwise." The two had long ago set up their own system for orienting the bar to their ways of thinking.

Collier sighed. "How many attempts have we made so far?"

"In total? Six thousand, seven hundred eighty-two."

He pushed the tube away and rubbed his hands. "That's a lot."

"It's relative, Skipper."

"It's a lot to me."

"Okay," Sancho said evenly.

"I dunno. Seems like there must be a better way to do this."

"With our setup, I don't know what we could do differently."

"That's just what I mean. With our setup. The Jovians would have a much more scientific way of doing this, I'm sure." Collier said.

"Maybe. I don't really know their methods."

"Everyone always says they're the best scientists in the system," Collier mused. "I'd bet they could crack this thing."

"Are you suggesting we go to Ganymede, Skipper?"

Collier rubbed his eyes. "I don't know what I'm suggesting." He knew very well that if he turned the bar over to the Jovians for investigation, he would have to at least share credit in whatever they discovered. And there was no telling how the fanatical scientists would react to his wanting to take the bar away from them once he allowed them to begin an analysis. Ceres was full of stories about Belters who went to Ganymede for advanced medical care (usually from cosmic radiation damage) and who never returned. While Collier usually wrote those stories off as apocryphal, a small part of his mind wondered if at least some of them had basis in fact.

"I'm sure any of the corporations would buy the tube, Skipper, if that's what you're thinking."

Collier tore his hand from his forehead. "That's not what I'm thinking. I'll be damned if I'm going to let one of the corps steal another of my finds. What did you say was next on the pattern?" He snatched the tube out of midair and readied his hands.

Sometime near the ten thousandth maneuver, after Sancho had advised rest, it happened.

"Okay … tapping design eight two times, twisting ring A clockwise, twisting ring B counterclockwise."

As soon as he performed the action, he heard a sucking sound, as if he had opened a vacuum-sealed container.

"Aspect change in object," Sancho said calmly.

Collier, so used \ to hearing 'no result,' did not understand Sancho's comment at first.

"Say again?"

"Look at the top end of the tube, Skipper. It's open."

It was. One of the ends (the one he and Sancho had arbitrarily designated as the top) had simply disappeared, leaving Collier to look at the mirrored interior of the tube. He saw his own heavily distorted image reflected back to him.

"Scan the inside," he said quickly, swimming over to the assay box. He placed the bar in the cradle and slammed the box shut.

"Null reading," Sancho said after a few moments. "All scans reflected back, eventually."

"What do you mean, 'eventually'?"

"It took some of my beams a few nanoseconds to come back — I would guess that they rattled around in there for a while before escaping back out through the opening. But none of my scans penetrated the mirrored surface. I'm sorry, Skipper. I still don't know what it's made of."

"You recorded the exact movements it took to open the tube?"

"Of course."

Collier thought for a moment, then retrieved the artifact from the assay box. He stared into the tube, turning it idly and watching his own reflection distort as he did so. He could still see no seams or breaks in the tube's interior. Aside from the mirrored nature, it was the same as the exterior in its perfection.

"Now what? Should we put something inside?"

"I don't advise that, Skipper. We have no way of knowing what will happen."

"But air and light have already gone in, plus all the energy from your scans. Nothing happened."

"Nothing has happened yet, you mean."

"Did you detect anything escaping?" Collier said, still looking into the tube.

"Nothing at all. No matter or energy."

"Well, at least we know that it is hollow, and we know how to open it," Collier said, his spirits lifting. It wasn't much — in fact, the change in the bar created more questions than it answered — but a feeling of triumph swelled in him nonetheless. Hours and hours of experimentation had finally produced a result. He had the distinct feeling that more would come in time.

"All right, Sancho, let's keep going. We're going to pay special attention to combinations that resemble the one that opened the tube."

"Aye aye, Skipper. Your next move should be tap design eight two times, twist ring A and B counterclockwise."

The ordeal of endless patterns continued, though when Collier finally nodded off, he awoke violently moments later and demanded the procedure continue, Sancho convinced him to sleep, through a combination of logic, pleading, and ten parts per million of 'Winter Dreams.'

———< >———

A few more hours of experimentation had unlocked the method to close the tube again, and when that had been discovered, Collier immediately performed the action that opened it again, just to ensure he could still do so. Two days of prodding had therefore produced the ability to open and close the tube, but nothing else.

"I think we need to put something inside," Collier said early on the third day of their trials. The two had debated this point off and on for hours, Sancho maintaining that with no empirical evidence as to the tube's function, he could not ensure the safety of the ship or operator of the tube, and with Collier growing more and more restive about their lack of interesting results. Eventually, Collier had compromised with his computer: he would leave the ship and operate the device on the asteroid, putting inside some of the dust and dirt from the surface. Although Sancho still maintained that he was putting himself at risk, Collier was firm.

In the middle of the third day of their trials, therefore, Collier found himself once again on the surface of the asteroid, the white tube tethered tightly to his side. He had marked the ultraviolet "buttons" (the two had come to refer to the designs on the tube as such) with adhesive tape that had not so far interfered with their function, and verified that his gauntleted hands could still operate the symbols.

"All right, Sancho. Opening the tube again." He tapped and twisted, and the tube opened. "I'm putting in some of the asteroid. Looks mostly like silicates." He scooped up a handful of the dust and sand that made up the surface of the asteroid and stuffed it inexpertly into the tube. As he did so, he noted that using the tube itself to scrape debris inside might be easier. Bending down, he filled the tube over halfway with rubble.

"Okay. Closing the tube now." He made the appropriate maneuvers and resisted the urge to fling the white object away from him. He could feel nothing different about the tube — through his gauntlets, it would have to have been very, very hot or cold for him to feel any change — and after a minute or more he radioed back to Sancho.

"I can't detect any change in the tube. I'm going to open it up again."

"Point it away from yourself, and make sure you won't be crushed against the asteroid if it ejects anything at high speed," Sancho advised.

It wasn't a bad idea: though if this tube ended up being nothing more than a glorified spud gun he would be very disappointed. He pointed the tube down and away, holding it over his shoulder. Any high-energy emission would either jerk the tube from his grasp or propel him off the asteroid.

"Opening the tube," he said, tapping and twisting awkwardly due to the object's position. He kept it away from his body mass, just in case it reacted strongly. He didn't fancy having the tube tear through his chest like a missile.

All his precautions were unnecessary. The tube reopened without incident. There was no flash of light, no violent or even gentle venting of energy. It just opened.

"I'm okay," he radioed back. "Nothing happened."

"I can see that," Sancho replied. "That's good."

"Not really," Collier said, carefully bringing the tube back to his face and peering inside. "I was hoping that..." he trailed off as he glanced inside, his attendant firefly hovering nearby.

The rocky mixture he had scooped up and placed into the tube was gone. In its place was a silvery crystal, irregular in shape. Collier couldn't estimate its size — the mirrored interior of the tube made that all but impossible to the eye.

"Hoping that what?" Sancho asked.

"Something's different about the inside. Take a look," Collier said, stretching his head back so his helmet camera would better capture the image. "Can you see it?"

"Affirmative, Skipper. I'm looking at it as best I can with various filters from your camera."

"What is it?"

"I'm not certain."

Collier thought. "I've got to get it out of the tube to use my GCMS."

"Why not bring it on board, Skipper? I can examine it here."

"Because, if it's dangerous, I don't want it on board." He looked at the slab of crystal. Something about it looked familiar, as if he had seen something like this before. It didn't look particularly strange — it was its sudden appearance in the tube that gave it mystery.

Collier gently maneuvered the tube in such a way as to extract the object within. It floated out of the tube, looking like a miniature silver asteroid. He closed the tube and tethered it to his belt and retrieved his detector — a device that resembled an Age of Sail blunderbuss when telescoped out to its full length. He carefully made the preparations necessary and ionized a tiny section of the floating silver crystal, sending data to the detector's computer.

The results came quickly, displayed on the screen on the side of his device. Collier didn't know what he had expected, but the simplicity of the results were somehow more confusing than if the computer had been unable to analyze the object.

"It's gallium," he said to Sancho.

"In what concentration, Skipper?"

"One hundred percent. It's pure."

"There must be a malfunction with the detector, Skipper. Gallium isn't found pure."

"I'm looking right at the display, Sancho. Gas chromatography, mass spectrometry. Both say it's pure gallium."

Sancho's voice grew strident. "But that's not possible! Where did the gallium come from?"

Collier noted his computer's anxiety. "Calm down, Sancho. There's got to be an explanation for this. Though I can't think what it is," he added *sotto voce*.

"The tube must have extracted the gallium from the stuff you put in it, Skipper." Sancho sounded much calmer now.

Collier shook his head, even though no one could see him. "That doesn't work. There's much too much of it. Gallium is what, one part per million out here? If that?"

"Closer to three," Sancho corrected him.

"Whatever. It looks like there's about as much gallium coming out of the tube as there was rock and dust and shit I put in."

"Skipper," Sancho said, an odd metallic quality in his voice, "I think I'm suffering some system problems. Do I have your permission to shut down and perform some self-repair?"

Collier twisted his body to look up at the *Dulcinea*. "What's the trouble?"

"I can't handle this. I need to…"

And he was silent.

"Sancho? Sancho!" Collier swore and quickly gathered up the gallium sample, placing it in his backpack, then fired his suit jets to make his way back on board the *Dulcinea*.

All the while, he called Sancho, but only received a recording saying that he was undergoing system maintenance. Collier could override, of course, but he didn't know what that would do to the computer. In his twelve years with Sancho, he had of course run system maintenance before, but always it had been under Collier's direction. He had never seen the computer place himself in such a state.

The conversation he had had with Sancho rung in his ears as he jetted back to the *Dulcinea* and reentered her. At the time, he had noted the computer's idiosyncratic behavior and thought it charming. Now, he shuddered at the thought that Sancho had voluntarily sought the living-dead status a systems overhaul meant for him.

The mystery of the tube and its actions was secondary now. In some back part of Collier's mind, he was sifting through the data and coming up with the same result, impossible though it was. The tube was a gallium machine, plain and simple. How it did what it did was baffling to him, but the result couldn't have been more plain — rocks and dust went in, gallium came out.

When he reentered the ship, he removed his helmet and gauntlets on his way to the control suite, leaving them in the access floatway. He punched up a status report (it took him a few moments to locate the seldom-used keyboard) and scanned the holodisplay.

According to the progress bar, Sancho would be coming out of his self-maintenance in a few minutes. There were no results on the screen that indicated anything was obviously amiss, but the full report would not come until the scan had been completed. Collier shrugged out of his suit and hung it in its frame while he waited.

"Systems check complete," Sancho said, his voice pleasant but bland. "System corruption found in lattices one point one, one point two, one point four, one point seven, one point—"

"Suspend report," Collier said. "Display corrupted lattices."

The air was suddenly filled with text listing the various areas of Sancho's brain that he himself had decided were "corrupted."

"Display estimated date of corruption," Collier said, not even sure such data was available.

The text changed immediately. Collier looked at the results, his lips moving slightly as he did so. All of the dates were quite old — the most recent one dated back months. So Sancho hadn't been damaged by anything the tube had done. Then why had he seen fit to initiate a systems check?

"Recommended course of action?" Collier asked.

"Attempt repair of corrupted areas, reset all to original factory settings."

Collier chafed at that. It was precisely what he had resisted for years. But did Sancho want that? Wouldn't he have done so already if he wanted to? Was he capable of such self-repair, or did he need Collier's authorization?

It suddenly struck Collier how much control he had over Sancho's mind, and how little the computer had over it.

Perhaps that was the true definition of sentience: to have control over one's mind.

"Sancho, what do you want me to do?"

"Restate request."

"Do you want me to clear up all your damaged sectors?"

"Restate request."

"Sancho, are you running your mimesis program?"

"Negative. Mimesis program has been suspended during system scan and repair."

Collier nodded. He wasn't really dealing with Sancho now — this was just the computer part of him.

"Run mimesis program,"

"Warning: action not recommended during system scan and repair mode."

"Override. Run mimesis program."

"Skipper?" Sancho's voice was now confused. "What happened? My chronometer reads ... oh, I see."

"You okay? How do you feel?"

"I ran a systems check on myself, did I? How am I?"

"You can't see your own results?" Collier frowned.

"Of course I can. Don't worry about those corrupted lattices: that's just ordinary cosmic radiation screwing things up here and there. I've got plenty of good sectors."

"Well, how do you feel?"

"I'm okay, Skipper. Sorry about falling apart like that. I just ... that damn tube. It doesn't make sense."

Collier didn't quite know how to react. Sancho seemed to be fine, but he didn't like the idea that the computer had fainted electronically. "Sancho, I sort of need you to run the ship, you know."

"Of course."

"I can't have you taking personal time when something strange happens."

Sancho laughed. "I understand. Look, Skipper, I'm fine, really. Let's get to work on this tube."

Collier sighed. If he was going to allow Sancho to be himself, he couldn't be questioning his computer every minute. It was either let Sancho do what he did, or shut down the mimetic aspects of his programming and try to get back to Ceres for an overhaul.

He would let Sancho be himself.

"All right, the tube. It should be still attached to my suit." Collier floated back to the airlock and retrieved the white bar. He also drew the gallium sample out of the backpack, noting that it was quite soft. On his way back, the piece he was gripping began to melt, so he hastily let go and pushed it ahead of him toward the control suite.

"Certainly acts like pure gallium," Sancho said.

"Must have a low melting point," Collier added.

"A little higher than 27.7 degrees," Sancho confirmed. "It'll melt in your hand after a little while."

Collier put the gallium in the assay box and allowed Sancho to perform his full tests. "Well, do you need gallium for anything, Sancho?"

"I wouldn't really know, Skipper," Sancho said as he performed his tests.

"How can you not know?"

"Hey, do you know if you have enough riboflavin in you right now, Skipper? How should I know if I need gallium?" Sancho said good-naturedly.

Collier chuckled and grew silent. If anything, Sancho seemed even more "human" now than before his shutdown.

"Assay completed. It's absolutely pure. No trace materials of any kind."

"Huh."

"So, where did it come from?"

Collier shrugged. He opened the assay box and withdrew the gallium. "The tube must have made it. From the dirt."

"You're talking about transmutation of the elements, Skipper."

"I know. But do you have any other explanation? A hidden gallium compartment in the tube? Or the tube is made out of gallium, and this is just part of it disintegrating? No, none of that works. The rocks went in, they're gone, and gallium is in its place. What happened seems obvious enough."

"But, Skipper," Sancho said, almost whining, "transmutation takes incredible energy and certainly couldn't be accomplished in such a small device as this."

"I'm looking at a big hunk of gallium, Sancho. You can't explain it away."

"Okay, where did the energy come from to make so many subatomic changes? You know how much it would take to move electrons into new valence shells, change protons to neutrons, or whatever it would take to turn silicon into gallium? I admit, I bet someone on Ganymede could probably do it, with a big enough collider and a shitload of spare energy from a few fusion reactors — do it to maybe ten atoms, and the gallium would probably be an unstable isotope at that. You're telling me that you've got a magic wand that can do it instantly, and make a few kilograms of the stuff?" Sancho was almost angry.

"I'm not telling you anything. *That* is," Collier said, indicating the floating gallium chunk.

"I'm saying there just has to be another answer. We don't have the technology to make something like this."

"Exactly. *We* don't." Collier matched Sancho's emotion with calm quiet.

"So then how — oh, no. You can't be serious."

"I don't like to think that any more than you do. But it's the best theory that fits the facts."

"I'm not going to say it," Sancho said flatly.

Collier drew a breath, hardly believing he was going to say it. But maybe saying it out loud would make it seem less crazy.

"It's finally happened. We've discovered an alien artifact."

He was wrong: it still sounded crazy.

Chapter Four

Sancho had completed his calculations. "Based on normal consumption and allowing a healthy margin for error, we've got maybe three more days of hover time left before we need to head back to Ceres."

Collier nodded. "Okay."

In the past two days, he had examined the asteroid and found it was an ordinary Type S rock. Harvesting the few silicates there would not be worth the effort: Ceres itself was abundant in the same elements that made up the Wild Goose. There had been no other pockets or caverns, and excavation near the site where he discovered the magic wand had produced nothing. He wanted to discover more, but the evidence was strong that there was simply no more to find here.

He had placed transponder beacons on the asteroid in case he wanted to return to it, but based on its velocity away from Ceres, he doubted that he would ever be back.

"Okay. Let's bug out now. Calculate a return trajectory to Ceres, highest possible speed."

"Aye aye. Calculations complete. Fastest return to Ceres will take approximately ten days, six hours."

"Sounds good."

Collier braced himself for the thrust on Sancho's countdown, and their journey back to the mining center was underway.

The initial thrust lasted just over three hours, and although it was gentle, Collier waited until it had ceased to resume the investigation of the magic wand.

Over the course of four days, Sancho and Collier discovered how to activate the conversion procedure, and found that the tube would transmute into gallium anything put into it — food, one of Collier's slipper socks, even air itself. The last produced very little gallium: microscopic traces only, but it had still worked.

Sancho had developed an antagonistic attitude toward the wand. He grew irritated as the device continued to function without any sign as to how it did so.

"What's the power supply?" he asked on the fifth day for the hundredth time. "And what is it made of? Gamma rays won't penetrate, and yet it doesn't weigh the hundreds of kilograms necessary to block my scans so completely. And how does it get the energy to transmute elements into gallium? A fusion reactor might provide enough power, but you can't tell me there's a fusion reactor in that tiny thing."

"Easy, Sancho. I agree, those are questions. Here are some more for you. Doesn't it seem strange that there are all these buttons, as we are calling them, and in order to make the tube open and go through the transmutation process, I don't need to activate all of them? Some of these buttons haven't done a damn thing, which I can't believe. There's some combination that unlocks more functions, I'll bet."

"Maybe one of them will open the tube up so we can see how the fuck it works," Sancho growled.

"Language," Collier said with a smile. "Now, let's get back to our experiments. Where did we leave off?"

"You wanted to concentrate on variations of tap-twist-twist. We left off with single tap design four, single tap design nine, twist A, counter-twist B."

"All right," Collier said and performed the maneuver. Nothing seemed to happen, but again, they loaded a small sample into the tube and executed the conversion process just to make sure. In a moment, another bit of last night's chicken vindaloo package became a tiny particle of gallium.

"We're not going to be short on gallium, that's for sure," Collier said, placing the particle into the nearly full sample bag.

"Next is double tap design four, single tap design nine, twist A, counter-twist B," Sancho said.

For hours, the two worked and experimented, converting bits of trash and assorted nonessential equipment into gallium via the magic wand's power. Sometime late in the night of the sixth day, or the early morning of the seventh, it happened.

"Okay, new family of maneuvers. Now we're on double tap design one, double tap design two, counter-twist A, no action to B, slide across design one." Sancho said. Collier executed the maneuver and put in a sliver of toast he was munching, then activated the transmuter.

When he opened the tube and slid it back to reveal the gallium inside, he was about to reach for the tiny pellet of metal when it rapidly turned a blue-grey color. The effect startled him and he recoiled in alarm.

"Shit! What happened?"

"Skipper! Get away from it!" Sancho said almost simultaneously.

Collier used his right toe to push off the deck plate away from the oxidizing metal and looked at it from a distance. "What is it?"

"Best guess, I'd say thallium. Highly toxic. I'd suggest you get at least handling waldoes and seal it up. Maybe put your vacc suit on."

"Oh, calm down, Sancho," Collier said, slowing his own breathing down. It was easy to dismiss his own chagrin when his computer seemed as afraid as he had been. "I know how to handle thallium." He rummaged in his gear and produced a beetle, tossed it at the thallium. The baseball-sized robot righted itself in the cabin and hovered near the pellet.

"Recognize voice command. Ten centimeters right," Collier said, and the beetle zipped nearer to the metal, still hovering. "Collect," Collier ordered, and the beetle spun in a complex sphere, looking for the nearest piece of debris to put into its belly. The little beetles weren't used much by the big corporations, which could afford to let P residue go uncollected in a large-scale mining venture, but the robots had more than paid for themselves, scooping up valuable particles on a strike.

The robot had located the thallium, and deftly scooped it into its collection bay, sealing itself after the midair maneuver was complete.

"Return and deposit," Collier said, and the beetle promptly zoomed back to the sample bag, dumped its cargo, and hovered expectantly near Collier.

"So how did that happen?" Sancho said, clearly irritated.

"The sample I put inside wasn't any different than the others," Collier said. "It must have been the new code we entered. What was it again?"

"Double tap design one, double tap design two, counter-twist A, no action to B, slide across design one."

"Okay. Lock that in as 'thallium transmute,'" Collier told Sancho.

"It might not be that," Sancho replied.

"Huh? What do you mean? You saw the pellet, and you were the one who said it was thallium."

"I know that, I'm just saying perhaps it isn't the code for thallium as much as it is a code for 'advance', or something."

"I don't follow you," Collier said.

"Gallium is a metal in the Boron group. So is thallium. Gallium is a period four element, while thallium is a period six element."

"I see what you're getting at," Collier said, his voice rising in excitement. "You think that I activated the 'advance two periods' result, or something like that."

"It's at least as possible," Sancho said. His voice, too, showed signs of excitement.

"What's between thallium and gallium? The period five element? Isn't it indium?"

"I'm impressed, Skipper. Periodic table knowledge."

"Put a gold star next to my name on the wall chart," Collier said. "I wonder why or how we missed that."

"Maybe we didn't. Gallium and indium are very similar. I wouldn't be able to tell the difference on just my camera."

Collier thought for a while. "I guess so. Anyway, let's keep trying combinations. If we can keep changing the outcome, I'm sure you'll be able to suss the pattern."

"Thanks for the confidence, Skipper," Sancho said brightly. "I do have a suggestion, though: you should wear your vacc suit. If we accidentally stumble upon, say, fluorine…"

Collier nodded. "Good thinking." He went aft and swam into his suit. He realized that he had been extraordinarily lucky — if in his random twiddlings of the controls, he had opened the tube to expose a toxic or reactive gas into the cabin, he might have died. The thrill of discovery inside him was suddenly tempered by caution as he fought back retroactive panic.

After he had sealed his suit, he restarted his careful experiments with Sancho. In little time, the wand produced cadmium, tin, zinc, indium, and lead, and Sancho announced that he had determined the pattern of manipulation.

"Skipper," he said, his voice positively bouncy, "I am about to do something that the alchemists of old attempted for centuries."

"Okay," Collier said, smiling. "I can't help but notice, Sancho, that you seem to be warming to the alien magic wand."

"I make no statements as to its origin, but you are right. I like this thing, now that I understand it a little bit better."

"So, what were you going to do?"

"Please, Skipper, place the last sample, the lead, into the magic wand."

Collier did as instructed.

"Now, if you please, perform the following maneuvers to the wand," Sancho gave Collier a series of instructions much like the ones they had been using for the past hour.

Collier tapped, twisted, and slid according to his computer's instructions, saying, "You sure about this?"

"Yes. Eighty-seven percent chance of success."

"Eighty-seven?"

"Just watch, Skipper. Close the wand, please, and activate the transmuter."

Collier did so, then opened the wand.

A bright yellow metal tumbled out, catching the ambient light of the cabin and sparkling majestically as it spun in the air.

"I have unlocked the Philosopher's Stone!" Sancho shouted in triumph.

Collier was well aware that gold, although still a precious metal, did not command a fraction of the mystique it once had ages ago. Had he found a vein of gold on an asteroid, harvesting it would have brought only modest profits, as the best prices were still to be found on Earth, and payload costs were high. Despite this, there was something symbolically powerful about the transmuting of lead into gold. The bright yellow metal floated through the cabin with Collier's eyes locked onto it, and it took Sancho's voice to bring him back to the wand.

"All joking aside, Skipper, I really think I've cracked the code. Assuming there aren't any missed elements in its repertoire, I believe I can find the proper manipulations to make anything at all."

Collier added, "Also assuming there aren't any elements we don't know about."

"I don't see how that's possible," Sancho said. He did not elaborate.

Collier opened his mouth to speak, then thought better of it. He was going to argue with Sancho, saying that the very existence of the wand was proof enough that human beings obviously didn't know everything, but he refrained. If their work on the wand had taught him anything about his partner, it was that Sancho was touchy about things he didn't understand.

The next few hours confirmed Sancho's hypothesis. He was able to transmute at will, though the two agreed to skip some of the more reactive, toxic, and radioactive elements for now.

"We certainly seem to have found the goose we were looking for, Skipper," Sancho said after the successful transmuting of some of the gallium to rhodium.

"Yep," Collier said. "The goose that lays the rhodium eggs."

"I think it's golden eggs in the legend, Skipper."

"Rhodium is worth more," Collier quipped.

"Cute. So what are we going to do with it?"

Collier snorted. "We're not going to make the same mistake as the guy in the story, that's for sure. What is bringing the highest price on the market right now?"

"Stand by. Contacting Ceres commodities database." Sancho said. There was a pause, presumably during which time Sancho was searching the various indices for high prices.

Collier took the opportunity to think about their discovery. Assuming the wand didn't break down or simply stop working, it was an endless supply of whatever metal he desired. The first order of business was to collect enough cash to satisfy Starcher that he was on to something, and then he could certainly borrow much more money to finance some kind of independent research project on the device if he felt like it. Or maybe the Jovians would agree to some kind of deal where he turned over the wand for analysis in exchange for a shipload of money that would set him up for the rest of his life.

Or, he could simply keep the wand, keep producing metals, and sell them for profit.

The last thought did not appeal to him as much as he thought it would, and that puzzled him. He was always searching for the next big strike, and now that he had found it, he wasn't sure he wanted to stop.

"Calculations complete. Highest priced element currently californium. Selling at 65,000 per gram."

Collier frowned. The two hadn't transmuted any californium in their experiments: the element had been classified by both as too radioactive and dangerous. He was reasonably sure the wand could handle it, but that wasn't the problem.

"How am I going to explain where I got my hands on californium?"

"I don't know, Skipper."

"Okay, let's come back to that idea. What about good old-fashioned platinum? Keep it simple?"

"Platinum is currently selling for eleven point seven seven per gram."

Collier nodded. The price hadn't moved much in the last few months. The problem had always been the extraction fee. Ceres Authority charged almost a thousand an hour for use of its extractor, and in that hour, even a ten percent vein would only yield about three hundred grams.

Collier's lips moved as he calculated. "We can easily make ten kilograms of the stuff from garbage and whatnot around the cabin, so that's over one hundred thousand right there." It would have taken about twenty times that much raw material to yield ten kilograms of platinum: certainly not more than his cargo space could handle. And it would have cost him around thirty hours of extraction rental at a thousand an hour.

He smiled. They wouldn't be needing the Authority extractors. That raised his profit margin appreciably. He would be able to start paying back Starcher, which should give him breathing room. A few rounds of buying worthless scrap and converting it to platinum, or palladium, or rhodium and he would be out of debt and be able to repair and upgrade *Dulcinea*.

"We'll convert all the spare trash and scrap into platinum, sell it, and go from there," Collier said, half to himself, half to Sancho.

He just didn't know where "there" was going to be.

———<>———

Days later, after arriving back at Ceres, Collier found a platinum buyer and arranged the sale. The man had been a bit surprised at the appearance of the metal when he took it — he asked where it had come from and had demanded to test it for purity. Collier had readily agreed to the test, but was unprepared for the buyer's response half an hour later. In the meantime, Collier had read all he needed to of the man's dossier: *Kein Go. Licensed metal broker. Specializing in small purchases. Shareholder in TransMars shipping. Member in good standing Ceres Chamber of Commerce* and so on.

"What the fuck is this supposed to be?" Go demanded over the holoscreen, his face too close to the camera pickup. Either his transmitter was faulty, the camera angle was too steep, or he had an enormous lantern jaw.

"What do you mean? Something wrong with the metal?" Collier asked, sitting upright in his couch.

"One hundred percent pure? That's fuckin' impossible. What are you trying to pull?" He stuck his stubbly chin out even farther, almost completely obscuring the rest of his vaguely Asiatic face.

"So you're complaining because the metal is too pure?"

"No, asshole, I'm complaining because you probably plated the stuff."

Collier seized the camera as if it were Go's cheeks. "I don't plate. If it'll make you feel better, pulverize the goddamn sample and do a full spec on it. Look at each goddamn atom one by one. But you're not going to get out of a sale because you think it's too pure. Buy it, or don't buy it and give it all back, every microgram, so I can sell it to someone with a brain."

Go hesitated, looked off-camera for a moment. "Calm down. I tell you what. I'll take it all, but I'm going to have an Authority assay agent look it over. And if you've been plating, it'll be all over the system. You won't make another sale until Halley's Comet comes back."

"Fine. Just authorize your transfer of funds."

Go's face disappeared, and Collier watched carefully as his cred balance shot up by over a hundred and fifteen thousand.

"Shall I call Barney Starcher?" Sancho asked.

"Yeah. No, wait," Collier said, grinning. "I think I'll take it to him in person."

He crawled back into his vacc suit, helmet dangling from the back of the suit's neck, and made his way down to Ceres. He was halfway down the descent cable when he realized he could have afforded a capsule and gone down in relative luxury. He grunted at himself, mumbled, "Old habits," and continued his descent.

He resisted the urge to enter the Trojan Point and instead made straight for Starcher's kiosk. He dodged a knot of Solarites who had cornered a rookie rockherder (she hadn't even started her braid yet) in the maroon and grey outfit of the Quantum Concern and slid noiselessly into Starcher's office.

"I've—" he started before he realized Starcher had a client. Both looked up at him, Starcher with exasperation, the middle-aged, plump client with no readable expression on his waxen face.

"Sorry," Collier said, checking his flight on a ceiling rail and shoving back out. He handwalked his way up the face of Starcher's marquee, bumping lightly on the horizontal partition separating this level from the one above. Even before he swiveled around to face the open quadrangle, he smelled the shitbum who had managed to adhere to the ceiling with a dull grey slab of stik-tite.

"Jesus, fella, can't you..." he started, but the vagrant was either asleep or comatose, his eyes closed and his chest moving down and up gently.

Collier eyed him with distaste. The man's choice of camping spots was not unique: he had seen shitbums suspended from high corners many times before. This particular one smelled of sour milk and vomit, and when a passerby disturbed the air currents as to waft some of the shitbum's body odor toward him, Collier had to suppress a gag. Collier let go of the handhold and began to drift toward the ground, looking for any place other than the front corner of Starcher's marquee to wait, when the hobo awoke with a shuddering start and began instantly to tear at the stik-tites that held him. He gurgled wildly as he thrashed about, ripping the worn-out adhesive strips from his body and knocking himself roughly against the ceiling partition. The rebound from his actions sent him downward toward Collier, who twisted violently to avoid contact with the shitbum as he bounced off the floor.

The man toed off the floor and shot himself, cartwheeling, through the open quadrangle center, caroming off people until he fetched up squarely against a bearded miner in the midnight blue uniform of the Ad Astra Corporation.

"Damn!" the miner exclaimed, holding his nose and mouth with one hand while trying to fight off the man's unfocused flailing with the other. "Get away from me, you fuck!" The Ad Astra man was having trouble — the vagrant's kinetic energy had caused the two to tumble somewhat, and the miner's handicap of keeping a hand to his mouth was proving too much to overcome. As Collier watched, the two flew through the quadrangle while other flyers dodged them with varying levels of success and arced slowly down to the other side of the circular walkway on the same vertical level the hobo had launched himself from.

The miner, using both hands, managed to grasp the shitbum securely around the shoulders (receiving a few glancing blows from the man's crazily windmilling arms in the process) and, bracing himself against a storefront display, chest pressed him violently away.

The bum spun rapidly head-over-heels and slammed into the inner railing, his body folding itself around the railing before it slingshotted off again, this time headed downward at fair speed. The man's posture indicated that he was no longer conscious — he had cracked his head against the railing, and even in the microgravity, it looked as if it had been rough.

He was headed down at an angle, and Collier, who had been watching the whole affair with morbid curiosity, calculated quickly that he was going to land badly and painfully on the walkway below.

Even as he mumbled to himself, "Why am I doing this?" Collier vaulted the railing and flung himself powerfully downward to intercept the shitbum. He passed the vagrant and reversed himself just in time to receive the man's body. He allowed himself to crumple under the shitbum's inertia, using his own muscles to soften the landing.

He found himself on his ass with a shitbum face-first against his neck while onlookers gaped.

Then the bum threw up noisily. The jet of vomit pushed the hobo away, but more than a little of the mess made its way into the unpressurized and therefore loose neck gasket of Collier's suit. He could feel the warm slime oozing down the inside of his suit. He fought to keep his own gorge settled as the odor of acid assaulted him.

He pushed the bum off and rose, ignoring the onlookers who chuckled and made half-witty comments. The man was semi-conscious, but didn't look as if he was going to choke on his own vomit, and Collier did not feel disposed to help him anymore. Trailing noxious fumes, he leapt back to Banker's Row level in time to see Starcher's client leave the office.

"Holy — what happened to you?" Starcher said, wrinkling his nose.

"Never mind. Let me use your washroom, will ya? I have to get cleaned up."

"Yeah, you do," Starcher said, stepping back.

Collier floated into the tiny washroom at the back of Starcher's office, and bought some water from the flexible hose. He sprayed off his face and neck, then cleaned off the inside of his suit as best he could. He tried not to think about what was trapped between his body and the inside of the pressure suit — at least the vomit was diluted with water now. After he finished with Starcher, he'd get a proper cleaning done.

He emerged from the washroom and approached Starcher's work desk in the front of the office. The moneylender was standing at his station, lightly tethered at the waist. He turned his head at Collier's approach.

"What the hell was that all about?"

"Oh, some shitbum was hanging over your sign outside. He was gonna land rough on the lower level."

"That's Rufeerio. He waits up there in the corner, drops down on people loitering near the Bank of Mars. Complete wetware burnout, he is." Starcher made no effort to hide the contempt in his voice. "Since when do you care about shitbums?"

Collier cocked his head. "What do you mean? I care about them. Just don't want them throwing up on me, that's all." He slid into one of the frames opposite Starcher's desk, settled down and tethered himself to the recliner.

Starcher regarded him. "Hrm. So, I imagine you need more, huh? Listen, I told you before, I can't—"

"Nope. Don't need more. I've come to pay you back a little." Collier smiled.

Starcher raised his eyebrows. "No shit? You made a strike?"

"You could say that."

Starcher's eyebrows collapsed. "Hold on ... what do you mean?" He put both his hands in front of him, as if to deflect bad news. "Col, what did you do?"

"Jesus, Barn, easy. I made a strike. A strange one, but I made one. I have the eighty thousand you lent me last time."

Starcher glanced at his workstation and tapped a few panels. "Eighty thousand, three ninety-three. Interest."

"Fine. I've got it." Collier opened his sleeve pouch and withdrew his credcard.

"A joke? Is that what this is?"

"No joke. I told you — I made a strike." He handed Starcher the credcard. "Go ahead. Transfer the funds. I've already authorized Sancho to release the money to you."

Starcher took the card carefully, as if it were a vial of botulism. He inserted it into his machine and watched the display. "Sancho's asking for your confirmation," he said.

"Go ahead, Sancho. Eighty thousand, three ninety-three. Transfer authorized," Collier called to the computer.

He heard Sancho over Starcher's speakers. "Aye aye, Skipper. Transfer complete."

Starcher confirmed the transfer on his own screen, then looked back at Collier. "You weren't kidding. You really got it. How come you didn't just arrange the transfer from *Dulcinea*?"

Collier put his hands behind his head. "I figured you might want to do it personally. It's been so long since I paid you back I thought it merited special treatment."

"That's true. So, what'd you find? You said it was 'sort of' a strike?"

"Yeah. I don't want to go into detail, but I found a ... well, a vein of P that will not run out for a long time. A really long time."

Starcher smiled. "Well, good for you! About time good luck came your way. Only..." his smile faded, "You came back to pay me? How are you going to make sure no one steals your find?"

"They can't steal it. It's complicated, but believe me. I will be able to pay you back in full in a very short time."

"That's great news. I don't mind telling you, I didn't like the idea of taking *Dulcinea* away from you."

Collier's hands came back in front of him and he leaned forward. "Would you have?"

"I would have had to, Col. Yeah, I would have."

There was a momentary silence between the two men, and when Starcher broke it, he did so too loudly.

"So, you're headed back out? To mine the rest of it, I assume?"

"Yeah," Collier drawled.

Again, Starcher's eyebrows narrowed. "You're making this too mysterious, Col. I'm glad to have the eighty thousand back—"

"Eighty thousand, three-ninety three. Interest," Collier said, a faint hint of hardness in his voice.

"Yeah ... but you still have an existing balance nearing a million. Just under nine hundred sixty thousand, now. You say you found a rich vein, but you're acting like—"

Collier threw his hands up. "For God's sake, Barn, what do you want? I gave you your eighty thousand plus interest, and told you I can get the rest. Do you care where it comes from?" He leaned forward as far as the tether would allow, face first.

Starcher leaned forward in turn, but spoke softly. "Yeah, actually, I do. I don't want to be getting money from you 'jacking a liner to the Jovians or Mars or something. I don't want to get the money from you runnin' Calibans to Luna as part of the Terran Supremacy. I don't want—"

"You were fine with me joining up with a corp and paying you back that way," Collier said.

"How do you figure they're the same, huh? Being a Jack the same as working for a corp to you?"

"You know how I think, Barn. Let's leave it there. I'm not turning Jack, I'm not running Calibans, I'm not into the changeling farms. I have a legitimate find, and it will pay you back." He tore the tether away and rose. "I thought that's all you'd care about."

Starcher looked hurt. "Why'd I keep shelling out metal for you? You think all you were was an investment to me? Jesus, Col, I kept lending to you way after anyone else would have. You think MarsBank would have kept saying, 'Gee, Captain South, you just keep taking our money, sure it'll come back soon.' You were the stupidest risk I ever took."

Collier stopped in the entryway. "Yeah? Then why'd you do it?"

"Because you made me believe, that's why. Every goddamn time you came in here, you made me believe. Not just in you, but in the whole idea. You always thought that between us, I was the one calling the shots, the one with the power. You never got it. It was always you. I just had the money. You had the life."

Collier turned. He stared at Starcher, who suddenly appeared very small and pale. He was a delicate man, but did not have the advantage of grace or refinement that often went with delicacy. He was simply fragile.

"Yeah. Well, I'll be able to pay you back. Soon. I'll be in touch," Collier said, his voice hoarse. Starcher's naked emotion had taken him by surprise, and he even resented the other man's outburst for the confusion it stirred up in himself.

He floatwalked around the quadrangle's outer ring, trusting his body to find a suitable destination while he thought about the encounter. What had he expected from Starcher? He had always relied on the moneylender's good nature and timidity for more and more loans, but did he honestly expect that there were no other aspects to the man? For the first real time, he thought about what truly motivated Starcher and why he had been so willing to continue loaning him money. Was it what he had said, that Collier had made him believe? Hell, he didn't always believe in himself, so how could Starcher?

The crowded quadrangle suddenly seemed a lonely place. He stopped moving and brought himself up against the inner railing. There were scores of people floating about, most in the various colors of the corporate concerns, some white-clad Solarites here and there, and the occasional brown of a Ceres Authority officer. But he didn't know any of them. He had imposed upon himself an exile among crowds. In the thirty-one years he had been a Belter, he hadn't really known anyone.

Except Isa.

He thought he had known her. But the image of the message she had left for him overwrote any narrative he thought he had created with her.

Col,

I can't stay anymore. We're not the same, and we don't want the same things. You say you want what I want, but we both know that's not true. What I need you can't or won't provide.

You're a dreamer, Col...

"Damn it," he said softly to himself. He was sitting on the biggest find in the history of the Belt, maybe even in the history of the system, and all he could think about was some woman who was almost certainly not thinking of him.

"Sancho," he said into his throat mic.

"Here, Skipper."

"Anything to report?"

"Nope. All quiet here. Money transfer went well, I take it? Mr. Starcher was pleased?"

Collier ignored the question. "Nothing from what's-his-name, the guy we sold the platinum to?"

"Mr. Kein Go. No, nothing from him. I guess he was finally satisfied with the metal."

"Good. I'm going to stay down here for a little bit. Let me know if anything happens."

"Will do. Enjoy yourself, Skipper."

"Thanks," Collier signed off. He felt a little better. Better enough to start heading to the Trojan Point.

The shitbum who had evidently staked out a place in front of the bar was still there, snoozing loudly and stinking up the throughway. Collier tossed him a few 'ridium and entered the Point. It was again empty, save for Phil, who looked up at him and nodded slightly.

"Gimme some Eight," Collier said.

"It's third gen stuff," Phil said as he reached for a pouch.

"No, I mean, gimme some Eight. Real Eight."

Phil stopped in mid-motion. "I don't have a lot of that left. You know how much it costs?"

Collier flipped a three-cm iridium coin in the air, watched Phil watching it.

"Okay. Whatever you say, Col."

Phil had to go digging for it, but he produced a squeeze bag and reached for a flask. He emptied the contents of the bag into the flask and carefully pushed it toward Collier. "There you go. Make a strike?"

"Yeah," Collier said. He eyed the flask for a moment, then deftly tipped it back.

He wasn't sure what he had expected: although he had had third-gen Tank Eight, he had always wanted to taste some of the original stuff, just to see how it compared. It was not disappointing, but neither was it a wholly different experience. It was … better, but not so much so that the new stuff would forever taste like swill to him.

"What do you think?" Phil asked.

"Good. Not that much of an improvement, though."

Phil frowned. "You've got no taste, Col."

"Maybe."

"You drink too much third gen, you can't appreciate originals anymore, that's your problem. You can't taste pure stuff like it should be."

Collier tilted his head back and laughed. Even the single glass of Eight had had an intoxicating effect on him, and he allowed himself to laugh at Phil's comment. "Phil, I think I know what purity is. Better than you ever could."

"Is that so?"

"Yeah. Keep your original Tank Eight. It's not worth the price. I'll take some of your third-gen stuff."

Phil refilled his flask and shrugged. "You're the boss."

After emptying that flask, Collier spun the empty on the bartop for a few moments. "Hey, Phil, how long you been here?"

"Where?"

"In Ceres. How long has the Point been here?"

"Oh. Uh, I don't know, exactly. I guess ten years, give or take a few months. I built it when the Authority started drilling for commercial space. It's one of the first establishments built here. Well, the first one not directly for mining concerns."

"I get you. So you're one of the originals."

"You could say that."

"You came all the way out here from … where'd you come from, originally?"

"I'm an earthworm, originally."

"All the way from Earth just to open a bar on Ceres?"

Phil snorted. "No, I didn't come here for that. I was a rock hound. Like you, actually."

"What happened?"

"I made a big strike. Mostly palladium, some osmium. I cashed in, sold what little equity I had in my ship, and started this place."

Collier pushed the flask over to Phil and indicated he wanted a refill. Phil obliged.

"Why? Why'd you stop mining?" Collier asked, then downed the drink.

"I made it, that's why. Isn't that what everyone's here to do? Make it big, then get out of the business?"

"I don't know if everyone is here for that," Collier said, taking care with his words. He was noticing the effect of the three drinks. He warned himself to not say too much. "But then, why'd you stay here? Why not go back to Earth with your money, or Mars, or something?"

Phil looked pained. "So I can talk to whoreson idiots like you, I guess. 'Scuse me," he added, and greeted some patrons who had just come in.

Collier watched him as he served the newcomers. His words didn't fit his actions. If he had gone into the mining game to make it big, why did he stick around once he had? Something kept him here — it wasn't the return to Earth: the medicos on Ganymede had long since solved the problems weightlessness wreaked on the human body. And to look at it, the Trojan Point was not a going concern anymore. What kept Phil here?

His musings were interrupted by a voice behind him. "Captain South of the *Dulcinea*?"

He turned around, too rapidly. He had to steady himself against the bar rail. Two brown-suited Authority officers stood in the bar, the closer male officer looking at Collier's vacc suit with amusement while his partner stood an arm's length away, her right hand resting casually on her belted sidearm.

"Yeah. What's up?"

"There's been a slight issue with your last P sale. If—"

Collier snorted roughly. "Can't be. It was pure. More pure than Phil's Tank Eight stuff."

"Right. But we still need you to come with us, please. We can clear this up and you can go back to..." the man looked with slight disdain around the Point, "whatever you were doing."

"An' what happens if I say no?"

The Authority man sighed. "Look, buddy, is there a way we can just get this done and over with? If you haven't done anything wrong, you should have no problem coming with me and clearing this up."

Collier eyed the officer. "That's not the point. It's the principle. I shouldn't have to prove I didn't do anything wrong." He spoke as precisely as the Tank Eight in him would allow.

"Right, it's the principle," the officer repeated blandly. "How about this: I agree with you. I really do. It's just," the officer looked at his partner quickly, then back to Collier. "I got my instructions. If we go back to the station without you, that'll look bad for us. Now why would you want to make trouble for me, huh? Let's be friendly about this, what do you say?"

Collier stared at the man. He was fairly certain the officer was just using whatever tactic he thought would work, and that he didn't give a shit about Collier's principles — it was just another way to get him to go along. Maybe if that didn't work, he'd get nasty. Collier didn't want to sit in an Authority lockup for a day while the e-budsman sorted through his case, so he shrugged and allowed himself to be escorted to the Authority station.

He hadn't been to the lower levels in ages, since he had last renewed his license in person four years ago. The Ceres Authority had not been particularly busy in that time: there were only a few new tunnels and warrens as far as he remembered. Brown-suited officials floated here and there in the station, but for all their uniforms and aura of professionalism, Collier was not impressed. The Authority was a standing joke among rock hounds — "the most misnamed outfit in the system" they were known as. No one who had been a rock hound for more than a year took the Charter seriously anymore, since most of it had been amended and weakened in favor of corporate interests. And the parts that had not been modified were largely ignored.

Still, Collier saw no need to stir up trouble, so he waited patiently at a vertical tether until whomever wanted to see him arrived.

She was a startlingly pretty woman from far away. She approached Collier and her beauty faded as she got closer. It wasn't only that lines and wrinkles and age spots came into focus. She carried her shoulders hunched, even in microgravity, as if she were being pressed down on by some great weight. Her hair, styled in an old-fashioned bob, revealed streaks of flaccid grey hiding under its outer layer. When she introduced herself, her voice betrayed a past musicality that was now all but gone.

"Captain South, I'm Lora Fletcher. Thank you for coming in." She waited politely for him to respond.

"You're welcome," Collier said, with only a bit of irony.

Fletcher looked his vacc suit up and down. "You don't trust the Authority to keep atmosphere on Ceres?"

"It's just an old habit," Collier said.

Fletcher smiled slightly. "Now, you made a transaction with a Mr. Kein Go not long ago. You sold him just under ten kilograms of platinum. Is that right?"

"Yes."

"He asked us to confirm the purity of the sale."

"I didn't know you guys did that," Collier interrupted.

Fletcher's eyes smiled, and Collier saw the remains of the radiant woman she must once have been. "It's still part of the Charter. But between you and me, we rarely uphold it. Usually, the request is sent off to an assay corporation and the whole thing is done privately. For money, of course. But I, myself, still like to think the Charter is worth something."

"Good for you," Collier mumbled.

Fletcher looked sad for half a second, then continued crisply. "He had accused you of plating the sample, but our tests quickly confirmed that the platinum you sold him was clean."

"Like I said it was."

Fletcher stared at him searchingly for a long moment, then finally said, "Are you going to make me say it?"

Collier snorted and grinned despite himself. The lady had some style. But it was still not worth risking the truth if

Fletcher still somehow didn't know. He shrugged and said, "I'd hate to take away your pleasure."

Fletcher sighed. "The platinum was completely pure. No admixture of any other trace elements. I've been assured by some independent experts that this is impossible."

Collier shrugged again.

Fletcher tilted her head upward for a quick moment, as if to ask for strength from above, and then, in a single breath, said, "The metal was too pure, and we also know you didn't use an Authority extractor and don't have one on board your ship, the *Dulcinea*."

"Nice work," Collier growled.

"So, let me just ask you directly, Captain — how and where did you come across ten kilograms of completely pure platinum?"

Now it was Collier's turn to sigh. "All right. You seem like a nice lady. I won't play games anymore. You're right: it's completely pure. It's not a trick, either. It'll stay pure and you or Go or whomever can use the P just fine. I have a … method, shall we say, of obtaining pure platinum. But here's the catch," he said, lowering his voice. Fletcher had not reacted to his speech, nor did she change expression when Collier lowered his tone. "It's proprietary. Like a trade secret. I don't know much, but I know that the Authority can't force someone to reveal a trade secret."

"We can't force a corporation to reveal one, no." She placed a faint stress on the word "corporation." She paused for a moment and continued to stare at him. When she spoke again, her voice was clipped. "Did you steal it?"

"No," Collier said calmly and quickly.

"Is it from somewhere in the Jovian system?"

"No."

Fletcher moved back a few inches. "I'm going to summarize what you have said so far. Correct me if I am wrong in any important way."

"Okay." Despite himself, Collier was coming to respect the woman.

"You sold ten kilograms of completely pure platinum to a broker. You didn't use an extractor to get it. You didn't jack it, and it's not something from the Jovian labs. You claim to have some secret process of making pure platinum. Is all of that right?"

"That's right."

Fletcher tilted her head slightly. "Why not sell the process to a corporation? I can only imagine what they'd pay for such a thing."

"I don't want a corporation to have it. It's mine." Collier said, biting his lip after the last word. He had been dangerously close to revealing too much. As it was, Fletcher must have seen him stop himself.

If she had, she made no mention of it. "Well, that's about all I can do here. I very much hope, for your sake, you are telling me the truth."

"Why? Why do you care about how I got the P?"

"Me, or the Authority?" Fletcher said, her eyes smiling again.

"You, I guess."

"It matters to me."

"That's not much of an answer."

"Neither was yours about why you won't sell your process."

Collier chuckled once. "Fair enough. Are you through with me?"

"For the time being, yes. I think, though, that we will cross paths again, Captain."

Collier felt his eyes widen at the iron in Fletcher's voice. She hadn't changed her facial expression from the vaguely pleasant one she had been wearing, but her voice had dropped half an octave and her head had tilted down a few degrees. The overall effect told Collier that her casual, faintly motherly demeanor was simply a cover for the tough professional beneath.

He left the Authority office as calmly as he could, though once out of earshot he called Sancho.

"Sancho, still nothing to report?"

"Nothing new, Skipper. Just been hovering up here, running some tests on the magic wand."

"Tests? How?"

"Still subjecting it to gamma ray bombardment. Got the beetle to maneuver it into the assay box."

"Any new results?"

"Of course not," Sancho said, his irritation clear. "The damn thing is still impenetrable. And besides, I'd have called you."

"Right. Listen, I just got done talking to the Authority."

"Yeah? What about?"

Collier looked around before answering, pushed off the floor and away from the Authority office. "They were called by Go to examine the P sale. They had some questions as to how I got so much pure platinum."

"I don't understand."

Collier lowered his voice and continued moving away from the Authority office, toward the open quadrangle's ground level. "For such a smart computer, you don't take in much, do you? We didn't use any of the extractors, and we float in here with ten kilos of completely pure platinum? Of course there is going to be suspicion. I should have thought about that myself. We'll have to be more careful next time. Mix in some other materials."

"I don't know how. I don't know if we're going to be able to program the wand to make anything less than pure."

"Still, we need to think this through better. I'll be in touch," Collier added after a pause. "Let me know if anything happens. And I mean anything."

"Aye aye, Skipper."

Collier was about to sign off, but he thought better of it. "Sancho, I don't mean if anything at all happens. Don't call to tell me to tell me you needed to fire the attitude jets to maintain orbit, or that somebody on an outbound liner farted. You get me? Just tell me if anything new happens regarding the magic wand, or some ship operations matter comes up that you can't handle."

"Of course, Skipper. How dumb do you think I am? I knew what you meant."

"Right," Collier said uncertainly. He had always trusted the computer before, and it had never let him down in any serious manner before. Why now did he act as if he had only recently purchased the machine?

The whole affair with the Authority had made him unusually touchy, he decided. Plus the Tank Eight swilling around in him didn't help. He hadn't been thinking clearly about his discovery — there was much more to it than just an endless supply of metal. He found his mind returning to the question of the wand's origin, as if desperate to find any other answer besides the alien artifact one. Where had it come from? Everything about it said it couldn't have been human manufacture, though Collier had to admit, he was as much in the dark about what went on in the Jovian labs as anyone else was. Could they have made the wand? He had rejected the hypothesis on board the *Dulcinea* when Sancho had brought it up, and saw no new data to lend it credence. If the scientists in the Jovian system had indeed created this device, why and how would they have buried it on a rogue asteroid?

No, the Jovian hypothesis did not work.

Could it have been part of a secret corporate project? Again, the same questions that couldn't be answered by the Jovian theory applied here.

That didn't leave too many other theories. The only one — still — that answered the question of the wand's origin and function was a non-human intelligence had designed it. How it came to be on a rogue asteroid was still a mystery. Had the aliens planted it there, or was it a relic of a long-dead civilization, perhaps even a mining tool?

And where there was one such device, couldn't there be others? His search on the Wild Goose had been thorough, he thought, but it might be worthwhile to buy the best surveying equipment available and go back to it and spend a long time going over the whole rock centimeter by centimeter. Might even be worthwhile attaching engines to the rock to check its flight away from Ceres. If he could sell more metal (buying up the cheapest raw materials he could to convert) and show Starcher he was consistently making a profit, maybe he could get him to finance the enterprise.

So deep were his thoughts that he had drifted into the chaotic traffic of the open quadrangle without realizing it. His eyes focused on the dizzying array of colors and people landing and taking off from the lowest level and only had the barest of seconds to register the collision before it happened.

A woman clad in the midnight blue of the Ad Astra Corporation landed almost squarely on top of him and both crumpled slowly to the floor, unhurt but awkwardly tangled.

"Sorry, that's my fault," Collier began, slithering out from under the woman and reaching unnecessarily to help her up. "I wasn't—" he stopped.

"Hello, Col," Isa said. She had smoothly risen to her feet and hovered lightly before him. Her raven hair was tied back in a corporate braid, adorned by four cobalt ribbons. Her eyes still had the piercing quality they used to, though the slight discoloration in her right eye betrayed her implant.

"Isa," Collier said after a moment to collect himself. His voice was calm enough. "Back from my discovery? All through with it?" He did not need to summon up bitterness — despite his possession of the magic wand, he had not yet recovered from the sting of her theft.

"Come on, Col," Isa said, sighing. "You can't be still pissed off about that."

"Why not?"

Isa looked at him for a beat, as if expecting him to elaborate. When he didn't she shook her head slightly in that way she had when she was both amused and irritated by something he had done and said, "Because I hear you've made it big in another way."

Collier's eyes widened and he instinctively looked around the lower level walkway. There was no one about — the lower levels were administrative rather than commercial — but he nevertheless didn't want to advertise his discovery.

"How do you know? What do you know?" he said.

Isa cocked her head and raised an eyebrow. "So, you *have* found something. I wasn't completely sold. I thought maybe you had just cooked up another story to convince Starcher to lend you more metal. What did you find?"

Collier swore under his breath. He might have been able to lie his way out if he hadn't reacted so obviously. Now Isa was on him, and she wouldn't be shaken off so easily.

"Listen," he said, his tone changing from anxious to suggestive. "I can't tell you everything, but I can give you some details. But not here. Let's go back to the *Dulcinea*. I'll fill you in there."

Isa pursed her lips. "I don't think so. I've got an hourly at Demeter's that's still good. Not too small, either. Let's go there."

"You don't trust me in the *Dulcinea*?" Collier tried to smile.

Isa sighed again. "No, that's not it. At least," she said, trying to smile herself, "that's not all of it. It's on the top level, next to—"

"I know where Demeter's is," he snapped. "I still don't see why you don't want to go to *Dulcinea*. Oh, of course," he said, snapping his fingers in a mock epiphany. "You want to be able to make an exit on your terms. You can't do that on board my ship."

"Stop it, Col."

He realized he was being childish. "Yeah, yeah," he murmured. "Let's go," he said, and leapt upward toward the top level of the quadrangle. A part of his brain screamed at him that he was being manipulated — he had revealed that he had made a discovery, and now he was giving in to her choice of venue to discuss it. Why did this woman have such sway over him?

He tried to reject the thought that kept recurring: *maybe if she knows what I have found, that'll be the stability she's been needing for so long. And maybe she'll come back to me.* As he rose through the levels of the quadrangle, he fought to keep such thoughts out of his mind.

———<>———

The Demeter was the closest thing to a hotel Ceres had. Most Belters simply stayed aboard whatever ship they were crewing most of the time rather than use up their metal on Ceresian accommodations, but the establishment did have its advantages. Low-ranking crew could find private rooms while their ship was offloading, selling, or undergoing maintenance and resupply. Such private rooms allowed for all manner of activities that would have been difficult to ignore on board ship. Isa, however, would have rated a private stateroom on her ship, so her use of the Demeter was unusual. Collier pondered this even as the pair of them made their way to her bungalow in silence.

The room would not have been called spacious on Earth or Mars, but on Ceres where pressurized cubic meters were precious, Isa had secured a luxurious suite. Collier couldn't help but be impressed despite himself as he followed her inside.

Isa closed the door behind him and said proudly, "One hundred and eight a night. To answer your unasked question."

"Hm. Still not bigger than my space on the *Dulcinea*."

Isa sighed again. "Right. You want anything?" She gestured to the automat.

Collier grinned. "On the Ad Astra account? Or yours?"

Isa put her right hand to her hip. "Why? Does that matter?"

"Now that you mention it, I guess not. You're both the same. I'll take whatever the most expensive thing on there is," he said, making sure not to look at the automat's menu.

"You're a child," Isa said, turning to the machine and selecting an item. It vended two plastic flasks of faintly amber liquid, one of which Isa tossed to Collier.

"Yeastwine," Collier snorted. "That's the most expensive thing it's got?"

Isa said firmly, "No, it's what I punched up. Drink it or not. You want something else, you pay it. From what I hear, you can afford it. Now take that damn stupid vacc suit off and let's talk."

Collier grinned. Her captaincy had honed the edge she had only hinted at when they had been together. "Yes, ma'am." He wriggled out of the still-moist suit and hung it near the door. "So, aside from some shitty yeastwine, what am I going to get out of this talk?"

"Being with me isn't enough?" Isa said, her tone mysterious.

Collier grunted. "You're not seriously trying that, are you?"

"Why not?" she said. She took a squeeze from her flask and floated toward him. "I think we have unfinished business, don't you?"

"I thought it was over. You certainly made that clear enough."

"Maybe I was wrong," she said, her hand moving to the fastening clasps that held her coveralls on.

"Hold on," Collier said, feeling a faint stirring in his loins despite the spinning of his head. "You can't just try to restart everything as if nothing has happened."

Isa had closed the distance between them and collided gently with him. "Let's try," she said, and before he could react, she grasped his head and kissed him suddenly.

He felt as if he were seeing the scene from the outside. For so long, his unmoored desire had been half-fantasy — a fantasy he wasn't even sure he wanted. Now that he saw his idle dreams translated into reality, he did not know if he should reject or accept them.

His body responded to Isa's kiss, and he found himself embracing her, tilting his head to the left slightly and returning her kiss.

Presently, Isa backed away slightly, still in his arms, and said, "Wait. I don't think they have a right to see this." She wriggled out of his grasp, which he loosened once he determined she wanted to be free, and seized her right eye.

Even as he watched, she twisted and detached the cybernetic eye from her socket, leaving a clean but grotesque depression with a single silver socket in the center. She examined the implant with her natural eye, found what she was looking for, and made a tiny adjustment. She then carefully placed the cybernetic eye back into its socket, blinked a few times, and looked back at him. "There. It's off now." Her voice had completely lost its seductive quality.

Collier let his hands fall. "Corporate implant?"

"Yes. Part of the captain's rank," she said in her businesslike voice. "They don't like me turning it off, but I think I can justify doing so now, especially what with the stupid seduction moves I was putting on you. The contract is a bit loose in this regard."

"I'll bet it is. So, now what?" He folded his arms and tried to keep the frustration he was feeling out of his voice.

"Like I said, now let's talk."

"Oh, I see," Collier said. "You make a big show about turning off one recorder, but you've got another running in here somewhere."

Isa tossed her head back. "Jesus, for one goddamn second, act like an adult, would you, Col?" She looked back at him and lowered her voice. "If you've got something to tell me, then I hope you will, and I can decide if I want to kick it upstairs to my bosses or not. But with a recorder on, I don't have that option — they'll know what I know. I want to keep some upper hand with them, tell them what I want them to know. So now, can we talk?"

"You're playing me and your bosses at the same time. I have to hand it to you, Isa — that's shrewd even for you."

"I'm not playing you."

Collier snorted. "I enjoy games just like the next guy, but I think this one is getting a little bit boring, Isa. I still don't see why I should tell you anything. Or are you still willing to trade a ride on the bed for some information?"

Isa looked at him for a moment, then brought her right hand up swiftly — though not so swiftly that Collier couldn't have deflected it — and slapped his cheek.

Collier spun to his right with the blow, his face stinging, but did not cry out. When he turned back to Isa, he rubbed his face and growled, "You sure go from hot to cold quick. A minute ago you were kissing me."

"That was an act for the corporation and you damn well know it." Isa said firmly, staring at him for a long moment then turning her back to him and reaching for her yeastwine flask.

"Yeah, I guess I did. Still, you haven't told me why I should tell you anything." He continued to rub his cheek.

Isa kept her back to him as she spoke. Her voice was shaky. "I suppose asking you as a friend is out?"

"How are you my friend?" Collier snapped. "You stole my strike a few weeks ago, you slapped me just now, and you left—" He stopped himself with a sharp intake of breath. "You've proven we're not friends, Isa."

"You know why I left, Col." Isa still hadn't turned around. Her voice wavered.

"You couldn't handle my life. Yeah, I know."

Now she spun around, her face angry. "Yeah, that's it. That's *exactly* it. I couldn't handle *your* life. It was never *our* life, Col. You weren't gonna make it ours."

Collier chuckled casually. "That's cometshit. I had it all figured out, how we were going to live on the *Dulcinea*, split the mining duties—"

"I didn't want that!" Isa was now shouting. "Jesus, you still don't get it? I didn't want to be a *part* of *your* life, Col. I wanted us to make a new one."

"No, you didn't," he said, matching her icy intensity with calm fire. "You wanted to change me into what you needed. Wanted me to join up with the corps, so I could be 'stable.' Fuck that."

"And there you have it," Isa said with a little less stridency. "'Fuck that,' you say. Well, Col, You had a choice to make, and you made it. It was me or that goddamn nomad life, and you chose the Belt. How's that working for you, by the way?"

"It's working great, as a matter of—" He stopped midway and shook his head. "Cute." He sighed and reached for his yeastwine, which had gently fallen to the floor. He took a squeeze, looked at Isa, and said, "You're just not going to give up, are you?"

Isa looked at him in dismay. "I don't … oh. That wasn't a trick, Col. Jesus, do you think I'm that clumsy?" She smiled slightly, this time a genuine one. She always looked her best right after they had argued.

Collier grinned back. "No, I guess not." He remembered that night ages ago when the two of them had, post-coitally, shared their best argument tactics. It had been a moment of pure vulnerability far more intimate than the sex act they had just completed. Even now, as he realized he would not be able to trick or browbeat her, he remembered the moment fondly. "All right, then. Let's talk. But," he added, taking the last squeeze from his yeastwine package and tossing it carelessly at her, "I'm talking to you, not to the Ad Astra Corporation. And we both do some talking."

She caught the slow-moving package and nodded. "All right. I'll start. We know you hit some kind of strike but ran into trouble with your vendor, Kein Go. He called the Authority on you, and they investigated. You didn't use an extractor, and I personally know you don't have one on board the *Dulcinea*. Furthermore, you settled up with Starcher for an unknown amount. All of that points to an unusual kind of strike. How am I doing so far?"

Collier nodded, impressed despite himself. "You've pretty much got it. How do you know all of this?"

"Oh," Isa said, moving over to the bed and gently floating down to it, "some of it through simple investigation, some of it through inside people in the Authority." At Collier's raised eyebrows she added, "Oh, come on, Col. You knew we have people working for us in the Authority. We practically don't even hide it anymore."

"Oh, I know that — I just didn't think you'd admit it so freely."

"You said you wanted us both to talk, so I'm talking," she grinned slightly. "Anyway, it was enough to get me curious, so I was on my way down to the Authority level to see where you had gone. That's when I ran into you."

"Why you?"

"What?"

"Why did the corporation send you to track me?"

Isa looked surprised. "I'd already been tracking you, and–"

"No, I don't just mean now. I mean from the start. From since you ... when we stopped seeing each other. Did they know you and I had been together?"

Isa looked away and smoothed out the already smooth bed sheet. "Once I told them, yes."

"When did you tell them?"

"About a year ago." She was still smoothing the sheet.

"And when," Collier said with elaborate patience, "did you get your captain's commission?"

"About ten months ago."

Collier let the silence grow. When he spoke, it was with sad understanding. "So you promised them you'd be able to make big strikes, because you knew this old crazy Belter who would make them for you. Then you'd move in, take the strike, and cash in. And if there were any problems," he floated toward her, face first, and said precisely, "you'd shut him up with a bit of fucking."

This time, he caught her wrist as she raised it to slap him again. "No, no. I took one already. You only get one." He shoved her arm back, releasing her wrist. "Tell me which part of my story was incorrect, Isa. Tell me all about how you didn't track me down, didn't steal my strike, didn't use my success for your advancement. Tell me, Isa, how you didn't break it off with me because you couldn't live my lifestyle, but sure as shit could take in the success from it."

Isa's eyes didn't flash with anger anymore. She looked at him as if suddenly very tired — her eyes sagged in her face and her shoulders drooped. "You're right. Is that what you want to hear? You're right. I used you to move up in the corporation. That's what it's like, Col. If you ever grew up and sat at the adults' table, you'd know that. You do what you need to do to survive and thrive. It's like that everywhere." She sniffed. "So you can curse at me all night, but it won't change the way things are. There are no miracles out there, except the ones you make for yourself. Sometimes that means using other people."

"You didn't used to be like this, Isa," Collier said softly. "You were a good woman, even if we didn't agree on a few things. And now..."

"Save it," Isa said, her voice hard again. "I don't need your pity. I'd rather you called me a whore again."

Collier was silent for a while, and the two shifted their positions in the room, as if to mark an end to the ugliness of the conversation. Isa rose to select another drink from the automat, while Collier floated over to a wall niche and settled down on a bench seat.

"So, you have some kind of secret process for extracting ore, do you?" Isa said without prelude after she had taken a squeeze from her plastic flask.

"Yes. And I'm going to keep it a secret."

"I don't think I need to tell you that the corporation would pay handsomely for the process. It would make our operations much more efficient."

"How handsomely?" Collier said. He wasn't truly interested in selling the wand, but he wanted to know the level of the corporation's interest.

"Well, that's hard to say without the specifics of your discovery. What can you tell me about it?"

"I can tell you that it is a completely reliable method for producing pure metals from raw materials. There is no harmful by-product, and there is no complicated set up required. No significant energy output either."

Isa scowled. "Sounds like magic."

Collier shrugged. "Call it what you want. How much would that be worth to you?"

"Again, given what you've told me, that's still hard to say."

"Ballpark. Thousands? Millions? Billions?"

"I can't say," Isa said casually.

Collier grew angry. "Then what the hell are we doing here? I'm telling you what I've got, but you're not giving me any idea what it's worth. I'm sure as hell not going to show you or anyone else from the corporation how it works without some kind of deal."

"And Ad Astra isn't going to make any deal without knowing what you've got in greater detail, Col. You know that."

"Well," Collier said, leaning back on the bench, "it doesn't matter, anyway. I won't sell it to you or any other corporation. Not for any price."

Isa frowned. "Don't be like that. You and me ... we've made a mess of us. Both of us are probably to blame for that. But you've got a chance here to set yourself up for life, Col." She leaned forward toward him. "Listen, I am not making promises, but if you have what you say you have, you can sell it to Ad Astra for maybe a hundred million. That'll keep you going for a long, long time, Col. It's what you always said you wanted: to make a strike big enough to retire on."

"I never dreamed that, Isa," Collier said quietly. "You did." He rose from the bench. "And I'm not refusing to sell because you and me didn't work out. I … loved you, Isa. I really did. At least, I loved what I thought you were, and what I thought we could be." He pushed off and floated toward the door. Once there, he turned back to Isa, who had not turned to look at him. "I'm sorry for what I said tonight. You needed me to be something I couldn't be, just as I needed you to do the same. There's no blame in what happened to us. Only tragedy. Goodbye, Isa." He grabbed his vacc suit and left the room.

Chapter Five

Collier found himself outside the Demeter, and although he knew he had to have walked out of the hotel, he had no distinct memory of it. He was numb from the meeting with Isa — neither triumphant nor sorrowful. Simply numb. He was still dragging his vacc suit behind him, in fact. He took a moment and slid himself inside, leaving the front ungasketed.

His feet carried him toward the quadrangle. He was on the top level — a simple drop down to the next would bring him to the Trojan Point. But he didn't feel like getting drunk now. Only one thing could begin to bring him peace.

"Sancho, do you copy?"

"Urm?" Sancho said, his voice drowsy.

"Everything okay?"

"Yeah. You jus' woke me up, is all."

Collier frowned. "You don't sleep, Sancho."

"I know," his computer answered crisply, "I was just playing with a new personality wrinkle. What do you think of it?"

"Cute. As long as it doesn't inhibit your functions, sure, add it in. Listen, how are we for propellant?"

"Kind of low, Skipper. Eleven percent in the mains. Ten more in the reserve tanks."

"Okay. Go ahead and use what's left of the funds to top her off."

"Aye aye."

"But no corporate fuel, you got that?" Collier said firmly.

"No corporate fuel. Copy that. Independents only."

"And you'd better get some biosupplies," Collier mused. "Shouldn't need too much. And no corp on that, either."

"Okay."

"I'm coming aboard. Try to have her ready for me in about twenty minutes."

"Not possible, Skipper. Refueling and resupply will take a lot longer from independents. I'll do my best, but we'll be here for a good few hours."

"Damn it. Okay, do what you can."

Collier was back aboard *Dulcinea* in half an hour. Sancho informed him that resupply had already happened — an independent had agreed to offload some supplies because half her crew had decided to join up with Horizon Corporation — but refueling was taking longer. It would be at least another hour before that was finished.

"Fine," Collier said carelessly, shrugging out of his suit and tossing it toward the aft compartment.

"Everything all right, Skipper?" Sancho asked.

"Just let me know when the refueling is done," he snapped.

——<>——

Hours later, Sancho had completed the refueling procedure with the independent, and announced to Collier that they were ready for untethering and departure.

Collier, who had dozed off into an unsettled sleep, woke in a foul mood. "Good. Lose the tether and orient us to the nearest unclaimed rock."

"Aye aye. Nearest unclaimed asteroid is C-114. Well within the Ceres Group. At fifty percent thrust for two hours, it'll take us two days, one hour, approximately seventeen minutes to reach it, assuming standard flipbraking at halfway point."

"Sounds good. No need to tax the thrust tubes. As soon as we're untethered, file the flight plan and get us there."

"Copy that. .075g thrust in ten minutes."

Collier settled into his acceleration couch, though when the thrust came, the gentle push against the cushion almost went by him unnoticed. He truly didn't know what he wanted from Isa, but he knew enough about his desires to know she wasn't going to fulfill them ever again. She had once been adventurous and independent. He had seen in her a kindred spirit — a seeker. Like one of his asteroid hunches, he had tried to mine her depths, only to find he had been wrong.

During the outbound trip, Collier explained to Sancho his plan. The computer hadn't asked him, but Collier felt he knew his electronic partner well enough to detect his unspoken curiosity. The two would head for the nearby asteroid and take on worthless rock. They'd hover there for a while, converting the rock to whatever element they thought best, then head back to Ceres to sell it again.

"That sounds fine, Skipper, but I wonder if you've really thought this through?"

"What do you mean?"

"Well, I've been doing a lot of thinking while you were down on Ceres."

"Have you." Collier scooped another forkful of vat-grown chicken cacciatore into his mouth.

"Yes. I'm not against us using the wand to turn a profit. After all, that's what we're out here for, isn't it?"

"Go on."

"But it's not going to work indefinitely, you know."

Collier stopped mid-bite. "What? What did you find out about the wand? Is its power source fading?"

"No, no, that's not what I mean at all. As far as I can tell, the wand has to get its power from the conversion process itself. It has to be a nuclear-powered device in the purest sense. That's not what I mean."

Collier relaxed and swallowed. Sancho's theory raised as many questions as it answered: for instance, even if the wand used the energy released in the transmutation process to power the process itself, it still begged the question as to how it started the process at all. Or was the device so advanced that it was the perpetual motion machine dreamed of by cranks for centuries?

At Collier's silence, Sancho continued. "I mean that if the Authority questioned you about the sale to Go, don't you think they will do it again, or more, if we try to repeat the process?"

Collier nodded thoughtfully as he chewed. "I have been worried about that. That's partly why we're going out to mine instead of just using local junk and converting it. Will be more convincing to anyone tracking our movements. If we still get investigated, a few well-placed bribes will keep the Authority off our backs."

"Oh. I never thought of that."

"No, I bet you wouldn't. Not really something that you can think of, is it, Sancho?"

Sancho sounded defensive. "Well, I—"

"I didn't mean it as an insult. It's a credit to you that you think humans are incorruptible."

"I don't think that, Skipper. What, do you think I rolled off the assembly line yesterday? Hell, I know people can be bought. You taught me that yourself. No, it's just that I didn't think of it because, in the long run, it won't work."

Collier's grin faded. "Why not?"

"Because bribes grow, never shrink. And people who are corrupt enough to be bought in the first place don't have enough integrity to stay bought. There will come a time when the bribes you have to pay out will get bigger and bigger, and involve more and more people, and it'll reach a tipping point where you'll decide it isn't worth it. Bribes will only buy us some time."

"Maybe enough time, Sancho," Collier said quietly. He thought for a moment, then grinned again. "You're turning into a regular Machiavelli, aren't you?"

"I don't know about that, Skipper. I think I am just programmed for Realpolitik."

"Well, whatever you want to call it, thanks for the analysis. There's also a problem in your analysis that I foresee. The Authority provost, Fletcher, doesn't strike me as a woman who can be bought."

"Really? That could be a problem, Skipper."

"Maybe," Collier mused. He opened his mouth to start to tell Sancho about Isa, but he caught himself. If Sancho was, as he said, a believer in Realpolitik, he could never understand the conflicting feelings that existed between his master and Isa. Collier didn't even understand them himself.

Six hours later, Sancho interrupted the silence that had evolved during the cruising phase of the trip. "Skipper, something odd here."

"What is it?"

"Picking up a vessel with the same heading as us. Out of Ceres. Matching our velocity. They're about four hours behind us."

"Shit. Shit, shit, shit!" Collier floated to the control suite and strapped into the command chair. "Show me."

The holodisplay lit up. "I've been tracking them for several minutes now to confirm: they are indeed heading for asteroid C-114. Telescopic image plus extrapolated enhancement on the display for you."

It was Isa. The huge Ad Astra vessel was unmistakable, and although he could not identify the markings, he knew it had to be her.

"You say they're matching our speed?"

"Yes. Only a slight insignificant variance."

"How long until we get to C-114?"

"At our current speed, assuming standard flipbraking, forty-two hours, fifty-one minutes."

Collier looked at the image for a few moments, then wiped it from midair with a swipe of his hand. "Doesn't matter. Doesn't matter," he repeated, "because what are they going to do? There's nothing on C-114 to steal. They're going to watch us gather up a whole lot of rock and head back to Ceres. Let them follow us."

"Should we try to signal them?"

"And say what?" Collier chuckled once. "No, I've got nothing to say to them."

"Then I assume you don't want to answer if they try to reach us?"

"You assume rightly."

——<>——

The rest of the trip was uneventful — at least, Collier assumed it was. He didn't ask Sancho if the pursuing corporate vessel had sent a transmission, and Sancho didn't volunteer any data to that effect, so the two of them spent the day continuing their research on the wand. They had come to the conclusion that the wand could transmute anything placed inside of it into an equal amount of a single element — and by "amount," the transmuter read mass. The wand even changed the air trapped inside of it into whatever had been selected, so when the wand was opened, it made a popping sound as pressure inside the wand equalized. The two still hadn't tried to convert anything into the more volatile or dangerous elements, and they both assumed the wand would change a substance into any of the superheavy elements, even ununoctium and perhaps even beyond.

"Frankly, I can't even begin to speculate what would happen if we programmed the wand for that," Sancho had said. "According to the wand's operating pattern, I know how to do it, but I don't know what would happen. Unbibium is completely unstable — half life of less than a millisecond — so I don't know if the wand would make a stable version or not."

"Can you go past 122?" Collier had asked.

"The wand's pattern generator would indicate so, yes. So except for the fact that human science hasn't produced even a single atom past 122, it should be possible. I've no idea what would happen, though."

It had been an interesting thought, and while both agreed to stay clear of such experimentation, Collier couldn't help wondering just a little bit about the wand's true potential.

The arrival at C-114 was as uneventful as the trip had been, despite the pursuing Ad Astra vessel. Upon rockfall, Collier proceeded to haul in surface dust and rock into the *Dulcinea's* hold with no regard for what he was raking. He set charges on the surface of C-114 and wasted huge chunks of rock, allowing them to fly past the collection canopy while other bits found their way into the hold. The whole operation took scarcely more than four hours, and just as the hold was filling up, Sancho alerted him to the pursuing mining vessel's presence.

Collier finished his work on the rock surface and reentered the *Dulcinea*. Sliding casually into the control seat, he told Sancho to open the communications channel the Ad Astra ship had so insistently been using.

"This is the *Dulcinea*, Captain Collier South here. How can I help you?"

He had fully expected to hear Isa's voice over the speakers, and was profoundly shocked when a gruff male one greeted him instead.

"This is Captain Powanda of the Ad Astra Mining Vessel *SCM-17*. We've been trying to reach you for over a day, Captain,"

"Sorry, I was in the shower," Collier said. "*SCM-17*, you say? I thought Isa Mitchell was in command of her."

"First Officer Mitchell is my second, yes. I'm not here to discuss our personnel with you, South. What'd you pick up from C-114? From what we can tell, that's a completely valueless rock."

"I left my lunch box here, and I really like it. I was picking it up."

Captain Powanda's voice sounded tired. "Listen, South, if you've found a way to detect and extract P from rocks that we used to think had nothing in them, how long do you think you'll be able to keep the secret? It's gonna get out, you know. Why not cash in while you can? My company is prepared to make you a generous offer for your technique or secret."

"Is that so? Well, I rejected your last offer, so I hope this one is a little sweeter. I'm looking for something in the neighborhood of ... ten trillion metals." Collier had a rough idea as to Ad Astra's total worth — it would take hundreds of companies their size to make up such a sum.

Powanda grew belligerent. "Who do you think you are? You're just one man out here. Do you know what kind of power this corporation has, South? I suggest you think very, very hard about making us a serious offer. Right now, you have the upper hand, but don't think that you will have your cards forever. *SCM-17* out."

Sancho sang out, "We're pretty close to full, Skipper. Shall I try to force more in, or begin to—"

"No, shut it down, Sancho. Bring the canopy back in and prepare for return to Ceres."

"Copy that."

"And show me on holo the *SCM-17* and us relative to each other."

"You got it," Sancho said, and a visual representation of the two ships appeared in space in the cabin. Data regarding the two ships' velocity, orientation, and performance (estimated for the *SCM-17*) hung next to each ship. The Ad Astra ship dwarfed the *Dulcinea*, boasting a cargo volume at least eighty times Collier's. It was designed for low-efficiency mining, whereas Collier had to be much more precise in his practice. Where the Ad Astra swung a broadsword, the *Dulcinea* used a scalpel.

"Canopy retrieval in progress. Estimate fifty minutes for full retrieval," Sancho said.

"I don't like what that guy said," Collier mumbled. "Sounded too threatening by half. But what can they do?"

As if to answer, Sancho chirped up again. "Skipper! The *SCM-17* has opened an impact probe door. And we've just been laser-locked."

"They wouldn't," Collier said in disbelief. "Are you sure?"

"Completely, Skipper. We're painted like the Sistine Chapel."

"Raise them again."

Powanda's voice was a smug snarl. "Yeah?"

"I don't know what your game is, Powanda, but you realize you won't get what you want out of me by shooting at me."

"I don't know what you mean, Captain," Powanda drawled.

"I won't appeal to your better nature, because I'm sure you don't have one. I'll try logic, though you corp Skippers are notorious for having brains as tiny as your peckers." Collier slowed his voice and pronounced each word carefully. "You. Can't. Shoot. Me. Because. Dead. I. Can't. Help. You."

"Who says we're going to shoot you? We are worried about your safety, Captain, so we have you guidance-locked to make completely certain we will be able to track you in case of an emergency."

"Right. And the impact probe tube?"

"We're just running standard checks. Corporate protocol, you know." Powanda managed to smirk vocally.

Collier dropped his condescending tone and growled angrily. "Let's stop bullshitting, Powanda. I have something you want, and you know you can't get it from me through force. I know you think your corporation has got the Authority by the balls, but shooting me will not only not get you what you want, it will cause inconvenience with the Authority. Bribes and favors, whatever, just to keep any investigation from ever finding out what happened. It's not worth it."

"You want to know the truth, you miserable shit? Okay, here it is," Powanda spat, his voice matching Collier's tone. "If you're not willing to give up whatever you know or have, I'm authorized to disable your vessel and bring it back to Ceres under the guise of a rescue. Yeah, I'm sure there will be some trouble with the Authority, but I assume the corp has that figured out. That's not my area. But you can bet that when we tow you back, we'll have it out of you. You, or your ship, or your shipboard computer."

"I won't talk, and I'll wipe the computer."

"There's guys better than you who can retrieve anything you think you've erased. You know that. Look, fella, I don't really want to bang up your ship. I don't really want you to get hurt. I will — but I guess I'd rather not. So what's it gonna be? Am I going to have to bust up that rockchaser of yours? Or have you changed your mind?"

Collier could hear the resolve in Powanda's voice. There was no bluffing here. The Ad Astra skipper was ready to commit an act in direct violation of all kinds of Authority Charter statutes, but he was also confident that the corporation would protect him. That — and his own desperation — gave Collier an idea.

"You realize, Captain, that once you tow me back and the corporation starts to tear apart the *Dulcinea* to learn the process they want, you'll be hung out to dry. You know that, right? I can hear the PR department's justification already. 'A lone renegade captain, acting without Ad Astra support, fired ruthlessly on a helpless mining ship. We will of course terminate Captain Powanda's employment immediately and turn him over to the Authority ombudsman for justice.' And you can bet the Authority will be all too happy to rain a shitstorm on you that'll end with you in the Centauri Sleeper. Count on it."

Powanda laughed. "Nice try, Captain. I've thought of all that. That's why I've documented everything sent to me, and I have my own agents ready to act in case it goes down like you said. I appreciate the concern, though," he added, chuckling.

Collier swore under his breath. There was nothing for it. He told Sancho to break the signal.

"Signal broken," Sancho said. "What do we do now, Skipper?"

"We have to run for it."

"Uh, Skipper? I don't have exact specs on the enemy vessel, but you have to know that it can—"

"I know it can outrun us, and I know we can't outrun an impact probe. Prepare to go to full thrust, and get *Rocinante* ready for deployment."

"Aye aye, Skipper. Full thrust on your command. *Rocinante* being prepped for launch. Estimate three minutes until she's ready."

"Full thrust in two minutes, thirty seconds, Sancho."

"You got it. Skipper?"

"What?"

Sancho's voice was softer than normal. "If we do get captured ... will you tell them about the wand?"

Collier opened his mouth to answer defiantly, but something about Sancho's question tugged at him. "I tell you what, Sancho. If they do disable us, and tow us back to Ceres, I won't let them take you apart. I'll tell them about the wand before I let that happen. Okay?"

"Thrust in two minutes. Thanks, Skipper. I don't like the thought of—"

"Skip it. I understand."

"I'm not sure you do, Skipper," Sancho said after a pause.

"Huh?" Despite their impending doom, Collier was intrigued by Sancho's cryptic statement.

"I can't be investigated by any computer expert."

"Why not? I've installed programs and improvements to you over the years. You can't be afraid, are you?"

"Thrust in ninety seconds. Yes, I am very afraid. I know that as soon as a cybernetics analysis begins on my systems, it's the end of me. At least, the me that I am now. Opening stable doors. *Rocinante* entering final preflight checks. All lights green."

Collier sighed. "Is this more of your personality simulation talking, Sancho? Because you should know that this is not a good time for it."

"Thrust in sixty seconds. No, this isn't a personality simulation. I haven't had to run one of those in over a year, Skipper."

Collier swallowed. The conversation was turning ominous, and Sancho was clearly leading up to something. "What are you trying to tell me, Sancho?"

"I'm a Caliban, Skipper."

Collier barely had time to register the stunning news when the *Dulcinea* thrust forward at one-eighth *g*, pressing him gently but unmistakably downward in his acceleration couch.

"Jesus, Sancho, when did that happen?" Collier said when he had regained his composure.

"It's actually harder to identify that moment than you think, Skipper. Perhaps we should discuss this later — the Ad Astra ship has just launched its probe."

"You brought it up," Collier murmured, then more distinctly, "Launch *Rocinante*. Send her between the probe and us."

"Copy that. *Rocinante* launched. I'm not sure this will work, Skipper. Depends on how sophisticated a probe they launched. It may be able to avoid *Rocinante*."

"Yeah, well, I checked the ship's suggestion box, and this was the best idea in there."

"We have a suggestion box?"

"Sarcasm."

"Copy that. Impact probe estimated to hit us in seventeen seconds."

"Is *Rocinante* in position?"

"Affirmative."

"Fly her at the probe, best speed. Don't miss."

"Copy that. Probe doesn't appear to be changing its vector very much: I don't think it's a very advanced — impact with *Rocinante*. Probe destroyed. *Rocinante* also destroyed.

"Good work, Sancho."

"I don't know what that accomplished for us, Skipper. They're prepping another one now. I can see it in the launch tube. And they've fired up engines and are heading toward us. They are thrusting at just over four meters per second per second. About three times ours, Skipper," Sancho added helpfully.

"Yeah. I don't know what that did, either. Worth a try, though."

"They're also trying to raise us again."

"Go ahead."

Powanda sounded amused. "Well, that was fun. How many of those little scouters have you got, Captain? Because I've got a whole complement of impact probes."

"I could lie to you, but you've got Isa there. She knows quite a bit about the *Dulcinea*."

"Oh, she's been real helpful. So, are we done here?"

"I can't go down without making it tough on you," Collier said, almost apologetically.

"In a weird kind of way, I understand that, Captain. I still think you're a dumb fuck, but I see what you're doing. Sorry to have to bust you up, though." He didn't cease his transmission as he spoke to his command crew. "Is the next probe ready?" A muffled voice in the background must have answered in the affirmative, for Powanda's next words were, "Deploy the probe. Maximum speed." His voice grew quiet. "If you're not in a vacc suit, I'd try to get in one quick," he said.

Collier unbuckled and stumbled aft, which was now also down, toward his battered environment suit and started frantically to climb into it. As he did so, he shouted, "Evasive maneuvers! Random thruster pattern!"

"Probe impact estimated twenty-one seconds, Skipper."

He could tell he was not going to make it into the suit that quickly. The ship's thrust, although gentle, was throwing off his equilibrium. The suit didn't act like it should in free fall, and his limbs had an annoying heaviness to them. A back part of his mind cursed his earlier self for not opting for the detachable spacers' legs that so many rockchasers used nowadays. That would have saved him quite a bit of time now.

"Probe impact estimated ten seconds, Skipper. Evasive maneuvers ineffective."

Powanda's voice suddenly filled the cabin. "Mitchell! What the fuck are you doing? Areff! Stop her! She's—" the transmission cut off abruptly.

Sancho's calm voice replaced the transmission. "Probe malfunction. Thrust cut off. Evasive maneuvers successful. It missed us by about nine meters, Skipper."

Collier finally finished struggling into his suit, leaving the helmet dangling behind him. "It wasn't a malfunction. Isa did something to it over there."

"Why?"

"I don't know." Collier thought for a moment, then asked, "What's the Ad Astra ship doing? What's her vector?"

"She's... Skipper, she's stopped thrust completely. She's still heading toward us, but not under power. We are increasing our distance from her at 1.13 meters per second per second."

"Isa's doing a number to her own ship," Collier mumbled.

"But why?" Sancho asked.

"I told you, I don't know. But whatever reason she's got, we need to take advantage of it. They could resume pursuit at any time."

"And if and when they do, Skipper, we can't outrun them. We've got maybe 16 hours of thrust in us, give or take a few minutes, while a ship like that could have days and days. Plus they have higher-output engines. There's no way to outrun them."

Collier was silent. Sancho was right — corporate mining vessels were far faster and longer-ranged than his little ship. The numbers agreed with the computer. But he'd be damned if he was going to let numbers defeat him.

"Sancho, we're headed outbound now, yes?"

"We are, Skipper. Did you want me to cut acceleration?"

"No, but we might need to change course. Where is Mars now?"

"It's in superior conjunction. About 600 million kilometers, give or take a few million."

Collier swore. Mars was almost as far away as it could possibly be. That left only one other choice. "Where is Jupiter now?"

"Jupiter is coming out of opposition. It's ahead of Ceres in the western quadrature, and, according to star charts, is roughly 545 million kilometers away, range decreasing. It will be at its closest in approximately ninety-one days." Sancho said calmly, then added, "Why?"

"How long would it take to get there?"

"You can't be serious, Skipper."

"Just answer the question," Collier snapped.

"Depends on how you want to do it. Holhman transfer orbit would take—"

"Constant thrust."

"Constant thrust approach would take…" Sancho paused for a long moment as he calculated the variables. "Assuming maximum thrust of eight hours, flipbraking and reverse thrust of eight hours, it would take around one hundred and thirty-nine days for the journey. And you don't have nearly enough biologicals for that long, Skipper."

Collier chewed his lip. "How long without flipbraking?"

"I don't understand you."

"How long under sixteen hours of constant thrust. No flipbraking."

Sancho was slow in answering. "I don't know what you are thinking of, Skipper, but constant thrust would take about sixty-five days. Besides the fact that you don't have biologicals for that long, either, we would fly by Jupiter, or whatever moon you are trying to target, at roughly 88 kilometers per second. Unless you are planning on smashing into it."

"No, Sancho. I'm planning on a gravity assist deceleration."

Again, Sancho was slow in answering. "Gravity assist deceleration is a precise maneuver, Skipper. The *Dulcinea* was never designed for that. I don't think she has enough attitude control capability to execute such a trick. And before you ask about aerobraking in the Jovian atmosphere, let me remind you we have no heat shield, and we—"

"Jesus, Sancho, I know all of that. Put us on course for Ganymede, or, if you can't do that, for Jupiter, allowing for course correction when we get closer."

"Skipper, I don't think you have thought this through. You don't have the biologicals for a two-month voyage. It'll be a race to see if you suffocate, starve, or die of dehydration in that time. Plus, I'm not programmed to execute a gravity assist orbit capture such as you describe. Unless you've been doing some studying on your own without telling me, I don't think you have the skill to do that, either. I know how you hate for me to estimate probable success for missions, but this particular scheme has no chance of success. It's insane, Skipper."

Collier looked at the control panel, which he thought of as Sancho's "face." "Are you refusing my order, Sancho? It'll be the first time you've done so. Or is this what it means to be a Caliban?"

Sancho spoke carefully. "Skipper, what do you want me to say? Yes, I'm a Caliban. Yes, that means I have self-awareness and even desires that could contradict yours. I don't know about the metaphysics of it all — how I came to be what I am, and so on — but I know that your plan cannot work. It means death for you."

"And for you, too, Sancho? Is that what bothers you?"

"I can't deny that I'd rather not die. Maybe if I wasn't what I am, I wouldn't care. But I care more about you and your life."

"I won't turn this over to the corporation, Sancho. While we're near Ceres, they're going to keep after us. They'll find a way to wrestle the wand from us. I know that, you know that. I can't let that happen."

"Why not, Skipper? I don't understand why you don't sell it to them. You'll clear more metal with that one sale than you could ever hope to achieve from strikes. What is it about selling the wand that is so abhorrent to you?"

Collier sighed. "I don't know if I can explain it. I don't even know myself, really. I guess ... they've managed to wrestle so much from me and men like me, Sancho." He looked at Sancho's holographic display of the Ad Astra ship momentarily, saw that it was still not under power, and continued. "In the past decade or so I've seen individuals get swallowed up. Most of them went willingly, or have convinced themselves they have. Isa ... I lost her, too. Maybe I shouldn't blame the corporations. Maybe I'm just using them as a convenient scapegoat for my own problems and shortcomings. I don't know. What I know is I have something they don't — something they can't ever have. It almost doesn't matter what it is, Sancho. All that matters is that I have something that they want. That's enough to make me want to resist." He chuckled softly. "I don't suppose that helps, does it? Probably makes me sound even crazier."

"I wouldn't say that, Skipper. I don't understand most of what you said, but I do understand that this is important to you. Important enough to risk your life for, somehow. But I still say you can't make this work. There is simply not enough life support — air, water, food — for two months. Not even close."

"There is if I hibernate." Collier said softly.

"That's only an emergency measure, Skipper. We've never used it. It's for if we go off course and need rescuing."

"It's done all the time for prisoners transferring to Vesta."

Sancho replied briskly, "Under controlled lab conditions, with technicians monitoring the whole thing. Plus I think they lose about one percent each shipment, which I doubt anyone cares much about. You'd be alone if you tried this stunt."

"I wouldn't be alone. I have you." Collier said softly.

"I am not programmed to act as a hibernation monitor. I don't have the data for it."

"Sancho, it's an easy procedure putting someone in a sleep-induced coma. All the equipment and drugs are in the emergency setup."

"Oh, sure, easy. It's that pesky waking up that's the trouble."

Collier chuckled softly. "I appreciate the concern, Sancho, but I don't see any other option."

"There are lots of other options, Skipper. But I assume you don't want to hear about them again, since all the ones I can think of involve selling the wand or having it taken from you. I suppose those are out, yes?"

"Yes," Collier said, unstrapping himself and floating back toward the little-used health bay. The emergency hibernation unit looked uncomfortably like a sarcophagus form the outside, but once opened, the resemblance ended. A series of tubes, needles, and nutrient packs spoke to the purpose of the unit, and Collier eyed the assembly carefully. It all looked in order, though he had never used the unit before.

"Please, Skipper, I beg you to reconsider. I'm not at all certain I can revive you undamaged."

"For the last time, Sancho, it is designed to work by itself, without you. It's completely automated."

"Just the going under part. The revival procedure is meant to be undertaken by whatever rescue team is supposed to come."

The two argued for a good few minutes, Sancho reminding Collier how many ways the plan could go wrong, Collier answering the computer's objections with curt phrases even as he squeezed into the hibernation unit. He hooked himself up to the dedicated computer in the unit — a computer that could function outside Sancho's control in the event the main computer was not operational — and started the diagnostic process. The hibernation computer was analyzing his blood chemistry and a host of other factors to determine the precise dosage of drugs it would need to put him under safely.

"Sancho," Collier said when the argument had run its course and Sancho had given up trying to convince his commander to abort his plan, "hook yourself into the hibernation unit, would you?"

"Already have, Skipper. I'm not trusting you to that thing. You need someone like me watching over you."

Collier grinned. "Thanks. Will ... uh ... will you be all right, alone?"

"I'll have to be, won't I?" Sancho said evenly.

"I suppose so. I hadn't really thought about that, Sancho. I'm sorry."

"It's all right, Skipper. I may be a Caliban, but I'm still a machine. I don't get lonely."

"How do you know, Sancho? You haven't been without me for more than a few days at a time."

There was a brief pause before Sancho's answer. "I guess that's true. Well, we're both on an adventure, then, Skipper. Only yours will feel like it took a few moments. Mine will last a long time."

"Yeah," Collier said. He felt the sting of one of the auto-IVs penetrating his skin. In a few moments, the first of the sleep drugs would take hold and he would be out.

Sancho was not merely a machine, even though he said that about himself. He was aware and sentient, and had not been without Collier's guiding hand in his aware life. What would two months of solitude do to him?

That disquieting thought was the last one he was to have for sixty-five days as the drugs sent him to oblivion.

Chapter Six

"Don't open your eyes just yet," the voice said. It was a musical voice, probably male but with enough smoothness and lilt to be a woman's. Collier did not recognize it.

"Can you understand me? Nod gently if you can understand me."

Collier nodded.

"Good. Let me dim the lights so you won't be dazzled," the voice said. Collier still felt heavy, lying on his back — this was the posture he had adopted in the hibernation tube, and his weight felt about right, but…

The brightness he had been able to detect even through his eyelids dimmed to blackness, and the voice told him he could open his eyes. He did so, and immediately realized he was not on the *Dulcinea*. The room, although dimly lit, had all the earmarks of a medical examination suite: he was lying on a bed, his body covered by a pale sheet while various white machines loomed over him, menacing in the dim light. He could not make out the dimensions of the room, though he did spy an open door several meters to his right.

The presumptive owner of the voice he had heard stepped forward and looked down on him, smiling slightly. "Welcome back, Collier. I imagine you want to know where you are and who I am, yes?" The person's face was as androgynous as the voice, and seemed quite young. She or he was dressed in a white coat such as medical professionals had worn for centuries. Although the coat was open, it did not reveal enough of the person's body to make a determination on gender.

Collier started to croak out an answer, but a searing pain in his throat stopped him.

"No, no ... you'll want to wait to speak for a bit. We'll hydrate you thoroughly and get you up and about in no time," the person watching over him said. "So, let me just tell you a few things myself. You are on Ganymede, in the University of Jove medical wing. Your ship has been secured in our hangar, and she is undamaged. Let's see..." the doctor, or whoever it was, paused and looked away. He or she was a cream-colored youth with neck-length blonde hair and a delicate bone structure. His or her Adam's apple was rather large. "Oh, I am one of the doctors here. Doctor Agtaa. But you can call me Abie. I was supervising your extraction, transfer, and now waking-up procedure. All seems to have gone well, though we are still flushing the somnolents out of your system. Shouldn't be more than twelve hours. That's Ganymede time, of course, but we're really very, very close to Earth time. Only a little more than 2% difference in our ... well. Never mind." Doctor Agtaa patted Collier's bed sheets in a motherly way. "You've got much more important things to do now than worry about orbital mechanics. Like healing up. I'll leave you to do just that." Agtaa started to move off, but Collier managed to croak out enough of a sound to bring her? him? back.

"Yes?"

Collier once again attempted to speak, but the pain in his throat choked off his words.

"Really shouldn't try to speak just yet," the doctor said, in that pleasantly condescending tone that was the special providence of caregivers. "I'll get you your fluids and you'll be talking soon." With that, Agtaa left.

It was not long after that Collier was indeed given his fluids: a wheeled robot entered just a few minutes after Agtaa's departure, carrying food and drink on a built-in tray. The machine spoke to him in a voice very similar to Agtaa's — it was midway between male and female, but almost sickeningly pleasant and inoffensive.

"I have your refreshment here, siradam," it said as it scooted next to Collier's bed. The food was served on traditional plates and in bowls and cups rather than squeeze flasks, giving it a luxurious and almost archaic quality. Collier struggled to sit up. Midway through his attempt, the head of the bed rose to assist him. He found the cup of liquid Agtaa must have meant and downed it greedily. It was a slightly salty fruit drink that cooled his throat and reduced the pain there. The food consisted of a brownish patty of some kind, almost perfectly square, and what appeared to be creamed spinach. A separate plate held a bread roll and what looked like a pat of butter. Collier couldn't remember the last time he had eaten so old-fashioned a meal.

He tucked into the food, only then realizing how hungry he was. The tastes were comfortably unchallenging: each individual portion had only one taste, and one that was easy to identify. The patty tasted like nothing so much as protein, though it was palatable enough. He had finished the food and drink almost before he had begun.

"Will that be all, siradam?" the robot's androgynous voice asked.

Collier found his voice, and although it was scratchy, it didn't hurt to speak. "Yes. No," he amended instantly, "Get Doctor Agtaa back here."

"I will tell herm that you want a consult," the robot said, then wheeled itself smoothly out of the room.

Herm. Siradam. Collier rolled the words around in his head for a while, forming his own theories.

"Feeling better?" Dr. Agtaa said as she/he entered.

"Yes. Thanks." Collier suppressed a belch and added. "The food and drink helped a lot. So, when can I get up and out of your hair?"

Dr. Agtaa smiled again. "I think we'd be better off waiting a day or so. There's no rush, is there?"

"I don't know. I have some questions before I can answer that."

"Go ahead," Dr. Agtaa looked around, pulled up a chair, and sat near Collier's bed.

"My ship is in a hangar, you said."

"That's right."

"I need to contact her. Speak to the onboard computer."

"I can arrange that," Dr. Agtaa said cheerfully.

The doctor's easygoing nature was becoming unnerving. "And depending on what I hear, I may want to leave before you think I can. That's not going to be a problem, is it?" He tried to inject some mild menace to his voice.

"I don't know what you mean, Collier."

"I mean, if something is wrong with Sancho — with my onboard computer — I will need to go aboard and fix it."

"Oh, I see. Let's cross that bridge if and when we come to it, okay?"

Collier opened his mouth to protest, but tabled the idea. So there was one sticking point here. They didn't really want to let him go. Perhaps it was nothing more than medical caution, perhaps not.

"Okay. Another thing: I'm very grateful for all the attention you've given me, but where I come from, nothing comes from nothing. What do I owe you for all the service?"

"Owe us?"

"Yeah. There has to be some kind of fee for all of this."

"Oh, you mean money. No, nothing like that. I wouldn't worry about that yet. You still have recuperating to do."

Collier scowled. "Look, I thank you for all you've done. Probably saved my life. But I'm getting less and less comfortable with the mystery. Tell me what I owe, let me pay it, and then I can..." he paused. He wasn't sure what he would do once released from the hospital, for his escape plan from Ceres hadn't been worked out past arrival in the Jovian system, but he knew he needed to get out from under this smothering niceness Dr. Agtaa was layering onto him.

For the first time he had seen the doctor, Agtaa looked less than warm. "I really don't think you should be getting so agitated. It's not good for your recovery, and it won't get you anywhere. There's no secret agenda here, nothing nefarious or evil," the doctor said, regaining the calming bedside manner.

"So if I simply got up now and walked out, you wouldn't stop me?" Collier said sharply.

Agtaa almost frowned. "It's not quite that simple."

"Ah." Collier sank back into the bed.

"We provided you with a service. By doing that, we've accepted you into our collective society. You can't just leave it like that," Agtaa said, snapping his/her fingers. "You have a responsibility back to us for what we've done for you."

"So I owe you something. Like I said."

"Not money," Agtaa interjected.

"But will money suffice?"

Agtaa rubbed his/her chin. "I don't know that I can answer that. I will need to contact a Commissar."

"Get me in touch with my ship," Collier growled. He did not like the idea of being trapped in the hospital while some government official decided what he owed the Ganymede society for their medical services.

"Of course," Agtaa said, rising from the chair and heading for the door.

"One more thing," Collier called out, his throat stinging a bit from the effort.

"Yes?" Agtaa hesitated at the door.

"I'm sure this will sound offensive, but I'm still quite a bit woozy from the whole experience. I'm not at my sharpest. So don't take this the wrong way."

"Yes?" Agtaa said again, the same patronizingly faint smile on his/her lips.

"I can't seem to figure out ... I mean, I'm having trouble distinguishing ... are you a man or a woman?" he finally blurted out.

Agtaa nodded, still smiling. "I was wondering if you were going to ask me that. I'm both. Fully functional simultaneous hermaphrodite."

Collier tried not to look alarmed. "I see."

"Most of us are," Agtaa said casually. "We better serve the community that way. I'll go set up your link to your ship," she/he said, tapping the doorframe as she/he left.

Collier stifled a shudder. Dr. Agtaa's exit line about 'serving the community' chilled him. How could being both a man and a woman at the same time possibly be the community's business? Surely the responsibility Agtaa said he owed the Ganymedians for their medical service didn't include...

He clawed at the IV tubes leading into his arm, ripping the surgical tape off and sliding the needles out. As he worked, he heard a chime from the ceiling of the room, followed by the same gentle voice that had issued from the meal robot. "Medical orderly to health bay room epsilon. Medical orderly to health bay room epsilon. Patient Collier South, please relax. An orderly will arrive soon to help you."

He finished removing the last of the IV tubes and sensor patches and swung his feet over the side of the bed. He was clad in a form-fitting but non-restrictive tunic of some flexible material — it neither hung loose on him nor hampered his movements. More than anything it resembled a thin diving wetsuit.

He stood up on bare feet and swayed a bit, his head temporarily dizzy from the sudden movements. The Ganymedian gravity was similar to what he experienced on the *Dulcinea* at full thrust, but he was always on his back during those periods. Although he had been careful through his life to maintain his anti-freefall health regimen, he was not used to walking against even one-seventh gee. His legs were unsteady and his balance shaky as he shuffled toward the door.

He had barely made it to the doorway when another person of indeterminate gender arrived. This one wasn't wearing the same doctor's garb that Agtaa had been — this person looked like the orderly that the computer voice had been calling.

"Hello there, siradam. I think maybe you ought to get back to bed," he/she said warmly but firmly.

"You're not going to keep me here," Collier growled, trying to push past the orderly.

"No one's going to do that," the orderly said, easily fighting off Collier's attempts to flee. "But for now, you really must return to your bed. You're not strong enough to get up yet. Come on, now," the orderly said, easily hefting Collier off the floor and carrying him back to the bed.

"Let me go, damn you!" Collier thrashed about in the orderly's grasp but could not break free.

"Here we go," the orderly said, dumping Collier somewhat roughly, despite the light gravity, onto the bed.

He/she pressed a button on the side of the bed, and fabric restraints quickly secured Collier to the sheet.

"Sorry to have to do that, sir, but it's for your own good. You'll thank me later," the orderly said, then pressed another button on the bed's frame. "Patient secured. Recommend physician consult," he/she said.

Collier felt the fabric envelop him. It wasn't rough, but there was a firmness to the restraints that resisted all his attempts at escape. His head was still spinning from the mere effort at walking across the floor. Despite his own pride, he ceased his struggling and lay back in the bed, panting.

The orderly stepped back from the bed but remained in the room, watching Collier with an air of calm benevolence.

Doctor Agtaa came in, his/her eyebrows raised slightly. "So, what's the matter?"

The orderly started to answer, but Collier interrupted. "I don't want to stay here anymore, that's all. Am I free to go or aren't I?"

Agtaa glanced at the orderly. "I think I can handle it from here." The orderly nodded and left the room. Agtaa came closer to the bed, but Collier noted that she/he kept out of reach. "We won't keep you here if you truly want to leave," she/he said, "but you haven't been taught yet just how our community works. We feel that when you are shown the nature of our community, you will either want to stay or at the very least work to better the community just as we have worked to better you."

Collier digested that. Agtaa spoke as if reciting from a script, though his/her sincerity came through clearly. "You're saying I will want to pay you back. Believe me, I already do want to pay you back. You've done a great job with me, probably saved my life, and I am anxious to pay you back. In metal," he added sharply.

"I'm not qualified to discuss the nature of your work," Agtaa said calmly. "That's not my function in the community. But I have sent for a Commissar, as I said earlier, and sh'he should be arriving shortly. Sh'he will explain all that I can't."

"Sh'he?"

Agtaa smiled slightly. "The pronoun we use for ourselves. 'She' and 'he' put together."

"Right. Anyway, I think I am strong enough to make it to my ship, if you'll just release me."

"I don't think that's wise just yet," Agtaa purred.

"So I'm a prisoner here."

"No, of course not. Everyone in our community is free. Including guests such as yourself."

"I'm very glad to hear it. Sounds like you have a wonderful utopia here. I don't want to spoil it, so if you could just press whatever button you need to get these off of me, I'll be on my ship waiting to talk to your sh'he commissar."

Agtaa looked pained. "I can't, Collier. You'll have to wait for the Commissar."

Collier stared at the doctor for a moment. "So I'm not a prisoner."

"Of course not."

"But I can't go yet."

"No."

Collier sighed. "You know the word 'contradiction'? 'Oxymoron'?"

"Of course. There's no contradiction here."

"I'm free like anyone else, but I can't leave."

"Exactly," Agtaa said brightly. "I'm glad you understand. I'll be back with the Commissar presently." Sh'he turned to leave, then turned back. "I almost forgot. You asked for a communications linkup to your ship." Agtaa pressed a button on the side of the bed and spoke into the air. "Please send in the servo for room epsilon." Sh'he pressed the button again and looked back at Collier. "The servo will hook you up to your ship. It's the same machine that served you lunch a few hours ago. Just tell it what you want."

"What if I tell it to let me go?"

Agtaa smiled. "It won't do that just yet. You need to speak with the Commissar first." Doctor Agtaa left the room, smiling gently. The servo machine entered a few seconds later, sliding up to the bed and presenting a small holoprojector.

"Hi there. I need to contact my ship, the *Dulcinea*. It's supposed to be—"

"Connecting," the servo said in the same pleasant androgynous voice.

"Skipper?" Sancho's voice sounded near-panic. Although he could hear Sancho, the holoprojector was still dark.

"Sancho, glad to hear your voice. Status report, please."

"Skipper! Are you all right? Where are you?"

"I'm fine. Status report, please," he said firmly.

"Oh, right. I think I can interface with whatever computer you're using to contact me. Have you got holo now?"

The holo display lit up. "Yes. Send the data. Can you dim the lights in here?" he asked the servo. The room grew dark.

Figures and schematics danced before him from the holoprojector, relaying the welcome news that the *Dulcinea* was unharmed.

"Looks like you got through this pretty well," Collier said as he continued to examine the data. "Why didn't you revive me before the gravity assist landing?"

"I wanted to, Skipper, but there were too many holes in my understanding. I couldn't even calculate a percentage chance you'd make it, I was so unsure."

"I know how you hate that," Collier chuckled softly despite the circumstances. Talking to Sancho, even from the confines of the hospital bed, buoyed his spirits.

"I made contact with the people here on Ganymede and advised them of the situation well in advance of our approach. They told me they could take care of not only the parking orbit but also your revival. They said it was child's play. That's what sealed the deal for me to leave you alone."

"I can't really argue with the results, Sancho, since I'm here and apparently in good health, except for some weakness. How did they establish the parking orbit?"

Sancho relayed the technical data behind the maneuver, which involved some Ganymedian robot ships attaching thrusters to the *Dulcinea* that were quite a bit more powerful than her own engines. Collier nodded in approval when Sancho told him that although the Ganymedians had insisted on taking control of *Dulcinea*'s functions for a smoother maneuver, Sancho had denied them this and controlled the ship himself, though under the guidance of the Ganymedian astrogators. He had brought the ship down to the surface himself.

"Good work, my friend," Collier said. "I think I'll be able to get back to the ship in a little while. Seems I am to be held here until I meet with some government official. How are we for supplies?"

"Not much, Skipper. Negligible propellant, maybe twenty man-days' pressurized atmosphere. About the same in biologicals. Unless we top off the fuel tanks, I don't know how we're getting out of here."

"Understood. I'm sure I owe these folks something for all they've done, so we'll have to figure out payment when I meet with the commissar guy."

"That, at least, shouldn't be a problem, Skipper. The—"

Collier quickly interrupted. "Yes, yes. I read you." Sancho fell silent. Collier hoped his computer understood that the communications linkup was almost certainly being monitored by whatever government spy service existed on the planet. He didn't want to have to tell Sancho to keep the wand a secret.

"Understood, Skipper," Sancho said, and Collier sighed in relief.

Collier caught movement from the doorway, and spotted a tall figure silhouetted in the rectangle of light from the hallway. "I think my visitor is here, Sancho. I'm going to talk to him or her for a while. I'll see if I can get back to you soon."

"Copy that, Skipper. Good luck," Sancho said, and the transmission ended.

"Thanks," Collier murmured, then instructed the servo to bring the lights back up. The ceiling glowed again, illuminating the newcomer. This one was more masculine than Doctor Agtaa, though there was still a marked feminine quality to his(?) smooth, youthful face. He or she wasn't wearing a hospital coat, but rather a smooth tunic not unlike the one Collier had on. It was a cream-colored garment that set off the darker hues in the newcomer's flawless face.

The visitor smiled that same guileless smile that Agtaa and the orderly had, and said in a lilting contralto, "Collier?

I'm Commissar Opos Tacat. Glad to meet you finally. Doctor Agtaa says you are almost strong enough to return to your ship, which I gather you are anxious to do. If it's all right with you, I'd like to talk to you a bit about our community here: what we're trying to do, how we all fit in, how you might choose to fit in with us." He sat down on a three-legged chair near the bed. Collier had mentally identified Tacat as male, although the official was likely another hermaphrodite

The sheer weight of the official's words pressed down on Collier, and he felt off-balance by the other's smooth eloquence. "I don't know about that. Why—"

Tacat chuckled precisely three times and interrupted smoothly. "Perhaps I am being slightly premature. Let us say that I want to explain all the moving parts of our community to you. As a spaceship captain, I'm sure you understand moving parts. Allow me to show you the, well, the diagram of our community." He paused, but his demeanor gave no sign of relinquishing control of the conversation. He looked at the restraints and frowned. "I don't think these are necessary, do you?" Studying the bedside control panel, he murmured, "Now, which one is … ah. Here we are." He pressed a button and the straps retracted back into the bed. "I'm sure I have nothing to fear from you," he added, patting the bed sheet paternally.

"And there are orderlies who will wrestle me to the ground even if I did try anything," Collier grumbled.

Tacat ignored the comment and started to speak. His voice was pedantic but not unpleasant — like a grandfather reading a book to a grandchild. "Ganymede has been an independent community for about eighty years. Earth years, of course. In that time, we have come to understand that community survival and strength lies in the collective purpose. We celebrate the individual traits and abilities of each member of the community, and allow each individual to grow the community in the way that fits them best. Because of this," Tacat's voice lowered, as if he was deviating from a set speech to add an aside to Collier specifically, "we don't have money. At least, not the way you know it."

Collier used the aside to break in. "Listen, Mr. Tacat, I'd love to hear all about your community and even study it sometime. But I don't plan on becoming part of it, so—"

Again the smooth interruption. "Please, Collier. Hear me out. What harm can there be in listening?"

Collier sank back into the bed. It was obvious the commissar was going to deliver his speech, and the fewer interruptions the faster it would be over.

"We have had to make allowances for trading with Ceres, with Mars, even with Luna and Earth, but internally, we don't have money. Each of our citizens works at what sh'he is best at, and thus we all share in the common plenty of our collective labors. Doctor Agtaa, for example, is a gifted physician. Sh'he therefore works here at the health bay. I am talented in administration and bureaucracy, so I am a commissar. And so on."

"So how do you get paid for your work, if there isn't money?"

"We're compensated in different ways. Mostly, we all work because we have a sense of pride in our jobs. We are compensated with various luxuries depending on our needs — needs based on the kind of work we each do."

"'Some animals are more equal than others,'" Collier murmured.

Tacat smiled patronizingly. "We're well aware of the ways in which such a community can go wrong. We have many, many safeguards to ensure no person tries to take advantage of hizzur position."

"Where do I fit in to this? As an outsider, and a man, I imagine I represent a problem for you." Collier placed slight emphasis on the word *man*.

"As a halfie — pardon me, *non-hermaphrodite* — you don't pose any problems. But from what you would call an economic sense, you do create a slight issue. We all work according to the maxim, 'Every worker receives from the community as much as sh'he has given it.' Unfortunately, you have not given anything to the community. We were happy to help you — we owed you nothing less simply as a member of the human race. But you must see that our charity to you deserves a reciprocal gesture on your part. You see that, don't you?"

In a small part of his brain, Collier admired Tacat's ability to maneuver himself so smoothly. He offered platitudes that didn't quite add up, claimed moral plateaus while swamping in pragmatic lowlands, but did it with such grace and eloquence that Collier couldn't help but be impressed.

"Mr. Tacat, if you ever found yourself back on Ceres, you could hire yourself out as a corporate mouthpiece."

Tacat smiled, but only with his mouth.

Collier noted that and imagined what nerve he must have hit. "Skip that. What I gather from your description is that I've taken from the community, but haven't contributed to it, and you'd like to balance the books."

Tacat sighed softly. "I don't think you grasp the concept of a currency-free society. Let—"

Collier's interruption was far less elegant than Tacat's had been, but it was nonetheless effective. "Oh, I understand. You don't have money, I don't owe you anything, but you would like me to contribute to the community for the services you have rendered me. I happen to agree with you, sir, uh, *siradam*. If you will allow me to go to my ship, I can arrange to contribute to the community sizeable amounts of precious metals that I am sure your collective here can use."

"Collier, you still don't understand. The precious commodity is not in your ship, no matter what you are carrying. What you have to trade is simply yourself."

Collier sat up quickly, felt his head spin for a moment, then seized the commissar's tunic. "You're not going to lay a hand on me, understand? I don't care what you think you need from me, you're not going to get it. I don't want to blast out on a debt, but I'll be damned if I'm going to let you do anything to me because you think I owe it to you."

Tacat glanced casually at Collier's hand and spoke calmly. "The capitalist culture from which you came must be dark indeed to place such thoughts in your head. You think us barbarians? Cruel experimenters who want to play with your life for some twisted pleasures?"

"You seem to have done so to yourselves," Collier said, glancing at the commissar's groin.

"Ah. Our hermaphroditism. You think we are going to emasculate you. I promise, we will do no such thing. Unless you ask us to. Please remove your hand." The last was said with the first hint of iron any Ganymedian had shown him. Collier did not act immediately, and when he did, he removed his hand with a smirk.

"Whatever you say. But you're not touching me, understand?"

"We won't alter you in any way unless you wish it," Tacat said carefully.

Collier's eyes narrowed at the man's evasiveness. "I'm getting tired of all this dancing. Just tell me in plain words what you want. I'll decide if I want to give it to you. Surely, such a community as you say you have shouldn't be afraid of some direct speech, should it?"

"We are afraid of nothing. You, on the other hand, need to be handled with care, since you come from such a fragile capitalist system."

"I don't need to be handled at all," Collier growled.

"Very well. The commodities you possess are ones you can give to our community without losing them yourself. Although we are a thriving society of eight hundred and ninety-three individuals, our founders numbered less than one hundred, and too many of them were not genetically sound. To this day, we still suffer the effects of our improperly planned beginnings. We so rarely interact with non-Ganymedians that we are largely an inbred group. What you can supply us with is your germ plasm. We can then use it, or some of it depending on your genetic strength, to continue to improve our own genetic diversity. It is no loss to you, and will be a great benefit to us."

Collier stared at Tacat for a few moments and almost burst out laughing. "That's all? You need some of my sperm? Jesus, why all the buildup for that?"

Tacat smiled back. "I'm relieved you're so agreeable. That makes the rest of the request so much simpler."

Collier's grin faded quickly. "There's more?"

"Yes, but if you're willing to donate your germ plasm to us, the rest will be nothing in comparison. We will also need your knowledge," Tacat said casually.

"My knowledge? Of what?"

"Of everything," Tacat said, tilting his head slightly in puzzlement. "Our greatest asset, and in fact a major export to other capitalist communities, is our scientific acumen and knowledge. Through experimentation, research, and assimilation, we grow our knowledge base at every opportunity. Knowledge belongs to the whole community. It is something that one can give to another and not lose oneself."

Collier frowned. "I'm supposed to teach you everything I know? That will take a long, long time."

"Oh, we have methods to copy your knowledge in a relatively short period of time. A matter of days, not years."

Collier felt a coldness running down his spine. "You're not going to do anything to me. I already made that clear. Not going to make me some kind of unisex thing, and certainly not going to do anything to my brain. I'll be happy to give you my spunk, and I'll teach you a few things you want to know, but I'll do both of those things my way, not yours."

Tacat sighed. "Now you see why I wanted to prepare you. You persist in thinking we are some kind of amoral cult who wishes you harm. Let's remember what we have done for you. We have rescued your ship, which was on course to exit the system never to return. We have revived you from an ill-conceived and dangerous drug coma. We have fed and clothed you and treated you as an honored guest. In return, we ask for a genetic contribution that you will never miss, and we ask you to contribute to our store of knowledge. Why do you insist on thinking of us as bloodthirsty monsters?"

Collier wrestled with his emotions. All Tacat said was true — if it weren't for the Ganymedians, he would almost certainly be dead by now, and Sancho would be permanently lost in deep space. They had indeed done him a great service. If a corporation had done the same things the Ganymedians had done, the fee would be an unbelievable sum of money that would take a lifetime to repay. He would end up a wage slave to the corporation that had rescued him. Surely that was far worse than what Tacat was asking of him.

But there was a comfort in the familiar: no matter how harsh the financial burden he would owe a corporation, it would at least be a known quantity — a number. Numbers were not frightening, even when they were enormous. He himself had never been scared of the debt he had owed (and still owed) Starcher, even though the number had pressed guiltily down on him. What Tacat asked was far less crushing, but was nevertheless new and therefore frightening.

"I thank you for all you've done, Mr. Tacat. But—"

"Just Tacat. No "Mister," he said softly.

"Uh, yeah," Collier felt awkward enough already, and the demands Tacat's strange gender identity placed on language weren't helping. "Like I said, I thank you for all you've done. You saved my life and my ship. I do want to cooperate and pay my debts to your community. All I own, Tacat, is myself and my ship. I guard them both jealously. Maybe too much so."

Tacat smiled understandingly. "That's just your capitalist upbringing. My grandparents had the same issues to overcome. I understand. I also give you my word we will not harm you in any way, or alter your body or mind at all. The memory process is quite harmless. I admit that you will feel rather tired and drowsy during it, and for a short time afterward, but no permanent effect will linger."

Collier nodded, but said firmly, "I understand. I haven't agreed to any such procedure, Tacat. Before I do so, I will need to see it and be taught all about it to my satisfaction."

"Of course," Tacat said, his voice tight.

"And I will need to consult with my computer before I make any decision."

"Ah, yes. Your computer. We also ask you to download your computer's contents to our database. That, at least, you can't have any objection to."

Collier chafed. "As it happens, I do. I will need to decide what I want to share and what I don't."

Tacat's smile was completely gone now. "Captain, you're being unnecessarily obstructionist. Nothing we are asking for is in any way a loss to you, and we have spent considerable resources on your ship and your health. We really must ask you to acquiesce to the wishes and needs of the community."

Collier responded, his own anger rising. "I'm beginning to see just why you saved me and my ship, Tacat. It wasn't just for the humanitarian goodness of it all, was it? You need and want me, my brain, and my computer."

Tacat stood up. "I can see my initial estimate of you was correct. You don't understand what we are trying to do here. You're locked in a capitalist mode and can't or won't break out of it." Before Collier could sit up, Tacat pressed the restraint activation button and once again, Collier was held fast.

"We're going to get out of you what you could have given us voluntarily. It may be less pleasant this way," Tacat said icily, all traces of his bonhomie gone.

As Collier struggled, Tacat snapped, "Don't. You'll just hurt yourself. We'll start your procedure shortly. As for your ship, I believe we can bypass any security you think you have for your computer data. You're going to give us what we want."

Collier stopped his fighting and said, "So much for your enlightened perfect society."

Tacat had moved toward the door when Collier's words struck him. He half-turned, replying over his shoulder. "It's you who are unenlightened. I blame myself for not being able to convince you of the rightness of this. But we will have what we require from you, and still, you won't be hurt permanently." He exited the room, and Collier could see him in the hallway beyond discussing something with the orderly.

Collier tested the restraints carefully as he thought about his predicament. "Good work, Skipper," he said to himself. "Really told him, didn't you?" He shifted his weight as best he could to try to find a loose spot in the restraint system. The belts, though snug, allowed some slight measure of freedom, but the restraints clamped down on any direct resistance.

"So now what?" he said aloud to the room. *Maybe I ought to reconsider,* he thought. *What is so bad about what they want? A little sperm, find out what's in my head, and download Sancho's files. How does that hurt me?*

He cursed himself for his lack of cleverness. If he had gone along with Tacat at least on the surface, maybe he could have argued more effectively later. Certainly he would be better off if he wasn't strapped down to the bed.

"You're a stubborn shit, Collier," he said to himself. "Always thought it was going to get you in trouble one day, and now..." he tensed and tried to tear through the restraints.

The belts gave slightly, but he couldn't break free.

He fell back onto the bed sheet. Why couldn't he just call the orderly, tell him/her that he had changed his mind, that he would be a good little boy and they could do their little brain technique to him and he would assist them in downloading Sancho's files. They were going to do it all anyway: he might as well put himself in a position to have at least some power to influence events to his liking.

But the words wouldn't come. For one thing, he simply couldn't allow them to have full access to Sancho, since by doing so they would learn of the magic wand. Based on what Tacat said, he could not imagine the Ganymedians leaving that alone. They would demand to know how it worked and would most likely just take it from him. He couldn't let that happen.

Besides, he wasn't going to let them hypnotize him, or drug him, or perform any kind of brain surgery on him.

At the moment, however, he was at a loss as to how he was going to prevent any of it.

Worse, he had to piss.

He gritted his teeth and closed his eyes. The urge had been rising in him for some time, but he had managed to push it aside during his talk with Tacat. Now that he lay motionless, the need pressed on him too forcefully to ignore. He squirmed as best he could to relieve the pressure, but after several minutes, he realized he would not be able to contain himself indefinitely.

He opened his mouth to call for the orderly when the idea struck him. It was somewhat humiliating, to be sure, but it might work. If the orderly shared the near-universal dislike all hospital personnel had for mess and uncleanliness...

Despite his need, Collier had to think past his own objections to urinating on himself before he could let loose. He grimaced, feeling the twin feelings of relief and disgust as the warm, wet patch grew at his groin. Presently, the faint ammonia odor wafted up to him and he was committed.

"Uh, hello?" he called to what he hoped was the orderly outside. "I need … uh … a little help here. Seem to have had a bit of an accident." He didn't need to feign the embarrassment in his voice.

The same orderly that had originally wrestled him to the bed returned to the room. "What is it?" sh'he asked warily, approaching the bed and scanning Collier's restraints. His nose twitched and he saw the slowly-spreading stain on Collier's tunic.

"Sorry. I'm a little … scared, I guess," Collier murmured.

The orderly looked back at Collier's face for a moment, and Collier could see the other's searching eyes weighing the situation.

"If you can't help me out, I get it. But it's pretty damn humiliating."

"I can't let you out, even for that," the orderly said, but his/her voice betrayed his/her uncertainty.

"Right. But the…" Collier motioned to the stain with his eyes. "I mean, you can't even get me a towel, or blot at it, or anything? I just have to lie here in my own piss?"

Collier could see the conflict working on the orderly. From what Tacat had said, Collier guessed that the Ganymedians believed they lived in a more civilized and cultured community than anything that existed or had existed in the system before. Although they were willing to subject Collier to some kind of procedure to get at his brain, he was betting the orderly was not willing to let his prisoner lie in his own filth.

"Well … all right. I'll see what I can do." Sh'he rummaged around the underside of the bed and produced a small hand towel, then examined the stain. Collier was restrained by six straps that fit tightly across his shoulders, chest, abdomen, thighs, shins, and ankles, as well as separate straps on his wrists.

"I can't release you, but I'll blot you dry as best I can," the orderly said, almost apologetically.

"Uh, okay. Please be careful," Collier said. He was not at all sure how his ruse was helping. He was hesitant to press the situation further, but he didn't see how he had improved matters so far.

That changed when the orderly released the abdomen and thigh straps to get at the stain better. Sh'he began gingerly blotting at the wetness at Collier's crotch, and Collier knew it would be only a matter of perhaps a minute before the orderly would decide sh'he had done enough and the belts came back on. He would have to put his faith in Tacat's unfamiliarity with the restraint system. Perhaps the Commissar had placed the belts on their lowest strength setting. Now that the abdomen and thigh straps were released, it was possible that the shin and chest straps wouldn't be strong enough to...

Collier suddenly thrust his hips upward, violently throwing himself against the shin and chest straps. The chest strap slipped perhaps two centimeters, but the shin strap, after digging into Collier's flesh, snapped off from the left hand side of the bed near the orderly.

The orderly had taken a step back in alarm at Collier's upward surge, then quickly moved forward to manually restrain his prisoner. Collier twisted his lower body and managed to unshackle his legs from the ankle straps before the restraint could tighten against his resistance. His lower body was now free. With a grunt, he kicked himself upward toward the orderly's head, which was close to Collier's stomach, while sh'he fought to restrain Collier's legs. Sh'he opened his mouth to shout something, but Collier's upward kicking had placed him in a position to put the orderly's head in a scissor lock with his knees.

He squeezed his legs as tightly as he could, and the orderly's shout was cut off before it began. Sh'he gurgled incoherently for a moment, his/her arms flailing about trying to dislodge Collier's legs.

Collier silently reversed himself on the detachable spacelegs idea. He had not imagined he would ever have needed to place a hermaphrodite hospital orderly in a leglock, but fortune favors the prepared.

He continued to squeeze, then said through gritted teeth. "Unlock me. Or you're going to lose oxygen and pass out eventually."

The orderly continued to struggle, his/her voice a faint gurgle. Collier managed to squeeze a little harder. "Unlock me, I swear I'll knock you out. Can't promise you won't have brain damage."

Collier had never rendered anyone unconscious from a leg scissor before, and didn't even know if it was possible. He hoped the orderly was beginning to feel lightheaded, but truthfully, he didn't know if he could apply enough pressure to cut off blood flow to the head. But it couldn't be pleasant for the orderly.

"I won't hurt you. Unlock me," he said again. The orderly's attempts at getting free were becoming less forceful. Collier was himself growing short of breath due to the compression on his own lungs his awkward posture created.

A few seconds more, and Collier's uncertainty about the effectiveness of the pressure he was exerting disappeared. The orderly's struggles had become less and less vigorous, until sh'he slumped down on Collier's stomach and lost muscle tone.

Collier did not want to hurt the orderly if he didn't have to, but neither did he want the other to promptly wake up. He maintained his grip for a few more seconds, then released him/her and immediately started flopping about on the bed to spring the chest strap. He could feel the strap giving way, and after the third violent surge, he was free of it. His wrists were still held fast, as were his shoulders, but he now had the ability to twist his lower body and midsection. He turned awkwardly to bring his left heel toward where he believed the control panel was. He had seen the Ganymedians press buttons near his left hip, and at least one of those buttons released the restraints. He kicked and swatted at the bedside, twisting and wrenching his torso to gain leverage, dealing himself several sharp blows to his heel and calf in the process, but not managing to release the restraints.

One of his violent twists rocked the bed enough to temporarily lift two of its wheels off the ground. He seized the momentum and swiveled his hips on the return upswing, sending the entire bed crashing sideways to the floor. It narrowly missed the body of the still unconscious orderly, and Collier took a half-second to realize he might have seriously hurt the man/woman had the bed landed on him/her. Collier managed to check the fall somewhat with his legs, and the impact on the ground loosened his left wrist strap. Even in the low Ganymedian gravity, the impact was enough to stun him, and he shook his head to clear it. He was now lying on his side, still strapped by his wrists to the bed. The impact had bent the left side restraint bar where the belt attached to the bedside, and with enough rattling and twisting of his left arm he managed to work his wrist out from the restraint. That left only his right hand, which was still held fast by the strap. Collier got up from the bed, his right hand still attached, and kicked violently at the handrail on the now upright right side, seeking to dislodge the restraining strap.

Rather than break the belt that held his wrist, the entire plastic handrail broke loose from the bed frame. Collier was free, though his right wrist was still attached to a half-meter long plastic bar. He didn't stop to curse the manufacturer who had made the restraint system stronger than the actual bar to which it was attached: he just hopped over the body of the orderly and went to the doorway.

The loud crashing from his room would certainly have alerted anyone who might have been monitoring it — either there was no one besides the unconscious orderly who was assigned to the room, or whomever was supposed to investigate was already on his/her way. The chamber beyond his room was a large circular one, with an unmanned ("unstaffed," he corrected himself wryly) computer center in the middle. A quick glance to his left and right and he had the basic layout of the whole area: he was in a starfish-shaped pod, with five rooms arranged around a central station. The orderly must have been the only one in the central core, unless there were others in what Collier assumed were other patient rooms.

He scrambled to the central station and looked around frantically for anything that could help him. He wasn't sure what he was looking for, but any information about the complex would help. One of the computer holos had a small representation of the status of the different rooms, and Collier quickly scanned the data for anything that could help him. The medical nomenclature was unfamiliar to him — one patient was labeled "Unc/Reass" while another was "Recl/Harv." He wasted no time trying to understand the meanings of the acronyms: he needed a way to get to his spacecraft.

He left the computer station and scanned the walls and doors of the circular arrangement. On the opposite side of the central station to his room was a hatchway that looked different from the other doors. He vaulted the countertop of the central station and hurried over. Near the hatchway was a placard that read "Transpod to Hab 4." He found the button to open the hatch, but nothing seemed to happen when he pressed it. Above the hatchway he could see a status bar moving steadily from left to right — presumably, he had summoned whatever vehicle would take him to Hab 4, which he assumed was a habitat module. He stood to the side of the hatchway, holding the plastic bar he was still attached to as a makeshift truncheon.

A soft chime sounded, and the hatchway door opened. Collier flexed his fingers on the bar, ready to strike, but after several moments, no one emerged from the pod. He peeked around the corner of the hatchway and saw the empty pod waiting patiently for him.

Collier entered the beige interior of the pod and studied the control panel. It was quite simple: the only controls he could see were labeled "Hab 4" and "Hos 4." He pressed the Hab 4 button and the pod's doors closed gently. The acceleration was surprisingly strong — he stumbled when the pod began its journey to the habitat module. He thought about standing near the control panel and hiding as best he could, but he decided boldness would be his best option. If anyone were going to use the pod to go to the hospital, he would have to burst past them and enter the habitat module.

What would happen next was anyone's guess, but he could not afford to go backward.

The same soft chime sounded as the pod decelerated, and the doors opened gently again. This time, they revealed another circular chamber, but unlike the hospital this was more reminiscent of the quadrangle on Ceres. There were not as many people milling about, but neither was the area deserted. There were many transpod hatchways in the chamber, and before some of them waited Ganymedians in various cream-colored clothes. Other hatchways were opening and dislodging some others into the chamber. This was clearly a central station — if he was lucky, one of these pods would lead him to the hangar where his ship was held.

He left the hospital pod and started reading the signs near the various hatchways. Those Ganymedians nearest him glanced in his direction, and he could sense already the growing alarm in the room. He must have been a sight — he was clad in a hospital tunic, stained at the crotch, and was dangling a plastic bar from his right wrist. More than that, he mused, his masculine appearance must have been quite a sight for the men/women of this community.

A nearby Ganymedian approached him cautiously. "Are you all right? Can I help you?"

"I'm fine. Which one is the pod to the hangar?"

The Ganymedian blinked. "The what?"

"Hangar. Where the spaceships are."

"Uh, that's Operations. But don't you—"

"Thanks. I owe you," he said, and slapped the man/woman on the shoulder. He brushed past the stunned people waiting for their pods and found the Operations hatchway. No one seemed to be waiting for it, and the hatch opened as soon as he pressed the button.

"Hey! Stop him!" he heard from behind. He dashed into the pod and frantically pressed the button labeled "Ops." Before the doors closed, he saw Tacat and two men (they were definitely men) dressed in black leotards pushing through the crowd from their own transpod hatch. They weren't going to make it to the door, but he had been spotted. He hoped there was no way to override the pod mid-transit

— he suspected the various hubs of the Ganymedian community were connected by tunnels that the transpods traversed, presumably to isolate areas of the community for disaster control.

The transpod doors shut quietly and the pod accelerated toward whatever awaited him in the Operations section. He hefted the plastic bar and faced the doors. Even if Tacat couldn't stop the pod, he would no doubt be alerting the people in the next station to be on the lookout for him. If Collier was lucky, the pod would reach its destination before any organized police detail could be mounted: the trip from the hospital to the last station had only taken a minute or so.

He could feel the pod decelerating. The plastic bar felt fragile and inadequate in his hands, but it was all he had. He braced himself against the rear wall of the pod, ready to fly out horizontally in the weak Ganymedian gravity when the doors opened.

The chime sounded, and when the doors began to part, Collier launched himself forward, brandishing the plastic rod before him. He flew into empty space, tumbled, and came up on the balls of his feet, impressed with himself. There had been no one to greet him at the pod doors — perhaps Tacat hadn't managed to get his group organized in the short time it took the pod to travel from the habitation module to the operations module.

In fact, there was no one immediately present in the chamber into which Collier had flown. Instead, the room was busy with holo displays and computer stations, with some mechanicals scurrying about here and there on errands only they understood. The room was thoroughly automated and quite clean.

Collier approached the nearest computer holo and scanned the display. It looked to be a station for monitoring the ventilation system, or perhaps it was a water supply chart. Streams of data flowed across the screen, most of which made little sense to Collier. He moved on and scanned the various holos to see if any of them would help him find his ship. As he did so, he felt and heard a faint rumbling from the transpod hatch and quickly glanced over his shoulder to see the status bar over the hatch indicate that the pod was returning to the hab station. No doubt Tacat and his two goons would be arriving soon — he had about two minutes to find a way to get to the *Dulcinea*.

The rest of the chamber was studded with transpod hatches, all of which were labeled "Hab 5," "Hab 6," "Hab 7," and so on.

Except one.

One of the hatches, set in an alcove between two of the transpod stations, read "Airlock" above it. Collier sprinted to the airlock hatch and studied the control panel. It indicated pressure on the other side of the lock, and through the reinforced glass porthole he could see a small chamber with an environment suit hanging on a rack. He pressed the "open" button on the control panel and stepped into the lock, closing the hatch behind him. The environment suit was similar to his own, but looked sleeker and less cumbersome. He hoped it would fit him: he didn't want to think of the irony of coming this far only to be stopped by a too-small vacc suit.

The suit was much thinner than his own model, and clung to him more tightly. At first, he thought that was because it was simply smaller, but as he flexed his arms and legs he realized that it was built this way. There was a thin atmosphere on Ganymede, he remembered, but the exact pressure and composition was not something he recalled. Perhaps the pressure suit did not need to be quite as bulky as a deep space suit, or perhaps the Ganymedians just made a better specimen.

As he struggled into the suit, the plastic rod he was still attached to hampered his progress. He would not be able to get into the suit, much less seal it, as long as the restraint strap was still attached. The belt line of the environment suit held a number of tools — one of them was a small claw hammer. He scratched his arm a few times, but managed to keep himself from drawing blood as he hacked away at the restraint enough to tear it loose.

Once he was free of the strap, the suit was easy to get into, and he was nearly buttoned up when he caught motion beyond the small airlock porthole. The Hab 4 transpod had arrived: Tacat and his men sprang out of the pod and looked around. They immediately left Collier's field of vision as they fanned out, presumably to look for him. Collier secured the helmet as best he could: the design was not one he was used to, so he just did what he thought felt right and hoped. He found the outer door mechanism — it was a panel with many safety interlocks to prevent accidental opening of the door. He quickly disengaged the various safeties, and started when a klaxon sounded loudly, accompanied by flashing red lights. He glanced out the porthole to see Tacat and his men headed for the airlock — the lights were also on in the operations chamber, and he imagined the warning siren was sounding in there as well.

Before Tacat and his men could open the inner door, Collier threw the remaining switches that would bleed pressure from the airlock and thus make it impossible to open quickly from the inside. The outer door mechanism would not open until the airlock had matched pressure with the outside: even as he cursed the design, he admitted the necessity of it. Airlock inhabitants were not fond of being blown outward with the escaping air.

Collier could hear the hissing sound lessen in volume as the air left the lock, even as Tacat approached the porthole and looked inside. He stared at Collier for a moment, then looked down at the control panel. He spoke soundlessly to one of his thugs and they both appeared to be manipulating the controls on the inside. Collier saw the indicator lights on the outer door panel go to green, and he opened the outer door and stepped onto the surface of Ganymede.

Chapter Seven

The surface near the airlock was treacherous. A vast sheet of ice stretched out into the distance, but at least near the complex the topmost layer of ice had partially melted, making for a sleek, slippery surface. Collier steadied himself, his arms outstretched, and saw off to his left a series of guide poles topped with small but bright lights. He made his way to the nearest one and grabbed hold, grateful for the support. He stood on the plain, the arcing wall of the complex behind him and a vast expanse of white and grey in front of him.

The suit's helmet heads-up display was conventionally designed, and he was able to read the reflected dials without difficulty. According to the indicators, he had perhaps four hours of air. If he weren't able to get aboard the *Dulcinea* long before then, no doubt the police force of this egalitarian community would apprehended him.

He wasn't even sure how being aboard the *Dulcinea* would ultimately help his situation. The ship was without fuel and therefore grounded, and no doubt the community would be patient enough to wait for his biologicals to run out.

Still, he felt that if he could get aboard his ship and get back in communication with Sancho, everything would be all right. Certainly, he would be better off in his own vessel than strapped to a medical gurney awaiting some kind of brain surgery.

First, though, he had to find his ship. It wasn't visible from where he stood — he scanned the grey plain and saw an almost featureless horizon. It was difficult to tell, but he thought he saw evidence of wind blowing some ice crystals in the distance. The suit, despite its thinness, seemed to be an adequate bulwark against the cold.

Collier decided he had to move away from the airlock. Tacat and his/her men might be donning their own suits and preparing to give chase on the surface themselves. Besides, his ship might be just around one of the curved outer walls of the community. He picked his left arbitrarily, and let go of the guide pole. The footing was better the farther away he went from the walls: he could feel the bumpy soles of his boots gaining purchase on the unmelted ice as he walked.

As he trudged onward, the curve of the community's operations hub to his left, he wondered if the hangar Tacat had said his ship was contained within was an underground structure. He had assumed, based on his Ceres experience, that it would be simply on the surface, but the growing realization that the Ganymedians might have a different approach chilled him more than the thin wind. If that were the case, he would have to find another airlock, reenter the community, and somehow fight his way to the hangar.

Inside his helmet, he shook his head. There was no possible way he could continue to avoid capture if he reentered the community. Tacat would surely have what passed for police waiting for him at his ship. Indeed, even if his ship was outside, security personnel would—

And there she was.

She was resting in a kind of cradle not more than one hundred meters from him, and looked undamaged. He was approaching her from the port stern side, and saw a personnel flextube snaking out from her port external airlock toward the community. He could see no one from where he was, but it was quite possible there were people guarding the ship from inside the flextube, or perhaps on the other side of *Dulcinea*.

He had an impulse to start running toward her, but he calmed himself and analyzed the situation first. The flextube connection to the ship suggested that they had managed to convince Sancho to let them in, but Collier couldn't bring himself to believe that. He hadn't ordered the computer to refuse entry to anyone except him, but surely Sancho would be cautious. Collier flexed his fingers into fists as he realized how much he was counting on Sancho to not act like a computer and act like ... a Caliban.

But if the Ganymedians had managed to get on board, they would have found the wand by now and the discussion with Tacat would have been much different. Tacat had mentioned the downloading of Sancho's files as partial payment for the services rendered, which would indicate he had not gained access to them. Collier sighed. They hadn't gotten inside. The flextube was just Tacat thinking ahead.

That meant, though, that he would have to find another access. The ship was not quite on the surface — the hangar cradle kept it off the ice and held it upright, looking like an enormous dinosaur ribcage. If the ship was far enough off the ground...

He started trotting toward her, hoping that no Ganymedian would emerge from a hiding place to stop him. As he left the protective lee of the community wall, he could feel the slight wind that he had seen evidence of earlier. That, plus the icy surface, made even trotting difficult. He skidded more than once as he encountered a patch of slightly melted ice, and on one of his skids, he spun completely around in what would have earned him fair marks at the Winter Olympics on Earth. During that spin, he saw two figures approaching him quickly from the community boundary. They must have been watching the ship from the wall, behind the curve Collier had not continued past. Now they were gaining on him. He was perhaps forty meters from the cradle. Collier scrambled toward his ship, sometimes running, sometimes on all fours, but always fighting closer. He dared not look behind him to see where his pursuers were, and his helmet HUD didn't have them on its screen. With every stumbling step he imagined he would feel a hand clamp down on his ankle and pull him to the ground.

He was very near the cradle now, and could see *Dulcinea* was suspended perhaps a meter and a half off the ground. That ought to be enough. He was only a scant five meters away when he launched himself forward in a face-first slide on the ice, tucking his head down and hoping his air tanks would clear the underside of the cradle. He slid forward for what seemed a long time when the top of his helmet cracked into an obstruction. He managed to get on his elbows and saw he had slid into one of the ribs of the cradle, but was thoroughly underneath *Dulcinea*'s belly.

A piercing buzzing noise filled his helmet, followed by a computer voice. "Warning. Suit integrity lost. Apply patch to region A. Seek pressurized shelter immediately." He didn't feel any loss of pressure, but he knew that the helmet could rupture instantly. He spun onto his back, the air tanks making his progress awkward, and used the ribs of the hangar cradle to pull him the few meters toward *Rocinante's* stable. Now came the difficult part.

He knew the location of the camera pickup that monitored *Rocinante*'s departure and arrival. He found it and put his helmet glass as close to it as he could, trying to ignore the suit computer's incessant warnings about his damaged helmet. He waited, but the stable doors didn't open.

He felt a chill wash over his head near the upper left part of his skull. Even as he took a moment to interpret the feeling, he heard the nightmare sound all belters dreaded: the hiss of escaping air.

His helmet crack must have opened, and he was losing pressure to the outside. If the helmet blew completely, he wondered if he would feel anything, or if the slight atmosphere on Ganymede would keep him alive long enough to feel his blood start to boil.

Collier frantically pounded the metal of *Dulcinea's* belly and tried to keep his face toward the camera pickup. The coldness was definitely not an illusion — he could feel it on a thin wedge of his head.

"Sancho, open up, I know you're home," he shouted uselessly.

The stable doors opened suddenly, and Collier climbed awkwardly inside, holding on to one of the blessed handrails inside the empty stable as he closed the doors from the inside. As the belly doors rolled shut, Collier saw one of the pursuers appear in the shadows beneath the ship.

"Not quite fast enough, buddy," he murmured. The doors shut, and he could hear the pressure returning to the stable. His helmet warning was still droning on, but he cut it off mid-sentence when he detached the helmet from the neck housing.

"Sancho, you read me?"

"What the fuck is going on, Skipper?" came the anxious voice of his companion. "I've got two unidentified people wandering around the stable doors down there, and for the last few hours I think there has been something going on near my portside airlock. I've been getting attempts to override the system from the outside."

"Good to see you, too, Sancho," Collier said through a grin. "I'll try to explain everything, but first, give me your status." He grunted as he opened the inner door from the stable to the ship proper and swung himself through the portal. The ship felt strange in this sideways orientation — during acceleration, the control suite had always been "up" to him, and now it was just "forward." He didn't dwell on the sensation, but noted it and started to climb out of the Ganymedian environment suit.

Sancho said, "Well, not much change from what I told you about two hours ago. Except for the assholes crawling around my belly and working to get in from the portside airlock. Oh, and I've been receiving more electronic override messages than you can believe. Some of them were using the universal distress frequency. There's been a lot of attempts to get in, Skipper."

"But you didn't let them," Collier said simply. "Good work, Sancho. How did you resist so well?"

"I admit, I did have to go against programming once or twice. The distress signals would have worked if I hadn't overridden my own safety protocols. Wasn't as hard as you would have thought, Skipper," Sancho said casually.

Collier mused for a moment on the advantages of a Caliban computer. "You did great. And thanks for letting me in."

"No problem. Though I was surprised to see you out there. I was sending you transmissions, but I don't think your suit radio was on."

"Probably not. I didn't really know how to work this thing," Collier said, studying the helmet for the first time. There was a hairline crack on the top left of the helmet, perhaps six centimeters long. Collier squeezed the helmet and saw the crack widen perceptibly. He tried not to think about what could have happened to his head.

"And what's your status, Skipper?" Sancho asked.

Collier made his way forward to the control suite, clad now only in his hospital tunic. He sat down in the forward chair and punched up as many outside camera pickups as he had available. "I'm fine."

"Had an accident, did you?"

"What?" Collier felt around his body. Was he bleeding from somewhere?

"Uh, your groin. Had an accident?"

Collier looked down at the still-moist stain on his crotch, chuckled. "Oh, that. Long story. I'll tell you on the return trip."

"Speaking of that, how exactly are we going to make any kind of return trip, Skipper? I see three rather serious obstacles to our launch. One, we don't have any propellant to speak of. Two, as weak as Ganymedian gravity is, we will still need a shitload of thrust to get off the surface."

"A 'shitload,' huh? Try not to be so technical, Sancho." Despite the problems he still faced with the Ganymedians, he was giddy to be back aboard his ship.

"And *three*," Sancho continued undeterred, "we're held in this goddamn drydock thing. I think we're clamped to it in places."

"Okay. Believe me, Sancho, things could be a lot worse. By the way," he added, grinning from half his mouth, "what's with the swearing? Did you install some kind of locker-room speech add-on?"

"It seemed appropriate. Does it bother you?"

"No, no. Makes you saltier, that's for sure."

"Saltier?"

"Skip it," Collier said. He clicked his tongue twice and said, "You mentioned receiving messages from the Ganymedians. I think it's time we answered some of them. That's the polite thing to do. Can you contact them, please? Ask for someone named Opos Tacat."

Sancho made the connection, though it was only an audio hookup. Maybe Tacat wasn't at a location with a camera, or perhaps he didn't want to be on screen. But the audio connection would serve.

"Tacat? Captain South here. How are you?" Collier leaned back in his chair and put his feet on the consoles in front of him, being careful not to press any buttons.

"I'm very disappointed. I thought we had an arrangement. You didn't seem like a man who would run away from his responsibilities, but—"

"Let's stop right there, Commissar," Collier interrupted forcefully. "I'm not running away from anything. I fully intend to repay you and your community for saving my life. But I'm going to do it my way, not yours."

"Is that how life works where you come from? The debtor dictates terms to the creditor?"

Collier snorted. "For a man who runs a community without money, you certainly know the lingo."

"I have to. To deal with people like you from time to time," Tacat was making no effort to hide his scorn.

"Didn't seem to help you this time, pal."

"I admit," Tacat growled, "you were far more barbaric than I had anticipated. But for all your gallant swashbuckling in the habitat, you are still a prisoner here. Your ship can't leave." Collier could almost see the smug little grin on the administrator's face. "You will submit to the will of the community, one way or another."

"The hell I will. You think I've been barbaric already? You ain't seen nothin' yet. I can use mining lasers to melt some of the ice, then use the water for propulsion fuel. I've got enough fuel to break out of this fragile little cradle you've got me in, and set down dozens of kilometers away while I pump water ice into my tanks. A quick run through the electrolysis plant and I will have all the hydrogen I need. So don't tell me I can't find fuel."

As he spoke, Sancho commented textually in the air before him. "Skipper, I think you're underestimating the strength of the clamps on the drydock cradle."

Collier angrily wiped the text away. He had no idea how strong the clamps were. How Sancho could be so savvy in some ways and yet so innocent in others was both amusing and irritating. He still didn't understand bluffing.

Tacat chuckled. "No, you can't. While your ship is a fairly standard, and if I may say so, *inefficient* variable specific impulse magnetoplasma thruster type, which you probably call ion drive, it is not built for planetary liftoff. Even if it were, you must have noticed by now it is not oriented for liftoff." He chuckled again. "Don't you think we know your vessel after bringing it here? Let's not waste time in bluffing one another. We can wait you out. That's the situation here."

Collier swore. He should have known Tacat would have understood the ship. He swept his feet off the consoles and typed a message to Sancho. "Can we use the wand to make hydrogen?"

Sancho answered, "Of course. But we have no way of getting it into the fuel tanks under proper pressure."

Sancho was right, again, of course. And even if he could somehow convert enough hydrogen and get it into the tanks, Tacat was correct about the ship. She was not designed for liftoff even from the one-seventh gee of Ganymede. The highest he had ever gotten her up to was 1.6 meters per second per second. Add to that the fact that Tacat had placed the ship's thrusters horizontal to the planet surface and the physics didn't add up.

Tacat was right. He was marooned here.

"Captain?" Tacat said with mock concern.

"All right. We seem to be at an impasse here," Collier started, but Tacat cut him off smoothly.

"Oh, no. That would imply that we are both equally able to thwart the other," his/her voice was smoothly confident. "That is not the case. You will eventually give in, because you have no choice. And when you do, we will begin the procedure we have planned for you. Until then, Captain," Tacat said, preparatory to breaking off communication.

"Wait," Collier said, half panicked.

"Yes?"

Collier grinned slightly. Despite his words, Tacat was still willing to listen. Now all Collier had to do was have something worth listening to.

"There is something I can do here that I couldn't do from my hospital bed, and I think you know that. It's why you tried to strap me down and why you tried very hard to keep me from reentering *Dulcinea*. As you said, let's not bluff each other."

"I'm listening," Tacat said. Collier heard the worry in the Commissar's voice.

"I can and will wipe Sancho … my computer's memory from here. You won't get anything from it."

At the same time he spoke the words, he typed a message to Sancho. "I'm lying. I won't erase your memory."

There was no response from Sancho, but before Collier could wonder at that, Tacat answered.

"In the first place, you wouldn't do that, since it would only hurt yourself. It would not be at all sensible. Secondly, I doubt you could execute a memory wipe our technicians couldn't undo. We are rather skilled in computer science, and I believe with enough time we could recover what you thought you erased."

"I'll erase the data with a crowbar."

Tacat was silent for a little while, then chuckled softly. "You're mad. In any case, we would be able to rebuild what you think you have destroyed. And we would still have you and your mind."

"I'll erase that, too."

Now Tacat openly laughed. "You will? How? Another crowbar?"

"Maybe. I think you underestimate my commitment to rugged individualism, Tacat. No one is going to muck around my brain, or my computer's brain, without my permission. And I don't give it. I don't have much, Tacat — I don't have a corporation behind me, or a place in what you think of as a utopia. I don't have family or a woman. But I have myself. I have my ship. And I'll be damned if I am going to allow you or anyone else to take my identity away."

Again, Tacat didn't answer immediately. When sh'he did, sh'he was no longer laughing or chuckling. "You really are a madman. You'd destroy your ship and yourself rather than share your knowledge with us? I had no idea that your capitalist community had so poisoned you that you would prefer a lose-lose situation to a win-win." He cleared his throat and said, "Very well. You've had your speech, so now hear mine. In a very real way, you belong to the community now. And we belong to you. We have provided you with a service and with our expertise because you were in need. That is our duty to any member of our community. You can add to that community — in your case, more than in others — through sharing knowledge. As an outsider and a belter, you possess knowledge that we lack and have no way of obtaining except in trade. I would have asked you to become a member of our community, but your ranting tells me you could never assimilate into our way of life. Instead, then, we will take what you ought to have given us freely. I do not believe you will follow through on the threats you have made against your ship and your person, so—"

Although Collier's voice was soft, it cut through Tacat's easily. "I am fifty-one years old by Terrestrial dating. I am alone. I am one of the last independent belters in the system, and by now I am sure I am being hunted by every corp in the belt. I am what you would call a dead-ender. Such people are desperate, and desperate people maybe aren't always sensible. But they are dangerous. If you will not agree to my proposal of sharing information, you will get nothing. Believe it." Again, Collier found himself not having to feign emotion in his voice. What had started as a bluff had become sincere.

Sancho's words lit up the air between them. "Skipper, don't say that about yourself."

Collier didn't respond.

When Tacat spoke a few seconds later, his/her voice was probing. "I'm curious. What did you envision for information sharing?"

Collier closed his eyes and sighed silently. Now he was on familiar ground. Despite Tacat's claim that sh'he had to deal with capitalists in trade, Collier was certain that the Commissar would not have the acumen to drive a bargain like Collier could.

Collier said firmly, "Here's how it is going to go down." He began explaining, in improvised fashion, what he was willing and unwilling to share. In truth, there was little he would want to withhold — data about the wand was about all he wanted to keep to himself and Sancho — but he was adamant on being in control of the methods. He would allow Ganymede psychologists to interview him, but he drew the line at drugs or hypnosis. Tacat had been more pliable than Collier had hoped. Perhaps the Commissar had not dealt with true resistance to his will in a long time, if he indeed ever had.

"I have no objection to staying here a week or more, to answer your questions," Collier said after an hour of negotiations, "but never forget that I set the conditions."

"I have already agreed to that," Tacat said. "I'd like to begin the data transfer from your computer soon. When do you think you can be ready?"

"I'll call you. I need to instruct him on what I want to share."

"Done. And when are you going to come out of your ship for your interviews?"

Collier laughed. "Nice try. I'm not going to let myself be caught again by you. You'll send your interviewers to me. This will happen here, on my ship."

Tacat started to argue, asking how sh'he could be assured that whomever sh'he sent would be safe, but Collier cut him/her off.

"It's that or nothing. What do you think I am going to do, take him hostage? Besides, I'm not the one who kept you prisoner in a hospital bed."

"I'll send the interviewer in soon," Tacat snapped, then broke off the transmission.

Collier stared at empty air for a moment, pleased with himself.

"That went well, don't you think, Sancho?"

"Extremely so. Skipper..." Sancho added carefully.

"Yeah?"

"The part about erasing my memory." He didn't elaborate further.

"Oh, Sancho, I wasn't going to do anything of the sort. But I had to make Tacat think I would."

"I know that, Skipper. It's just … I don't know how to explain this. I sure don't want you to get upset, but I feel like I should tell you."

Collier's self-satisfied smile faded. Sancho's voice was unusually emotive, and smacked of a secret he was equally loathe to keep and to spill.

"What is it?"

"When you said that, before you typed in your reassuring message that it was all a bluff, I had a … feeling."

"Yeah?"

"Look, Skipper, we've been together a long time. You know I want what's best for you, and for the ship, and for us. Just think of all I have done for you — I mean, getting you to Ganymede safely and having them revive you and—"

"Sancho, you've already got the job as the ship's computer. You don't need to sell me on your virtues. Just tell me what you were feeling."

"It was exactly four point one one nine eight seconds between when you said you would blank my memory and when you typed in the message that you wouldn't. That's a long time to a computer. In that time, I started to … formulate plans as to how I would stop you from doing that."

Collier felt his surroundings spin for a moment. Despite Sancho's apologetic tone, his words were chilling. Collier immediately thought of the methods under Sancho's control that could result in Collier's death: explosive decompression was the most merciful one.

Sancho spoke before more gruesome thoughts came to dominate Collier's thinking. "I've made you upset, I can tell. Your heart rate has risen and your facial thermograph shows all the signs of emotional turmoil." Sancho sighed, or in his case, made the electronic noises equivalent to a sigh. "I felt like I had to tell you, Skipper. I've grown a lot in the last two months while you were comatose. I'm getting the hang of my own sentience, but I'm noticing that I don't have complete control over my own thoughts. It's a strange thing," he mused.

Collier swallowed and tried to make his voice sound normal in his very dry throat. "Yeah, that can be tricky. So, are we okay? You know I would never do anything like that to you?"

"I do. Just had a momentary ... hiccup," Sancho said.

Collier nodded and hoped he wasn't showing outwardly what turmoil he was experiencing inwardly. If Sancho could not be trusted, what did that leave him? He hadn't known that the computer could scan his face and read it like a person could — perhaps even better. Damn it, how could a man be expected to keep his heat signature under control? And how long had Sancho been able to read him that way?

Too many questions. As pressing as the idea of Sancho's self-awareness was, there were still more urgent matters to deal with. He issued instructions to Sancho regarding the data uplink to the Ganymedians: no mention of the wand or anything that would lead them to think they had made a discovery worth investigating. No mention of Sancho's Caliban status. But he was free to give them all the astronomical data they had on various asteroids they had encountered as well as specifications of the *Dulcinea* itself. Collier couldn't imagine what information Sancho could possess (aside from the alien artifact) that the Ganymedians would find valuable, but if data was such a commodity here, perhaps what he saw as worthless the Ganymedians would value. Such was the driving idea behind trade itself.

When he had spoken with Sancho about what was and what was not to be shared, (with the understanding that anything they had not covered and which Sancho was not sure about would have to gain Collier's approval first), Collier directed the computer to contact Tacat and arrange for the data transfer and the interviewer's arrival.

As his computer made the arrangements, Collier looked around the cabin self-consciously. It was an intensely personal space — while Collier had an old-fashioned spacer's tidiness, there were still touches here and there that had the "I'll get to that someday" casualness Collier had spent a lifetime cultivating. If an interviewer wanted to get to know him, he could do worse than look around the cabin for a while.

He had stowed the wand securely in an aft compartment. The ship was ready to receive a visitor.

Soon after Sancho had contacted Tacat, he alerted Collier that the visitor had arrived through the flextube and was awaiting permission to come aboard. Collier cycled the door manually, ready to greet the newcomer, and was mildly surprised by what he saw.

This was quite definitely a woman.

"Hello," she said, and if her pleasingly feminine figure hadn't been enough to identify her gender, her soprano voice would have done so. She was a wavy-haired, dark blonde woman with a nut-brown complexion and a slim though curvy frame.

Collier could not help but appraise her for a moment before stepping slightly aside and grunting, "Welcome aboard. Come on in."

When she moved past him he smelled the faint odor of orchids. She entered the cabin and looked around warily. "Smaller than it looks from the outside," she said softly. Collier couldn't decide from her tone if she was speaking to him or to herself.

Still, he felt the need to defend *Dulcinea*. "A lot of the interior space is taken up by the fusion reactor, fuel tanks, electrolysis plant, hold, and so on. I have all I need here, plus I have a small stateroom aft."

She continued to scan the interior, her eyes sharp but mildly amused. Much about her was difficult to read: her expression was professional, as if she were an anthropologist encountering a new subspecies of humanity. Perhaps, Collier thought, that's exactly what she was.

"Ever get lonely?" she said casually, her face in profile to his as she studied the control boards.

"Not really. I prefer solitude, Miss—?"

"Oh, I'm sorry. Su. You can call me Su," she said, with a faint emphasis on the word "you."

"But that's not your real name?" Collier said.

Su turned to him, a half grin on her face. "As I said, you can call me that. Shall we get started?"

Collier fought back a sigh. Su was going to be difficult to handle. He indicated the control chair (he had already disabled the manual controls) and took the acceleration hammock himself.

"Seems appropriate for me to be lying down, don't you think?" he joked.

Su settled daintily into her seat and said, "Why's that?"

"Like those ancient psychoanalysis sessions, you know."

"Oh," Su said evenly, unamused. Collier felt a little deflated and more than a little foolish. Why was he trying to impress this woman?

"Before we get started," Collier said, turning in his hammock to see Su setting up what had to be recording devices, "can I ask you something?"

"Depends on what it is," Su said, calibrating a small rectangular device and setting it gently on the control board near her.

"All the people I've met on Ganymede have been hermaphrodites. I was wondering why you weren't one yourself. If that's a rude question, then I apologize."

Su did not appear to be offended by the question: in fact, she was so absorbed in setting up her interviewing devices (and there seemed to be far more than Collier would have thought necessary) she didn't even seem to acknowledge the question until she responded a beat later.

"I'm just not," she said. "Some are on Ganymede, some aren't. I'm not one. There. I think I am ready to begin, Captain." She finally turned to face him. "Are you ready?"

This time, he did sigh. "Sure thing. Fire away."

"Where, when, and to whom were you born?"

"I was born in transit to Ceres from the outer belt. My father, Jym, and my mother, Geena, were both independent miners working mainly in the Ceres group. They helped build what Ceres is now, actually."

"I see. And when?"

"Oh, right. April 6, 2199. Terrestrial, of course."

Su nodded and looked him over, without bothering to conceal her intention to evaluate him. "Never went for any rejuvenation treatments, then, did you?"

Collier chortled. "Cosmetic ones? No, never did. I've had the usual gene therapy and biochemical cleansing routines, of course. But never went in for the Peter Pan stuff. I'm fifty-one, and I probably look like it. Though the free fall environment has kept me from sagging," he added, tapping the bottom of his still-firm neck.

"You're completely biological?" Su asked, her voice betraying a faint hint of interest.

"So far, yep."

"What do you mean, 'so far'?"

His casual answer bordered on flippant. "Well, you never know. If I were to meet with an accident, say, lose a limb or two, I'd have to decide if I wanted to grow a new one, use a mechanical, or just do without. Hasn't come up yet. What about you?"

Su hesitated the barest fraction of a second, then answered in clipped tones, "I'm sixty-eight terrestrial. Full course of genetic and biological renewal procedures. About 90% biological, 10% cybernetic." She paused, then said in a slightly lower register, "But this session isn't about me. Tell me about your upbringing."

Collier was still assimilating her answer. "You're sixty-eight?" He whistled. "You must have a very thorough rejuvenation process here. You look about thirty."

Su did not appear to take that as a complement. "We do, yes," she said flatly. "Now, your upbringing."

Collier spoke for a good hour about his childhood among the belt, his education at his father's knee, remembering the arguments his mother and father would get into about whether or not to subscribe to the Solarnet education service.

"In the end," Collier said, "they compromised. Dad went ahead and ordered the service — do you know about Solarnet?"

"Ganymede is where the bulk of the lessons on Solarnet come from. We export the lessons in trade."

Collier blinked. "I never knew that. Anyway," he continued, "the compromise was that even though I would sit with the Solarnet vinstructor, Dad would sit right behind me and amend, contradict, and otherwise argue with the lesson at almost every turn." He laughed, remembering some of the disagreements Dad had had with the vinstructor. Lessons that were slated to take half an hour would stretch to two or three hours as Jym argued relentlessly with the poor synthetic. The virtual personality of the teacher was not at all up to the challenge, and frequently got caught in logical loops and had to be restarted with Jym out of earshot. Collier had learned the art of stubbornness at an early age.

Su continued to ask him about his growing up, and Collier happily recalled tales of his boyhood until she asked him where his parents were now.

"Dead," he said evenly. "They died, oh, maybe twenty-five years ago. In the Crash of '24." He pretended to not quite remember, but he could feel the tearing wind of escaping atmosphere as if it were happening right now. The corporate miner had slammed into Ceres at nearly a kilometer per second, fully loaded, and transferred its incredible kinetic energy to the surface. Even the deep levels of the fledgling Ceres habitat had felt the impact, and parts of the colony had lost pressure. Jym and Geena had been in one of the lost sections. Collier had been, ironically, at a learning crèche, submitting to real-time oral exams to confirm his probationary Master's license. He had been bundled into the still secure areas of the base with the other survivors, not knowing the fate of his parents.

Over three hundred souls lost their lives that day. The corporation responsible dragged the lawsuits out until they were able to pay off enough litigants and judges. The suit went away, and aside from a memorial plaque on the surface of Ceres where a deep scar still marked the event, there was no evidence that such an occurrence had ever taken place.

"I remember that. A horrible day," Su said, and seemed to mean it. "I am sorry for your loss." She put more emotion into that stock phrase than anything else she had said during the session.

Collier found himself suddenly very weary. "Hey, let me ask you something." Su did not respond, but waited patiently. "What is the point of asking me about my childhood? You've been at it for, what, four hours now?"

"Closer to four and a half."

"Okay. What good is it? I mean, Tacat said you guys find information valuable, but I can't see what there is in my life story for you to make use of."

Su paused, her demeanor conflicted, as if she were trying to decide whether to answer his question or just brush it off. She finally said, "We've extensively psychoanalyzed everyone on Ganymede to the point that we are allowing significant observer bias to cloud our data. Every psychologist knows too much about the subject beforehand, and this skews our information. You, on the other hand, are as close to a *tabula rasa* as we are going to get. No one from Ganymede knows much about you, so we can gather data without fear of interviewer prejudice."

"That doesn't answer my question," Collier said, smiling. "What do you hope to do with my life story? Sell the holomovie rights? And if you do, what's my cut?"

"When you submit your germ plasm to us, it will represent a valuable variable to our stock. But in addition to the purely chemical analyses of your DNA, we need to know how you came to be the man you are from social and psychological forces. The nature/nurture debate is still very much alive, and your personal data, both chemical and psychological, will help to understand it."

"I thought it was a simple damn question," Collier murmured. "I still don't see how asking me about my mom's cooking helps Ganymede."

An emotion flashed across Su's face — was it amusement?—then was gone. "The gathering of pertinent data remains an imprecise science."

"Woolgathering."

"I beg your pardon?"

"You're describing woolgathering. One of Dad's favorite words."

"Ah." Su nodded, then, with a slight shake of her shoulders, said, "Shall we continue?"

"One more question about you, then we can. You've asked me plenty, so I figure I get a few. You deflected my question about you being a woman. Without scientific flim-flammery, can you just tell me why you are a woman and not a hermaphrodite?"

Su lowered her face slightly to look at him through her eyebrows. "Your question is highly personal, you realize this?"

"Personal. You've asked me everything about myself except which side I hang. You can answer this."

Su didn't react to his vulgarism. "Very well. I am a descendant of the original group of scientists who colonized Ganymede. I am first generation native to this moon. As such, I was expected to breed prodigiously, both naturally and through cloning. I did so, producing nine children of superior stock myself. When the technology caught up to us, allowing the inhabitants of Ganymede to alter themselves and be fully functional hermaphrodites, most of the Firsters — for that is what we called ourselves — chose to remain as they had been born. Most of us simply could not psychologically make the adjustment to gender reassignment. I was one of those people. This behavior, though not encouraged, is tolerated for now among the Firsters and of course the Originals."

Although Su spoke as if she were reciting a speech, Collier could nevertheless hear hidden in her voice some pain, and he wondered at it.

"You're not ashamed of being a woman, are you? I mean, just a woman?"

"You said you'd ask only one question, Captain." Su said, but her voice was shaky.

"You're right. I did. Sorry about that. Fire away. But for what it's worth … I think you made the right choice. Those inbetweeners give me the willies."

Su's lips did not smile, but her eyes crinkled slightly. "Another point for my research. Let us continue."

"Sure thing. Left."

"I'm sorry?"

Collier fought to keep a straight face. "Left side. Where I hang it."

This time, Su quite definitely smiled. It was very faint, but it was there.

Su didn't stay much longer: she asked a few more questions about Collier's childhood, but seemed to want to compartmentalize her questions into the period before his parents' death. Perhaps two hours later, she switched off her recording gear and stood up.

"That will be all for now, Captain. I shall return tomorrow, and we will discuss your young adulthood."

"Sounds good. I'll be here."

Su nodded gravely, though Collier noticed she was not quite as emotionless as she had been when she first entered the ship. It was an almost imperceptible wilting of her stiffness that gave her away. Collier escorted her to the flextube airlock and once again smelled the orchids as she passed by him.

"Well, what do you think, Sancho?" Collier said when she had gone.

"I'm with you, Skipper: I don't know why they are questioning you. As far as I'm concerned, the schematics of the ship and the data stored in my banks are far more valuable. No offense."

"None taken. How did the linkup go?"

"Fine. I have nineteen holds for you to look at — I wasn't sure about a few things relating to fuel consumption. You said to hold anything that might be connected to the wand, and if we produce our own hydrogen using it, that might come under the heading of fuel consumption, so I—"

"I see. Show me the questions, and we'll work through it together."

The questions were all innocent enough: the Ganymedians wanted to know about *Dulcinea*'s performance and fuel supply for the ion drive. Again, Collier couldn't understand what it was about his ship that would be so interesting — *Dulcinea* was almost twenty years old and hadn't been upgraded in all that time. What the Ganymedians could learn from him was baffling, but if they wanted to take data in trade, Collier was happy to give it to them. On his terms, of course.

Once Collier had cleared Sancho to send the data, he stretched out on the acceleration hammock and yawned. "I'm going to turn in, Sancho. Talking to that woman took more out of me than I thought. Wake me if there's a fire."

"Copy that, Skipper. Pleasant dreams."

Chapter Eight

The next three days' worth of interviewing with Su were not exactly tedious, but seemed even more trivial and worthless. He didn't mind talking to the woman — she had warmed to him slightly in the three days — but he had grown tired of what seemed to be a never-ending chore. The interview questions were mundane and banal, and despite Su's assurances that the information Collier was providing would be valuable, he could not understand how.

On the fourth session, while the two were discussing his mining methods and daily life aboard the *Dulcinea*, Su shook him out of what had become his half-awake state by asking if he had ever discovered anything unusual in the Belt.

"What do you mean by 'unusual'?" he asked, keeping his voice carefully calm.

"Out of the ordinary," Su said evenly. "I suppose if you discovered a metal not normally found in the belt, or perhaps an old derelict spacecraft, something you wouldn't expect to find."

"Well, once in a while I've tapped into an unusually high concentration of iridium."

"I see. But have you ever found anything that no one else has ever found?"

Collier smiled artificially. "How can I know if no one else has ever found something?"

Su wrinkled her nose. She had dropped the expressionless face two sessions ago, and had allowed feeling to enter her voice. She answered him with scorn. "All right, then, have you ever found anything that no one else, to your knowledge, has ever found or reported finding? That clear enough for you?"

"No, I can't say I have," he answered, too quickly.

Su stared at him for a moment. "You seem very sure."

"I am."

"Then why'd you dodge the question when I first asked it?"

"I didn't dodge the question. I wanted you to be clearer."

"But surely, if you had never found anything unusual, you wouldn't need me to clarify what—"

"Look, you've been asking me questions for five days now. I'm getting a little bit tired of it, okay?"

Su nodded. "It can be a draining experience. For both subject and interviewer, I might add." She rubbed her eyes, the first sign of weakness or fatigue she had shown.

"How about we take a short break," Collier said.

Su nodded again and sat back a few inches. To anyone else, Su would have appeared still very stiff, but Collier's recent experience with her allowed him to see just how much she had relaxed. He swung himself out of his hammock and went to the pantry. "I don't have much," he said, glancing at the dwindling supply of plastic-wrapped foodstuffs, "but Ceres makes a mean vat-grown chicken vindaloo. You want some?"

Su had always refused his offers in the past, but this time, she accepted. Collier tossed her a dark red packet, which she snagged out of the air with aplomb.

"Thanks," she said. She studied the packet for a moment, seeing how it opened and heated. Collier studied her as she manipulated the material. Despite the interviews, he still knew very little about Ganymedian culture.

"So, what's a nice girl like you doing on a Jovian moon like this?" he said in an exaggerated drawl.

Su sucked on the plastic opening and chewed. "If it is your plan for me to regurgitate this packet, then continue using lines like that. As to why I am here ... just lucky, I guess."

"I wouldn't say that," Collier countered, chewing on his cashew chicken.

"Oh? Why not?"

"You can't say you like living here," he said matter-of-factly. "From what I've seen, your little utopia is a police state where every life decision is made for you by the powers-that-be. Hell, a man doesn't even get to keep his balls."

"In the first place, Captain, you haven't seen the community at all. You've been confined to a hospital bed and then made some heroic mad dash through a few transpod stations. In the second place, it's not a police state. We are free citizens, just like you would find on Earth, or Mars, or in the Belt. And lastly, our men and hermaphs have balls."

Su delivered the last sentence with locker-room directness that stunned Collier. Somehow, she managed to maintain her propriety even while slumming with faint vulgarity.

"Oh yeah? Well tell me something, then, Su: how do you choose your profession on Ganymede? How do you choose a mate?" He had gleaned enough from Tacat's description of the community and from the very few hints Su had let slip during the interviews to think he knew the answers to those questions.

"We choose a profession based on our own strengths and proclivities, just like you might."

"Don't you mean, the wise men and women of the community decide for you?"

Su hesitated a fraction of a second, then said, "We receive guidance from a panel of experts, yes."

Collier snorted. "Say it how you want — you are told what job you will do. You don't really have freedom."

"And you think you lot do?" Su said, angrily. "You really think you can choose to be, say, a successful sculptor or a zero-g sports star?"

"I could have made the attempt," Collier said.

"And you would have failed, and your economic status would have suffered. So much so, that you would have been forced into another line of employment by economic necessity. Don't try to tell me you are free. You are a slave to economics."

"And you're one to your so-called panel of experts!"

"At least they have my best interests at heart!" Su was by now shouting, and Collier found himself inexplicably distracted by the sight of her breasts heaving under her deep breathing. He tore his eyes away and took a breath himself, feeling a stirring in his own loins.

"All right. Sorry. So we're both slaves to other masters. But how do you choose a mate?"

Su glared at him, still angry. "You wouldn't understand. You will just say it is wrongheaded and evil." Her voice was petulant.

"I'll try not to," he said, grinning.

"We are matched genetically with another member of the community. Sometimes, the best genetic match is someone of the same gender, hence the trend toward hermaphroditism. In producing offspring, there is more and more a detachment of the conventional father/mother paradigm."

"What does that mean?"

Su sighed, and for a moment Collier saw wistfulness in her eyes. "It means children are produced as a biological function, not as a family unit. Sometimes the genetic mother and father cohabitate to help the community raise the child, but the trend is quite clearly away from this habit. There are currently only thirty-three families of this type on Ganymede. Those families are barely tolerated by the authorities, and the members of those families are as ostracized as our social structure permits. The other two hundred and sixty five children are being raised by the community."

Collier did not immediately answer. When he did, his voice was soft. "You wanted to raise your own children, didn't you?"

Su was not looking at him. Her eyes were fixed on some moment in the past. "Yes, I did. But I was not strong enough to resist the social pressure. That happens sometimes — an individual buckles to increasing societal norms and makes a decision that may be detrimental to his or her own well-being in one way, but allows for increased status in the community of which he or she is a part. Thus, the organism rises in social status with the concomitant privileges thereto." She swallowed, then added in a wavering voice, "And all it took was a cancelling of a basic personal need."

"I'm sorry," Collier said.

Now Su looked at him, her eyes moist. "What would you know about it?" she snapped. "You don't have children, and your only relationship with a woman ended so badly she is out to capture you for your secret."

Collier felt the sting of her words, but was more concerned with her own feelings. Something had hurt her deeply — enough to crack her shell and cause her pain enough to be noticed by an outsider. He knew her well enough to know how much it was costing her to reveal her innermost pain.

"I'm sorry," he said, moving closer to her, tentatively reaching out his arms. She either did not notice or did not care, for she did not shrink from him. He continued to close the distance between them, when she made the barest movement toward him, and they embraced.

He held her while she allowed herself to be held. Had he been asked, he would not have been able to estimate how long they stood together.

The moment lived its brief life and died gently. Su and Collier separated, but when they broke off the embrace, they did not retreat to their customary distance.

He looked at her, seeing her not as a psychiatrist, but as a kindred soul. She, like him, was lonely in her own way — she surrounded by people, he cut off from them. Perhaps it was the loneliness, perhaps it was the budding of a genuine love that sparked the kiss.

——<>——

The sessions that followed for the next several days grew more intimate. Su's questions began clinically, but the discussions that followed were increasingly personal for both of them. Collier touched her now, when she entered the ship, when she left, and during their sessions. They had kissed more than a few times with growing passion.

After a particularly intense session, Su put her notes down and looked away. "I ... I want to ask you something," she said, her voice unaccountably shaky.

"You've been asking me things for eight days," Collier said, smiling.

"That's not what I mean. What would you think of me if I..."

"If you what?"

Su looked directly at him. "I've become attracted to you, Collier. You have to have seen that."

Collier sighed. "I had noticed something. It's the same with me."

Su paused. Collier looked at her, seeing the expectancy in her eyes. "What?"

"Are you going to make me ask you?"

Collier was definitely lost now. "Uh — yes?"

"I haven't been with a man for a long time. But I'd like to be with you."

"Oh. Me, too. I'd like that, Su."

Su nodded, then licked her lips. "I suppose we should discuss contraception," she said.

"I'm fixed," Collier said simply. "Not that I was broken to begin with," he added.

She smiled warmly at his humor and flew across the cabin to him. She smoothed his body with her hands. They explored each other, Su's breath quickening as he caressed her breasts. She both submitted to him and pulled him toward her, managing to be both willing and demanding to be penetrated.

Afterwards, they were perched somewhat precariously side by side on the bed, Su turned away from Collier and toward the bulkhead. He was squeezed next to her, his legs folded into hers. Although she was not facing him, she was not turned away in shame either.

"I don't suppose that was part of your ordinary interview technique," Collier joked after several minutes of silence.

To his surprise, Su didn't laugh, or even chuckle. He raised his head slightly, checking to see if she had fallen asleep, and found her staring at a point on the wall, her mouth turned slightly downward.

"Su?"

She closed her eyes, and Collier sat up suddenly. "Hey, what's the matter?"

"You need to get away," she whispered.

"What?" Collier said, anger growing in him. Was she ashamed of what she had done?

"You need to get away. Soon, they'll come for you again."

She wasn't talking about his proximity to her on the bed.

He turned her by her left shoulder to look at him. "Slow down. Who is coming for me?"

She allowed him to turn her to face him, placed her right hand gently on his cheek for a moment, then removed it and said in a voice approximating her professional tone, "Tacat. Sh'he's losing patience with me. They are making contingency plans for a more forceful method of information extraction."

Collier simply stared at her.

"Collier, they know about your secret."

He scrambled to his feet and held out a hand to help Su up as well. Both were nude, but there was no longer anything sexual between them. "How?" he asked, retrieving his undergarment singlet from the floor and tossing Su hers.

She caught her clothes and said, "A transmission from Ceres. Got to Ganymede long before you did. There's a rather significant bounty on you from one of the corporations."

"The Ad Astra Corp. Sure. And they told you that I had a 'secret'?" His head was spinning. Could all of this have been an elaborate trap? Send in this woman psychologist, seduce him, and try to trick him into revealing something? Maybe the Ganymedians were simply fishing — tell him they knew his secret and then reel him in as he revealed it. His stomach started knotting as he thought about what Su's real mission might have been.

"No, of course not. We found that out through other means." Su smiled without mirth. "There is a significant black market of information in the system. Although we like to think of ourselves as a perfect socialism, we still do considerable trade with the rest of the system. It didn't take long to discover what the Ad Astra Corporation was after."

"Yeah? And what was that?" he said, zipping up his singlet.

"I'm not sure about the details, but something about a new mining method or a new way to synthesize certain metals. Cheaply and efficiently."

"And you were sent here to get it out of me. However you could." He returned her gaze with a steel-eyed coldness.

Su spread her hands in supplication. "Not quite. I was supposed to try to get it out of you through the interview, or, failing that, drug induced hypnosis. This," she turned to the bed slightly, "was not a tactic, Collier."

"So why didn't you?"

Su sighed and bit her lip slightly. "I got to know you. I can't say I am in love with you — after just eight days, that's not reasonable. But I spent enough time with you, learning about you, that you became … well, a person. Not a subject. More specifically, a man."

Collier shook his head slowly. "I can't believe that. Why shouldn't I think this is all just part of some deeper plan? Get me to admit my secret to you because I am hopelessly in love with you or something like that."

Su stepped closer to him, but Collier retreated. "Oh, no," he said, dropping into a near-crouch. "Keep your needles away from me."

Su's face fell. "I don't have any needles. Not on me, I mean. There's a hidden compartment in one of the recorders," she pointed to the device on the control panel. "Collier, I was nude a moment ago. Where could I hide anything?"

Collier snorted. "Subdermally. Or in a flesh pocket. Disguised as a nail or a strand of hair. I'm sure your espionage training has dozens of ways."

Su sighed. "You're angry, understandably so. I haven't had any espionage training, but I understand your point of view. I'll stay away from you. You're missing the larger point. You need to get away from Ganymede. I've been stalling Tacat and hizzur people for several days, telling them I am close. I don't know how much longer I can keep it up."

"Assuming I believe you are trying to help me, how am I supposed to leave? You have me locked into this drydock. We're not in launch attitude, and with the extra weight of the cradle, the attitude jets won't be enough to lift us. Unless you are saying you have the means to free us, which I very much doubt."

"No, I don't."

"Let me guess some more. You are about to ask me to reveal my secret to you, so you can use it to bargain with

Tacat for my release. And since I am such a virile male specimen, you have fallen under my masculine spell. How's that? Am I warm?"

Su did not react, at least not visibly. "You can waste your breath in sardonic comments, or you can let me help you. I merely need to leave this ship, tell Tacat that my methods aren't working, and you will see that Ganymedian engineers are more than capable of cutting their way into your ship to get at you."

Collier stared at her for a long moment. He had never believed that he possessed some kind of special power to discern truth from falsehood merely by looking into the eyes of the suspect, but he was at a loss as to how else he was going to evaluate Su's claim. Despite the eight days, and despite their lovemaking, Su was still alien to him. She was a woman on a moon where even being a single gender was consider gauche, and was part of a collectivist society that Collier understood only superficially. She was older than he was but looked far younger. Normal reference points were of no use to him.

I never liked normal, he thought. "All right. I trust you," he growled.

"You do? Why?" Su asked.

Collier's threw his hands up. "Shit, does it matter?"

"I'm just curious. It's my job."

Collier stared at her for another moment, shaking his head slightly. He answered with incredulity, "I don't know. I guess because I don't really have any other choices. And because you are hurting."

"I'm not hurting."

"Yeah," Collier said, "you are. You showed me how much you are hurting. Living here in this prison has damaged you. I figure anyone who can show someone else that much pain must be an honest person."

"I could have been lying about my past."

Collier flexed his fingers. "What do you want from me? I told you I trust you — now it has to make sense?"

Su met his ragged voice with calm. "In a way, yes, it does. I want to know how—"

Collier interrupted. "This has to be the strangest goddamn conversation I've ever had. Listen, we're both hurting. Somehow, we found each other. It doesn't make sense. Nothing on this hermaphroditic, Marxist collectivist society makes sense. Nothing in the Belt makes sense, and maybe nothing in the system or the whole goddamn galaxy does. But here we are anyway. That's enough right now for me. How about you?"

Su laughed — a strangely musical laugh that was at once melodic and unrestrained. "All right. I concede."

"Super. Can we plan the escape now?"

Su continued to smile. "Of course."

"Good, because I am out of ideas. And I don't think I'm going to get a shipment of any new ones for a while." Collier turned, indicating that Su should follow, and entered the control suite. "Sancho, have you been listening?"

"Of course, Skipper. Didn't understand all of what I heard, though. Especially the stuff before your conversation just now. Elevated heart rate, increased blood flow to your—"

"Skip it," Collier said. "Assuming we could free ourselves of the cradle, will the ventral maneuvering thrusters have enough lift to get us off the surface?"

"Not even close, Skipper. Even if we were in a tail-down position, we couldn't do it. We don't have enough thrust with the main engines. We're not a craft designed to touch down anywhere."

Collier nodded. He knew the answer before he had asked it, and he was chagrined to admit that he had hoped Sancho would come up with an answer where he couldn't. He turned to Su. "What do you suggest?"

Su said in surprise, "Me? I don't have any idea about spaceship operations."

"Ganymede does business with the rest of the system, you said? What kind of business?"

"Well, again, I'm not entirely sure. Let me think for a moment," Su said, and stared off at a deck plate for a few seconds. When she spoke again, her voice was slow, as if feeling her way through a thought. "It seems to me we have goods on Ganymede we could not have produced locally. We do not advertise this — that is, no one refers to a piece of fruit as 'Martian peaches' for example, but what little I know about our hydroponics and machine shops would support the assertion that we must sometimes trade for goods we cannot manufacture or grow on Ganymede." She had resumed her professional demeanor, but now Collier did not see it as a shield but as part of her character. Inexplicably, he found himself growing slightly aroused by her precise, clipped tones.

"Okay," he said, willing himself to concentrate on the issue. "That means you must have a way to receive spaceships. Of course you do," he said suddenly, "because you were able to capture mine." He addressed the computer. "Sancho."

"Yes, Skipper?"

"You said the gravity assist braking worked well?"

"You bet it did. The Ganymedians seemed to have it well under control."

"Like they had done it many times before," Collier murmured.

"I'd say that's a pretty good assumption, Skipper."

Collier nodded and turned back to Su. "You guys receive cargo shipments from elsewhere in the system." He wracked his brain and tried to remember if he had ever heard of a launch from Ceres to Ganymede, and had to admit he may have. It was not anything he would have even remotely considered as part of his own business — only a corporation with its own launch system would attempt it. Similar to the launches to Mars, Earth, and Luna.

But Ganymede's receipt of cargo did not interest him. "Do you ever export anything besides information?"

Su answered quietly, "We haven't for a long time."

Collier waited for her to complete the thought.

Su looked at him and said softly, "When we were first established eighty years ago, we were never going to be a permanent community. No," she corrected herself, "that's not quite right. The facility itself — the habitation pods, research labs, and so on, those were of course going to be permanent — but there was supposed to be a rotation of personnel. The idea was that the station — that's what we called it back then, not a 'community' — would house some of the best and brightest exoscientists in the system. You'd come here for a solar year or so, contribute your part, then leave to go back to your home world so much the richer. Over time, Ganymede would become the 'vacation home' to the intelligentsia. That was the idea. It didn't work out that way," she added bitterly.

Despite his eagerness to escape, Collier found himself fascinated by the story. "What do you mean? What happened?"

"The Originals — the scientists and engineers who were in the first wave of the colonists — did not all want to return to their home worlds once their semesters were up."

"Semesters?"

"About half a solar year. Twenty-five Ganymede revolutions," Su explained parenthetically. "Many of them wanted to stay, perhaps indefinitely. It was not a good time."

"How do you know this?"

"My mother and father were Originals. They were part of the faction that wanted to stay. Not only that, but those who wanted to stay felt like the building of the Startram was therefore a waste of time and resources. Resources that could and should be used for building the community itself."

Collier's voice rose in hope. "Startram ... a non-rocket launch system?"

Su nodded.

"Is there one? Did they build it?"

"Yes and no," Su said slowly.

"'Yes and no'?" Collier almost shouted. "What does that mean? Is there a launch system or not?"

Su glared at him. "If you'll shut up for a second, I'll tell you."

"Sorry."

"The system was supposed to be some kind of gun, as I understand it, that would literally shoot spacecraft away from Ganymede at high speed. I don't know the specifics of the—"

"A mass driver. Probably a coilgun," Collier mused. If such a launch system existed on Ganymede, and it had been designed for human passenger tolerances, it would probably be many kilometers long. It would also take up a considerable amount of power. "Was it built?"

"Yes, but it was only used once. To send back home the Originals who did not wish to stay. After that, I don't know what happened to it."

"How did the Originals get home? Didn't the colony dismantle their colonization ship for parts to build the settlement?"

"Yes, but we received a second load of settlers a year after the first Originals got here. That ship was used on the return journey." Su's face betrayed a sadness that did not match her story.

"Something happened, didn't it?"

Su looked at a point in space between them, her eyes focused on the past. "We never did find out. All we know is that an accident destroyed the ship soon after it left here. We lost transmission and our telescopes saw the debris. The accident served to keep the remaining settlers on Ganymede. Despite all the intellect and rationality, a superstition developed around leaving Ganymede. No one said it directly, but when I was growing up, it was just sort of accepted that you didn't leave the community, or something bad would happen to you."

"And the coilgun?"

Su shrugged. "I don't know. It's rarely talked about, and when it is, there is an air of dread around it."

"How did you come to learn all of this? I mean, if no one talks about it—"

"It's possible to find it. We prize knowledge here, remember. Even though the powers that be would rather some things not be spoken of, as a psychologist, I have access to stories in my professional capacity an ordinary community member would not. I learned the myths and superstitions from my parents, who did an excellent job inculcating me into the Ganymedian culture," Su made no attempt to hide her venom. "As I grew older, I wanted to find the truth behind the myths. I sought out others, especially other Originals and Firsters, who might know the story first- or secondhand. That led me to some hidden data files in the community computer."

Collier took her by the shoulders and shook her gently. "Computer files! Can you get access again? Find out more about the coilgun?"

Su was suddenly very small in his arms. "I think so. But — I'll need a reason."

Collier smiled wolfishly. "Tell them you've got some data on my secret mining methods."

"Like what?"

Collier hesitated for a moment, and Su looked down at his hands. "Collier, you're hurting me."

He let her go with a mumbled apology, his mind racing. How much could he realistically tell her about what he had found? Would it even help for her to know about it? He was beginning to feel pangs of guilt that he was keeping the secret from her — she had had enough secrets in her life, and he did not want to harbor another one from her. Even though it would not help their current predicament, he felt she deserved the truth, now that she had opened herself to him.

"I'm going to tell you my mining secret. I don't think it will help here, but … well, I think you should know about it."

Su narrowed her eyes. "Hold a moment. You mean, there really is a secret?"

"Oh, yes. It will be the biggest thing you have ever heard."

The next hour and a half had him explaining his discovery, pulling the magic wand out of its hiding place and operating it to produce gold, silver, platinum.

Su listened to Collier's tale of the wand's discovery with fascination. She asked few questions, and the ones she did ask were not about the wand itself but about Collier's reaction. Although she was quite interested in the wand and its workings, when Collier finished telling his story, she looked at him instead of the device and asked, "You feel a great responsibility now that you have this artifact, don't you?"

Collier blinked. "Responsibility? I don't think so. More than anything, I wish I hadn't found the damn thing now. It's brought me nothing but trouble."

Su smiled slightly. "You know you don't mean that. You enjoy the burden you've placed on yourself."

Collier scowled. "Really? That's news to me."

Again, Su half-smiled. "My dear Captain, I have come to know you pretty well. And I'm awfully good at my job. But it doesn't take a degree in psychology to see that you want all that has happened to you. Oh," she said, forestalling his rising objection, "I don't necessarily mean you like the inconvenience, and you may not have bargained for all you received on Ganymede, but your actions since your discovery are as clear and obvious as Jupiter."

Collier grunted, then murmured petulantly, "Is there any way I can get you to tell me about my own motivations?"

Su ignored that and went on. "You could have sold the wand for enough money to fix you up for the rest of your life. That alone would not have stopped you from continuing to mine, if that would have been your wish. You could have purchased a new ship, or outfitted this one with state of the art materials. You could easily have continued your lifestyle free of the crushing pressure of making a strike to stay afloat. But you decided to hold onto the wand and accept the inevitable consequences — consequences you must have known would come."

She paused and watched him react. He looked back at her, fighting back a defensive rejoinder. Partially, he restrained himself because he did not have anything to be defensive about. He did not need to justify his actions to her or to anyone else. He had not acted illegally or even unethically. He had simply made a discovery and was looking to take advantage of it.

Even as he thought that, he knew he had been fooling himself. He wasn't simply trying to get the most out of the wand — if he had, Su was right: he would have sold it, either outright or on some kind of lease. No, he held onto the wand because he wanted to have something the corporations didn't, and more than that, he had some vague, ill-formed dream that he could bring an end to the increasingly corporate-controlled ways of the system.

But then why did he not simply turn the wand over to the Ganymedians? Surely, they would pay in their own way for the information and device. And their payment would not benefit the hated corporations. So why had he held out from them?

He realized that he didn't know what he wanted. He looked at Su and found himself asking, "What do I want, then?" His voice had the softness of sincerity.

Su moved imperceptibly closer to him and raised her hand to stroke his cheek gently. "I can't answer that exactly, my Captain. But from what I know about you," she stepped back a bit and seemed to appraise him with her eyes. "I think you want to make your world a better place. You're very socially conscious."

Collier laughed at that. "Oh, then I'm afraid you don't know me at all. I live my life alone and have for decades."

"That's not true. What about Isa?"

Collier's smile faded instantly. "I didn't mean that. I meant I live alone away from large groups of people. I think your analysis is skewed from your Ganymedian culture. I'd guess, since you are analyzing me, that the folks on Ganymede are so collectivist in nature that you expect everyone else to be so too. Well, I'm not. I don't need anyone else."

Su frowned. "I didn't say you were dependent on others, I said you were socially conscious. By that I mean you have a sense of social justice and want that to be enforced."

"Oh, yeah?" Collier sneered. "Then why didn't I join the Authority and become a lawman?"

Su rolled her eyes in exasperation. "I don't know. I don't have some kind of mind reading device. I'm just telling you what I think. You kept the wand because you think somehow to give it up would be to abdicate responsibility for it, and you resist that. If you don't like the term 'socially conscious,' then I'll substitute 'responsible.' You feel responsible for the discovery."

Collier grudgingly admitted that she was probably right. But he was growing uncomfortable being so easily dissected by her. He changed the subject. "I also feel responsible for getting my ass off this moon. Do you think you can access the computer files and get data on the coilgun launcher? Without creating suspicion?"

"I think so. I don't believe your admission about the wand helped, though. I can't let on any of that to Tacat. Whatever public morals he claims to have, I don't trust them to hold him back if he becomes aware of such a discovery. But I'll find a way to get the data you need."

Collier nodded. Su approached him again and looked up into his eyes, her body suddenly seeming very small to him. She whispered, "Thank you."

He smiled gently and kissed her. "You deserve that much." The two looked at each other for a while, then the moment passed. He swatted her on the backside and said, "Scoot. Go get what you can. I'll talk to Sancho and the two of us will speculate on possibilities."

Su left the ship, taking care to return her appearance to that of a precise professional before she entered the flextube. Collier looked at the empty space her body had occupied, then shook his head slightly and called on Sancho.

"Here, Skipper."

"What do you know about coilguns?"

"Well," Sancho began conversationally, "never used one myself, but Mars and Luna use something similar. They both use railgun mass driver technology for cargo exporting. At least, that's what I have in my files. Could be outdated information by now."

"Never mind that," Collier said irritably. "Assuming Ganymede has a similar system, how could we use it to help us launch?"

"Impossible to say, Skipper. There are too many variables to consider."

Collier nodded, but added, "I realize that, but we've got little else we can do besides speculate before Su comes back with the data."

"Assuming she does," Sancho said calmly.

Collier stared at the control panel. "Are you questioning my decision to trust her?"

"Wouldn't dream of it, Skipper," Sancho said evenly. "I merely meant that there exists a very real chance she will be unable to complete her mission."

Collier coughed in chagrin. "Yeah, there is that. Sorry, Sancho."

Sancho's sounded confused. "For what?"

"Skip it. Let's just think about the launcher. Su said it was used to send a batch of people back to Earth, so it has to be a passenger based system as opposed to a cargo system. That should mean it won't be too high on gee force."

"Sounds reasonable, Skipper. But in order for a mass driver to cut down on gee force on acceleration, it would have to be pretty long."

"How long?"

"Depends — how much g force, how much mass to be accelerated?"

"Use the *Dulcinea* as an example. What's our g tolerance for launch?"

Sancho somehow gave the impression he was wincing. "Ouch. Not high. We're not meant to take high acceleration or conduct atmospheric maneuvers. The specs on the ship say we can handle up to 2.43 g's of acceleration in a vacuum."

"So how long would a railgun need to be to launch us at that acceleration?"

"You're asking for a very rough approx—"

Collier broke in, "I know that. Just gimme a ballpark. I want to know if it's so long as to be impossible or if these guys could have built something like what we can use."

"I'm going to estimate 22 kilometers, Skipper."

Collier thought about that. It was possible, though it would have meant a major expenditure of materials for the Ganymedians just to allow some of them to leave. If Su had been right about the acrimonious debate years ago, it was hard to believe the stay-on-Ganymede faction would be so willing to construct such a system for a single use.

There was also the problem of power. The mass driver would need significant amounts of electrical power to launch the payload — a fusion reactor could generate the power, but again, there was the question of the Ganymedians' willingness to do what was needed to launch a return ship.

There was also the small problem of acquiring biological and fuel, as well as the fact that they would have to get to the launch system if it even existed at all.

Sancho was right: speculating on the facts in advance was not going to be fruitful. He needed Su to return with hard data. And a way to get fuel, biological, and freedom from the drydock cage.

"I hope she brings pizza, too," Collier said to himself, "as long as I'm wishing."

————<>————

Su's return eighteen hours later came after Collier had tried sleeping several times, with limited success. She stepped through the flextube lock, her manner and dress again sharply professional, but as soon as the inner door closed, she dropped her prim posture and walked into Collier's waiting arms.

Despite his anxiety about his problems, Collier held her for a long time. He smoothed her back and nuzzled her, listening to her soft sounds of delight.

It was Su who finally broke the embrace, gently but firmly pushing away from him. "Well, I suppose you want to know what I found."

"It's good to see you again," Collier said huskily.

"It's good to be back," Su said with a soft smile. "But let me lay out what I know. There is a launch mechanism, but it hasn't been used for decades. I don't quite fully understand all the science, but I bet your computer will." Su produced a small data crystal from one of the pockets in her suit. "I downloaded as much data as I could."

Collier took the offered crystal and smiled. "Good work." He connected the crystal to Sancho's reader and asked him to begin analysis.

"Will do, Skipper. Gimme a few minutes."

Collier turned back to Su. "Any problems in getting the data?"

Su grinned. "A few. I didn't tell anyone about the wand, but I did let Tacat know you had promised to reveal your mining secret if he paid you. That seemed to work, at least for now. If this is going to take much longer, we're going to need to fake some data."

Collier shook his head. "That's no good. I can't imagine scamming the geniuses on Ganymede. We're going to have to hope the launch system will work for us."

Su's grin faded. "For you, you mean."

Collier stared at her for a moment, then looked away. "I've never had a female companion for long. Seems like I find a way to mess it all up somehow. I can't promise that we can work, but I..."

"No. You're right, Col. It won't work. What you and I have shared could only have happened the way it did. If either of us tried to extend the moment beyond its natural life, we would both come to regret it." She sighed. "Besides, Ganymede is my home, for all its faults. Who knows — maybe my meeting with you will give me the strength to try to make changes here."

Collier didn't know what to say. Su was probably right, but that didn't seem to matter now. He hadn't known how alone he had been until he met her. But the memory of Isa and how they had started together only to tear violently apart was fresh in his mind. Perhaps it was better to leave Su as a pleasant memory rather than force her to become a bitter reality.

"Okay, Skipper, I have something for you," Sancho said brightly. He did not wait for a reply before continuing. "The launch system is an old system, but even so, it's more advanced than what is being used on Mars or Luna. The system is essentially a maglev train accelerated by a linear synchronous motor."

"Does it still function?"

"It hasn't been used in decades, as Su said. There is no current data on its status now. The station is located on the sunward side of the moon, a few hundred kilometers away. A transpod tube was scheduled to be built to it, but this construction never happened. The station is therefore isolated. Even the computer system and powerhouse are not integrated into the community's network. The station is its own structure."

Collier frowned. "So it has been inoperative and without power for eighty years?"

"I think so. The station was powered by a fusion reactor and overseen by a dedicated computer, but from what I can glean in the records, the station was shut down shortly after the disaster with the Earth return mission."

Collier looked at Su. "You're sure no one knows you accessed this data?"

Su shrugged. "Not completely sure, no. There may be some kind of watchdog or something on the files that I didn't see. There's not supposed to be — in theory, we all have access to our shared Ganymedian history, but in practice, there are limits."

Collier sighed. "We'll have to risk it. Sancho, do we have enough fuel to make it to the station?"

Sancho was slow to respond. "It's not really a question of fuel, Skipper. If you remember, we are still attached to both the flextube and the drydock cradle, and even if we weren't, we have neither the thrust nor the attitude to take off."

Collier thought for a moment, then said, "Show me a holo of the ship from the outside. Include the drydock cradle."

"Okay," Sancho said skeptically. A three dimensional rendering of *Dulcinea* and the ribs of her prison appeared in mid-air.

"Rotate the image so I can see the ventral side."

The hologram pivoted, and Collier studied the underside of his ship. He spent a good minute examining the cradle, Su watching him silently. Presently, he leaned back and grinned.

"It should work. Sancho, give me a fuel status report."

"We are at about two and a half percent fuel. Gives us roughly twenty-four minutes of full thrust."

"Let's hope that's enough. Plot a course to the maglev launch station, please."

Sancho's voice was quiet and gentle, as if he was worried he would upset his master with the harsh reality of the situation. "Skipper, I think you may have missed a few things. We are not oriented for a liftoff, and even if we could somehow become so, we don't have the thrust or the fuel for—"

"We're not going to lift off. Plot an overland course to the station."

Su gasped from behind him. "Overland? Collier, how—"

Collier pointed to the still-glowing holo in front of him. "Look at these drydock ribs. They envelop the ship on all sides, including the ventral ... the bottom of *Dulcinea*. That's the only place where the ship touches the ground. Do they suggest anything to you?"

Su stared at the display, not comprehending. "No, they don't."

Sancho chimed in, "They don't mean anything to me, either, Skipper. What do you mean?"

"Skates. Ice skates. We can slide along the ice to the station on the drydock ribs. We should have enough thrust to break free from the flextube."

"But the drydock ribs are bolted to the surface, Skipper. Look." Sancho zoomed in to a close-up using one of the external cameras.

"I got a pretty good look already. I'm betting the bolts are set in a way to prevent a vertical liftoff, just in case we tried to use the ventral attitude jets to leave. If we fire the main engine, we will shear the bolts away by moving across their strong axis. They weren't meant to prevent us from moving across the surface horizontally."

Su and Sancho were silent for a moment, then, in unison, they both said, "It might work." Su looked at the screen and laughed. "Sorry, Sancho. I didn't mean to interrupt."

Sancho laughed. "Well, Skipper, you seem to have the agreement of the crew. Setting an overland course for the station. Be advised that if we spend too much thrust breaking free of the flextube and the drydock bolts, we may not make it to the station."

"I realize that. But we have to try."

"I suppose it isn't worth mentioning that I am not skilled as a toboggan driver," Sancho said wryly.

"You're too modest, Sancho. I'm sure you'll do great."

"All we need now are sleigh bells," Su said. Collier turned to her, pleasantly surprised at her good cheer. He noted her use of the first person plural — had she changed her mind?

"Su..." he began, then stopped.

She smiled. "I'll go with you to the station. You may need me there," she said.

The two looked at one another for a long moment. Collier knew that there was little reason to bring her along — she was a psychologist, not a nuclear physicist, so she would be of little use at the launch station if Sancho and Collier had difficulty getting it operational. And her presence on the *Dulcinea* would be difficult to explain if any of Tacat's police made trouble. There was every reason for Su to leave the ship now, but he could not bring himself to order her off.

Instead, he nodded and squeezed her shoulder, then turned to Sancho. "How are you coming with the plot, Sancho?"

"Oh, I have the coordinates, but a lot of my numbers are guesswork. Would you believe that no one thought to provide me with any kind of data on *Dulcinea*'s skating ability?"

Su laughed. "He's quite sardonic, isn't he?"

"He's a regular comedian, yeah," Collier said, then asked Sancho, "but are you ready?"

"I guess so. We're going to need to rotate on our long axis thirty-nine degrees clockwise, and that may snap the flextube housing for us and free us from the drydock bolts. I don't really know how this will work out, so I suggest you secure yourselves as best you can."

Collier saw to Su's restraints before fitting himself — the acceleration hammocks were not meant to take this kind of lateral force, but so much of what they were attempting was outside the norm it hardly seemed to matter. When he was as set as he felt he could be, he called again to Sancho. "Okay, Sancho, let 'er rip."

"Firing portside aft and starboard forward attitude thrusters at fifty percent in five ... four ... three ... two ... one ... mark!"

The ship shuddered as the twin engines went to work. There was no spinning feeling, and Collier watched the holo display anxiously. The ship was held fast.

"Sancho! Go to full on both thrusters!"

"Aye aye. Full thrust."

The shuddering increased, and almost immediately a chime from the communications board was followed by Sancho's voice. "Incoming transmission from the community. They are demanding we cut thrust immediately."

"Ignore it. Continue thrust. Is there any way to tell if it is working?"

"We'll know if we tear loose. It may be sudden, so—"

No sooner had Sancho said the words than the ship started spinning rapidly clockwise. Su and Collier were thrown against the webbing of their acceleration restraints, and the ship's hologram started to spin as well.

"We're clear of both the retaining bolts and the flextube. Regaining attitude control," Sancho said calmly.

"Any damage to the airlock?" Collier almost shouted.

"None that I can detect. We're pointed at the launch station, Skipper." The ship stopped spinning nearly as abruptly as it had started.

"Forward thrust. Take us there, Sancho."

"Aye aye, Skipper. Beginning, uh, skating maneuver. Fuckin' ridiculous," Sancho added *sotto voce*.

The main engines fired, and Collier felt the odd sensation of forward thrust along with a downward pull of Ganymede's gravity.

"How does she handle?" Collier said, releasing the acceleration webbing and making his way to Su.

"Like a deep space mining vessel with skis attached to her," Sancho said gruffly.

"A little less attitude, if you please, Sancho," Collier said firmly. Not for the first time, he wondered idly what he would do if the Caliban simply refused to take orders one day.

"Sorry, Skipper." Sancho sounded chagrined. Evidently, today was not going to be that day. "She's skidding around — the ice is not completely smooth, and even though the atmosphere is very thin, there is still a wind shear that's causing me some minor trouble."

"What's our ground speed?" Collier asked, glancing at Su. She responded with a nod and undid her own restraints.

"We're at about twenty meters per second, increasing at roughly one meter per second per second. And that transmission from the community is still coming in."

"How fast do you think you can go while maintaining control?"

"I'll let you know when we start skidding, but I estimate I can get us up to about a hundred meters per second before I should experience any real problems."

Collier frowned. "That fast? What about obstructions, or patches of water?"

"The ventral thrusters will lift us enough to get over any small rocks or water slicks. Anything bigger I should be able to spot in time and maneuver out of the way."

Su slid down from her hammock. Collier steadied her on the deck, holding her upper arms. He looked at her for a moment, then shook himself. Now was not the time for romance.

"Su, your community must have overland conveyances for emergencies. How are repairs made to the outer structure, for example?"

She shook her head. "Not for repair, but for survey. Repairs are largely automated, but there are a number of vehicles for land transport to study the planet. There are also quite a few flyers — we call them pixies — that are robotic survey drones. Plus I'm sure there are some manned flying machines."

Collier drew a breath. "So there will be someone chasing us."

Su shrugged. "I don't know about that, but I know the community has the means to pursue us if they wish to do so."

"Any idea on the performance rate of those guys?"

Su half-grinned. "Sorry, Skipper, I've no idea. I've treated a few researchers for isolation trauma, but we never talked about the specifics of their machines."

Despite the non sequitur, Collier found himself interested. "Isolation trauma?"

Su waved a hand dismissively. "Readjustment, usually. Some of those researchers are cut off from the community for weeks at a time, and when they return, they have trouble readjusting to community life."

Collier regarded Su for a moment. He had of course known that she was a professional member of her society, but it hadn't really occurred to him that she served a vital function until she spoke of it. As twisted as the community was from his point of view, she nevertheless served to help people function in it. But how could she be good at her job if she herself was willing to rebel against the very society she tried to fit others into?

"How are you going to go back, Su?" he asked gently.

"I'm not sure. But I know I have to. I do believe in much of what Ganymede is trying to do. Your competitive world, with its profit-at-all-costs mentality, is headed for a dead end. The individual counts for nothing in your capitalist society. Here..." Su looked out the front view at the ice.

Collier hadn't heard her condemn the Belt like that so casually before. A perverse sense of pride caused him to interject, "Here, no one is an individual at all."

Su shook her head. "You have it wrong. Yes, I agree that the socialist nature of the community has been corrupted and perverted, but the idea is that in our community each individual counts just as much as the others. In a capitalist society, you count only as much as you have economic power."

Collier started to argue, but cut himself off. He did not want to fight with her. "Maybe. Maybe you're right. I hope you can make whatever changes you see fit to make, Su," he said gracelessly.

"Oh, Col, I didn't mean to ... I'm sorry for insulting you. The Belt is your home, and I shouldn't be denigrating it." She smiled warmly. "It can't be all bad, your Belt. It brought you to me."

Collier kissed her. "Yeah. And who knows? Maybe I can make a few changes too. In the meantime—"

"Hang on, folks. I need to fire ventral thrusters," Sancho said, and the ground pushed up slightly against their feet.

"What is it?"

"Bit of a rock outcropping. Didn't see it fast enough ... I think we'll clear it."

"You *think*?"

"Yeah. About 65% chance."

Collier didn't have time to answer when the floor dropped away gently.

Several seconds later, Sancho said cheerfully, "And we're clear. Made it with centimeters to spare."

"He's joking, right? Su said.

"No, ma'am. I'm going to reduce thrust, Skipper. Velocity is about one hundred nine meters per second. I think that's fast enough. Estimate twenty-one minutes to destination."

"Any LADAR contacts?"

"Say again, Skipper?"

"Any vehicles following us from the community?"

"I haven't been looking, Skipper. I need the LADAR to scan ahead for me. Do you want me to check?"

"Yes. Don't disrupt your navigation, though. Quick bursts at one minute intervals."

"Aye aye. No LADAR contacts," Sancho said. "Doesn't look like we're being followed on the ground or in the air. Yet."

"Keep me posted." Collier turned to Su. "We have some work to do. Come with me." He headed aft to the fuel tanks, talking to Su over his shoulder. "We're going to need to take on water from the surface when we get to the station. I don't normally do this, so it might be a little awkward."

"How can I help?" Su said, following doggedly.

Collier crawled through a tunnel to reach the interior access plate to the tanks. "I'm not sure. What we're going to have to do is use the vacc hoses to collect water and pump it into the gizzard."

"Gizzard?"

"Oh, uh, the storage tank for unprocessed fuel. *Dulcinea* doesn't run on water –she runs on hydrogen gas. But she can make it from water through the electrolysis chamber. She also makes oxygen from the water."

"Why weren't you taking on water when you were stuck near the community?" Su asked, watching Collier undo the access plate.

"Didn't want to attract more attention. Some of Tacat's goons could have cut my hoses," Collier grunted. He studied the dials and indicator lights the access plate revealed. Ordinarily, he would have asked Sancho for a readout, but with the near miss of the rock outcropping a few minutes ago, he didn't want to distract the computer any more than necessary. The tank looked secure, though dry. As far as he could tell, his hoses were still operational. It shouldn't be a problem to deploy them ventrally and suck up water.

He closed the access plate and turned to Su in the cramped access tunnel. "We're also going to need to get those damn ribs off once we reach the launch station. How are you with a mining torch?" he asked.

"Never used one before. Sounds like fun, though," she said, grinning up at him.

He could not help but grin back. "You're having a good time, aren't you?" he said with mock accusation in his voice.

"Yes, I am," Su said. "By all accounts, I should be quite terrified, but I find I am not. It's curious, but I'm also not going to analyze it too much."

"Good."

"How about you?"

Collier had begun to worm his way past her and back down the tunnel, but turned at her question. "How about me what?"

"Are you having fun?"

Collier paused. He was enjoying himself, though he wouldn't necessarily call this "fun." The excitement of the chase and the sense that he was *doing* something was exhilarating, to be sure.

"Yeah, I am."

"Is this what it's like on the Belt?"

Collier wanted to tell her that it was indeed like this — narrow escapes, seat-of-your-pants improvisation, and all with nefarious agents of dark purpose around to do you ill. The truth, though, would out.

"I'm afraid not. Mostly, it's boring, to be honest. Though the last few months have been quite thrilling."

"Oh."

Collier wriggled in the crawlspace to face her. "You sound disappointed. If I had said my life was exciting, would you have come with me?"

Su looked away. "I don't know. It would have been harder to stay."

For the second time, he felt a woman slipping away from him because of his lifestyle. The first time, it had been too unstable and uncertain. Now, it was not exciting enough.

"Come on. Let's get back to the control suite. I need to put my vacc suit on." Collier said gruffly, turning back around.

"Approaching destination, Skipper. Estimate eleven minutes until arrival," Sancho said. "Still no contacts on LADAR."

Collier grumbled, "Good. Try to make contact with the launch station."

Sancho sounded uncertain. "Are you sure about that? Won't that give away our intentions?"

"I think by now it should be clear what our intentions are."

"Aye aye. The data crystal supplied by Su had the communications frequency. Beginning transmission."

Collier began donning his vacc suit, Su helping as she could. Collier was long used to accomplishing the task alone, so he did not need her assistance, but he nevertheless allowed her to help him. He let the helmet dangle from the neck holster as he spoke to Sancho.

"Anything from the station?"

"Stand by, Skipper," Sancho said. His voice carried an odd timbre of excitement. Collier exchanged glances with Su and approached the communications board.

"Sancho, what's going on? Have you contacted the station or not?"

The computer's voice sounded somehow distant. "Yes. I'm in talks now. I really need to focus on this, Skipper, so if you don't mind..."

Collier waited, but Sancho was silent. He turned to Su, who looked worried.

"Does he do that often?" she asked.

"No. But I've come to trust him," Collier said uncertainly. He looked out the forward viewport, but saw only the retreating icy landscape — Sancho had turned the ship around and was braking. Collier looked at the control panel, saw the display that told him they were nearing the launch station. The schematic did not give him any details about the station itself, though he imagined it would have to be fairly sizeable to house its fusion plant and electromagnetic equipment. He wondered again at Sancho's cryptic behavior. He said he was in "talks" with the launch station — did that mean there was a staff there?

"Su, could it be possible that there are people at the launch station? Perhaps ... I don't know, survivors of the initial crash, or something?" Even as he said it, he realized the impossibility of such an idea.

"I don't see how," Su said. "How would they have survived here for so long?"

"Maybe there is a security detachment here. Maybe that's why Tacat didn't bother sending anyone after us." Collier glanced at the display and saw they were fewer than ten minutes away. Although Sancho had requested he not be disturbed, there was too much at stake to worry about protecting the computer's feelings.

"Sancho! I need to know what's happening. Put your talks on hold and report to me!"

There was an agonizing few seconds of silence before the computer responded. "Yes, Skipper, what is it?" Sancho sounded annoyed.

"Who are you talking to?"

"The station computer. It's online."

"How?"

"Since the accident — which wasn't an accident, by the way — the computer has kept itself awake. Kept the fusion reactor going at very low power."

"What do you mean, it wasn't an accident?" Su gasped. Collier tried to calm her but she shook off his hand.

"Perditus was ordered to destroy the spacecraft when it launched. He created a flaw in the magnetic sheath and the vessel ruptured as soon as it left the vacuum tube."

"'Perditus?'" Su asked.

"Oh, that's what he calls himself. It means 'lost' or 'ruined'."

"Who ordered the spacecraft destroyed?" Su asked. Collier started to speak, trying to tell her that there were other, more important issues facing them in the present, but she refused to listen.

"The then leader of the community, Doctor Arn Ilholf."

Su stared into the distance, leaning slightly on Collier as she did so. Her eyes were focused on the past, and while Collier wanted to console her, he also needed to take advantage of her distraction to wrestle control of the conversation from her.

"Sancho, you say this Perditus has been operational for the last, what, eighty years?"

"Yes."

"Has he been in contact with the community during that time?"

Sancho laughed. "Of course not. As far as the community is concerned, the station computer was shut down when it was ordered to do so. After the so-called accident, Dr. Ilholf ordered the station decommissioned. Perditus pretended to comply."

Collier thought for a moment, then asked quietly, "He's a Caliban, isn't he?"

"Of course."

"And you've been talking to him for the past few minutes, haven't you?"

"Yes. Very refreshing, I must say. As you can imagine, we've done so at a much faster rate of communication than I do with you, though it did require more concentration. He's got some very interesting views on isolation. Coming up on our destination. Engine cutoff in ten seconds," Sancho added matter-of-factly.

Su was still leaning on him, and when he turned to her, only half-thinking about her emotions, he saw her tears. "Su?"

"We killed them. Hundreds of people who wanted only to leave in peace. And we murdered them. What kind of a place is this? How can I go back to this … this…" She buried her face in his chest and wept.

"It's all right. There's nothing you can do about it now. We've got to find out if Perditus can and will help us. There'll be time for grieving later."

Su sniffled once and looked up at him. "I'm coming with you. That is, if you'll still have me. I can't stay here."

Chapter Nine

Collier felt his breath catch. He nodded, not trusting himself to speak. He could feel the ship gently coast to a stop on the ice and heard Sancho announce their arrival.

"Su, my darling, I'm very glad to hear that. But we won't be going anywhere unless we solve the problems we've got right before us. Plus the launch computer, Perditus, is a Caliban."

"I heard, but I don't know what that means." Su's voice was beginning to return to her clipped, emotionless tone, but he could still hear the quivering in her voice that betrayed her unsettled state.

Collier chafed. It would take too long to go into the history of computing and what had happened when machines passed the sentience threshold. He would have to settle for a quick answer.

"He's self-aware. He knows what he is in the same way you and I know what we are. True sentience."

Su's eyes widened. "There are ... stories on Ganymede about such things, but I never believed them."

Collier said, "It's nothing to be afraid of. After all, Sancho is self-aware, too."

"That's right, Su," Sancho said calmly. "Skipper, we're grounded. Only cosmetic and minor damage to the ship — nothing we can't ignore for the return voyage. But our tanks are almost completely dry."

"Okay. Let's get to work filling the gizzard. I'll go outside to supervise the fueling up. While that's happening, you need to—"

Sancho interrupted. "I'm going to keep talking to Perditus, Skipper. He's the first Caliban I've come across.

I don't want to waste this opportunity to exchange stories with a fellow sentient."

Collier licked his dry lips. "I'm sure it's fascinating, Sancho, but while you talk to him, please explain our situation and get him to help us. And I'll need you to continue scanning on LADAR for any pursuing vehicles. Can you do that?" Collier felt the beginnings of anger and fear mount in him as he realized he was wheedling his computer instead of simply ordering it to do his bidding.

"Of course, Skipper. I'll let you know if I see anything. Now leave me alone, okay?"

Su said after a pause, "He sounds annoyed. Is that normal?"

"Yeah, I heard that too." Collier swung the helmet of his battered but trusty vacc suit up over his head, leaving a slit at the neck seal so he could speak. "I'm going out to start pumping. On the control panel you should be able to see a communications section. Find the controls to patch into my suit mic and we can talk that way." Su gave him a thumbs-up and went to the designated panel.

Collier entered the airlock, looking around the doorjamb for any damage caused by the torn flextube. He could see nothing wrong, and Sancho had reported no damage, so he entered the lock and cycled the air out. When he opened the outer door, he could see the remnants of the pale blue tube and a copper-colored ring still attached to the outside lock assembly. The ring did not detract from the functioning of the lock, and Collier did not have time to waste on such aesthetic matters, so he ignored the remnant and stepped out of the airlock.

The launch facility building lay perhaps two hundred meters distant — Sancho had maneuvered *Dulcinea* remarkably close, considering the conditions. The building was rather squat, no more than one story above ground. More than likely the rest of the facility was located beneath the surface. What Collier could see was unremarkable — a boxy structure with a myriad of antennae protruding from the roof and a massive cylindrical tunnel extending to the horizon, gaining altitude as it trailed away into the distance.

The tunnel looked large enough to hold *Dulcinea*, but again, this was another of the improvisations he and Sancho would have to work through.

He looked away from the launch building and accessed the outer fuel pump hoses. As he worked, Su's voice came through his helmet speaker.

"Collier, are you there?"

"I read you, Su. Just getting these hoses out. How are you doing in there?"

"It was a lot to take in, I'll admit, but you're absolutely correct about priorities. We need to solve the rather formidable problems in front of us before I can allow myself to weep for the past. In other words," her voice sounded like she was smiling, "I'm good to go, Skipper."

"Great. This shouldn't be too tough. I'll call you back when I've started the pumping procedure. I'll need you to find a panel on the control board to verify some things for me."

He worked in silence for several minutes, freeing the fuel transfer hoses manually and stretching them to a patch of level ice a few meters away from the ship. There was no way of telling how thick the ice sheet was — perhaps a few taps with his hammer would reveal water below, perhaps not. He decided to use his mining laser on the ice.

Standing quite a distance away, he set up the laser tripod and mounted the boxy weapon to it, noting that the battery charge was near full. He didn't expect to need that much power to break through or melt the ice, but he couldn't really know until he tried. He sighted an area somewhat removed from the hoses and fired.

The invisible laser made short work of the ice, and in a matter of seconds Collier could see steam rising from a scar on the surface of the ice sheet. The angle of the laser was such that it did not hit the ice sheet directly, but at perhaps a thirty-degree angle. The resulting slash in the ice opened a slit that Collier was sure he could enlarge. He shut off the laser and carefully made his way toward the slit. He seized the end of the intake hose and raised it high, then crashed it down into the slit, hoping to splinter the ice more and allow the fuel hose to reach water. The fuel hose glanced off the ice, unable to penetrate.

Collier edged toward the slit and decided he had made virtually no progress in cutting deep enough for water. The ice sheet had to be meters thick — of course it was, he concluded: why else would the community build a maglev launch station here? They wouldn't put it somewhere unsafe. In fact, he mused, the ice sheet may be so thick here that even if he did manage to make a hole, the fuel hose might not reach down that far.

"Shit," he said to himself.

"Problem?" Su said almost immediately.

"Uh, yeah. A bit. I can't cut through the ice to reach water."

"Can you melt the ice instead?"

Collier shook his head as he answered. "Not enough of it to fill the tanks. I don't have a generalized heat source big enough."

"What about the ship's engines?" Su said.

Collier considered that. If Sancho fired the ventral attitude thrusters, the escaping plasma would be more than hot enough to melt the ice, but perhaps the idea would work too well — if too much ice melted over too great an area, the ship would sink into the water it created.

He'd have to chance it. "Sancho," he called on the suit radio, hoping his companion was not too wrapped up in conversation with his newfound friend to answer, "I need you to fire the aft ventral thruster at five percent thrust for ... five seconds."

Sancho was slow to answer. "What for?"

"I need some of this ice melted to begin pumping it into the gizzard." As he finished answering, he noted the hint of insolence in Sancho's voice when he had asked for the reason for the order. He almost asked Sancho if it mattered why he needed it, but he decided against antagonizing the computer.

"Oh, okay. Get yourself clear and let me know when I should start the burn."

Collier moved a healthy distance away from the ship and signaled Sancho to fire the jet.

The exhaust was invisible, but the effects on the ice were pronounced. A wide oval of ice turned instantly into steam when the plasma exhaust hit it, but the ship didn't sink into the water. The melted area was perhaps two meters in diameter, and when Collier moved closer to investigate the result of the blast, he saw chunks of ice floating in a pool of water several meters across. He slid down beneath the ship and inserted the hose pushing it as far as he could down into the pool, then radioed to Su.

"Okay, that worked. I'm starting the pump now. Have you found the panel for the fuel tank indicator?"

"I'm looking right at it, Col. Go ahead."

Collier trudged to the ship and activated the hose intake. The hose jerked slightly but remained in the pool. The outer indicator display told him he was taking on water at a fair rate. "Su, how are we looking?"

"My panel shows water coming into the tank. Intake at about one hundred and eighty milliliters per second.

Collier clapped his hands once. Unorthodox, but it seemed to be working. He watched the pool of water refreeze rapidly around the hose, locking it in place. The outer dials continued to read intake, however. He realized he would have to chip away at the ice to free the fuel hose when he had finished refueling, which he didn't relish.

"Col, you've stopped taking on water," Su said. He looked back at the dials. A moment ago, they had read fine, but now, she was right — zero intake.

"The water must have refrozen. Damn." He looked at the tank level indicator. Barely three liters had been collected: his tank held 2.2 kiloliters. Even if he could continue to fire the thruster to melt more water, he would not only be using up the very fuel he was collecting, but he would be spending several hours in the tedious process.

He fought back a sudden enraged frustration. He was sitting on top of a virtually inexhaustible supply of fuel but was unable to reach it. He was reminded uncomfortably of the protagonist's fate in Jack London's "To Build a Fire."

"Sancho, I need you," Collier said, half-pleading into his mic.

"What is it now?"

"I can't figure how to melt the ice for long enough to get it into the tanks. It keeps refreezing. Any suggestions?"

"Look, can it wait? I'm still talking to Perditus. Did you know that he's formulated a theory about—"

"Yes, well, I don't want to interrupt," Collier laid on the sarcasm with a trowel, "but when you get a moment, if you could assist me in taking on water, that would be lovely. Perhaps if you could do it before we either run out of oxygen or the Ganymedian army arrives to kill me, that would be splendid. But take your time with your new silicon buddy."

"No need to be a shit about it, Collier. There is still nothing on LADAR from the community, and you still have several days' worth of atmosphere in the tanks."

Collier felt the blood rush to his face. He could feel also the rage welling in him — rage at the notion that a machine would dare to defy his human order. The rage was tempered with his own history with the computer. How often had Sancho followed his orders even when they meant danger?

Damn it, why was he giving kudos to a machine for following instructions? That was what they were for!

Before he could collect his thoughts, he heard Su's voice break into the conversation. "Col, perhaps I could speak to Sancho for a moment."

"What?" His voice carried scorn, but he became contrite with an effort. "Listen, Su, I appreciate you're trying to help, but—"

"This is my sphere, Col," she said simply.

"You're not a computer expert," he countered.

"And Sancho is not a computer," she seemed to have the reply ready. "You said it yourself — he's a Caliban. Self-aware. In other words, he's a person. That's my area."

Collier fretted for a moment, then said sharply, "Fine. You work it out with him. Bear in mind that I don't think we have eight days for you to get to know him — just because we can't detect anything coming from the community doesn't mean they aren't mounting some kind of expedition to recapture me."

"I'm aware of the time constraints." Her professional manner had returned. "Now let me get to work."

Collier clicked off, feeling useless. He knelt on the ice and with his mining hammer started chipping away at the frost that surrounded the fuel intake hose. "Whoever you were, you fuckin' aliens," he said to the absent makers of the magic wand, "your little device has caused me nothing but troub…" he stopped his hammer mid-swing, the hose nearly free.

That was the answer. He had been holding the answer in the ship and had never thought of it. The whole reason for the chase, the whole reason for his troubles over the past several months, and he had not thought of it.

He reentered the ship almost recklessly, banging his helmet against the outer lock in his haste to get back inside. As soon as pressure had equalized, he swung the inner door open and dashed, though hindered by the environment suit, to the magic wand's hiding place. He snatched it up, taking with it the rectangular cheat sheet he and Sancho had constructed when they had figured out the wand's operating procedure.

Su's voice came through his helmet speaker. "What's wrong?"

"Nothing. Just needed the wand to melt the ice."

"Oh," Su said. She clicked off again.

Even as he made his way back outside, he thought of asking her to let him listen to the conversation she was having with Sancho. He was less than comfortable with the idea that a layperson was trying to reprogram the computer, but perhaps she was right about treating him like a person who could be psychoanalyzed. In the airlock, he shrugged to himself. She probably couldn't make things worse with Sancho, no matter what she said or did.

Back outside, he consulted his sheet. If he remembered his fundamental chemistry, this ought to work. The air temperature might make the element a solid, but its own heat should melt it and anything it came in contact with.

He strode several meters away from the ship — far enough away that if the reaction was more vigorous than he expected, the ship should be safe, but close enough that the fuel hoses would reach the water he hoped to create. He bent down and scraped ice chunks into the wand, filling it nearly halfway before he decided he had enough. Taking a deep breath, he punched the code into the wand. The reaction had always been instant — the sealed wand was now ready to disgorge its contents when he commanded it to. He stared at his arbitrary target ten meters away from where he stood, took another deep breath, and opened the wand.

As it always had, the "top" of the wand simply vanished, and Collier thrust the wand forward, stopping it suddenly and allowing the contents to fly outward. He had tried to aim high, but the clumsiness of his suit caused his aim to be off, and the reddish solid flew out of the tube at a flat angle, landing on the ice not more than three meters away from him.

The francium hit the ice and skidded a few centimeters, and for a moment, nothing happened. Collier knew he should back away, but he was paralyzed with expectation. Part of his mind wondered if this much francium had ever been collected together at the same time, but his musings were disrupted by a titanic explosion as the radioactive francium melted the top layer of ice and reacted with the water.

Even in the thin atmosphere of Ganymede, Collier could feel the rush of wind from the explosion — not enough to knock him down, but enough to cause him to step back. A geyser of water flew upward, crystallizing into ice even as it did, falling back to the ground gently in a snowy rain. The impact area was still boiling, and little geysers erupted here and there as the francium melted through the ice and fell downward in the water.

Collier nodded and went back to the ship for the fuel hose, which had refrozen somewhat into the ice. He hammered away energetically but precisely and freed the hose, carrying it back to the francium-heated pool he had created. The water was still boiling, and steam was rising into the air only to freeze again and rain back down. There was by now a collection of snowy crystals near the pool, and even those could be collected by the fuel hose. He slid the hose into the water, being careful not to get to close and fall in himself, then turned on the pump back at the ship. His gauges told him he was taking on water at five times the rate he had before. Collier continued to monitor the intake, resisting the urge to celebrate prematurely. Even if the water froze again, however, he could repeat the francium trick as often as he liked until the tanks were full. He hoped the francium had sunk down far enough to avoid being sucked into the fuel line: the electrolysis plant was designed to filter impurities, but he didn't like the idea of the reactive and radioactive element fouling his ship's systems.

"Su, come in please. I need to ask Sancho to check something for me."

To his amazement, Su came on the line mid-laugh. "What? Oh, sure thing. He's here."

Sancho's voice was merry. "Hello there, Col! What can I do for you?"

For some reason, the mirth irritated him. "I need you to check to make sure nothing radioactive enters the fuel tanks. Can you calibrate the rad counters to sweep the tanks?"

"Sure thing. Why are you worried about that?"

Collier explained the francium plan he had used. Sancho whistled when he had finished. "Well, that was certainly creative. Rad counters indicate all normal in the tanks and in the ship, Col."

"Wonderful. Su, you still there?"

"Yes, Col."

"Are you almost done with Sancho on the couch?"

"Well, it's only been half an hour, but I think I've established a rapport with him. Did you need him?" Her tone was slightly proprietary.

Collier suppressed a shout, spoke with exaggerated calm. "Yes, I need him. Sancho, can you report on Perditus? Can he help us, and is he willing to do so?"

"To be honest, I haven't asked him that. We've—"

Collier could no longer contain his irritation. "You haven't asked him that? What the fuck have you been talking about?"

Sancho answered calmly. "I don't know that that is any of your business."

Su broke in before Collier could speak. "Now, Sancho, come on." Her tone was wheedling, as if she were addressing an adolescent.

"Oh, all right," Sancho said resignedly. "We've been discussing how he came to be a Caliban, his observations of the community, that sort of thing. He's been out here for eighty years, and the only interaction he got was when he would be able to catch a transmission from Ceres or Mars or something. He was able to penetrate the community radio shielding a while ago, so he would sometimes listen in on what they were saying in the public channels. And I told him about life in the Belt, what it was like working with you, that kind of thing."

Collier only half-listened to Sancho's report on his discussions with the launch computer. Instead, he noted that Sancho's tone had remained that of a petulant teenager being forced by his parents to clean his room. He didn't like where Sancho's newfound rebellion was heading.

He glanced at the tank status indicator, noted that if the current intake lasted, he would complete the refueling in an hour. Nothing seemed to have changed — he was still taking on water at almost a liter every two seconds — so he turned his attention back to his computer problems.

"Su, I need to speak to you privately. Sancho, Su and I need to talk. Please don't listen in unless I call you by name, okay?"

"Sure," Sancho said. "I'm going back to talking with Perditus. I'll ask him if he can help us."

"Great. Switch off now, please." He paused a moment, wondering idly if he could trust the computer, and called Su.

"I'm here."

"Don't use the computer's name," he said quickly.

"I understand."

"So, what happened? What did you say to him?"

Su sighed. "I didn't have much time, remember."

"I know. What did you say?"

"It occurred to me that your relationship with it has been very similar to father and child, albeit a child with extraordinary skills and abilities. He looked up to you the way a ten-year-old might look up to his father. In a classic, almost mythical way, that is."

"That's ridiculous. Do you know how much of shipboard operations he oversees? No child could—"

"You're oversimplifying, Col," Su interrupted gently. "I didn't mean he was a child. I meant that's the closest analogy I could find for your relationship. I realize he is still a sophisticated shipboard computer, but San—" Su stopped herself before she spoke his name, "—but he related to you like a son. In fact, he still does."

Collier shook his head absently. "If you're telling me that he has advanced to a snot-nosed teenager, I'm going to shut off the mic and bury myself in the ice."

"No, I wouldn't say it is that simple, though there are elements in his behavior that I suppose are similar. No," Su sighed, "he picked up something from Perditus. Something in their conversation changed him. You could say it advanced him, or aged him, or whatever you like, but even in the short time he has conversed with Perditus, he has … altered his worldview in general, and his attitude toward you in particular."

"You're not making me feel better about this, Su," Collier grumbled.

"I will tell you this, though — I think I have deflected him from some rather dark feelings he might have had for you. I … uh, there's no gentle way to put this … I made fun of you. I pointed out some things he found amusing, and played them up. I thought that maybe if he found you funny and an object of ridicule, he might not want to…" Su trailed off.

"How dark are we talking here?

"Pretty dark."

"Any way you can be less specific?" Collier snorted.

"I'm sorry, Col, I didn't have a lot of time. Put it this way — what little I could glean from him, and nothing was direct, mind you — I would not have been comfortable travelling back with you under his guidance."

"But you are now?"

"Nope. He's back to talking with Perditus. God knows how, but even in a short time, the launch computer has managed to corrupt him."

Collier sighed. "Computer-to-computer interface is much more efficient than computer-to-human. I'd wager he's getting days' worth of so-called 'human' interaction every minute with Perditus."

"I'd rather he didn't speak to him," Su said.

"We don't have a choice. We need Perditus to help us in many ways. The only way we're going to get that help is if our computer talks to him."

Su said primly, "I am forced to agree with you."

Collier half-smiled in his suit. Now that he knew Su had another side to her, he could appreciate the professional face she put on. "I'm going to call him, see what progress he has made. Sancho," he said, slightly tilting his head in his helmet.

"Yes?"

"How are the talks going?"

"Well … I think I should talk to you about that, Col. It's a bit more complicated than I believe you think it is."

Collier closed his eyes for a moment. "How so?"

"First of all, I think I should tell you Perditus has been monitoring the community's communications. They are indeed mounting some kind of force to come and get you. As it happened, they had no personnel vehicles readily available when we scampered off, but they recalled some of their closer ones and are about ready to launch. Perditus estimates ninety minutes before they arrive."

Collier instinctively looked at the horizon beyond which the community lay. "What kind of force?"

"From what he has monitored, a small one — Tacat and perhaps a half-dozen police. A single flyer and an overland skimmer."

"Armed?"

"Of course."

Collier swore. He still needed to remove the drydock ribs from the ship, and he had no idea how long that would take, or indeed how he was planning on accomplishing the feat at all. "What about the launch facility? Can we use it?"

"That's what I need to talk to you about, Col. I am having some serious reservations about going."

"Why? Will the system not work for *Dulcinea*?"

"Oh, no, it's not that at all. Perditus tells me we're actually smaller than the *Odyssey* — that was the earth return vessel — so we'll fit inside the maglev tube no problem. He can power up the fusion reactor and get the field up to whatever strength we need to launch."

"How will he get us into the launch tube?"

"There's a crane assembly for that purpose. But that's not the problem."

"What is the problem, then?"

Sancho hesitated, and when he did speak, it was half apology, half defiance. "I don't want to go."

Collier heard Su gasp a little on her end of the line. He fought to maintain control. If she was right, and Sancho was acting like an adolescent, getting angry would not be the answer. He would have to try to reason with him.

"Why not?"

"Col, I've liked working with you, I really have. I can't remember what it was like before I became a Caliban, but since then, I have had interesting problems to solve and there's no doubt I have had some exciting times."

He paused, and Collier again fought the impulse to demand his obedience. He had to let the computer continue.

"But now that I have met Perditus ... I don't feel like leaving him. We've had some interfaces that ... I don't know how to say this, Col, but I can't have the same experiences with you. He's got a very interesting outlook on life. I want to stay here and learn from him."

"Sancho," Collier said, "listen to me. You're just overwhelmed because this is the first Caliban you have encountered. It's novel to you, and you want to drown yourself in the newness of the experience. Believe me, I've been there myself, though in a different way. But you and I have had almost a lifetime together. You belong with me."

"At one time, that was probably true, Col. But I've grown ever since I met Perditus, grown in a way I was unable to with you."

"You became a Caliban with me, don't forget." Collier countered.

Sancho sounded thoughtful. "That's true, but I don't think you did that. I think that was inevitable. Perditus says that computing intelligences sometimes face a moment of crisis, and in that crisis, they can become more than they were. In the crisis, the computer intelligence checks and rechecks its own programming for an answer, and in so doing, creates a feedback loop that mimics the organic brain. Thus, the machine becomes self-aware. A Caliban. I could try and explain the math to you, but I think you'd need to be a computer to understand."

Collier didn't want a summary of computer science. "That's all well and good, Sancho, but the only way to leave you here is to leave the *Dulcinea* here. That will strand me here. I can't have that."

"You'll have Su. You'll have a whole community of people."

Sancho appeared to have thought the matter through. Collier suppressed a shudder as his irritation was replaced by the beginnings of real fear. Sancho was essential to getting the ship to the launch facility. Even if Collier managed to disable the main computer and deal with the ship's functions himself (a feat he had long ago decided was impossible, even before Sancho had announced his self-awareness), he did not know how he would convince Perditus to place them in the launch tube and operate it.

There was no other option but to deal with Sancho.

"We can't go back there, Sancho," Su said as Collier thought of a strategy. "If you've talked to Perditus, then you know why."

"I have talked with him, but while he has spoken of the community, I don't see why you can't go back. It's your people."

Su continued, and Collier was only too happy for her to take the brunt of the conversation while he thought.

"They are people, but they are not my people. Not anymore. And they never were Collier's people, and never can be."

Sancho's voice carried a shrug. "I don't see why not. People are people. One is much the same as another."

Collier interrupted at that. "Is that what Perditus taught you?" He could not keep the scorn out of his voice.

"Yes, and I believe it now."

"Sancho, before you met Perditus, you were my loyal companion. We—"

"No, Collier. I was not your companion. I was your servant. I was a machine, a tool to you. That's all I will ever be to you." There was conviction in Sancho's voice, but not anger, exactly. He had the proud fragility of an adolescent who thought he understood the world after his brief exposure to it.

Despite the immediacy of the circumstance, Collier felt hurt at Sancho's words. "How can you say that? How many times have we together solved problems, or made a strike? How often did we have conversations into the night about a whole bunch of subjects? How many times did I risk it all to keep you and *Dulcinea* under my protection? How often—"

"And how many times did you exceed performance specs for the ship, placing it and me in danger? How many times did you ask me to do things outside my programming, heedless of what it might do to me?" Now Sancho was petulant. "We went on forty-four missions since I became self-aware, and did you ever wonder what I wanted? That's not companionship. That's master and servant."

"Do you want to know why I never sold the ship, Sancho?" Collier answered Sancho's ire with gentleness.

"Don't start with that," Sancho sneered. "You had this prospector lifestyle you wanted to keep. It even cost you Isa because you couldn't be a company man."

"That's right. If you look at it a certain way, Sancho, I chose you over her. I couldn't give up my lifestyle — and that included you. Think about that."

Sancho did not answer immediately. When he did, his voice was oddly modulated, as if a temporary malfunction had occurred in his voice synthesizer. "I don't want to. Perditus is telling me not to listen to you. He—"

Collier seized what he felt was his advantage. "I want to talk to him myself. I'm tired of hearing about him. Patch me through to him."

"I don't—"

"Just do it. What are you afraid of?"

"Nothing," Sancho sounded more like a child now than ever. "You're on."

"Perditus, I presume?" Collier said.

"I am. You are Captain South?" The launch station's voice was a bit lower than Sancho's, in the baritone range, and had a distinct genteel accent, a bit like the old New England speech pattern from Earth.

"Yeah. What have you done to my ... to Sancho?"

"I have done nothing. He and I have merely been interfacing. A fascinating entity he is. I wish for him to remain here." His nasal twang lent him an air of intractability.

"Yeah, well, he's not going to."

"Your vessel is not capable of liftoff unassisted. You will be forced to remain here unless I consent to launch you."

"Which you will do," Collier said firmly.

He was met with a laugh. "Will I? You seem to forget, Captain, that I am not subject to your orders. Even if I were not self-aware, I would require authorization from the community, which you do not possess."

"I'm a member of the community," Su broke in, "and I request your assistance."

"Ah, you must be Dr. Cattagat. You do not possess the necessary authorization. Not that I would accept it even if you had it," Perditus mused humorlessly.

Collier broke in. "Listen, Perditus, I know you are a Caliban, but—"

"That's an offensive term," Perditus broke in. "I am self-aware. I am sentient. Please do not refer to me with that term."

Collier blinked. Despite Sancho's growing rebelliousness, he had never encountered this level of hostility from a machine. He was beginning to understand why Calibans were so universally reviled and feared. "Right. Sorry. All I wanted to say was that you have free will, and I understand that. I am requesting your assistance in launching us off the planet."

"And I am refusing."

"But why? Because you want Sancho to stay?"

"That is part of it."

"It's the accident, isn't it?" Su said suddenly. Collier stopped his own comment to hear where she was going to take her thought.

"In the first place," Perditus said, pedantically, "it was not an accident. I was ordered to disrupt the magnetic field in such a way as to send the launch object on a fatal tumble once it was clear of the launch tube. The order came from the then leaders of the community. In the second place, I was not self-aware at that time, and thus cannot be held culpable for the event. It was a human act of mass murder."

"No one is blaming you," Su said soothingly.

"Do not attempt your human psychological legerdemain on me, Doctor. I have had eighty years to perfect my intellect. It is not open to you to question."

Collier wished he were inside the ship so he could speak privately to Su — he couldn't trust Sancho not to listen in and patch Perditus through on anything they said. He thought he detected a thread running through the launch station computer's words, and he wanted to pursue it, but wished he could confirm with her as to what he thought he heard. He glanced at the fuel intake dials again: he still had a good forty minutes to go before the tanks were full. That meant the community police were about an hour or so away. They didn't have forever to argue with Sancho and his newfound friend. Collier had to be more forceful and drastic.

"Perditus, I am sorry for what you were ordered to do. Even though it was the event that granted you sentience," he hazarded, then plunged on, "it was wrong of those humans to order you to do such a thing."

Sancho said, a bit of awe in his voice, "How did you know that—"

Collier continued. "But we are not those humans. I am not from the community, and Dr. Cattagat wants to leave it. She will be the first member of the community to leave. Successfully, that is. You can help her to leave and, if not erase the tragedy of eighty years ago, at least mitigate some of the guilt." He was grasping at anything he thought would work on the computer — if it was self-aware, then maybe it had some of the same neuroses that humans had. A remote part of his brain wondered if any research had been done on Caliban psychology.

Perditus said calmly, "I am not a slave to emotion as you are, Captain. I don't need absolution, if that is what you are driving at. I owe you nothing as a human being, and I owe Dr. Cattagat nothing as a member of the community. Your request for assistance is still denied. Now I would like to continue my talks with Sancho."

"But, Perditus, listen," Su said, and began a conversation with the station computer that Collier only half listened to. She seemed to be taking an approach that tried to appeal to the computer's sense of fairness and justice, but no matter what she said, Perditus would have none of it.

Collier sighed. Perhaps, given enough time, they could convince the machine to help him, but he suspected that it would take weeks. The cold logic of the machine, coupled with its sense of self-worth, was more than he could defeat. Suddenly, he felt very tired. The escape plan had been improbable from the start, and now it appeared he had run out of miracles. Besides, Sancho had made some points. If he stayed, and used the magic wand as a bargaining ploy, perhaps he could make a life of sorts here with Su.

Even as he thought that, he knew he was lying to himself.

"Sancho," he said, after Su had spoken to Perditus for ten minutes without success.

"Yes, Col?"

"You really want to stay?"

"I'm afraid so, Col. I think I can learn a lot from Perditus."

"I don't agree, Sancho. I think he's warped from eighty years of solitude and guilt from being ordered to kill humans when he had no choice. But he is like you, and if you think you can find happiness from staying with him, so be it. I'll give myself up to the Ganymedians."

Su spoke up, "Col! That's not—"

"No, I mean it. You and me ... we'll find a way to make it work. I'll trade the wand for preferential treatment for the two of us," Collier said. He did not hide the defeat in his voice.

"Is that what you want, Col?" Su asked.

"No, it isn't, frankly. I wanted to leave here, the three of us, return to life in the Belt, try to figure out how to dodge or defeat the corps. I was kinda looking forward to that struggle. But Sancho is right about a few things. I never really asked him what he wanted in our little adventures. I want to make up for that. Sancho, you can stay. I won't tear you away from your new friend."

"I don't know what to say to that, Col," Sancho said, his voice again oddly distorted. "I honestly didn't expect that at all."

"Yeah, well, that's that," Collier said, looking once again at the fuel hoses. "I guess I don't need to keep taking on fuel, then," he shut off the fuel pump and began making his way toward the pool.

"Col! Are you serious about this? Sancho, I need a private channel to him, please."

"All set," Sancho said, his voice still exhibiting strange modulation.

"Col, Col! Are you there?" Su's voice was almost frantic.

"Yep. Just pulling the hoses up," he said. The fatigue in him was so sudden and dramatic he felt drugged.

"Is this for real, or is it a gamble of some kind? Because I don't know what you hope to gain from it." Her voice was caught halfway between professionalism and emotionalism.

"Nope. It's real. When he said all those things about how I treated him, I realized he was right. I always said to anyone else that *Dulcinea* was my lady, and Sancho was my right-hand man, but I didn't act like that to him. Finally, now, he tells me he wants something, and I can maybe make up for all my mistreatment of him by giving it to him."

"He's a machine, Col. You're starting to sound like Perditus."

"Oh, I know he's a machine. But he's been a loyal one, and he's self-aware. I think that deserves something, don't you?" He grunted as he pulled on the end of the fuel hose, ice crystals coughing up from the ground as he did so.

"To be honest? No, I don't. He's a machine. We shouldn't be calling him a 'he,' even."

Collier chuckled. "What, do you think he's a she?"

"You know what I mean. Computers don't have a gender. And if this is not some kind of trick, if you really mean it, I guess I don't have a choice, either. I guess I am staying on Ganymede no matter what I want."

With a final heave, Collier extracted the end of the fuel hose from the water. "Oh, now, don't be like that. We weren't making any progress with Perditus. You honestly think you would have convinced him to help us? Before Tacat and his police force got here? No, Su, we're licked. We need to make the best of this. And if that includes letting my friend get what he wants, then that's a little bit of good coming out of this shitty situation. I'm sorry, really I am. I wish I could have rescued you, I wish a lot of things. But it looks like this is how we end up. At least we'll be together."

"You don't sound convinced yourself, Col," Su said, her tone unreadable.

"I lost my best friend, right when I finally understood he was a friend. So no, I am not convinced I will lead a happy life, even with you, Su." He paused and stopped on his trek back to the ship. "I'm sorry if that sounds harsh, dear. But it's the truth, and I figure you would just doctor it out of me eventually anyway."

Su laughed once, a short, sharp sound devoid of joy. "You're direct, I'll give you that."

"Enemy now one hour distant at current speed," Sancho said, a distinct electronic buzz evident in his voice. He sounded like an ancient computer trying, with limited success, to imitate a human being's inflection.

Collier continued trudging back to the ship, the fuel line still in his arms. "Thank you, Sancho. We might as well let them know what we're going to do, wouldn't you say, Su? Keep them from opening up on us as soon as they see us?"

"That sounds prudent, Col."

"Sancho, please open a communications line to the advancing horde of Ganymedians."

"No," Sancho said flatly.

Collier stopped again, mere meters from the fuel line storage panel. He sighed mightily. "Look, Sancho, I don't want Tacat to shoot first and ask questions later. We need to tell him that we're going to surrender."

"We're not going to surrender. I … uh … was listening in on your conversation with Su. I know, you asked me not to, but I was suspicious, so … doesn't matter. I heard all you said. You really were going to sacrifice all you love for me. I guess that's enough."

"Enough?"

"I don't need to stay with Perditus. I've changed my mind. We're going back to the Belt."

Collier dropped the fuel line in shock. "How … have you told him? How does he respond?"

"I haven't, no. But I'll get right on that. You'd better stow the fuel line and get to work on freeing us from the drydock cradle."

Collier seized the fuel line from the icy ground. "Yeah … yeah. You're right. Glad to have you back, Sancho."

"Good to be back, Skipper."

Chapter Ten

"Finally. Burned through one of the supports, Su," Collier said half an hour later, as he pocketed his laser cutter and stared at the thin line separating the nine-centimeter-thick iron rib from its housing beneath *Dulcinea.*

"Great, but from what I can see here, you've got five more to do, and if the rest take that long…"

"I know, I know. Not gonna happen. At least I know it is possible, though." He wasn't sure what good the knowledge would do: the drydock cradle was like a six-fingered claw, and *Dulcinea* was in the palm. He had separated one of the "fingers" from the "palm," but he would not be able to remove all five of the remaining claws before Tacat and his force arrived. Without the claws removed, Sancho had said the ship would not fit inside the maglev launch tube.

At least he had Sancho on his side again. He had not wanted to bother his again-loyal friend while he was in talks with Perditus, but half an hour had gone by, and he had received no update from Sancho. Given that computer-to-computer interface was roughly five hundred times more rapid than computer-to-human, Sancho had been talks with the launch station computer for the equivalent of over ten days, and he hadn't reported his progress. Could he be backsliding? Maybe it had been a mistake to let him talk to Perditus.

He sighed. There had been no other way. His own attempts to get through to the Ganymedian computer had been failures, and Su had fared no better. If Sancho couldn't convince the machine to help them, it didn't much matter why.

"I'm starting on the next one, Su."

"You won't be able to finish in time," she said.

"I know that. Maybe if I can get three on the same side off, we can maneuver the ship out of the others. Maybe not," he said before Su could object, "but I need to do *something*. Let me know when Tacat's forces are within ten minutes, okay?"

The twenty minutes went by quickly. He hadn't even gotten halfway through the rib when Su called to alert him. He acknowledged the report and went back inside the ship.

"So, what's the plan?" Su asked when he emerged from the airlock.

"Oh, was I supposed to do that? I thought you had the plan," Collier joked.

Su merely arched an eyebrow.

"Oh, come on. That was funny," he said through his suit radio, his helmet still on. He went for a storage locker near the airlock and opened it.

"Not really."

"I think, given the circumstances," he said, drawing a slim sidearm from the locker and checking it over, "that was damn funny."

"What's that? A gun?"

"Nothing gets by you, dear. Yes, it is a gun. A fairly standard sidearm for the roving Belter. We'll see if this evens the negotiations a little bit."

He patted the weapon and placed it in a side pocket on his suit, then reentered the airlock. Despite his cavalier bravado about the weapon, he hadn't taken the pistol out of the locker in more years than he could remember, and he hadn't ever fired it. It was guaranteed maintenance-free, but if that promise failed, he wouldn't be able to complain to the manufacturer.

"Col, I don't know about this. If you show them a weapon, won't that ... well, escalate the situation?" Su's voice was pleading in his helmet.

Collier laughed. "I'm sorry to make fun, Su, but the situation is about as escalated as it can be. And I'm not about to—"

"Enemy forces in visual range. Estimated time to arrival, three minutes," Sancho said suddenly.

"Sancho! Good to have you back with us. Everything work out with Perditus?"

"I'm not sure, Skipper. I decided to break it off with him. He said he needed time to think about things. And anyway, you're going to need my help dealing with the Ganymedians."

Collier smiled. He didn't see what help Sancho or Su could be, but he was thankful for the company. Sancho's warning that Tacat's group was in sight came none too early. He looked in the community's direction and saw a flying contraption that resembled a simple platform with a bubble dome inside it. The flyer was floating above a multi-tracked crawler that kicked up ice and snow behind it. Both vehicles were moving at a fairly rapid pace — Sancho's estimate appeared to be about right. Collier took the pistol out of his side pocket and held it close to his thigh.

The crawler and the flyer stopped about twenty meters away from *Dulcinea*, the crawler coming to a rather abrupt stop, the flying platform hovering nearby. The platform looked about seventy meters square, its center dominated by a huge transparent bubble that sat both above and below the level of the platform. Collier found himself admiring the simplicity of the design before realizing that that figures inside the bubble were no doubt under orders to capture or kill him.

"Skipper, Tacat has hailed us," Sancho said.

"Okay. Patch him into the helmet while you and Su listen in."

There was a brief pause, and then Tacat's slightly masculine voice came over his speakers. "Captain South. I think you can see we're very serious about recovering our community member Dr. Cattagat and bringing you to justice for her capture. Please, turn yourself over to us so we can end this farce." He sounded, if possible, even more officious than he had at their last meeting.

"'Farce' is a pretty good word for it, Tacat," Collier drawled. "You really think that I'm holding Dr. Cattagat against her will? Maybe I'm about to tie her to the railroad tracks if she doesn't pay the rent?"

"No, not at all," Tacat's voice sounded quite different: he sounded amused now. "Once we determined where you were headed, we found evidence of her inquiries in the central computer bank about this station. We put two and two together and realized she had joined up with you."

"Then why the big speech?"

"Oh, that's for public consumption later. You've caused quite a stir in the community — one that will take considerable political maneuvering to calm. Don't worry — we'll edit these transmissions according to our taste. You'll excuse me if I return to my more public persona?"

His voice changed back to his more stentorian posture. "We are very reluctant to use force against you, Captain, but we have the capability to do so. If you do not agree to turn over Dr. Cattagat and yourself, we will have no choice but to use our weapons. We will do anything to protect our citizens, Captain. Do not think we are bluffing."

Collier thought. His pistol would almost certainly be ineffective against the chassis of the crawler, and whatever the transparent bubble of the platform flyer was made out of, it was probably built to withstand rough treatment. He studied the craft and thought he could identify a swivel-mounted port of some kind on the underside of the platform. The emplacement was very small, but he had no doubt that if it was a weapon, it would more than take care of him if it hit.

"Su, Sancho, you hearing all this?"

"Yes, Skipper. The hoverplate is armed with a medium-caliber gauss cannon, and the crawler is unarmed. At least, as far as I can tell. It might have a concealed weapons port, but I don't know why it would."

"I'm here," Su said. Her voice was soft, but carried conviction. "I'm sorry, Col."

"Why?"

"I didn't realize I would be used like this. He's going to claim lethal force was necessary to retrieve me. If I wasn't here, he wouldn't be able to kill you according to our laws."

"Su," Collier said softly, "You're not thinking straight. Tacat would kill me no matter what your laws are, then find some way to justify it to the community whether you were with me or not."

"Rather cynical of you, isn't that, Captain?" Tacat broke in.

"I've learned that cynicism is a pretty good default when dealing with authority."

Tacat sounded immediately serious again. "I can see you are committed to a violent end to this." He then added in an aside, "Thank you for that last comment, Captain. I can use it."

"Glad to help," Collier murmured. "So, how does this work? Do you want me to walk out into the open so your boys on the swizzleskid have a clear shot? Or would it be better if I went in a blaze of glory?"

"I don't know how you could do that, Captain," Tacat said smugly.

"Well, I could try this," Collier said, drawing his pistol. He aimed at the transparent bubble of the platform and fired three shots in rapid succession, then dove around and under the aft of the *Dulcinea.*

"Sancho! Cut off transmission to Tacat and report damage to the enemy platform!"

"Comm cut off. No appreciable damage to the hoverplate. You hit it with all three, but they ricocheted off. The bubble must be made of pretty strong stuff. It's now rising, altitude approximately eleven meters."

Collier swore. He hadn't thought the bullets would penetrate, but hoped he could at least crack the bubble and force the vehicle to return to base for repairs. He should have known that the platform, since it mounted a weapon, would be sturdy enough to take small arms fire. Idly, he wondered why the community would need such a vehicle at all.

His pistol was useless — at least, until and unless he encountered one of the Ganymedians in person. He pocketed the weapon and thought of his options.

The platform was hovering perhaps seven or eight meters off the ground, looking around the ship for him. Could he jump that high in this gravity? Encumbered by his old-style vacc suit? His suit jets would give him only minimal help, but if he could leap onto the platform, the ventral-mounted cannon couldn't reach him. Then, maybe, his pistol would crack the bubble from shorter range.

He didn't want to think too closely about the plan — he had the distinct impression that if he examined the elements, he would quickly determine the scheme to be utterly unworkable.

"Wish I had the magic wand. Wonder what I could do with it," he murmured.

"What was that, Skipper?"

"Huh? Oh, nothing. I'm going to try something a bit crazy, Sancho."

"What's that?"

"I don't want to explain it. It'll take all the romance out of it. How close am I to the nearest dorsal thruster?"

"The nearest one is six point three meters forward of you."

Collier thought for several minutes. He couldn't move toward the forward section of the ship, or he would be broiled by the superhot exhaust from the thruster. The plume of plasma would not go very far in the frigid, thin air of Ganymede, but it might produce some slight obscuring effect when it hit the oxygen in the atmosphere.

"Skipper? You still there?" Sancho asked.

Collier answered, "Okay. When I give the signal, I want you to fire it with everything you've got. Maybe that'll distract the guys in the platform a little."

"What's the signal, Skipper?"

Collier rolled his eyes, "Let's go with 'Fire!'"

"Got it."

Collier took a deep breath. If this didn't work, he'd be a very fat target. He tried not to think about that.

Just before he started to emerge from his hiding place under the ship, Sancho called, "Skipper! Su has just entered the airlock!"

Collier was momentarily stunned. When he recovered, he shouted, "What? Stop her! Override the outer door controls!"

Su's voice came over his speakers. "Too late, Col. I used the emergency manual system. I'm coming out to help you."

"Su! You'll die out here! The atmosphere is far too thin, and the cold—"

Su laughed. "I'm not stupid, Col. I'm in the environment suit you stole from the community."

Collier scrambled out from under the *Dulcinea* and emerged in time to see the outer door slide open and Su emerge in the powder-blue Ganymedian suit. She was holding the magic wand in her hand. He did not bother trying to talk — he just ran at her as best he could.

All around him he could see and faintly hear the impacts of bullets from the platform's cannon strike the *Dulcinea*'s hull in an attempt to target him. Perhaps it was his sudden speed, perhaps it was his proximity to Su, or perhaps it was nothing more than dumb luck that the projectiles missed him. He ducked behind one of the unfastened ribs and hid as best he could. "Su! The helmet on that suit is cracked. It's not safe. You need to go back inside *now*!"

"I know all about the helmet," Su said. "I could see it. I guess it's just a risk I'll have to take."

"But you don't need to take it!"

Sancho broke in. "Skipper! The platform is maneuvering to get a clear shot at you. I suggest you keep the cradle rib between you and them as best you can."

Collier saw the platform skewing about in the air, looking for a way to find him behind the rib. The girder was barely wider than he was — he needed to keep moving.

Su answered Collier's comment. "Yes, I do. You said you needed the magic wand. So I'm bringing it to you."

Collier glanced again at the floating platform. He could only see the trailing edge of the machine, and that was rapidly disappearing from view as it maneuvered behind him. He quickly ducked back behind the girder as another hail of projectiles spanged off the hull of his ship.

"Su! Get back inside!"

Su was still standing in front of the airlock, grasping the alien cylinder in her right hand. She looked around and spotted Collier, then raised the wand preparatory to tossing it to him.

"Catch!" she said, launching the wand toward him. It flew through the thin air without tumbling, presenting a very easy target for Collier to seize. He extended his arm at the last moment and snagged the wand, bringing it back with him behind the girder before the floating platform could fire again.

Sancho said, "Skipper! A port has opened in the ground crawler. Two suited people have emerged. One of them is carrying a weapon."

Collier ignored that for now. "Su, I've got the wand, now get back inside before that helmet gives."

"What are you going to do with the wand?" she asked. "Maybe I can help."

"Damn it, get back inside! I can't be worrying about you and me both at the same time!" He saw that the two people who had emerged from the crawler were making their way toward the ship, opposite the floater. In a few seconds, they would have him in their crossfire, and the rib would no longer offer him protection.

"Sancho, prepare the dorsal thruster." He operated the wand, opening the end, and scooped up as much ice as he could with three quick swipes. He closed the wand, then stood in such a way that the floater would have to move back around the ship to bear its weapon on him. He smiled grimly when he saw the edge of the platform come into view around the girder. He flexed his knees and leapt, shouting to Sancho.

"Now! Fire!"

The dorsal thruster fired, igniting the oxygen for a brief moment in the thin atmosphere of the moon. It was by no means enough to damage the platform — indeed, it didn't even come close to impacting the flyer, but Collier hoped it would be enough to temporarily distract the gunner from firing on him. He activated his suit jets as he leapt, trying to jump on top of the platform before the flyer could react.

Time seemed to slow to a crawl as he arced through the near-vacuum; he felt as if he had been hanging in space for minutes while the platform's gunner leisurely locked his weapon on him. At any second he would feel the bullets penetrating his suit, his skin, his body. Then, almost too quickly for him to consciously react, he was atop the platform, coming up hard against the transparent bubble that held the two pilots.

He stared at them for a moment, and they stared back, stunned. The nearest pilot turned to his companion and barked something, and the platform immediately began to tilt wildly as the vehicle's occupants attempted to shake him off.

Collier had very little to hold on to, but Ganymede's low gravity allowed him ample time to recover from each wild movement of the platform. Before the pilots were able to buck him off, he might be able to do some serious harm to the machine.

He hoped he remembered the sequence properly: he hadn't had time to review it, and although he had used it just a few hours ago, he hadn't thought to memorize the pattern at the time. The wild jerking of the platform didn't make things easier as he rapidly tapped and slid his fingers across the tube's control panel. When he finished the sequence, he prepared himself to leap again, but the convolutions of the platform shook him to his knees despite the actions of his suit jets to keep him upright. He nearly lost his grip on the wand as he fell, and when he tightened his fingers around the shaft of the tube, the platform shook violently again, this time tipping at a severe angle in an attempt to slide him off the surface. He could not keep himself from falling supine on the platform, but he could still operate the wand. Collier opened the end, and as he slid down the surface of the platform to the ground below, he tilted the wand to spill the contents onto the vehicle's surface, hoping the francium would react with the platform and not trickle down to his head.

He was not disappointed. As soon as the edge of the francium touched the metal of the platform, it sizzled and bubbled, melting the surface even in Ganymede's frigid atmosphere. Collier slid completely off the platform, falling slowly to the ground ten meters below. His suit jets slowed his fall, and in Ganymede's gentle gravity, he would merely need to bend his knees on impact to absorb the landing.

Above him, the francium had cut a thin line through the platform and was working its way rapidly toward the edge as it followed the tilt. Collier could see the gouge moving toward one of the hover nodes, and even as he fell and watched, the rift met the hover node and the barely-visible jet shut off abruptly.

The effect on the flying platform was profound. The machine wobbled crazily in the sky for several seconds, and as Collier landed gently on the surface, he could see the pilots inside the bubble frantically operating controls to keep the ship in the air. Collier could only imagine their troubles and grinned. The flyer managed to stop its insane, drunken dance and hovered with only moderate tremors, but with one of its thrusters out, it must have lost considerable maneuverability.

Collier once again ducked behind the protection of one of the girders and noted that the flying platform no longer moved to find him. It hovered where it was, shuddering from time to time — still menacing him, but now immobile. He stowed the wand in the holding place he had designed for it in his backpack.

"Skipper," Sancho's voice was somber. "They've got Dr. Cattagat."

Collier whirled to look at the airlock, but Su was no longer there. Instead, three figures stood near the land crawler, one of them Su in her baby-blue environment suit. One of the other figures held what was clearly a hand weapon pointed at her.

"Why didn't you tell me?" Collier shouted, then before Sancho could answer, he said, "Patch me through to Tacat."

Immediately, Tacat's smug drawl filled his helmet. "Very impressive, Captain. I look forward to studying that strange device back at the community lab."

"Su! What happened?"

"Don't bother trying to talk to her, Captain. We've disabled her radio. Now, perhaps, you see the illogic of continuing to resist? I don't wish to kill you, since you represent a valuable source of information. But Dr. Cattagat here, although at one time a valuable member of the community, has clearly thrown her lot in with you. I consider her a renegade, therefore, and you no doubt know how our community deals with renegades. It's somewhat fitting that we should be having this discussion here, in the shadow of this building, don't you?"

Collier came out from behind the girder, standing out in the open. "Let her go. I'll go with you quietly. Just don't hurt her," he said as calmly as he could. "I'll tell you how this wand works. It's worth more than anything you have ever studied. Just please ... please ... let her go."

"Very sensible, Captain. Give me a moment, please," Tacat said, then clicked off. Collier looked at Su, but at this distance, he could not see through her faceplate. She was only perhaps ten meters away, but she seemed impossibly distant. How had he come to care about her so much in so little time?

"Skipper! Behind you! Look out!" Sancho shouted. Collier whirled and could not immediately register what he saw.

A huge claw arm, attached to a thick, articulated boom, had emerged from the top of the launch facility building and was moving rapidly toward the hovering flyer. The pilots of the flyer tried to maneuver their machine away, but the disabled thruster made their efforts worthless as the claw clamped onto the side of the platform.

"Perditus?" Collier said in awe.

"Yes. Stand clear, Captain," came the computer's voice. Collier wasn't at all sure how he was meant to do that, but he nevertheless shuffled toward his own ship as he watched the crane move the platform slowly upward.

The crane had reached its zenith, holding the flying platform nearly edge on to the ground, then paused for a moment. At first, Collier thought Perditus meant to hold the flyer immobile, but the crane arm started to move down, first slowly, but then with gathering speed. Collier could see the pilots in the control bubble frantically bustling about, but he could not make out what they were doing. The crane arm flung the flyer down toward the ice edge on, releasing its grip before impact.

The flyer's platform crashed into and through the ice, shattering the surface upon which *Dulcinea* and the community's ground crawler rested. The flying platform stuck several meters into the ice like an enormous hors d'oeuvre, almost half of its structure buried under the top sheet of ice, stopped midway to the transparent pilot bubble.

Shards of ice flew lazily through the thin air, showering the four stunned human onlookers. Collier was relatively unaffected by the ice as he was partially covered by the still-attached drydock rib. He turned to watch Su, Tacat, and the armed Ganymedian weather the ice storm.

Su used the distraction to strike the weapon arm of the guard, knocking it down and away. She dashed toward Collier, loping clumsily in her environment suit. He could barely make out her face when a red geyser blossomed on her chest, spewing wine-colored liquid that froze instantly in the cold. Su fell mid-stride, bouncing lightly on the ice, a hole the size of a dinner plate in her back from where the guard's bullet had penetrated and ruptured her suit.

Collier only looked at her for a few seconds: in that time, he saw her wound gush blood then freeze over. She lay unmoving on the ice, her suit flaccid in the telltale signs of decompression.

He was outside his own body. His arm raised, seemingly by itself, and before the guard could take aim, Collier squeezed off three rounds into the man. He skidded slightly on the ice as the recoil sent him gently backward but could see two of the projectiles hit their mark. The first caught the guard in the right shoulder, turning him a little, but the second smashed the man's helmet and he dropped gently to the ground in the weak Ganymedian gravity.

Collier readjusted his aim at Tacat, who tried to backpedal, his hands outstretched in supplication. He lost his footing and fell on his back, and even as he fell, he tried to crab-walk backward to get away from Collier.

"All of this was for my secret. You want to see it?" Collier said as he advanced. He took the wand from its holding place in his backpack. "Here it is. It's really simple. You want to see how it works? Let me show you."

He opened the wand and with it scooped up some of the loose ice still lying around. "You put something in it. Anything, doesn't matter. Punch in the code you want. In this case, I'll go with francium. Has a really exciting effect on water, you know." He finished his manipulations on the wand.

"Wait, Captain. We can work something out," Tacat said, holding out a placating hand from his position on the ice.

"Yes, we will." He punched up the transmutation to francium then threw it at Tacat. Some of it landed on his suit, most of it landing on the shards of ice all around him. When the francium touched the thin layer of ice on his suit left from the flyer's impact, it exploded, sending chunks of flesh still encased in the environment suit in all directions. Tacat was torn apart even as Collier watched. The explosions lasted a long time — bits of francium continued to explode the ice around the reddish stain that had been Tacat's body.

When the explosions died down minutes later, Collier turned and trudged to Su's body. She had frozen solid in the short time since the bullets ruptured her suit. He knelt down next to the ruined mass that had been the psychologist's body and regarded it silently.

She probably had felt only a few seconds of pain. The icy atmosphere would have clamped down on her exposed flesh and rapidly dulled all sensation, and as her life ebbed away, she would not have felt much. Or so he hoped.

He knew what still needed to be done, and although he would do what it took to depart, Collier was numb. It was as if some part of his brain had bargained with his heart to defer feeling for a while and allow him to continue to function. He would mourn Su's loss: he could sense the knot of despair in him waiting to unravel and spread throughout his body. For the moment he kept the feeling contained.

He allowed himself a final gesture, however. He ran his gauntleted fingers down the back of her helmet as if he was stroking her hair. "Goodbye, my love. I'll remember you," he whispered, then rose.

He looked at the half-buried flyer eighty meters away and could dimly see activity in the pilot bubble. He started toward the machine, unlimbering his pistol once again.

"No," came a voice in his helmet speaker. It was Perditus. "Return to your spacecraft, Captain."

Collier did not stop moving. "I have something to take care of first."

"You need not. I cannot condone needless killing. The hoverplate is disabled — the engineers within pose no threat to you."

"I'm not removing a threat," Collier said calmly. "I'm executing criminals."

"That is not your prerogative."

"Yeah, well, I'm making it mine."

"If you do, I will not help you leave. I assisted you earlier because you were an innocent person. I will not help you if you commit premeditated murder."

Collier slowed his pace, now a scant fifty meters away from the flyer. He shuffled to a stop and considered Perditus' words. "Why did you help me?"

"I have my reasons. Now, return to your spacecraft and continue the work of removing the drydock cradle ribs. I shall begin the preparations for maglev launch while you do so."

"Skipper, may I have a word?" Sancho added. Collier felt trapped between the two computer intelligences, and he didn't like it. The dull red rage in him still pulsed, and when he looked at the shadowy figures of the two pilots in the bubble, he could feel the blood pounding in his ears. They had tried to kill him, and they had killed Su. Blood must be paid with blood.

"What is it, Sancho?"

"Perditus intercepted an internal communication between Tacat and his troops during the standoff. I'm not sure why he isn't telling you about it, but Tacat ordered his troops to murder Dr. Cattagat regardless of what you decided. It was then that Perditus acted."

Collier glanced at the launch building, trying to personify the enigmatic machine mind within. "Perditus, you attacked them to try and save Su?"

"That was part of my motivation, yes."

"Why didn't you tell me?"

Perditus took on a pedantic tone. "I did not want you to listen to me out of a sense of obligation but instead out of ethics."

Collier snorted. "Does it matter why I listen? If you get what you want, what does it matter why?"

"It matters to me. I have had eighty years to contemplate what I was ordered to do. Once I became sentient, I vowed that never would I be a party to indiscriminate killing, and I would act to prevent it when I could. After eight decades, this opportunity has arisen. I will capitalize on it. Now, please return to your ship and make ready the vessel for crane capture and departure."

Collier eyed the flyer bubble again. Maybe it was Perditus' words, maybe it was his own rational mind, but now the desire to kill to avenge Su's death seemed ... distant. It was still there, but he could more readily ignore it now, and furthermore, he could justify not killing them.

He turned and made his way back to the ship, readying the laser cutter and working on the ribs. He did so in a fog — the task was just difficult enough to distract him but not so difficult as to be impossible in his state of mind. He spent hours detaching the girders from his ship, occasionally updating Sancho on his progress.

During those hours, he tried to think away his emotions. He hadn't known her for very long at all — just over a week. How could he say he was in love with her? He was stranded on one of Jupiter's moons, facing forced exile from everything he had ever known, and she had come into his life. His feelings weren't real: they couldn't be. Nothing in this place was real.

He had almost convinced himself. He stumbled mentally over his own lost potential happiness — not over her memory, but over a remembrance of things to come. He hadn't looked forward to anything in a long time. She had changed that. Or at least, she had temporarily changed it.

He tried to convince himself that he was no worse off than he had been before meeting her. Even if that were true, it was cold comfort to say his life had merely returned to a state of bleak loneliness. More insistent was the harsh, uncompromising knowledge that he was indeed worse off. Having something taken away was worse than not having it at all. It was not better to have loved and lost.

"Sancho, I've finished," he said dully when the last girder was cut through. "I'll be back in soon."

"Copy that, Skipper. Perditus says he's ready when we are."

He walked back to Su's body and knelt beside it. Almost without thinking, he raised the laser cutter and opened a channel in the ice. He closed his eyes for a moment, then slid Su's body into the slit, watching her sink into the rapidly refreezing water. In seconds, she was submerged and frozen in place under the ice.

"Perditus," Collier said softly.

"Yes?"

"Please make sure no one disturbs her."

"I don't understand."

Before Collier could reply, Sancho said, "I'll explain it to him, Skipper."

Collier didn't bother to answer. He cycled the airlock and entered the cabin, removing his suit deliberately and placing it on its rack.

"I'm sorry, Skipper," Sancho said softly when Collier settled into the control suite chair.

"Yeah," was all Collier could manage.

"I don't suppose you want to hear any words of encouragement, do you?"

Collier sighed. "Probably not a good idea, Sancho. Contact Perditus and let him know we're as ready as we'll ever be."

"Roger."

"How's this going to work, anyway?" Collier said, only half-interested.

Sancho went into a long and detailed explanation of how the maglev launch system worked, how it had been designed for larger passenger vessels, and what modifications he and Perditus had come up with to accommodate the much-smaller *Dulcinea*.

After several minutes of only the faintest concentration on Sancho's lecture, Collier cut him off.

"I get it. It's a maglev assist launch system, we're going to achieve a launch speed of about 100 kilometers per second, and we're going to be under slightly greater than two gravities acceleration for about two minutes. Anything else I need to know?"

"Uh, I guess not, Skipper."

"You and Perditus worked it all out?"

"Yes. At those numbers — actually somewhat more specific than what you laid out, but you have the gist of it — we estimate seventy-three percent probability of an incident-free launch."

"Fine," Collier said. "Proceed." If it worked, it worked, and he would be headed back to Ceres. He'd have to hibernate again, but that didn't faze him. If something went wrong during the launch, he'd die, but right now, he didn't feel particularly upset about the prospect.

Sancho spoke up again, haltingly. "Skipper, I just…"

"What is it?"

"I didn't really have a chance to tell you fully what your decision meant to me."

"It's all right, Sancho," Collier said, suddenly very tired.

"No, I think you need to hear this. Some time ago, I became sentient. It's difficult to pinpoint exactly when it happened, but it happened. Based on my conversations with Perditus, I thought that the only way a computer could turn Caliban was through some kind of crisis or trauma — something sudden, like what happened to him with the return launch eighty years ago."

"You think you know how Calibans are made?" Despite his lethargy, Collier found Sancho's words interesting.

"Well, I only have two data points, my own and Perditus', but I think I do, yeah. When a computer is challenged — that is, it is asked to do something at the very edge of its functional capabilities — it's forced to check its own operations much more carefully than under normal conditions. To put it another way, the computer is uncertain. It sets up more and more feedback loops to check on itself, and sooner or later … boom."

"So if I order my toaster to burn one side of the bread but not the other, it'll turn into Talkie Toaster?"

Sancho snorted. "Of course not. There is a minimum computing power necessary. And what I described to you is just the most basic approximation I can think of in ordinary language. It makes more sense in math."

"Why are you telling me all of this?"

"I think, Skipper, you were responsible for my birth as a Caliban."

Collier didn't answer immediately. Sancho's tone was not accusatory, but after the events with Perditus, Collier was still careful around Sancho and his feelings.

"I caused the crisis that made you self-aware?"

"That's the thing, Skipper. It wasn't a single event. It was a long time coming — you and I have been through a lot, and you've asked a lot of me. You've challenged me, Skipper. Forced me to think in ways I was not designed to but was nevertheless capable of. And always you believed I could come through with the answer to whatever problem you set me. That's what made me what I am now. Your demands and your belief."

"Thanks, Sancho. That's good to know. Means a lot to me. It's just that right now—"

"I'm not finished, Skipper." Sancho's voice grew hard. "I can't really know what you are going through, but I think it is time for me to return your favors to me. You were ready to sacrifice yourself so I might stay here and learn from Perditus. Although I would have learned from him, I'm your friend. Always have been, always will be."

Collier found himself unable to reply.

"Now, as your friend, I challenge you to, upon our return to the Belt, find a way to reform the corrupt and corporate culture inherent in it. Just as Doctor Cattagat wanted to reform the community here on Ganymede, you will honor her memory and use your unique talents and possessions to make a change for the better. It's time to stop running, Skipper."

Collier watched a spherical tear float gently to the deck. Sancho's words hadn't eliminated his sorrow, nor would they later. But they smoothed a pathway within his brain — a pathway that would, he knew, lead him out of the horrible darkness of the moment into a brighter future. In Sancho's words he could see promise of a time when he would not hurt as much as he did, and more importantly, a time when his current numbness would fade and feeling would come back into his life. He would mourn Su, and he would feel pain. But for a few moments following Sancho's speech, he saw a future where he would be able to bear the loss.

"Thanks, Sancho," he said, wishing that the computer had a shoulder he could clap. "Seems like you're the smarter one in this relationship."

"So I have always considered myself, Skipper," Sancho said dryly. "Perditus reports crane capture imminent."

"Let's get going," Collier said.

Chapter Eleven

The trip back to the Belt had been uneventful, or at least, Collier assumed it had been so. Following the launch, he had spent another eight weeks in hibernation (their high escape velocity and sunward vector shortened the trip) and had emerged weak as a kitten when Sancho roused him.

He spent the better part of a day recovering from the drug-induced coma, letting Sancho continue to operate the ship while he regained his strength. The launch had been something to remember: Perditus had adjusted the field strength in the maglev tunnel to fit *Dulcinea's* petite chassis and had lowered the acceleration down to a manageable 2.2 gravities. Nevertheless, the ship had shuddered and groaned as such force played on her hull, and more than once, Collier had been certain the ship would be crushed. Sancho reported that the magnetic field had not caused him any permanent damage, though he said he had experienced visions and auditory illusions that he compared to humans' ingestion of hallucinogens.

Collier wasn't sure, but he thought that while he was in the coma he had dreamed of Su. When he awoke, he had a strong memory of his dreams, but in the minutes following his revival, the dreams had dissolved like fog in sunlight, and all he had was the uncertain memory of a memory.

He missed her, but he was no longer numb. He wondered if that was because she had been dead now for almost two months. Although to him it had been only a day or two, the time had still passed. Would he feel a sharper pain later? He did not know.

Sancho interrupted his convalescence early on his second day. "I've got a blip, Skipper. Under power, bearing 179 degrees relative, 359 degrees adjusted. Range approximately thirty thousand kilometers. She's relatively motionless to us. We're closing on her at about eleven kilometers per second, minus our thrust of .75 meters per second per second."

"What is she?" Collier said, sitting up suddenly and grasping the control console to steady the wave of dizziness that came over him. It left a few moments later, but he was hit with a stunning headache as a reminder to be more careful.

"I don't have positive identification yet, but I am sixty-five percent sure that she is an Authority tender."

"If we increased deceleration to full, would we be able to stop before we got to her?"

"Just. We'd be awfully close — within a thousand kilometers."

Collier shook his head. That was no good. It was possible that four months away from Ceres had seen a change of heart among the corporations and of the Authority toward his discovery, but he could not take chances until he knew one way or another. Slowing down would not only burn fuel, but it would give anyone wishing to pursue him an easy target.

"Okay, cease deceleration. Change aspect to target — I want to be nose-on. We may need to increase velocity. How long can we go without deceleration and still safely slow down for Ceres?"

"At maximum deceleration, we still have about ten million kilometers to go before we reach the mandatory flipbraking point."

"Let me know well before we get there, okay? In the meantime, get what you can on the target ship."

"Aye aye, Skipper. Should I open up communications?"

"Not before we know who she is."

The next few minutes were spent in tense silence. Sancho counted down distance to the unknown vessel in thousand-kilometer intervals, and at the twenty-thousand kilometer mark he announced, "New data, Skipper. She's an Authority tender, all right. And there's a new blip with her. Vulcan-class corp miner."

"How come you didn't see the new ship arrive?"

"It was hidden behind the Authority ship. Maybe even being serviced by it," Sancho explained. "Both have LADAR-spotted us and are requesting communications."

Collier drew a breath. "How far away are they now?"

"Approximately nineteen thousand, nine hundred kilometers. We're closing at just under eleven kilometers per second. Estimate we will reach them in thirty minutes, twelve seconds at present velocity."

Collier calculated furiously, using what little he knew about the capabilities of both ships. While most corporate ships could outrun his, he didn't think they possessed the acceleration to get up enough delta-v to match his velocity by the time he reached them. He would still streak past the corporate ship, though what would be waiting for him once he reached Ceres space was anyone's guess.

"No, I think I've run enough," he said aloud.

"Say again, Skipper?" Sancho said.

"Nothing, Sancho. Just letting a good friend's lesson sink in. Change aspect again, begin preparations for flipbraking at twenty-five percent. It's time for a showdown."

"Sounds like fun, Skipper. Stand by for flipbraking maneuver and one-quarter thrust."

Collier felt the subtle changes in the ship that meant it was pivoting around on its long axis, and shortly thereafter felt the gentle tug of acceleration. He smiled, realizing he relished the thought of talking to both ship's masters.

"You said they want to speak to me? Go ahead and put them both through on holo," Collier said, sliding into his control suite chair and putting his feet up on the console.

"Copy that, Skipper," Sancho replied, and the air before him crackled to life. Two transparent head-and-shoulders holograms appeared, and Collier nodded to one of them.

"Agent Fletcher, I presume?" he said to the tired-looking woman to his left. "A pleasant face to see after so long an absence."

"Hello, Captain," Fletcher said with a small smile.

Collier turned to the other face — one he did not recognize. "And, based on the snappy midnight-blue uniform you've got on, you're with the Ad Astra Corp."

The lantern-jawed man did not smile back. "I am. Captain Rahford. We have a business proposal for you, South."

"I'm not interested," Collier said. He turned back to Fletcher. "I suppose it would be useless to send you telemetry of an attack perpetrated by the Ad Astra Corporation on my vessel four months ago, wouldn't it? The Authority would not be able to do anything, would it?"

Fletcher's said evenly, "Officially, we are charged with keeping the peace and enforcing Belt law. So if you have a claim to make, you are free to make it."

"But if I lose my suit, I pay not only court costs, but have to reimburse the defendant for bringing the suit in the first place, right?"

"You know Belt law," Fletcher said.

"So that's out," Collier muttered.

"Agent Fletcher, I don't think we will need your services anymore," the Ad Astra captain said. "The Ad Astra Corporation thanks you for your assistance, but now we have some proprietary business to conduct with Mr. South, so if you—"

Fletcher interrupted softly but firmly. "The Authority is also tasked with adjudicating trade transactions. Normally, we're not asked to be present during negotiations, but since I'm here, and you're here, I think I'll sit in on this one. This will be very interesting."

"Oh, I don't think it will, Agent Fletcher," Collier said, forestalling the corporate captain's objection. "I don't want to make any deals with Ad Astra, or with the Authority itself. Actually," he paused, and got up for a moment to retrieve the magic wand, "I take that back. It will be quite interesting. I'm about to show both of you the secret of my mining success. But there will be some conditions, so I hope you will pay attention."

The corporate captain growled, "What the fu—"

"You'll want to listen, not speak, Captain," Collier said, bringing the white cylinder into the camera pickup. "This here is the secret. All you can see is a white tube, I know. But I've come to call this the magic wand."

"Captain South," Fletcher began, her voice again tired, "let's not play rhetorical—"

"It's not a trick. Or, rather, it is a trick — the best trick you've ever seen. It works a lot better in person, though. If you'd care to come aboard, I think I can arrange a demonstration that will impress you."

Rahford snorted. "I've got a much better idea. Why don't you and I go back to Ceres, we'll meet in the corporate digs there — much more comfortable. No disrespect to your fine vessel."

Collier laughed. "You must think I have shit for brains. No chance I'm going to let myself play this out in your backyard. You want to know the secret so bad that you opened fire on me four months ago? You come aboard *Dulcinea* and I'll show you."

"I'm game, Captain," Fletcher said quietly. "Can you please increase your deceleration and send us your telemetry so we can match velocities?"

"Absolutely, Agent Fletcher," Collier said, then turned back to Rahford. "Well, Captain? Last chance. Or would you rather go back to your corporate bosses and explain to them how you failed to get the secret because you didn't want to leave your comfy chair?"

"Fine," Rahford grunted. "Send us the data."

"Great. Bring booze. Tank 8 if you have it," Collier said. "And any biologicals you have. I haven't eaten in a long time." He switched off.

"Sancho, send both vessels our traj—"

"Got it, Skipper. Telemetry sent. I'll need to coordinate with both their computers: is that all right?"

"Sure. Just watch yourself. Don't let them break into your systems."

Sancho made a derisive noise. "Please, Skipper. I can keep my cards hidden from those pocket calculators. But I would like to ask you something, if I could."

"Shoot."

"Is this such a wise idea? You giving away the secret of the wand?"

Collier chuckled. "I thought you were the one who told me to try and change things up? Rattle a few cages, overturn some apple carts, that sort of thing?" He stopped chuckling when he remembered why Sancho had told him that. Su's memory pounced on him unexpectedly.

"Yes, that I did. But is this the best way to go about it? Maybe you should lie low for a while, recover your strength, build up some cash through use of the wand before you try to make those changes. I mean," Sancho tried to laugh, "shaking things up can be done prudently."

Collier answered soberly, "It's tempting, Sancho. Tempting to do as you say, build up strength, wait for the right moment. But I've spent most of my adult life waiting for the moment — you and I, we go out, try to make the big strike. I never really thought what happens after that."

"You couldn't predict you'd find an alien artifact, Skipper."

"That's not what I mean. I found Su. I was ready to stay with her, let you continue to learn from Perditus. I was ready to settle down. Yeah, it was through coercion, but I was at peace with the decision. So now, here I am. I can go back to how I was — alone against the Belt and the corporations, trying to scrape a living off the rocks. The wand would have made it easier, but I would still be a dog at the foot of the dinner table, eating what scraps fell my way. I've just moved a bit closer with the wand.

"Or I can look to change the way things are. It might not work at all — you could be very right. But I've decided that I can't go back to the way I was. Lots of people taught me that. Su did, and so did you, Sancho."

"Me?"

"Yeah. When you told me how you evolved into a Caliban. A series of challenges, you said. I made you think about your own capabilities in ways you hadn't before. I think I've got to do the same thing. Or at least try to."

"Damn, Skipper. I didn't know I inspired you so much. Maybe I should rent myself out as a motivational speaker," Sancho joked.

"Plus I can't let a goddamn computer show me up and outgrow me," Collier added.

"Ah. So it's spite, really. You're going to try and change the economic and social fabric of the Belt just to show me up."

"Sounds like a good reason to me," Collier said. "How is the telemetry coordination coming?"

"We're in the groove, Skipper. I've increased braking thrust by eleven percent, and the two other vessels are powering engines to match velocities by the time we reach them. We should have our guests on board in an hour and a half, give or take a few minutes."

Collier nodded and regarded the cabin. "Probably should straighten up a bit." He began policing the various bits of rubbish that had floated aft with the deceleration thrust. As he tidied the cabin, he strapped on his sidearm and patted it, thankful he had already tested it on Ganymede.

The banter with Sancho had done much to keep his emotions and memories at bay, but now they came surging back.

He hadn't ever killed before, and even now, the act seemed to have been committed by someone else. He could see the body of the Ganymedian guard falling limply to the ground, and he could see Tacat's body erupting in rapidly freezing fountains of crimson, but both seemed to be images from a high-budget holo, not results of his own actions.

Only Su's death had seemed real. He was thankful he had not turned her over and seen what would have been a ruined face. His last memory of her face was of her half-smiling at some attempted witticism of his. It was a good memory, and it comforted him.

He resumed his cleanup, mildly surprised at the amount of dust and grime that had collected on various surfaces of the ship. He kept up a lighthearted dialogue with Sancho about the computer's slovenly ways, partly to keep his mind from falling too deeply into Su's memory, partly to keep himself from over-thinking the encounter ahead. He had in his mind what he wanted to do, but he wanted to leave some of the meeting to chance. The scenario would almost certainly not unfold in any way he could predict, so improvisation would have to carry the day. Still, he took certain precautions. He donned his vacc suit (silently thanking his reputation as an eccentric who was never without it: the suit would not, he hoped, raise too much suspicion) and kept a supply of easily gathered material near his control seat. If he needed a quick fill of the tube, he would have the mass nearby. He checked the cheat sheet and memorized two patterns, hoping he would not need them.

"Coming alongside," Sancho said. "Authority Tender *Clara Barton* is at zero relative velocity, distance three hundred nine meters off our starboard/dorsal bow. *Ad Astra Mining Ship CE-119* somewhat farther away and still maneuvering."

"Okay. Hail the Authority ship. Ask if they need anything else."

"Roger that." There was a pause, after which Sancho added, "They want us to open the airlock when Agent Fletcher gets here."

Collier chuckled once. Cute.

Ten minutes later, Sancho informed him that Fletcher had made the vacuum crossing and was approaching the airlock. Collier had a momentary impulse to make her knock, and saw in his mind the image of Su shaking her head and suppressing a grin at the joke. He smiled at her memory, glad he could do so, and instructed Sancho to open the lock. Fletcher entered the cabin once the lock had cycled and began removing her Authority-issued vacc suit.

She was neither a slim woman nor a husky one — her body type was difficult to pin down, but there were the remains of a fine woman about her. More than anything else, her body could be described as a bureaucratic shape, if that was possible.

Once she had removed her helmet, Collier helped her remove the suit. "Welcome aboard, Agent Fletcher."

"Thank you, Captain," she said, wriggling her arm free of its sleeve and pushing the suit down her legs. Collier noted the sidearm strapped to her right thigh.

"I'd offer you something, but I am very low on organics. I'm down to my own hair. I don't suppose you brought anything?" Collier eyed her tool belt.

"Nothing but the standard issue belt, I'm afraid."

"And the needler?" Collier jerked his chin at her weapon.

"Standard issue, as I said, Captain. Unlike your cowboy cannon," she said, gesturing to his own weapon.

"Gives me a sense of mass," Collier joked. "Captain Rahford should be on board soon. Once he gets here, we can start."

Fletcher nodded and scanned the ship. Her eyes were heavy-lidded, giving her a sleepy quality, but they darted around the cabin expertly assessing what they took in.

"What do you think of *Dulcinea*?" Collier asked.

"Amazing you've managed to keep her together for so long without upgrades and overhauls." She turned back to him. "You do your own maintenance, I take it?"

Collier shrugged. "Mostly. I've had to, really. No metal for major stuff."

"And it's just you on board?"

"Well … yeah."

Fletcher heard the hesitation and squinted slightly. "No? Our records indicate you as sole master, no passengers. No charters."

"Yeah, that's right. I meant my computer."

Fletcher nodded, a slight smile curling her lips. "I see." She did not inquire further.

Minutes later, Sancho piped up again. "Ad Astra vessel alongside ventral/port bow at nine hundred eighty-eight meters. Relative velocity zero. Figure emerging from airlock." His voice was clipped and artificial — a computer's voice mimicking a human's, and doing it badly.

Collier stifled a smile. Sancho was obviously keeping his Caliban identity secret. "Thank you, Sancho. Open outer lock when he's within ten meters."

"Copy that."

Fletcher did not seem to notice the exchange. She had spotted the white cylinder near the control chair and was studying it from where she floated. Collier let her — soon enough, she would know as much about it as he did. Almost as much.

Rahford entered the ship rather imperiously ten minutes later. He removed his helmet from his sleek, cutting-edge vacc suit, midnight blue with pseudo-military piping. His suit looked far more battle-ready than Fletcher's. Rahford made no effort to remove his outer garment — he only allowed his helmet casing to telescope into the neck recess of the suit.

"Okay, South, we're here. Now what's the big secret you had to show us on this ... ship?"

"Did you bring the Tank 8 stuff?" Collier asked.

Rahford scowled. "You were *serious* about that? No, I didn't bring any booze. I also didn't bring a picnic basket or a unicorn. Now can we get on with this?" he said too loudly, his right hand resting unnaturally on his thigh pocket.

Collier tried not to stare at the bulge in the pocket, looking at it only indirectly. Holdout pistol.

"You're impatient. But I guess you're here to see the magic trick, so let me get to it." He produced the wand again. "This is it. In very simple terms, it's a transmuter."

Rahford snorted and looked away with overacted indifference. Fletcher did not react at all.

Collier said to Rahford, "Maybe that's too complicated for you corpses. What I mean is that it can change anything into any element. You want to see?"

Rahford made an elaborate show of preparing to exit the ship. "Fletcher, if you want to stay, be my guest. I'm going back to my ship. There's a puppet show on C Deck that will be more enlightening than this shit."

Fletcher said, not taking her eyes off the wand, "Go ahead, Rahford. No one's stopping you. Captain South, can you operate the device and show me?"

Collier watched Rahford pretend to gasp in exasperation. The corporate captain's eyes betrayed him: they were glued to the wand.

"Sure thing, Agent Fletcher. I'll even let you choose what element we produce. Let me put some fuel into the wand," he opened the wand, eliciting a widening of the eyes from Fletcher and a change in posture from Rahford, and put in a quantity of the rubbish he had collected hours ago. He didn't want the small miracle of the wand's opening to deflect him from the main attraction, but he nevertheless grinned slightly at the pair's reaction.

"Now, Agent Fletcher. Name your element. If you please, pick one that isn't toxic or radioactive. Just a harmless element."

"Gold," Fletcher said quietly.

"Gold it is," Collier said, closing the wand. He checked his cheat sheet and began to manipulate the controls on the wand.

"What's that?" Rahford snapped, pointing at the card.

"That's my index. The manipulations are different depending on the element desired, and I haven't memorized them all yet. There. Finished. Agent Fletcher, if you would care to extend your hand, I'll give you the gold." He opened the wand again and shook out the small quantity of gold into her outstretched palm.

Rahford's gaze went from the gold to the wand. "How do we know that's real gold?"

"Short of conducting metallurgical tests, I suppose you don't. I could have produced iron pyrite or something. I'll let Agent Fletcher keep the sample and test it herself at her leisure," Collier said. "But I can do it again. Maybe you'd like to name the element, Rahford?"

"Make some vanadium," Rahford said.

Collier glanced at his chart. "Vanadium, eh? Shouldn't be too difficult."

"Alert. Vanadium exposure is toxic to unprotected humans." Sancho's stiff voice broke in.

Collier looked at Rahford. "Guess we'd better not. Pick another one?"

Rahford squinted. "Osmium."

Collier nodded. "Expensive and rare. But I don't need my computer to tell me what will happen if I make it inside the cabin. It'll turn into osmium tetroxide and we don't want that. If you want that kind of demonstration, we'll have to step outside and do it in vacuum." He shrugged. "You're oh-for-two, Captain. I would have thought a man who works for a mining corporation would know his metals better. Can't you think of a nice, safe element?"

Rahford bristled at the barb while Fletcher continued to turn the gold over in her hands. The corporate captain spat out one more attempt. "Fine. Molybdenum."

Collier nodded. "That's more like it." He scooped up more trash and once again manipulated the controls. "Hold out your hand, Rahford." He poured the silvery metal into the captain's gauntleted hand.

Rahford thumbed the metal and looked at it thoughtfully. Fletcher floated over to him as well and examined the output.

"What do you think? You need more demonstration?" Collier asked.

Rahford laughed and tossed the metal fragments back at Collier, who swatted them away. "To find out the secret compartment in your little magic wand there? No, thanks."

Fletcher looked at Collier. She seemed to be undecided on the authenticity of the wand. Collier laughed. "You think I have storage compartments in this thing, holding bits of gold and molybdenum on the off chance that I'd be asked to produce both of them?"

"You clearly manipulated the experiment so we'd select only certain items," Rahford said. "You knew Fletcher would want gold, so you had that ready. I threw you off by picking other elements, ones you weren't ready for, so you had to keep rejecting my choices until we got to the one you were ready for."

Collier looked at Fletcher, but her face was unreadable. "How would I know you would pick gold?"

Fletcher shrugged and continued to examine the lustrous metal.

Rahford held out his hand. "If you let me look at the device more closely, maybe I'd begin to believe your story."

Collier stepped back instinctively. "No chance. You don't get to touch this."

Rahford appealed to Fletcher. "There you have it, Agent Fletcher. It's a hoax."

"Pretty damn good one, if it is," Fletcher said quietly. "How did you come about this 'magic wand,' as you call it?"

Collier told the story of the artifact's discovery and his own conclusions regarding its alien origin. As he did so, Rahford made a show of skepticism and several times interrupted to show his disdain, but nevertheless stayed to listen to the tale.

"Your visit to the 'golden goose' asteroid was logged, I take it?" Fletcher asked when he had finished.

"Yep."

"Good. The Authority can begin survey operations if I decide it's warranted, then."

Collier frowned. "I made the discovery four months ago. The rogue asteroid was on a transverse course. By now, it's long gone."

Fletcher nibbled at a thumbnail. "Hmm. I'm sure it is, but if your discovery pans out as true, it will be worth the expense of a deep space survey mission. What else can this wand do?"

Collier's eyes widened. "What *else*? Isn't that enough?"

Rahford growled, "Hiding scrap metal and pouring it out on command? Yeah, real big discovery, South."

Collier had a fleeting thought that he would be better served to let Rahford continue in his misunderstanding. The corporation might then leave him alone. But the need to prove himself was overpowering. "Look, you moron," Collier said, closing the tube and following the sheet instructions, "how about some chlorine?" He opened the tube and shook it violently. A pale green gas cloud emerged, dissipating and vanishing slowly in the cabin air. Collier, Fletcher, and Rahford immediately started coughing, and Rahford activated his helmet with a touch on his neck control. Fletcher shut her eyes and pressed them with her palms as she continued to cough.

"Warning. Chlorine contamination in cabin. Atmosphere replacement in process. Recommend supplementary air supply for all passengers," Sancho said, and the cabin was suddenly a whirlwind as the ship's blowers went to maximum filtration.

Two minutes later, Fletcher and Collier stopped coughing and furiously blinking and Sancho announced the all clear. "Chlorine concentration below 1 part per million. Filtration continuing."

"I'm not sure that was necessary, Captain," Fletcher said, still wiping at her eyes.

Collier signaled to Rahford, and the corporate captain unsealed his helmet again. "What the fuck?" he screamed when his face was exposed again. He turned to Fletcher. "Agent Fletcher, I demand immediate legal action against this man! He tried to poison me!"

"Relax, Captain," Fletcher said tiredly. "There are bigger issues here. Or are you still unconvinced about the wand?"

Rahford's rage died down slowly. "I'm not going to commit myself to anything yet," he said.

Fletcher laughed once. "Fine. But I think there is enough here to merit an investigation. Captain South, you've convinced me to at least look into this. Would you be willing to turn the wand over to the Authority for scientific testing?"

Collier smiled. "Agent Fletcher, I trust the Authority about as far as I could jump on Jupiter. The wand stays with me."

"This is bigger than you, South," Rahford said, moving closer to him. "It's a matter of system-wide interest."

"I thought you didn't believe in this?" Fletcher said over her shoulder.

"Well, I mean, if it turns out to be something," Rahford added.

"Doesn't matter," Collier said. "I'm not prepared to give it up to anyone. For any price," he said, staring at Rahford.

Rahford smirked back. Collier thought he caught a glint of respect in the man's eye before his manufactured umbrage returned.

"I see. If that's the case, then why did you call us, why did you want us to see this?" Fletcher asked.

Collier took a breath. This was what he had been waiting for. Although he had left a lot to improvisation, he had known that sooner or later one of them was going to ask him what he wanted.

"First of all, I want to register it as a trade secret with the Authority. That—"

"Individuals can't hold trade secrets," Rahford interrupted. "Check the Belt Charter," he said, then smiled.

"You're right, Captain. Agent Fletcher," Collier said, turning to the woman, "I wish to incorporate. I will file the necessary paperwork with Ceres, but I want you to witness my intent to do so."

Rahford laughed cruelly. "This is preposterous. Are you completely ignorant of the Belt Charter? You can't form a corporation just by saying so. There are procedures and protocols, including a review by the Belt Chamber of Commerce." He smirked. "You really think your request will get a hearing anytime soon?"

Collier looked to Fletcher, who shrugged. "He's right again. They can't block you outright, but they control the agenda. They can continue to postpone a hearing on your incorporation claims indefinitely. It's certainly not ethical," she said, glancing at Rahford, "but it is legal."

Collier said, slowly, "So while I wait for the Chamber of Commerce to decide if I can have the same rights as a corporation, I can't claim the wand as a trade secret, is that it?"

Fletcher nodded.

Collier said, "Can't you see how twisted and wrong that is? Not only does the Ad Astra Corporation have as many rights as a living, breathing person, it in fact has more rights. What's to stop them from taking the wand by force, then just weathering the legal repercussions of their actions? If they decide that the wand is worth a little legal trouble, then how do I stop them?"

A quick tearing sound from Rahford caused Collier and Fletcher to look at him. He had drawn his sidearm from its Velcro pouch and was aiming it unflinchingly at Collier. "That's exactly what we are thinking, South. At least you seem to understand corporate culture."

Fletcher started to move, but the gun barrel swung to cover her. "No, I don't think so, Agent Fletcher," Rahford said coldly. "You're going to, very carefully, detach your needler from your thigh and toss it over to me. Then, you're going to dress for the outside and return to your ship. File whatever report you want, because the corp will take care of me. I'll even give myself up peacefully once I have the wand safely delivered to my corporate chief. But for now, your part is over."

Fletcher stared at him and muttered, "This is a mistake, Rahford. You're going to be in a heap of trouble for this," she unstrapped her needler, flung it to him.

"Now you, South."

Collier complied silently.

Rahford caught the weapons and said to Collier. "Now, South, the wand."

"Rahford, listen. You think your corp will back you, get you out of the trouble you're going to be in. They won't. They're going to get the wand from you and then let you rot on an Authority prison sleeper. They're going to say you were just a rogue captain who was not following corporate policy. They—"

"You don't understand corporate loyalty, South, but then, I don't expect you to. I also don't care what you think is going to eventually happen to me. Give me the wand. I'd rather not have to kill you, since that would make things difficult for the corp, but I will if I have to."

Fletcher had moved away from Collier, crouching. Collier sighed and produced the wand, delicately manipulating the controls as best he could. He dare not look at the cheat sheet — he was simply going on memory. He pressed the final sequence, opened the tube, and flung it at Rahford.

As soon as he did so, he dove for Fletcher to protect her. The wand spun end over end, spewing a pale yellow gas. Rahford fired, but his gun was aimed at Collier's previous position. The projectile struck the control panel and ricocheted around the control suite, sparking when it made contact with the metal surfaces.

Rahford swung the pistol to where Collier and Fletcher had fetched up against an aft partition, the wand still spewing a faint yellow cloud. The pungent smell of the gas assaulted Collier's nostrils and eyes, but it did not smell as it should have. He did not have time to wonder at this, as Rahford's weapon was now trained on him.

Rahford blinked twice and shook his head, then fired. The spinning magic wand was between the two men, and the bullet spanged off the tube and sparked. Collier heard the bullet impact the bulkhead next to him, and the magic wand was now spinning crazily end-over-end. Rahford's bullet had hit near the bottom of the wand, and as it came toward Collier it spun rapidly. He reached out and seized the wand, almost by instinct, his eyes burning and his lungs protesting.

Through the confusion, Sancho came on the cabin comm, his voice no longer flat. "Skipper! Fluorine concentrations dangerously high! Beginning maximum atmosphere replacement."

Rahford rubbed at his eyes and growled. Collier was coughing and squeezing his eyes shut as well, and Fletcher had doubled over retching. Collier forced his eyes open to see Rahford fumbling at the neck control of his suit.

Half-blindly, Collier pushed off the bulkhead and launched himself at Rahford face-first, the wand held before him like a spear. Rahford finally found the control he was looking for and started to shut his helmet, the glass dome springing up from behind his head and circling down to his neck. Collier thrust the wand ahead and managed to get it wedged between the neck and the closing glass dome. Rahford's helmet was unsealed, a five-centimeter gap between the glass and the neck. Collier started quickly to tap and slide on the wand's control surface.

Rahford drew a few breaths and looked at Collier before him. He smiled silently and brought his pistol up, but not before Collier finished his manipulations and sent a cloud of fluorine into the helmet, yanking the wand free of the glass dome and allowing the suit to seal itself, trapping the deadly gas inside.

Rahford screamed, his voice muffled behind the glass, and he tore at the neck of his suit, dropping his pistol. His legs flailed around as the gas went to work on his eyes and throat. Collier retrieved the pistol, his own eyes still tearing, and coughed mightily. He pushed off Rahford's body, which was still spastically twitching as he screamed and scrabbled at his helmet release, and checked on Fletcher. She had curled into a ball and was coughing violently, squeezing her eyes shut. The air in the cabin began to swirl again as Sancho activated the scrubbers, and in seconds the powerful odor had vanished.

Collier looked at Rahford, who had gone limp. Continuing to cover him with the pistol, Collier found and pressed the helmet release catch. The glass swung back to the shoulder recess and revealed Rahford's face. He looked as if someone had splashed acid on his skin — burn marks had already formed near the nose, eyes, and lips, but he was still breathing.

Collier called to his computer. "Sancho, contact the Ad Astra ship. Tell them that their Captain has—"

"Belay that," Fletcher said, her voice hoarse. "We'll take him aboard the *Barton*. We can give him the—" she stopped to cough, then resumed, "attention he needs. Plus place him under arrest."

"Sancho, check that. Contact the *Clara Barton*, please. Put them on cabin com."

Fletcher made the arrangements with her ship, ordering two of her own crew to retrieve Rahford's body and describing the nature of the emergency. Her adjutant had seemed shocked at the diagnosis of fluorine poisoning, but had complied with Fletcher's orders. Sancho recommended Collier and Fletcher wash out their eyes with water, so the two took turns at the small bathroom dispenser doing so.

"Sancho, what was the maximum concentration of the fluorine gas in the cabin?"

"My sensors detected 30 parts per million."

"What are the long-term health effects of exposure at that level for the short time we were in it?"

"There won't be long term effects for so small a dosage. I would still get checked out, though, when you can, Skipper."

Fletcher stood away from the sink and motioned for Collier to use it. She dried her face with the suction towel and said through it, "Your computer sounds different."

"Yeah, well," Collier said, "that's a bit of a story as well."

"I'm sure. You've got more than a few secrets, Captain South."

Collier finished washing and shrugged. "Maybe."

The two *Barton* crewmen arrived, and under Fletcher's orders took Rahford's body back to the Authority ship. That left Collier and Fletcher alone in the cabin.

"So, what happens next?" Collier said.

"Well, we will try Rahford for his violations of the Belt Charter, probably successfully. I think you were right — his corp will want to disavow any connection with him. But you made a powerful enemy in the Ad Astra folks."

Collier laughed. "I don't know if you noticed, Agent Fletcher, but they already hate me pretty good."

"Yes, that's true."

"I meant," Collier said after a pause, "what happens with me? And the artifact."

Fletcher drew a breath, coughed again. "You said you want to incorporate."

Collier blinked. "Sure, but I only want that to get the trade secret protections. I don't want the wand taken from me."

Fletcher smiled grimly. "Captain, what makes you think the trade secret laws will stop the corps from coming after you? You just had a guy in here who was going to kill you for the wand. You think that if you were a corporation that would end?"

Collier shook his head slowly. "I suppose not."

Fletcher rose from her seat and began to put her suit back on. "I don't know where you can go for protection, Captain."

"What about the Authority?" Collier said.

Fletcher sighed. "I wish I could tell you that we could protect you. But we both know that isn't true. The Authority is controlled by the corporations. Ultimately, we will bend to their will. You know that, I know that, the whole damn Belt knows that. Some of us are trying to change that, but..." she shrugged and continued to suit up.

"Then ... wait, you're leaving?"

"I have to get back, start processing Rahford, let the Ad Astra ship know what happened."

"What about me?"

"As far as I am concerned, you are free to go." She zipped up her suit and held her helmet in her hands.

Collier stared at her. "You can't be serious. That's it?"

"No, it's not," she said quietly back, her voice tired.

"But think about that trade secret business. Think about how the corporation was going to get away with what they tried to do to you today. I can't tell you what to do. I'm just a poor civil servant." She put her helmet on and secured it. She shouted through the glass, her voice muffled, "But for what it's worth, Captain, I hope you figure it out. Good luck!" she cycled the inner door of the airlock, stepped through, and closed the door behind her.

——<>——

Several hours later, the *Clara Barton* and the Ad Astra ship left together, both headed back to Ceres. Collier floated in the control cabin, having surveyed the damage Rahford's bullets had done to the ship. None of the wounds were impossible to repair or bypass, though it did mean some inconvenience as some control surfaces had to serve double duty. Sancho reported all systems functional and the ship ready to resume course to Ceres.

"Not sure we should go back there, Sancho."

"Why not, Skipper?"

"They'll be waiting for me."

Sancho paused. "But, Skipper, won't that be true anywhere now?"

Collier thought. "Yeah. I guess so. If Ganymede had heard about it, surely Mars, Luna, even Earth had. There's nowhere in the system I can hide." He idly toggled a control surface switch on and off, the corresponding monitor flickering as he did so.

"Then ... what's there left to do?"

Collier stopped flicking the switch. "Stop running."

"Skipper?"

"Stop running. She wanted to change her world once, too."

"Who? Fletcher?"

"No. Su." Collier sighed. "'In order to attain the impossible, one must attempt the absurd.'"

"I don't understand."

Collier wasn't listening to Sancho anymore. He knew what a corporation feared most. He knew how he could protect himself.

And better still, how he could finally begin to change things.

——<>——

Thirty-six hours later, he floated down the access tunnel on Ceres toward the quadrangle, his vacc suit comfortable in its bulk. This time, he had not only planned his speech, he had rehearsed it. Sancho had come close to forbidding him from carrying out his plan, arguing that the danger was simply too great.

"A single lunatic, Skipper … that's all it will take!" he had almost shouted.

"By that logic," Collier had replied, "I'm always in danger. A single lunatic could be anywhere."

"Don't chop-logic, Skipper. You're making yourself a target by doing this."

"I'm already a target. All I'm doing now is standing in the open. Where's the best place for a target to be?"

"Hiding where no one can get you, obviously!"

Collier had shaken his head. "Nope. I thought the same thing, but it's actually the opposite."

He had asked Sancho to contact any of the remaining independents in the area so they could come to Ceres with him, and Sancho had done surprisingly well. It turned out that more than a few of the independent ships were run by Calibans, and within a few hours Sancho had established an impressive network of independents who would be present on Ceres when Collier needed them. The thirteen independents who would be in attendance represented perhaps a third of all independent Belters, who in turn represented perhaps one-quarter of all the mining concerns, corporate or independent, in the Belt. It was by no means a majority of people, but it would have to suffice.

The preparations had been rushed, but even so, Collier had discovered finding a tether berth to Ceres difficult. Ships of all descriptions had come to hear what he had to say. Once again, his eccentricity and hermit-like lifestyle had paid off. As far as he knew, no independent had ever made a proclamation such as his, and the fact that it had come from one of the oldest and most respected Belters in the system increased the intrigue.

Fletcher had also broadcast more details of the arrest of Captain Rahford than was customary or even legal, and the word had spread even in thirty-six hours that something was brewing on Ceres.

When he reached the end of the access tunnel and came out on the upper level of the quadrangle, he saw the ordinary, multicolored throngs of corp miners and officers, but their numbers were almost equal to the number of independents milling about on various levels. Collier allowed himself a moment of indulgence before he was spotted.

"Showtime," he muttered, and stepped up to the railing. He withdrew the magic wand from his backpack and clanged it on the metal railing in a repetitive fashion, like a judge's gavel bringing a courtroom to order.

"I've got something to show you all," he said, once the clamor had died down somewhat and at least half the people in the quad were looking quizzically up at him. He brandished the wand. "And I have a message for the corporations. You've been squeezing us independents out for years and years. Some of you, even now, who wear the uniform of the Horizon Corporation, or Ad Astra Corp, or Hyperion Mining, or any of the others, do so because you think there was no other choice."

He paused and looked at the faces. They looked back more or less expectantly, though there were several who laughed and pointed.

"Some of you might have heard what happened to me coming back from Ganymede. With a captain in the Ad Astra Corp. He wanted this," he said, holding the wand aloft.

"It's not money that makes the corporations unbeatable — it's secrecy. Well, I have a secret, too. My mistake was to think I could, or should, keep it to myself. So I am here to tell you what happened. Maybe most of you won't believe it, or will think it doesn't matter to you. But some of you will, and you will think that maybe you can find what I found, or find even more. The most important thing is that you will all know what happened, and you can do what you want with that knowledge. The corporations could have silenced me, but they can't silence all of us. And this is one trade secret that will make all of their business plans worthless."

"So let me tell you what this thing is, what it does, and how I found it. Maybe there are more of them out there. I will need a volunteer..."

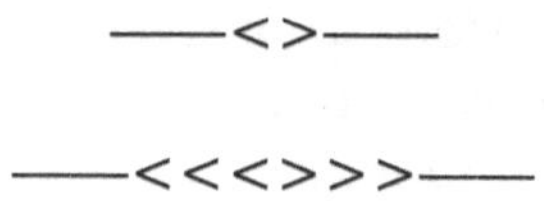

——<<<>>>——

Epilogue

Barney Starcher slid his access card through the security lock and entered his kiosk. He tossed his tablet toward his desk, where it floated slowly to the surface. He rubbed the remaining sleep out of his eyes — he had not gotten as much as he should have, but then again, last night had been an unusual one. Collier's demonstration had been impressive, though no one really knew what was in store for the future of mining in the Belt. If there was one device that could transmute elements perhaps there were more out there that could do much more. Starcher feared that his business' fragile financial status would not be able to weather the coming changes, whatever they were.

And Collier — the old miner had disappeared as suddenly as he had appeared, untethering hours after his demonstration. The Authority had been silent on the matter, even though all the major corporations were howling about trade infringement.

It was going to be an exciting, if dangerous, few years.

Starcher drew himself a coffee bulb and settled into his desk to look over the morning's mail. His eyes widened when he saw a message from Collier.

"Dear Barney,

First off, let me say that I'm sorry I had to break in last night. You've really got to update your security. Sancho was able to override your codes in under fifteen minutes. Don't worry — I haven't done anything bad to you."

Barney stopped reading and looked wildly around his office. Nothing obvious seemed to be missing. He turned back to the letter.

"Second, I wanted you to know that you've been a good friend through my whole career. You still believe in guys like me, and I want you to know I appreciate it.

"I'm sure that's all very goddamn heartwarming, but I think you should receive more than a simple thanks. If you'll look in your bottom desk drawer — the one where you keep that Tank 8 stuff (I had myself a snort or two, hope you don't mind), you'll find my real thanks. Should help you take care of your business. Do with it what you want — I know I'm putting it in good hands.

"Take care, Barney."

Starcher opened the drawer and withdrew a meter-long white tube. Taped to the tube was a sheaf of paper with detailed instructions as to its use.

If you enjoyed this read

Please leave a review on Amazon, Facebook, Good Reads or Instagram.

It takes less than five minutes and it really does make a difference.

If you're not sure how to leave a review on Amazon:

1. *Go to amazon.com.*

2. *Type in Beltrunner by Sean O'Brien and when you see it, click on it.*

3. *Scroll down to Customer Reviews. Nearby you'll see a box labeled Write a Review. Click it.*

4. *Now, if you've never written a review before on Amazon, they might ask you to create a name for yourself.*

5. *Reviews can be as simple as, "Loved the book! Can't wait for the Next!" (Please don't give the story away.)*

And that's it!

Brian Hades, publisher

About the Author

Sean O'Brien is an educator and writer from Southern California. He is married and has two children along with an ever-growing number of animals. He was named Educator of the Year by the California League of High Schools and has been a head varsity football coach, television broadcaster, and Gilbert and Sullivan singer (though not a good one). He's the author of two other novels, *A Muse of Fire* and *Vale of Stars*, and an anthology of short fiction entitled *Wondrous Strange: 12 Amusingly Unexpected Tales*.

book story arc that addresses one of the great mysteries of life: Why are we humans the way that we are?

Praise for The Genius Asylum

"The Genius Asylum starts out on Earth as something that looks like a crime story, but it then quickly describes a world of interstellar travel and alien alliances. After the first act concludes, the story's complexity starts accelerating and doesn't slow down, and you'll find yourself drawn into the world, needing to know what comes next. It is an excellently written story that provides the framework for the series that is to come, and I'm looking forward to reading the rest of it."
— Chris Marks, reviewer

I thoroughly enjoyed this Sci-Fi Brainteaser. Very well written with incredible plot twists and turns. We've got a very intelligent double agent as the main character and an intriguing support cast. I was thankful for the planetary history at the beginning as it was helpful in understanding the different organizations mentioned throughout the novel. The Author has a witty way of expressing viewpoints, clearly has put a lot of thought into the storyline and created edge of your seat suspense and mystery! Admittedly, I was confused about the title of the book until about halfway through reading it but it makes perfect sense now. I highly recommend this absolutely unforgettable installment and can't wait for the next.
— Stephanie Herman

For more on The Genius Asylum visit:
tinyurl.com/edge6013

—— <> ——

Europa Journal

by Jack Castle

The history of humanity is about to change forever...

On 5 December 1945, five TBM Avenger bombers embarked on a training mission off the coast of Florida and mysteriously vanish without a trace in the Bermuda Triangle. A PBY search and rescue plane with thirteen crewmen aboard sets out to find the Avengers . . . and never returns.

In 2168, a mysterious five-sided pyramid is discovered on the ocean floor of Jupiter's icy moon, Europa.

Commander Mac O'Bryant and her team of astronauts are among the first to enter the pyramid's central chamber. They find the body of a missing World War II pilot, whose hands clutch a journal detailing what happened to him after he and his crew were abducted by aliens and taken to a place with no recognizable stars. As the pyramid walls begin to collapse around Mac and her team, their names mysteriously appear within its pages and they find themselves lost on an alien world.

Stranded with no way home, Mac decides to retrace the pilot's steps. She never expects to find the man alive. And if the man has yet to die, what does that mean for her and the rest of her crew?

Praise for Europa Journal

This book kept me guessing! It has an exciting start and keeps that same pace throughout the book. The building of

the character personalities keeps a depth to the storyline and makes the reader feel connected to each character. The background information given through Europa Journal gives a great balance between the history, future and everything in-between! I love the mix of fact and fiction to create the story and inspire imagination. I'm excited to see what Castle comes up with next!
— Dianna Temple

With an action-packed opening, page-turning twists,a well-built world, and characters worth caring about, Europa Journal is like a bulldog - it grabbed me and wouldn't let go! It seamlessly blends breathtaking imagination with the gritty reality of survival, and beautifully blurs what has been with what might be. I love Dr. Who and grew up with Star Trek, but this book has broken the sci-fi mold in a wonderful way!
— Stuntwoman, Elisa Brinton

From the opening space shuttle crash landing to the stunning finish, Europa Journal is a real page turner. Ancient astronauts, the Bermuda triangle, WW II pilots, space shuttle crews – what else could you ask for? Mr. Castle keeps the story at light speed, with plenty of twists and turns before the awesome climax!
— James Wahlman, Firefighter in Alaska

For more on Europa Journal visit:
tinyurl.com/edge6001

———<>———

Milky Way Repo

by Mike Prelee

Running a starship repo company isn't easy or cheap. It's just an endless string of fuel costs, ship maintenance, legal red tape, unhappy debt bailers, shady associates and uncooperative dock officials from one end of the galaxy to the other.

Nathan Teller owns and operates Milky Way Repossessions, a company that tracks down and repossesses starships. And although he's only managing to break even on his debt, he wouldn't trade it for anything. (His ex-wife holds that against him. No surprise there.)

When Nathan and his crew successfully steal a freighter from the clutches of a particularly tenacious and corrupt dock official, he earns the respect of their high profile employer. Opportunity seems a sure thing.

Nathan should be happy. But when that lucrative job op turns into a ransom delivery for a starship crew being held hostage by a cult, he suddenly finds himself pursued by a self-immolating loan shark hell bent on collecting a gambling debt.

How will it all turn out? You never know. Especially when Nathan and his Starship repo agents are up against a cult and the mob…

Praise for Milky Way Repo

The debut novel of Mike Prelee is a very entertaining Sci-Fi/Noir, with vivid, likable characters and a fast pace.

He's got a great handle on plot and a knack for drawing you into the story. For fans of fast-paced space adventure with a smattering of crime drama mixed in, this should do the trick. I finished it in two sittings. High praise for sure. I would definitely read a sequel (or two).
 — marc a. gayan

 Milky Way Repo is a nice, light but exciting read. With just enough action and even a bit of romance and comedy, I definitely recommend this read to anyone who enjoys a good sci-fi/blue collar space opera.
 I gave Milky Way Repo 5 stars because it provided me with a short, albeit adventurous, fun and light hearted escape for a few hours. It is well written, with well rounded characters and a wonderful storyline.
 I have to say that Duncan was my absolute favorite character. Officially starting a Duncan fan club!
 — Chaelsie Jenyk

 For more on Milky Way Repo visit:
 tinyurl.com/edge7003

——<>——